'A masterful storyteller, carefully crafting ... that keep readers
on the edge of their seats'
USA Today

'Perfectly plotted . . . sin-tillating suspense'
People magazine

'Millions of readers clamour for the compelling novels of
Sandra Brown. And no wonder! She fires your imagination
with irresistible characters, unexpected plot twists, scandalous
secrets . . . so electric you feel the zing'
Literary Guild

'Lust, jealousy, and murder suffuse Brown's crisp thriller'
Publishers Weekly

'Brown's novels define the term "page turner"'
Booklist

'Fast fun'
Cosmopolitan

'An edge-of-the-seat thriller that's full of twists . . .
Top stuff!'
Star

'Virtuoso plot twists . . . Brown's thriller
engages the primal senses'
Kirkus Reviews

Novels by Sandra Brown

OUTFOX

SANDRA BROWN

HODDER

First published in the United States of America 2019 by Grand Central Publishing
A division of Hachette Book Group, Inc.

First published in Great Britain in 2019 by Hodder & Stoughton
An Hachette UK company

This paperback edition published in 2020

1

A CIP catalogue record for this title is available from the British Library

Paperback ISBN 978 1 473 66953 6
eBook ISBN 978 1 473 66952 9

Typeset in Baskerville MT Std

Printed and bound in Great Britain by Clays Ltd, Elcograf S.p.A.

Hodder & Stoughton policy is to use papers that are natural, renewable
and recyclable products and made from wood grown in sustainable forests.
The logging and manufacturing processes are expected to conform to the
environmental regulations of the country of origin.

Hodder & Stoughton Ltd
Carmelite House
50 Victoria Embankment
London EC4Y 0DZ

www.hodder.co.uk

OUTFOX

Prologue

———◦◦◦———

A cheerless drizzle blurred any view of the body on the beach.

Mist formed halos around the lampposts along the pier, but didn't diffuse the glaring portable lights that had been put in place by first responders. In a grotesque parody of catching someone in the spotlight on center stage, they shone a harsh light on the covered form.

A police helicopter swept in low. Its searchlight was unforgivingly bright as it tracked the length of the pier. Its beam skittered over the marina where boats rocked in a lulling current that was out of keeping with the surrounding chaos.

Before shifting out onto the surf, the searchlight cut a swath across the corpse. The chopper's downwash flipped back a corner of the garish yellow plastic sheet to expose a hand, inert and bone-white on the packed sand.

Since the discovery of the body, officers representing several law enforcement agencies had converged on the scene. The colored lights of a search-and-rescue helicopter blinked against the underbelly of low clouds hugging the harbor. Beyond Fort Sumter, a US

Coast Guard cruiser plowed through the waters of the Atlantic, its searchlight sweeping across the swells.

TV satellite vans had arrived, disgorging eager reporters and camera crews.

On the pier, the inevitable onlookers had congregated. They vied for the best vantage points from which to gawk at the body, monitor the police and media activity, and take selfies with the draped corpse in the background. They swapped information and speculation.

It was said that the deceased had washed ashore with the evening tide and had been discovered by a man and his young son while they were exercising their chocolate Lab on this stretch of beach.

It was said that drowning was the obvious cause of death.

It was said that it was the result of a boating mishap.

None of these conjectures was correct.

The unleashed Labrador had run ahead of his owner, and it was the dog, splashing in the surf, that had made the gruesome discovery.

One of the spectators on the pier, overhearing the exchanges of facts, fictions, and laments, smiled in self-satisfied silence.

Chapter 1

Three weeks earlier

The automatic doors whooshed open. In one surveying glance, Drex Easton took in the hotel lobby. It was empty except for the pretty young woman behind the reception desk. She had a porcelain-doll complexion, a glossy black ponytail, and an uncertain smile as she greeted him.

"Good morning, sir. Can I help you?"

Drex set his briefcase at his feet. "I don't have a reservation, but I need a room."

"Check-in isn't until two o'clock."

"Hmm."

"Because...because for the convenience of our guests, checkout isn't until noon."

"Hmm."

"Housekeeping needs time to—"

"I realize all that, Ms. Li." He'd read the name badge pinned to her maroon blazer. He smiled. "I was hoping you could make an exception for me."

He reached behind his back to remove a wallet from his pants pocket and, in doing so, spread open his suit jacket wide enough to reveal the shoulder holster beneath his left arm. Upon seeing it, the young woman blinked several times before rapidly shifting her gaze back up to his, which he held steady on her.

"No cause for alarm," he said quietly. He flipped open the wallet that contained a badge and photo ID that classified him as a special agent of the Federal Bureau of Investigation.

He didn't like to overplay this card, doing so only when he needed a shortcut through rules and red tape. It worked on Ms. Li, who was automatically willing to please.

"Let me see what I can do."

"I would consider it a big favor."

Graceful fingers pecked across her keyboard. "Single or double?"

"I'm not picky."

Her eyes scanned the computer monitor. She scrolled down, then back up. "I can have housekeeping service a nice double room for you right away, but the turnaround could take up to half an hour. Or, there's a less nice single available now."

"I'll take the less nice single available now." He slid a credit card across the granite counter.

"How long will you be staying with us, Mr. Easton?"

She was no slouch. She'd noted his name. "I'm not sure. Two other... Two associates of mine will be arriving shortly. I won't know how long I'll be staying until after our meeting. I'll have to let you know then."

"No problem. You may keep the room until you notify me of your departure."

"Great. Thanks."

She ran his credit card and proceeded to check him in. She had him initial the room rate on the form and sign his name at the bottom; then she returned his credit card along with the room key card. "That key also unlocks the door to the fitness center on the second floor."

"Thanks, but I won't be using it."

"The restaurant is just down the corridor behind you. Breakfast is served—"

"No breakfast, either." He bent down and picked up his briefcase.

Taking the subtle hint, she pointed him toward the elevators. "As you step off onto your floor, your room will be to your left."

"Thank you, Ms. Li. You've been a huge help."

"When your associates arrive, am I at liberty to give them your room number?"

"No need, I'll text it to them. They can come straight up."

"I hope your meeting goes well."

He gave her a wry grin. "So do I." Then he leaned forward and said in an undertone, "Relax, Ms. Li. You're doing a fine job."

She looked chagrined. "This is only my second day. Were my nerves that obvious?"

"Probably not to anyone else, but sizing people up quickly is a large part of what I do. And if this is only your second day, I'm even more impressed with how you handled a troublesome guest."

"Not that troublesome at all."

He gave her a lazy smile. "You caught me on a good day."

___

The less nice single wasn't a room the hotel chain would feature in an ad, but it would do. Drex opened his briefcase on the desk and booted up his laptop. He texted Mike the room number, then went over to the window. It afforded a fourth floor view of a freeway interchange and not much else.

He returned to the desk and checked his email in box. Nothing of importance. He went into the compact bathroom and used the toilet. As he came out, the hotel telephone was ringing. He picked up the extension on the desk. "Yes?"

"Mr. Easton?"

"Ms. Li."

"Your associates are here."

"Good." Sooner than he'd expected.

"Would you like for me to send something from the kitchen up to your room? Perhaps a fruit platter? A selection of pastries?"

"Thank you, but no."

"If you change your mind, don't hesitate to call down."

"I'll do that, Ms. Li. Thanks again for accommodating me."

"You're welcome."

Although the open drapes let in plenty of daylight, he switched on the desk lamp. He adjusted the thermostat down a few degrees. He glanced at his reflection in the mirror above the dresser and thought he looked presentable, but hardly spiffy. He'd showered and dressed in a rush.

At the soft knock, he went to the door and looked through the peephole before opening it. He stood aside and motioned the two men to come in.

As they filed past him, Gifford Lewis said, "The girl at the desk stopped us to ask if we were Mr. Easton's associates. She's moony for you."

"Anything Mr. Easton wants," Mike Mallory grumbled. "As long as she was offering, I could have done with the fruit platter and pastry selection. You could still call down."

Out of habit, Drex checked the hallway—which was empty—then shut the door and flipped the bolt. "You wake me up at dawn, say, 'Find a place where the walls don't have ears.' And don't waste any time doing it, you said. I don't waste any time, I find a place, and here we are. Never mind the fruit platter and pastries. What's up?"

The other two looked at each other, but neither replied.

With impatience, Drex asked, "What's so top secret we couldn't communicate through ordinary channels?"

Gif stationed himself against the wall, a shoulder propping him there. Mike rolled the chair from beneath the desk and wedged his three hundred forty pounds between the protesting armrests.

Drex placed his hands on his hips, his expression demanding. "For crissake, will one of you speak?"

Mike glanced over at Gif, who made a gesture that yielded the floor to Mike. He looked up at Drex and said, "I've found him."

Mike's tone conveyed all the gaiety of a death knell. The *him* didn't need specification.

For years Drex had been waiting to hear those words. He'd imagined this moment ten thousand times. He'd envisioned himself experiencing one or more physical reactions. His ears would ring, his mouth go dry, his knees buckle, his breath catch, his heart burst.

Instead, after his hands dropped from his hips, he went numb to a supernatural extent.

Gif and Mike must have expected an eruption of some sort, too, because they looked mystified over his sudden and absolute immobility and silence, which were downright eerie, even to himself.

A full minute later, when the paralyzing shock began to wear off, he walked over to the window again. Since last he'd looked out, nothing cataclysmic had occurred. Traffic hadn't stilled on the crisscrossing freeways. No jagged cracks had opened up in the earth's surface. The sky hadn't fallen. The sun hadn't burned out.

He pressed his forehead against the window and was surprised by how cold the glass felt. "You're sure?"

"Sure? As in positive? No," Mike replied. "But this guy looks real good on paper."

"Age?"

"Sixty-two. So says his current driver's license."

Drex turned his head and raised his eyebrows in a silent question.

"South Carolina," Mike said. "Mount Pleasant. Suburb of—"

"Charleston. I know. What name is he going by?"

"Un-huh."

That brought Drex all the way around. "Excuse me? What does that mean?"

Gif said, "Means that you're not getting a name until we know what you plan to do with the information."

"What the hell do you think I plan to do with it? First thing is to haul ass to Charleston."

Gif exchanged a look with Mike, then pushed himself away from the wall and squared off against Drex. He didn't take a combative stance, which would have been laughable because Drex was physically imposing and Gif was nowhere near. But he set his feet apart and braced himself as though Drex's self-restraint was iffy and reasonableness was way too much to hope for.

He said, "Hear me out, Drex. Mike and I talked about it on our way over here. We think you should consider…That is, it would be advisable to…The smart course of action would be to—"

"What?"

"Notify Rudkowski."

"Not a fucking chance in hell."

"Drex—"

Louder and with more emphasis, Drex repeated his statement.

Mike shot Gif a droll glance. "Told ya."

Drex's ears had begun to clamor after all. Now that the reality was setting in, his blood pressure had spiked. The window glass had felt cold against his forehead because his face was feverish. The blood vessels in his temples were throbbing. His scalp was sweaty beneath his hair. His torso had gone clammy.

He pulled off his suit jacket and tossed it onto the bed, wrestled off the shoulder holster and dropped it on top of his jacket, loosened the knot of his necktie, and unbuttoned his collar, all as though he were preparing for a sparring match, which, if necessary, this argument might result in.

Willing himself to at least *sound* composed, he asked again, "What name is he using?"

"Assuming it's him," Mike said.

"You assume it's him, or you wouldn't have suggested this secret meeting. Tell me what you have on him, starting with his name."

"No name."

Mike Mallory was an all-star when it came to excavating information from a computer, but a people person he wasn't. He harbored a general contempt for his fellow man, considering most to be complete morons, Drex and Gif being the only possible exceptions.

He was so good at what he did that Drex put up with his truculent attitude and lack of social graces, but right now he muttered an epithet that encompassed both Mike and Gif, who, on this point, had taken Mike's side.

"Fine," Mike said, "call us nasty names. We're thinking in your best interest."

"I'll think for myself, thank you."

"After you hear everything, you may decide against taking matters into your own hands."

"I won't."

Mike shrugged. "Then it'll be your funeral. But I'm not digging your grave, and I'm sure as hell not climbing in with you. Fair warning."

"Fair enough. I'll find out his frigging name myself. Just put me on the right track."

Mike nodded. "That I'll do. Because I don't want him to get away, either. If it's him."

Drex backed down a bit and rolled his shoulders, forcing them to relax. "Does the mystery man hold a job?"

"Nothing I could find," Mike said, "but he lives well."

"I'll bet," Drex said under his breath. "How long has he been in Mount Pleasant?"

"I don't have that yet. He's lived at his current residence for ten months."

"What kind of residence?"

"House."

"Leased?"

"Purchased."

"Mortgaged?"

"If so, I couldn't find it."

"Cash purchase, then."

Mike raised his beefy shoulders in an unspoken *I guess*.

Gif speculated that maybe the property had been inherited, but none of them really thought that, so no one pursued it.

Drex asked, "What's the place like?"

"Based on the real estate listing, it was pre-owned, not new," Mike said. "But an established neighborhood. Upscale."

"Price?"

"Million and a half and change. Looks spacious and well kept on Google Earth. It's all on here." Mike groped beneath his overlap for his pants pocket and produced a thumb drive.

Drex took it from him.

"Won't do you any good without the password, and you're not getting it till we've talked this out."

Drex scoffed. "I can get the password cracked. When applied to you, the word *geek* sounds ludicrous, but you're not the only computer geek around, you know."

Mike raised his hands. "Be my guest. Get a geek to go digging. But if you're found out, how are you going to explain your interest in this seemingly law-abiding citizen?"

"A bribed hacker won't care what my interest is."

"A bribed hacker won't blink over taking your money, then—"

"Stabbing you in the back with it," Gif chimed in.

"Your hacker would get the man in South Carolina on the phone and tell him there's a guy in far-off Lexington, Kentucky, who's spying on him."

Gif picked up. "For more coin than you're paying him, the hacker would sell you out."

"Then it would be *you*, Special Agent Easton," Mike continued, jabbing a stubby index finger at him, "who would be spied on, caught committing God knows how many violations and crimes, civil and criminal, and that would squash this and any future chance you might have to finally nail this son of a bitch, which has been your main mission in life." He wheezed a deep breath. "Tell us we're wrong."

Drex sat down on the end of the bed, propped his forearms on his thighs, and dropped his head forward. After a moment, he looked up. "Okay. No hacker. I'll moderate my approach. Satisfied?"

The other two exchanged a look. Gif said, "Exercise a little caution, some discretion."

"Don't go off half-cocked," Mike said.

Gif added, "That's all we're saying."

Drex placed his hand over his heart. "I'll be cautious, discreet, and fully cocked. Okay?"

Neither approved of that last bit, and they didn't look wholly convinced of his sincerity, but Mike said, "Okay. Next question?"

"Do you have a picture of him?"

"Only the one on his driver's license."

"And?"

"Looks nothing like he did the last time he surfaced."

"Key West," Gif reminded them, although they didn't need reminding.

"You'd never know it's the same man," Mike said. "Which means I could be dead wrong about this fella."

"If he is," Gif said, "but you rush in hell-bent and create havoc in this guy's life, you'll land yourself in a world of hurt. Especially if Rudkowski were to get wind of it."

"Rudkowski can go fuck himself."

"Rumor is, he's tried, but can't quite figure out how to go about it."

Gif's quip got a rare snort of humor out of Mike and a reluctant grin from Drex. Gif was good at defusing a tense situation. Of average height and weight, with thinning brown hair, and not a single feature that was distinguishing, Gif's averageness was his camouflage. He could observe others unnoticed and unremembered, which made him a valuable asset to the team. He was also a reliable predictor of human behavior, as he'd just demonstrated.

Drex's impulse had been to rush in hell-bent and create havoc.

Needing a moment to collect his thoughts, he motioned toward the minibar. "Help yourselves." He stood up and began pacing in the limited space between the bed and the window.

Mike and Gif made their selections and popped the tops off soda cans. Mike complained that he needed a crowbar to get the lid off the jar of mixed nuts. Gif offered to give it a try. Mike scoffed at that and called him a weakling.

Drex tuned out their bickering and focused his thoughts on his quarry, a man he first knew as Weston Graham, although that could be just another of his many aliases. Having eluded the authorities for decades, he could have turned up enjoying a Frosty at the Wendy's across the freeway or burning incense in a monastery in the Himalayas, and neither would have surprised Drex.

He was a chameleon, exceptionally good at altering his appearance and adapting to his environment. Among the ones in which he'd lived comfortably and without arousing suspicion were a penthouse on Chicago's Gold Coast, a horse ranch outside of Santa Barbara, and a yacht moored in Key West. Other locales that he had oozed his way through—those that Drex knew of—weren't that ritzy. They hadn't had to be. All had been extremely profitable for him.

When his cohorts had resettled, Drex asked, "What put you onto the guy in South Carolina?"

"I run my trot lines continually, but what finally tipped me?" Mike said around a burp. "An online dating service. Figuring he vets his victims somehow, I troll those services periodically just to see if something clicks. Day before yesterday, I came across a profile that did. The wording of it jostled my memory. Felt like I'd read it before.

"Took me a while to find it, but there it was. Except for the physical description of himself, it was word for word, comma for comma, identical to this most recent one. Likes, dislikes, five-year goals, philosophy of life and love. All that bullcrap. But the kicker? It was posted six months before Pixie went missing."

Patricia Montgomery, known as Pixie to her friends, had vanished from her Tulsa mansion, never to be seen again.

"Coincidence, Mike," Drex said. "Acquaintances of Pixie's who were interviewed swore that she never would have used a dating service to meet men."

"The acquaintances of all the missing ladies have sworn that. They've also sworn their friend was too savvy to be taken in by a con man. But Pixie disappeared within days of selling her stocks and emptying her bank accounts of her oil fortune."

Gif said, "The only thing missing from her home was her PC. Her seducer left behind tens of thousands of dollars in jewelry and furs but took an outdated computer."

"So there wouldn't be evidence of an online flirtation," Mike said. The leather seat beneath him groaned as he leaned forward to take the near-empty jar of nuts from Gif. "You're frowning," he said to Drex.

"I want to be excited, but this is awfully thin."

"You're right. Thin as onionskin. So I went back to his victim after Pixie. At least the one we *suspect* to have been his victim."

"Marian Harris. Key West."

"Eight months before her disappearance, the same damn profile was posted. Different dating service, but one that also caters to 'mature' clients with 'discriminating tastes.'"

"Word for word?" Drex asked.

"Like a fingerprint."

"Bad joke," Gif said.

The man they sought had never left a fingerprint. Or if he had, no one had found it. Freakin' Ted Bundy.

Mike shook the last of the nuts straight from the jar into his mouth. "Pittsburgh didn't take him as long," he said as he noshed. "He solicited 'companionship' with 'a refined lady' only three months before Loretta Doan's disappearance, more than six years ago."

"Are all the services you scanned nationwide?"

"Yes. Relocation isn't a deterrent to him. I think the asshole likes the changes of scenery."

"When was this most recent profile put out there?"

"Couple of months back."

Drex grimaced. "He's looking for his next lady."

"That's what I deduced. So I gave it a test run. I replied, using buzzwords I figured would make me sound like a prime target. I described myself as a childless, fifty-something widow who's financially secure and independent. I enjoy fine cuisine, good wine, and foreign films. Most men find me attractive."

"Not me," Gif said.

"Me neither," Drex said.

Mike gave them the finger. "He must not have, either. He hasn't taken the bait."

Gif thoughtfully scratched his forehead. "Maybe you oversold yourself. You sounded too self-assured, sophisticated, and smart. He looks for women with a dash of naïveté. Vulnerability. You scared him off."

"Or," Drex said, "he picked up on the buzzwords, smelled a rat, figured that this dream lady was actually a fed on a fishing expedition."

"Maybe," Mike said. "But another, more likely possibility—the one I fear—is that he jumped the gun. Solicited too soon. He hasn't responded because he hasn't ditched his current victim yet."

It was a reasonable theory to which Drex gave credence because it caused his gut to clench. "Meaning that she's in mortal danger as we speak."

"Worse than that."

"What's worse than mortal danger?"

Mike hesitated.

"Give," Drex said.

The heavy man sighed. "I repeat, Drex, I may be wrong."

"But you don't think so."

He raised his catcher's mitt–sized hands at his sides.

"Why do you think it's him?" Drex asked.

"Just promise me—"

"No promises. What makes you think this guy is our guy? *My* guy?"

"Drex, you can't go—"

Gif said, "Rudkowski will—"

"Tell me, goddamn it!" Drex said, shouting above their warnings.

After another pause, Mike mumbled, "He's married."

Drex hadn't seen that coming. "*Married?*"

"Married. Do you take? With this ring. I now pronounce you."

Gif confirmed it with a solemn nod.

Drex divided a perplexed look between them, then shook his head and huffed a laugh of bitter disappointment. "Well, that shoots everything to hell, and you've wasted my morning. If we hurry down, the restaurant will still be serving breakfast." He pushed his fingers through his hair.

"*Shit!* Here I was getting all excited, when what it looks like is that our lonely heart has struck out again and is still seeking his soul mate. But he's not our man. Because a wife doesn't jibe."

"It did once," Gif reminded him.

"Once. Not since. Matrimony, do you take, with this ring, hasn't fit his profile or MO in years. Not in any way, shape, or form."

"Actually, Drex, it does," Mike said solemnly.

"How so?"

Gif cleared his throat. "The wife is loaded."

Drex looked at each of them independently. The two men couldn't be more dissimilar, but they wore identical expressions of fear and dread.

He turned away from them, and where his gaze happened to land was on his reflection in the dresser mirror. Even he recognized that, since he'd last looked, his countenance had altered, hardened, become taut with resolve. There was a ferocity in his eyes that hadn't been there only minutes ago, before he had learned that a woman's life hung in the balance. Delicately. And dependent on him to save it.

He kept his voice soft but put steel behind it. "Tell me his name."

Chapter 2

———◆———

"Need help?"

Drex set the empty cardboard box on the curb, turned, and had his first face-to-face with his nemesis.

If this was indeed Weston Graham, he was around five feet eight inches tall and, for a man of sixty-two, extraordinarily fit. His golf shirt hugged firm biceps and a trim waistline. He had a receding hairline, but his graying hair was long enough in back to be pulled into a blunt ponytail. His smile was very white and straight, friendly, and wreathed by a salt-and-pepper door knocker.

Drex swiped his dripping forehead with the ripped sleeve of his baggy t-shirt. "Thanks, but that's the last of them."

"I was hoping you'd say that. I only offered to be nice."

The two of them laughed.

"I'll take one of those beers, though," Drex said. "If you're offering."

His neighbor had crossed the connecting lawns with a cold bottle in each hand. He handed one to Drex. "Welcome to the neighborhood."

"Thanks."

They clinked bottles, and each took a drink. "Jasper Ford." He stuck out his right hand and they shook.

"Jasper," Drex said, as though hearing the name for the first time and committing it to memory, as though he hadn't had to wring it out of Gif and Mike, as though he hadn't spent the past week gleaning as much information on the man as he possibly could.

"I'm Drex Easton." He watched the man's eyes for a reaction to his name, but detected none.

Jasper indicated the pile of empty boxes Drex had stacked at the curb. "You've been hard at it for two days."

"It's been a chore to lug everything up those stairs. They're killers."

He chinned toward a steep exterior staircase that led up to an apartment above a garage that was large enough to house an eighteen-foot inboard. The structure was a good thirty yards behind the main house. Drex figured it had been positioned there to take advantage of the concealment provided by a massive live oak tree.

He squinted up through the branches and pretended to assess the apartment from a fresh perspective. "Moving in was worth the backache, though. It's like living in a tree house."

"I've never seen inside," Jasper said. "Nice?"

"Nice enough."

"How many rooms?"

"Only three, but all I need."

"You're by yourself, then?"

"Not even a goldfish." He grinned. "But, despite the ban on pets, I may get a cat. I spotted some mouse droppings in the kitchen area."

"I can see how a mouse could sneak in. The owners are snowbirds, down here only during the winter months."

"So Mr. Arnott told me. They come down the day after Thanksgiving, stay until the first of June."

"Frankly, when I learned the apartment had been rented out, I was concerned."

"How'd you hear about it?"

"I didn't. You showed up and started carting boxes upstairs."

Drex laughed. "And going through your mind was 'WTF?'"

By way of admission, the man smiled and gave a small shrug. "I have Arnott's number in case of an emergency, so I called him."

"I was an emergency?" Drex glanced down at his ragged shirt, dirty cargo shorts, and well-worn sneakers. "I can see where you might think so. You got one look at me and thought 'there goes the neighborhood.'" He flashed a grin. "I clean up okay, I promise."

Jasper Ford laughed with good nature. "Can't be too careful."

"That's my motto."

"Good fences make for good neighbors."

"Except that there's no fence." Drex looked across the uninterrupted expanse of grass between the two properties. Coming back to Jasper Ford's dark gaze, he said, "I'll confine my rude behavior to this side of the property line. You'll never know I'm here."

Jasper smiled, but before he could comment, his cell phone signaled a text. "Excuse me." He took the phone from his shirt pocket.

While he was reading the text, Drex arched his back in an overextended stretch that caused him to wince, and took another swallow of beer.

"My wife," Jasper said as he thumbed off his phone. "Her flight has been weather delayed. She's stuck at O'Hare."

"That's too bad."

"Happens a lot," he said somewhat absently as he glanced over his shoulder toward his house, then came back around to Drex. "How about some surf and turf?"

"Pardon?"

"I've got crab cakes ready for the pan. Steaks marinating. No sense in half of it going to waste."

"I couldn't impose."

"If it was going to be an imposition, I wouldn't have invited you."

"Well..." Scratching his unshaven cheek, Drex pretended to ponder it. "I haven't stocked the pantry or fridge yet. I've been subsisting on fast food."

Jasper chuckled. "I can do better than that. See you at sunset. We'll have drinks on the porch." He reached out and took Drex's beer bottle. "I'll toss this for you."

Drex stepped out of the shower and reached for his ringing cell phone, which he'd balanced on the rim of the sink. He looked to see who was calling, then clicked on. "Hey."

"How are you faring?" Mike asked.

"Right now, good. I'm standing naked and wet under a ceiling fan."

"Spare me."

"The fan squeaks, but this is the coolest I've been since I got here. Why didn't you tell me this apartment wasn't air-conditioned."

"You didn't ask."

Once it had been decided among the three of them that Jasper Ford warranted further investigation, Drex flew to Charleston. He wasted no time in driving to Mount Pleasant and locating the Fords' home.

Google Earth hadn't done it justice. The two-story house was built of brick, painted white. Classically southern in design, a deep front porch ran the width of the façade, twin columns framing a glossy black front door with a brass knocker in the shape of a pineapple. The house was surrounded by a sprawling lawn and shaded by decades-old trees.

The residence looked lived in. Blooming flowers in all the beds. Thriving ferns on the porches. An American flag hanging from the eaves. Newspaper and mail delivery.

By contrast, the house next door looked less tended, and for the three nights Drex surveilled it, lights came on at the same time, went off at the same time. Timed to do so. No flowers, ferns, or mail.

He returned to Lexington, briefed Mike and Gif, and instructed Mike to find out who owned the property neighboring the Fords', which appeared to be a second home or otherwise infrequently occupied.

Mike did his due diligence, got a name and contact info off tax records.

Then Drex did his thing. He made a cold call to Mr. Arnott, who, with his wife, resided most of the year in Pennsylvania, but, upon retirement, had purchased the place in South Carolina to escape the cold and snow.

Drex, laying it on thick, told him of his situation, which was a complete fabrication. Then he got down to the heart of the matter. He was seeking temporary lodging in or near Charleston. During a scouting expedition to see what might be available, he'd crossed the Cooper River into Mount Pleasant, and as he was driving around getting the lay of the land, so to speak, he'd spotted the garage apartment. It was ideal: Secluded. Quiet. A "cabin in the woods," within the confines of a scenic and safe neighborhood.

The apartment would provide all the space he required. He would live there alone, no pets. He was a nonsmoker. And, in the bargain, he would keep an eye on the main house.

"Honestly, Mr. Arnott, if I'd been a burglar, I'd have chosen your house to break into. It's obvious that you're an absentee owner."

When Arnott hedged, Drex was tempted to play his FBI card. He didn't, fearing it would be tipped to Jasper Ford that he had a fed moving in next door to him. Instead he provided Arnott several fictitious references, all written by Gif, whom Arnott actually called to confirm his high recommendation. Mike also got a call to verify the reference letter signed by him. Between them, they convinced

Mr. Arnott that Drex Easton was a man of sound mind, good character, and everything he claimed to be.

Arnott agreed to lease him the apartment for the requested three months, although Drex would be there for only two weeks—his allotted vacation time. Only Mike and Gif would know how his time away was being utilized. Until he had a major breakthrough, he was keeping everyone else in the dark.

Besides, asking Arnott for a three-month lease lent credibility to his story and made him seem like a stabler, more responsible tenant. He paid the full amount of rent up front.

"Besides no AC, how is it?" Mike asked now. "Are you moved in?"

From the open bathroom door, Drex could see practically the entire apartment, and virtually every square inch of it was empty, as had been most of the boxes he'd carted up the stairs for the benefit of his audience next door. The apartment had come furnished, though sparsely. He'd brought only the essentials needed to keep himself clothed and groomed. He'd brought a coffeemaker, but he hadn't lied about a steady diet of fast food.

"All settled in," he told Mike. "My laptop is on the kitchen table. My pistol is between the mattress and box spring."

"In other words, it's the same as your place here," Mike said. "And you've lived here for how long?"

"Is there a reason for this call? If so, get to it. Because I don't want to be late for my date."

"In two days' time you've already lined up a *girl?*" Mike said. "When you said 'fully cocked,' you really meant it? I'll have to check my charts, but I think this might be a record."

"There's no girl, and cut the bullshit. Is Gif with you? Put me on speaker." When Drex could tell that Mike had switched over, he said, "Jasper Ford invited me over for dinner tonight."

After a second or two of stunned silence, Mike and Gif exclaimed their surprise.

"Here I have my high-powered binocs focused, all set up to spy on him, and he comes over today with a cold beer and a hand-shake, welcoming me to the neighborhood. I'm glad he made the first move. That saved me from having to devise a way to put me in his path and make his acquaintance."

He gave them a run-down of their conversation. "It was casual, friendly, but definitely an appraisal. When he saw me moving in, he called Arnott to check me out."

"Paranoid, you think?" Gif asked.

"Or just a watchful property owner, cautious of strangers," Mike said. "Anybody in that kind of neighborhood would be."

"It could be either," Drex said. "I should have a better feel for him after our dinner."

"What about the missus?" Mike asked.

It had been a worry to them that, although Drex had spotted Jasper coming and going over the past two days, he hadn't seen any sign of his wife. "He told me that she's been out of town, which I hope is the truth and that she's still alive. While we were talking, he did receive a text ostensibly from her." He told them about the delayed flight.

"Why Chicago?" Gif asked.

"He didn't say. But he did say that her being delayed happens a lot, indicating that she flies often."

"Makes sense," Mike said. "She was in the travel business."

"Yes, *was*," Drex said. Mike had discovered that the sale of Shafer Travel, Inc., had been the source of Mrs. Ford's mega bucks. "Question is, why is she still frequently on the go?"

When no answer was forthcoming, Drex said, "I'll feel better when I can confirm she's still with us. Maybe I'll get a lot of questions answered tonight. Speaking of…" He glanced out the window. The sun was sinking. "I've got to go now, get dressed, make a run to the liquor store."

"What for?"

"It wouldn't be neighborly to show up for dinner empty-handed."

As he signed off, he was thinking how neighborly it had been of Jasper to bring him a beer and then offer to toss the bottle for him.

However, wouldn't it have been more neighborly to let Drex finish drinking the beer? But no, Jasper Ford had wanted that bottle back.

———◆———

"White for the crab cakes. Red for the steaks." Drex held up the bottles of wine in turn as he approached the screened porch where Jasper was sitting in a rocking chair beneath a twirling ceiling fan.

He got up and held open the screen door. "You didn't have to do that, but thank you." He took the bottles from Drex. "How about a drink first?"

"What are you having?" Drex motioned toward the highball glass on the wicker table next to the rocking chair.

"Bourbon on the rocks."

"Water?"

"No."

Drex grinned. "Perfect."

"Have a seat." Jasper put the white wine in the mini fridge beneath the built-in bar and poured Drex's drink. As he handed it to him, he said, "You do clean up okay."

Drex raised his glass in a quasi toast. "I try." He'd shaved, but had left a scruff. He'd worn casual slacks and a button-up shirt, the shirttail out. Docksiders, no socks.

Jasper resumed his seat in the rocker and sipped from his drink. "So, you're a writer."

Drex pretended to strangle on his sip of whiskey and looked at his host with surprise.

"Your literary agent was one of the references you gave Arnott."

"Oh! For a second there, I thought you were a mind-reader." Looking abashed, he said, "I'm trying to be a writer. Can't claim the title yet. I haven't published."

"Your agent told Arnott that you have real potential."

He waved that off. "All agents say that about their clients."

"She must believe it or she wouldn't be representing you."

"He."

"Sorry?"

"My agent is a he."

"Oh. My mistake."

My ass, Drex thought. That had been a test.

"Are you writing full-time?"

"Lately I have been."

"How do you support yourself?"

"Frugally." Jasper gave the expected laugh. Drex said, "My dad died a couple of years ago and left me a small inheritance. Nothing to boast about, but it's keeping a roof over my head while I work on the book."

"Fiction or non?"

"Fiction. Civil War novel."

Jasper raised his eyebrows, encouraging him to continue.

"I don't want to bore you," Drex said.

"I'm not bored."

"Well," Drex said, taking a deep breath, "the protagonist takes a sort of Forrest Gump journey through the conflict, from Bull Run to Appomattox. He grapples with divided loyalties, his moral compass, mortal fear during battle. That kind of thing."

"Sounds interesting."

Drex smiled as though he realized that was a platitude, but appreciated it all the same. "My agent likes the story, and said my research was factually sound. But he felt the narrative lacked color. It needed more heart, he said. Soul."

"So you came down here to get color, heart, and soul."

"I hope to soak up some while working on the second draft. And," he said, stretching out both his legs and the word, "I needed to get away from the distractions of the everyday grind."

"Like a wife?"

"Not anymore."

"Divorced?"

"Thank God."

"You sound bitter. What happened?"

"She accused me of cheating."

"Did you?"

Drex looked at him and cocked an eyebrow, but didn't answer. Instead he sipped his bourbon. It was a smooth, expensive one. "The divorce cost me dear and taught me a hard lesson."

"You'll never cheat again."

"I'll never marry again."

"Ah, never say never," Jasper said, shaking his index finger at him. "After the loss of my first wife, I grieved for her and stayed single for a long time. Thirty years, in fact."

"Man, that's loyalty. How'd she die?"

Looking Drex straight in the eye, he said, "In pain." He held the stare for a beat, then finished his bourbon in one shot, stood, and headed for the kitchen. "How do you like your steak?"

The medium rare rib eye had been seasoned and grilled to perfection. Jasper apologized for serving the meal in the casual dining room, rather than the more formal one, but the table was set a lot fancier than Drex was used to, and he confessed as much.

While they ate, Drex probed his host for more personal information, but in a manner he hoped would seem natural. "This house is really something."

"Thank you."

"You hire a professional decorator?"

"Only to consult. Talia knew what she wanted."

"Talia? That's your wife's name? Pretty." He glanced around. "She has good taste."

"She has great taste."

"Expensive taste?"

Jasper only smiled at that, but didn't respond.

Drex took a sip of the Cabernet he'd brought, blotted his mouth, and then picked up his utensils and cut into his steak again. "You seem to do all right," he said, applying his knife to the meat. "What's your line of work?"

"I work at enjoying the fruits of my labors."

Drex stopped chewing and looked across at Jasper to gauge whether or not he was joking. Jasper's expression didn't change. He didn't even blink. Drex swallowed and laughed out loud. "Lucky you. You retired early?"

"Several years ago."

"From what? Must've been a healthy business."

"I created some software that proved to be lucrative."

Or did you accumulate a fortune by rooking women out of theirs?

That's what Drex was thinking when Jasper smiled at him congenially and said, "I have lemon sorbet for dessert."

Drex declined the sorbet. And since it was obvious that Jasper didn't want to elaborate on his former field of endeavor, Drex let the subject drop. He also declined to have coffee, not wanting to outstay his welcome.

Although he offered to help with the cleanup, Jasper refused.

As Drex was about to leave, he mentioned that the apartment didn't have air-conditioning. Jasper insisted on lending him a box fan. He fetched it from his garage and told Drex to keep it for as long as he needed it.

"Thanks. Thanks for everything." Drex extended his hand.

As they shook, Jasper said, "Talia texted that she should be home by midnight. We're taking a boat out tomorrow afternoon. Not too far offshore. Just puttering around. Why don't you join us?"

Drex was anxious to meet his wife, gauge her, but didn't want to appear too eager. "Nice of you to offer, but it's been days since I looked at my manuscript. The move-in and all. I really should work tomorrow."

"You can't take off a Sunday? I'm sure the Lord would understand."

Drex pretended to have been persuaded. Jasper gave him the name of the marina and the number of the slip. "Meet us there around noon. We'll go ahead and get things ready. Come hungry. We'll have a picnic lunch on board."

"Sounds great." Drex thanked him again for the evening and carried the box fan across the lawn and up the stairs.

He began undressing by reaching under his loose shirttail and removing the holster from his waistband at the small of his back. Call him a cynic, but surf and turf had seemed a little over the top for a first visit even if the meal hadn't originally been prepared with him in mind.

Fifteen minutes later, he was stripped down to his underwear, the fan was on high, all the lights were off, and he was at the window watching through binoculars as Jasper went about cleaning up. When he was done, he locked the doors and turned out the lights. A few moments later an upstairs light came on. Minutes after, that light was also extinguished.

He hadn't waited up for his wife. Talia.

Drex repositioned the fan so it would be blowing across the bed. He lay down on his back and stacked his hands on his chest. But, tired as he was, he was still awake when he heard a car. He returned to the window that offered the most advantageous view of the Fords' house.

Turning into the driveway was a late-model BMW sedan. Drex checked his wristwatch. Mrs. Ford had overshot her ETA by twenty-seven minutes. She must have opened the garage door with a remote. She drove in, and the door went down.

Drex never distinguished more of her than a shadowy form, but by the lights being turned on, then off, he tracked her progress through the house. The last light to go out was behind a shade in a small upstairs window. He presumed it was a bathroom. Drex stayed at the window for several minutes more, but the house remained dark.

He returned to bed but lay awake, his mind troubled with thoughts of Talia Ford, lying beside her husband. When she got into bed with him, had she whispered good night, kissed his cheek, snuggled against him, reached for him, and initiated lovemaking? The thought of it made Drex ill.

At least she was alive. But for how long? Because if Jasper was the man Drex suspected him of being, his wife's days were numbered. If Jasper Ford was the man Drex had first come to know by the name of Weston Graham, then this woman would be the next of many whom Jasper had befriended, wooed, and robbed of millions before they disappeared without a trace. Drex was convinced that he had disposed of those women.

How'd she die?

In pain.

The words, Jasper's implacable doll-like stare when he spoke them, had made the hair on the back of Drex's neck stand on end. In that moment, it had felt as though Jasper was baiting him.

Drex hadn't taken the bait, but he'd wanted to.

He had wanted to lunge across the short distance separating them, grab the man—the good cook, the perfect host, the friendly neighbor—by the throat, and demand to know if he was the psychopathic cocksucker who had killed his mother.

Chapter 3

The vessel moored in the designated slip wasn't just a boat, but a yacht. It wasn't the largest in the marina, but it held its own among them, being impressively sleek and shiny. Drex felt like he should be wearing white pants and a blue blazer, maybe with a jaunty pocket handkerchief, and have a hat with gold braid and a shiny black brim.

Instead, he was in khaki shorts, a chambray shirt, and baseball cap.

Jasper waved to him from the aft deck. The woman beside him called down, "Ahoy, Drex. You're just in time for Champagne." She hefted a magnum by the neck.

He gave her his best smile and started up the ramp. "I'd settle for a beer."

"We have that, too."

A decade younger than her husband, she was very pretty in the soft and—what was the word Gif had used? Naïve? She had that dash of girlish naïveté that a con man would target. Her hair was blond, short, and artfully tousled. She was dressed in white capri pants and a bright pink sleeveless top with a scooped neckline that showed off a deep cleavage. The best that money could buy, Drex guessed.

As he joined them on deck, he and Jasper shook hands. "Have trouble finding us?"

"None at all." He took in the yacht, then divided a look between Jasper and his wife, landing on Jasper. "You're a lucky bastard. This is some beauty you have here." Then he leaned in, adding, "The boat's not bad looking, either."

All three of them laughed. Mrs. Ford flattened a hand against the swell of her breasts, the diamonds on her fingers flashing rainbows in the sunlight. "Why, thank you. Jasper warned me that you were a charmer. I'm so glad you joined us today, even though I understand we're dragging you away from your work."

"Thank you for the invitation, and it didn't take much arm-twisting to get me here. A writer looks for any excuse not to write."

"I would be completely daunted by the prospect of writing a book," she said.

"I'm completely daunted by it, too, Talia. I'm sorry, is it okay if I call you Talia?"

She and Jasper looked surprised, then both began laughing. She said, "You could call me Talia if that was my name. I'm Elaine. Elaine Conner."

Taken aback, Drex was about to stammer an apology when Jasper looked beyond him and smiled. "*Here's* Talia."

Drex did an about-face.

A woman dressed all in white was coming up the steps that led from the galley, a tray of canapés balanced on her right palm. Hearing her name, she tilted her head back and looked up through the hatch, straight at Drex.

His stomach dropped like an anchor, because, in that instant, he knew: *I'm so fucked.*

As Talia cleared the doorway onto the deck, the tall stranger stepped forward. "You could use a hand." He relieved her of the tray.

"Thank you." The sun was behind him. She shielded her eyes against the glare to better see him. The bill of his cap cast his eyes in shadow, but his bristly jaw and smile were visible. He didn't appear to be quite as "rough around the edges" as Jasper had described. "You must be our new neighbor."

"Guilty."

Jasper placed an arm across her shoulders. "Talia, this is Drex Easton. Drex, my wife."

"Pleased to meet you, Drex." She proffered her hand. He was holding the tray in his left, so his right hand was free to shake hers. It was a firm handshake, but not a bone-cruncher.

"Pleased to meet you, too, Talia."

"Jasper told me about the pleasant dinner you had together."

"It's a shame you missed it. Your husband is an outstanding cook."

"Which works out well, because I'm dreadful."

"This doesn't look dreadful." He nodded down at the array of hors d'oeuvres on the tray.

"The deli," she whispered.

"But the rémoulade for the shrimp salad is homemade," Jasper said. "I whipped it up this morning."

"And I recommend it highly," she said.

Elaine got their attention by clapping her hands. "Gather 'round. I insist on everyone having at least one glass of Champagne." She had filled four flutes and placed them on a cocktail table. "This is an occasion. We've made a new friend. Welcome, Drex."

"Thank you. I'm glad to be here."

Although he was the outsider, he looked at ease as he carried the tray to the table and set it in the center, then held out a chair for Elaine before seating himself.

"You forgot your hat, Talia." Jasper came up behind her and placed her wide-brimmed straw hat on her head.

"Thank you. It wouldn't have taken long for me to miss it."

"Wise girl," Elaine said to Drex. "She avoids sun exposure. Too late for me."

"You acquire a gorgeous tan. I freckle," Talia said.

"She's practically a vampire," Jasper said.

Affronted and embarrassed by his insensitive remark, she looked at the newcomer of the group, who was sitting directly across the table from her. He had slid on a pair of sunglasses, but she could tell that he was looking into her face, as though seeking the referred-to freckles.

What could have become an awkward moment was saved by Elaine, who prompted them to raise their glasses. She made a toast to everyone's good health then turned her attention to Drex and began plying him with questions.

Jasper spoke quietly to her. "I believe I embarrassed you with the vampire comment. I'm sorry."

"No harm done."

He patted her hand, then turned toward the other two and joined their conversation. Talia was content to let it flow around her without being required to either lead it or participate to any great extent. The tedious hours she'd spent in O'Hare, the bumpy flight to Charleston, then the drive home from the airport had left her exhausted. Jasper didn't wake up when she got into bed, for which she'd been relieved. It was his wont to ask for detailed accounts of her trips.

Over breakfast, she had suggested that she sit out today's excursion. "You and Elaine go without me. Enjoy yourselves. I'll be perfectly happy to stay behind and lounge all day."

"We've had this planned for days. Elaine will be disappointed if you don't come. Besides, I've invited a fourth."

That's when he'd told her about the man who'd moved into the garage apartment.

"Is it even livable?" she'd asked.

"He seems to think so. But I doubt his standards are very high."

"Why do you say that?"

"I'll let you form your own opinion. He's rough around the edges, but I will credit him with knowing which fork to use for each course, and the two bottles of wine he brought were passable."

"If you weren't that taken with him, why did you invite him to come along today?"

"Curiosity."

Drex Easton was more refined than Jasper had led her to believe, but then Jasper *did* have very high standards. Gauging by Elaine's body language, which had her leaning toward the writer across the armrest of her chair, she found him magnetic.

He seemed unfazed by her avid interest, answering her barrage of questions with humor but, Talia noticed, little elaboration. He was self-deprecating and unaffected.

But when he glanced across the table and shot her a smile, Talia wondered if perhaps he was exercising reverse psychology. Maybe his seeming disinterest in making a good first impression was a calculated attempt to make one.

Not so long ago, she would have accepted his open and friendly nature for what it was, rather than to look for duplicity. Jasper was more disinclined to take people at face value. She supposed that tendency of his was wearing off on her.

They finished the remainder of the Champagne, then Jasper pushed back his chair and stood. "Shall we get underway? Or would you rather serve lunch first, Elaine?"

"Let's go out a way and anchor for lunch."

Jasper saluted her. "After you, captain." He bent down and peeped beneath the brim of Talia's hat. "You don't mind if I play first mate, do you?"

"I know you can't wait to get your hands on the wheel. Go."

He pecked her cheek with his lips. To Drex he said, "Beer and soft drinks are in the fridge in the galley. Help yourself."

"Thanks. I'm good for now."

Jasper followed Elaine into the wheelhouse and closed the door behind them. The absence of Elaine's chatter was immediately noticeable. Drex was the first to remark on it. "Has Elaine ever met a stranger?"

Talia laughed. "Not since I've known her."

"Which is for how long?"

"A few years."

"How'd you come to meet?"

"She and her husband frequently cruised down here from Delaware. After he died, she decided to move here. She and I met when she joined the country club."

He gave a look around. "I assumed the yacht belonged to you and Jasper."

"No, it's Elaine's."

"Does she pilot it herself?"

"Usually only out of the marina."

"That takes some maneuvering skills."

"According to her, the late Mr. Conner was an avid boatman. He taught her how to pilot in case there was ever an emergency and she had to take over for him. She's coaching Jasper. Once we clear the buoys, she lets him have the wheel."

"He seemed eager to be at the helm."

"He loves boats and all things aquatic."

"What about you?"

"I enjoy our outings, but I don't have a passion for the water."

"No? What turns you on?"

Possibly she was reading innuendo into the question when none was intended. Otherwise it bordered on being inappropriate. Since they were going to be trapped on a boat together for hours, she chose to make a joke of it rather than an issue.

"Nutella," she said. "I eat it with a spoon straight from the jar."

He laughed.

The lighthearted mood had been reestablished. Feeling more

comfortable, she settled in her chair, tucking her right foot beneath her hips. She motioned toward his cap. "Did you go to Tennessee?"

"No. A buddy of mine is an alum and gung-ho fan. We went camping last summer, and I came home with his cap mixed up in my stuff. I never gave it back." He grinned. "It's ragged. I doubt he's missed it."

She smiled, then looked away, distracted by another boat passing them as it entered the marina. She waved to those onboard, and they waved back. But once the boat was past them, she again got the feeling that Drex Easton was studying her, and when she turned back to him, she caught him at it. "What?"

He pointed toward her empty glass. "You passed on a refill of Champagne. Can I go below and get you something else?"

"You shouldn't be waiting on me. You're the guest."

"But you didn't invite me. Jasper did. You probably would have preferred not having to entertain today. You got in late last night."

She tilted her head inquisitively.

"I heard your car when you pulled into the driveway."

"I'm sorry I disturbed you."

"You didn't. I wasn't asleep. I haven't slept through the night since I moved in."

"A new place takes some getting used to. Give it a few more nights."

"I don't think a few more nights are going to improve the lumpy mattress. The fan Jasper loaned me helped with the heat."

"He lent you a fan?"

"His generosity knows no bounds."

She smiled. Then, to her chagrin, she yawned. "Forgive me. The truth is, I didn't get a full night's sleep, either, and the Champagne has made me drowsy."

"Then I'll shut up and let you doze. Or would you rather I leave you in peace and...relocate?"

When he smiled in a certain way, an attractive dimple appeared in his right cheek behind the piratical scruff. She figured he knew that dimple was attractive and doubted he would relocate if she took him up on his offer.

"You may stay," she said.

"Ah, good. I'm drowsy, too. And after two days of moving in, it feels good to sit and do nothing." He slouched deeper into his chair, pulled the brim of his cap down to the top of his sunglasses, and linked his fingers over his lap. No rings. A sizeable but unadorned wristwatch with a black leather band.

His hands were large and long-fingered, with plump veins crisscrossing the backs of them. His sleeves were rolled up to midway between wrist bone and elbow. Even though he appeared relaxed, she sensed tensile strength in his limbs.

She looked away and followed a solitary cloud drifting between them and the horizon. A minute passed. He didn't move. The silence between them began to feel ponderous. She searched for something to say. "Drex is an unusual name."

He flinched and sat up straighter. "Sorry? I was about to nod off."

"No you weren't."

The moment the words were out, she wished she could call them back. Too late now, however. Above his sunglasses, one of his eyebrows arched to form a question mark.

With a trace of challenge in her tone, she said, "You were staring at me. I could see your eyes through your sunglasses."

He thumped the arm of his chair with his fist. "Damn! Busted." He shot her that smile again. "I *was* staring at you."

"Why?"

"Welllll, if I told the absolute, swear-on-the-Bible truth, Jasper would probably sew me up in a tow sack and pitch me overboard."

Talia couldn't help it. She laughed. He was a shameless flirt, and, since he made no secret of it, it was harmless. "Like the Count of Monte Cristo."

"My favorite book," he said.

"Oh? Why?"

He thought about it for a moment. "He was committed."

"To getting revenge."

He bobbed his chin. "He let nothing stop him, not even imprisonment. He was patient. He did his homework. He pulled off the best undercover guise ever. Got his man." He paused and then grinned wickedly. "And woman."

"His enemy's wife."

He sat up straight and leaned forward with his forearms crossed on the tabletop. "I called Jasper a lucky bastard when I mistook Elaine for his wife."

"You no longer think he's lucky?"

He didn't answer immediately. Then, "I think he won the Powerball. Twice. At least."

The dimple had disappeared, and so had the mischievous smile. Of a sudden, the flirting didn't seem quite so harmless.

Chapter 4

Elaine chose that moment to open the wheelhouse door and poke her head out. "Hold onto your hats and watch to see that those flutes don't slide off the table. We've cleared the marina, and Jasper's about to give it the throttle." She ducked back inside. The yacht gathered speed and moved out into open water.

Elaine had interrupted an uncomfortable moment. But Talia thought perhaps she had imagined the intensity in Drex's tone, because now his teasing grin was back.

"Why was I staring at you? I was contemplating. Here I am a wordsmith, but I'll be damned if I can think of an adjective that accurately captures the color of your hair. When I saw you coming up the stairs, I thought 'russet.'"

"Adequate."

"Adequate but lacking nuance."

"You need nuance?"

"Yes. Because when you got in the sunlight, I saw that your hair is shot through with strands of gold and copper. So what word would I use to describe it?"

"Why would you need a word? Why would you be describing

me? Unless you're planning to use me as a character in your book."

"Oh, God no! I think far too highly of you to do that."

Her laughter was followed by a comfortable silence as they stared out across the chop. He resumed the conversation by asking what had taken her to Chicago.

"I went to assess a hotel." Reading his puzzled expression, she smiled. "It's a prototype. New concept. Very minimalist. I tried it on for size."

"What for?"

"It's a long story."

He spread his arms. "I've got nowhere to go."

"Okay, but remember you asked."

"Fire at will."

"I was trying out the hotel for my clientele."

"Clientele?"

"My parents had a travel agency. I started working in the office when I was in high school. When I graduated college, I was made manager, and they semi-retired. Then Dad died, followed by my mother a year and a half later. I was their only child and heir. Shafer Travel, Inc., became mine."

"That sounded like the expurgated version. Go on."

"Well, I expanded the business, first by opening an office in Savannah, and then another in Birmingham. Those did well. I paid off the business loan that got those up and running, then took out another loan to open two more offices, one in Dallas, the other in Charlotte."

"Wow," he said. "This at a time when most people started booking everything travel-related online."

"Most people, yes. But when even the best travel agencies began cutting back on personnel and services offered, a market was created for white glove service. My agencies responded, and began catering to clients who didn't need to, or wish to, shop online for the cheapest airfare or haggle over a room rate."

"You stopped booking bus tours to see fall foliage?"

"And started booking private jets to see the seven wonders of the world. Word spread about our specialized service."

"Millionaires talk."

She smiled. "Before too long, Shafer Travel got the attention of a company that has dozens of agencies nationwide. It didn't look kindly on the competition mine were giving them." She raised her shoulders. "They made me an offer I couldn't refuse."

"You sold out."

"Lock, stock, and barrel."

"Congratulations."

"Thank you."

"So if you no longer have the business, why were you trying out the hotel in Chicago?"

"Are you sure you want to hear all this?"

"I don't know. How much more inept and underachieving am I going to feel when you're finished?" The dimple reappeared.

She tented her fingers and tapped them against her lips as she regarded him thoughtfully. "I don't quite trust you."

"I'm sorry?"

"Your self-denigration. I think you use it to disarm people so they'll form a lower opinion of you than they should."

He placed his hand over his heart. "What a relief. Here I thought my inadequacies were real. I'm glad to learn they're faked."

She didn't laugh as he obviously expected her to. Rather, she continued to wonder why he downplayed the shrewdness she detected in the eyes behind the dark lenses. Not that his psychology was of any consequence to her, she reminded herself. She went on with her story, but only because he motioned for her to do so.

"I discovered I wasn't cut out to retire at the age of thirty-two," she said. "Inside of a month, I was bored. So when I began getting calls from former clients, complaining about the lack of attention and personal service they were receiving, I agreed to handle their travel arrangements, everything from the time they left their front door until they returned. Down to the most minute detail."

"You do this for fun? Goodwill?"

"No, for a percentage of how much they spend on the trip."

"Ah!" He grinned. "I doubt I could afford you."

"Few can," she admitted. "That limits the number of clients I cater to. I get to keep my toe in, but only to the extent I want."

"Still giving the big boys competition?"

"I'm an...irritant. Especially to the company that bought me out."

He barked a laugh. "I'll bet. You're keeping the big spenders under your wing." He flopped back against the chair cushion. "For ingenuity alone, I'd give you a five-star rating."

His flattery made her feel good in a way it probably shouldn't. She experienced a warmth she wanted to bask in.

"How did you like the minimalist prototype?" he asked.

Glad to be pulled back on track, she said, "There were an overabundance of outlets in which to plug in devices."

"But?"

"The room was sterile. No personality or character. No—"

"Ambiance?"

"Good word."

"Whew! Maybe I have promise as a writer after all."

She gave him an arch look before continuing. "Everything was so high tech, it took me fifteen minutes to figure out how to turn on the lights and keep them on. I'm not particularly fond of baroque or chintz, but I do like a chair that conforms to the human body, one that I can actually sit in."

"You won't be recommending the place."

"No. My clients appreciate having their travel streamlined, and having plenty of electrical outlets for their gadgets, but they also insist on creature comforts."

"I'm a creature who likes his comforts."

"Then why did you move into that tiny space with no air-conditioning and a lumpy mattress?"

"I hadn't suffered enough yet. To be a good writer, one must suffer."

"Self-flagellation?"

"I haven't tried it yet, but I'm almost to that point."

They shared a smile, then he asked, "When you go on these research trips, does Jasper ever go along?"

"Not that often. Only if I'm looking at something a bit more exotic than a hotel for the business traveler."

"Do you ever go overseas?"

"I go two or three times a year. Jasper, never."

"Why not? I'd think those would be the trips he'd want to take."

"He doesn't like the long flights."

"I see."

She sensed there was more to his dismissive comment than the mere two words. "What?"

"Nothing."

"What?"

"Well, I think Jasper must be the most secure man I've ever met to let you go traveling the world on your own and be okay with it."

"I didn't ask his permission, so it's not as though he *lets* me," she said coolly. "And I didn't say he was okay with it."

"Then he's not?"

"He is, but he keeps track of my itinerary."

"So he knows where you are at any given time."

"Yes." Minutes earlier, she'd been thinking how glad she was to have avoided one of Jasper's debriefings late last night. Now, she was defending his husbandly concern. "It only makes sense. It's a safety precaution."

"Me? I'd want to put a chip in your ear."

Again Drex's grin lightened the tenor of the conversation and relieved the tension inside her chest that had begun to collect. She had disliked having to justify Jasper's vigilance over her schedule.

Drex looked toward the wheelhouse. "How long have you two been together?"

"Together, a year and a half. Married, eleven months."

"That was a short courtship."

"Relatively."

"He must have swept you off your feet as soon as you met. How did you?"

"You wouldn't believe it."

He came back around to her. "Oh, no. Don't tell me you found each other online."

"Well, in a sense, but not on a match-up service. We corresponded by email for several weeks before we met in person."

His eyebrows bobbed above his sunglasses. "Do tell."

She laughed. "It's not at all salacious. He'd booked a trip—domestic—through our office in Savannah. When he returned, he had a complaint about one of the hotels we'd booked him into, and wanted to take up the issue with the top dog."

"That would be you."

"He was given my email address. I looked into his complaint, and found that it had merit. I got him a full refund for that night. He was impressed by the excellent service."

"And proceeded to email you flowery compliments for weeks."

"Then gave me flowers for real."

"Smooooooth. What did the card say?"

"There wasn't a card. He drove from Savannah to Charleston to deliver the bouquet in person."

He whistled softly. "Even smoother."

"It was a change from being asked out via text."

"The suave move worked, and here you are. Happ'ly ever after."

She looked down at her wedding band and turned it around on her finger. "Here I am." Her soft comment was followed by a ding. She raised her head and looked across the table. "Is that your phone?"

"Yeah." Looking resentful of the interruption, he stretched out his leg and dug into the front pocket of his shorts for his phone. He looked at the readout. "I set myself a reminder. I'm supposed to call my agent. But can I get cell service out here?"

"It extends offshore for ten or fifteen miles."

"Then I'd better make the call. He's expecting it."

⸺◆⸺

He was about to stand when she motioned him back into his chair and got up herself. "I'll go inside."

"No, stay here. I'll go forward. Once he gets wound up, he tends to ramble."

"It would be hard for you to hear above the wind. Besides, I need to make myself useful."

Drex was reluctant to end their private conversation. He watched her until she was inside before he tapped in the number. It was answered immediately. "Sheriff's office, Deputy Gray speaking."

"Agent Easton. Did you locate the file?"

"Yes, sir."

Early that morning, Drex had called the Monroe County sheriff's office in Key West, Florida, figuring that whoever was working the undesirable Sunday morning shift would be junior in rank. A more senior officer wouldn't be as impressed to be speaking with a federal agent and would have given Drex a lot more hassle.

As good fortune would have it, Gray was just such a rookie.

In their earlier conversation Drex had told him that his field office in Lexington was investigating a missing person case. "Single, affluent, middle-aged woman. It's almost certain a kidnaping. One of our data analysts determined that some of the particulars of this disappearance are similar to a case your department investigated a few years back."

There was no such active case in Lexington, but there was a cold case in Key West, where Marian Harris had disappeared, abandoning her yacht in a private harbor and leaving her bank accounts empty.

It could be sheer coincidence that within hours of meeting Jasper Ford, Drex had been invited to go out on a boat with him. The man might never have spent a day of his life in Key West. But Drex had played a hunch and called the sheriff's department that morning anyway.

He was glad he'd had that foresight, and unapologetic for lying about an investigation in Lexington, because, since talking to Deputy Gray this morning, he'd learned from Talia that Jasper had a passion for being on the water and at the helm of a yacht.

Gray had asked for a few hours to locate the file. Drex had told him he would call back at a designated time. It wasn't the most ideal time to talk, but Gray was due to go off duty soon, and, besides that, Drex was eager to hear anything the deputy could tell him.

"What have you got for me? And you'll have to speak up. I'm outdoors."

"This case was before I joined the department. In between performing my other duties, I've been reviewing it, so I have a general grasp. It would help if I knew what you're looking for, specifically."

"In particular, I'm seeking information on one of Ms. Harris's acquaintances. A Daniel Knolls." Drex spelled the last name.

He could hear Gray tapping on a keyboard. "After she went missing, Knolls was interrogated and released. He owned up to staying overnight on her yacht on several occasions. But other people did, too. Their relationship was platonic, not romantic. He was never considered a suspect. He cooperated fully with investigators."

Drex already knew all that. Daniel Knolls had cooperated fully, then he'd bolted. He had vacated his apartment and had left no forwarding address. So far, Daniel Knolls hadn't been heard of again. No credit card charges. No activity on the Social Security number attributed to him. No passport. Taken at face value, he had ceased to exist within two weeks of Marian Harris's disappearance.

Drex looked toward the wheelhouse. He could see Jasper silhou-etted behind the wheel. "Is there a photograph of Knolls in the file?"

"One."

Drex knew the picture. The quality was lousy. A merging of smiling people whooping it up on the deck of Marian Harris's yacht. Blurred figures backlit by a blazing setting sun. It could have been Drex himself standing there in the background, face averted from the camera.

He said, "Can you scan that photo and send it to the email ad-dress I gave you this morning?"

"Of course, sir."

"Is there anything new on the case? Any recent info on Knolls?"

"Let's see. Says here he was sought for questioning after Marian Harris's body was discovered, but he—"

"Excuse me, *what*?" He plugged his free ear with this index fin-ger. "Did you say her body was discovered?"

"Yes, sir."

Drex's heart began to pound. None of the previous victims had ever been found. "When was this? Where?"

"Give me a sec here, please."

It took more than a sec. Drex thought his head would explode before the deputy said, "Okay. Here's the skinny. A construction crew in Collier County was dredging a creek so they could replace old bridge abutments with new ones. Backhoe dug up a box."

"Box?"

"Like a shipping crate. Wood. Dimensions were six by three by four feet. Lid was nailed shut. The remains were inside."

"When was this?"

"Uh...Only three months ago. FBI was given a heads-up. Everything was sent to an Agent Rud...rud..."

"Rudkowski."

"That's it."

That son of a bitch. Drex removed his ball cap, put his elbow on the table, and rested his forehead in his palm. The Champagne was churning hotly in his stomach. "The remains were positively identified as Marian Harris?"

"Using dental records."

"Cause of death?"

"Suffocation." Then, "Oh Jesus."

"What?"

The boat was slowing down. They would be anchoring soon. Through the glass walls enclosing the lounge area, Drex could see Elaine and Talia laughing together as they set the dining table for lunch.

Drex said, "Gray, you still there? What?"

He heard the deputy swallow. "Man, this is grim."

"Tell me."

"There was blood inside the crate. On the underside of the lid. Streaks of it, like claw marks. Appears the vic was buried alive."

Chapter 5

———◆◆———

Gif shared Drex's horror. "Buried alive?"

As soon as Drex had returned from the yacht cruise, he'd showered off the salt spray as well as the taint of Jasper Ford. He'd parked himself in front of the borrowed fan and placed a three-way call to Gif and Mike. They'd been waiting to hear about his afternoon excursion, but the news about Marian Harris was unexpected. It had rocked them, just as it had Drex.

"A minute after hearing that, I had to sit down across the table from him and eat chilled watercress soup and shrimp salad with his homemade rémoulade."

"Mild or spicy?"

"Fuck, Mike," Drex said. "That's crass, even for you."

"You're right. Sorry. I'm deflecting my guilt. How did I miss that her body had been discovered?"

"Don't beat yourself up," Gif said. "It really wouldn't have done us any good to know before today."

"At the time she was found, she'd been missing for almost two years," Drex said. "A widow, no children. Most of her friends in Key West were snowbirds, vacationers, jet-setters from the U.S. and

49

abroad. Word eventually would have gotten around to them, I'm sure, but I doubt there was a groundswell of reaction. Local news in southern Florida may have made the recovery of her remains a headline. 'Authorities hope the discovery will provide clues into the Key West's woman's kidnaping and apparent murder.' Then, on to weather and sports.

"I don't know if there was a memorial service or observance of any sort. But it didn't warrant national news coverage, so it was easily overlooked, Mike."

Marian Harris's fate was upsetting to Mike and Gif, but, because of his mother, it affected Drex in ways they couldn't relate to.

He didn't have any substantial memories of her, only infinitesimal snatches of recollection lurking in the dark corners of his memory. But they were meaningless because he couldn't fit them into any context. He had no points of reference. By the time he was old enough to retain memories, she had been long absent from his life.

When he reached an age to become aware of and curious about this deficiency and had asked to see a picture of his mother, his dad had claimed not to have one. Then, as now, Drex figured that he'd been lying, or, if telling the truth, it was because he'd destroyed any pictures of his ex-wife.

Their separation had been bitter, absolute, and permanent. His father even went so far as to have his and Drex's names legally changed so that, even if she had rethought her decision and wanted to reconcile, she wouldn't have been able to find them. Though Drex didn't learn of that until years later.

In his early teens, when he was going through a rebellious phase, he'd demanded to know how he could contact her. His father had refused to provide him with any information, describing their severance as an extraction and an exorcism.

The only picture Drex had of her was the one that had been circulated by the Los Angeles PD when she went missing, and he hadn't seen it until years after the fact when no one was still actively looking for her.

It was then that he had assumed the search. He didn't really expect to find his mother living somewhere in obscurity. He had reconciled that she'd been killed and that her remains had been left where they were unlikely ever to be found.

No, he didn't begin searching for his mother. Rather for the man responsible for her disappearance. He had vowed not to stop until he found him. And he wouldn't.

However, from the outset of his quest, he had avoided speculating on his mother's manner of death. But after what he'd heard today about Marian Harris, to imagine the woman who'd birthed him suffering a similar fate, to envision how horrific her end might have been, made him break a sweat despite his recent shower and the whirring fan.

Plowing his fingers through his damp hair, he left his chair and went to stand by the window. The Fords had returned home only a few minutes behind him. He hadn't seen either of them since. There was no sign of them now.

Were they upstairs or down? Sharing a room? A bed? A kiss? Was he caressing Talia with the same hands that had nailed shut that shipping crate with a breathing Marian Harris inside?

He inhaled deeply through his nose, exhaled through his mouth, whispering, "He buried that woman alive."

"You say that like it means something," Gif said. "I mean more than the obvious."

Drex said, "We've been on the hunt for a con man who kills his victim solely to eliminate a witness. After learning about Marian, what's obvious to me now is that this guy is more than that. He likes the killing."

"Thrill kills?" Mike asked.

"Maybe not that extreme," Drex said thoughtfully. "Close, though. He could be evolving into that."

"His version of middle-age crazy?"

"You're joking, Gif, but that makes a weird kind of sense. He's getting older. He watches the news. He sees the new generation of

degenerates outdoing him. To compete, he's got to up his game."
He cursed softly. "Which means I do. I've got to rearrange my
thinking, start looking for traits in Jasper that—"

"You don't know that your neighbor is Knolls," Mike said. "Or
Weston Graham, or whatever the hell his real name is."

"It's him. I know it."

"No, you *don't*, Drex."

He was annoyed by his cohort's denial of what he felt—knew—
in his bones, in his gut. "Did you get the picture?"

Drex had asked the deputy in Key West to send the party shot to
a dummy email account to which none of the three could be linked.

"Yeah," Mike replied. "I magnified it and compared the guy in
the background to Ford's South Carolina driver's license picture.
There's no resemblance."

"I trust my gut more than I do photography. Look more closely."

"Drex—"

"Blow that picture up to the size of a fucking football field.
Count every pore on the bastard's face if you have to. It's him."

Quietly, Gif said, "You want it to be him."

"All right, yes!" Drex fired back, in an angry hiss. "I want it to
be him."

Staring at the Fords' house was only making him crazy. He went
to the fridge, got a bottle of water, and returned with it to the chair.
Neither of the other two spoke.

After taking a long drink and calming down a degree or two, he
said, "Find out everything you can about Elaine Conner."

He told them what he had learned about her through conversation. "The yacht is named *Laney Belle*, her husband's pet name for
her. It's registered in Dover, Delaware, where he hailed from. I get a
sense that he was older and had old money, but I'm guessing. She's
an attractive, rich widow."

"Our guy's type."

"That occurred to me," Drex said. "Although Elaine is more
bubbly than the others. More self-assured and less needy. Gregari-

ous. Life of the party. But he's very courtly toward her, and she eats it up."

"His wife isn't jealous?" Gif asked.

"If she is, I didn't pick up on it. She and Elaine come across as good friends."

"What's she like?"

"I just told you, Mike. Bubbly."

"Not her. Talia Ford."

"Shafer. I learned today that she goes by her professional name."

Mike, who had no regard for political correctness, huffed, "Women these days."

Gif repeated Mike's question. "What's she like?"

I took her tray, she took my breath. Her eyes are the color of wood smoke and just as hypnotic. A smile I wanted to eat.

He cleared his throat. "She's damn smart, I'll say that. Told me the history of her company. Inherited, but she expanded it, sold it, and then trumped the buyer. I was intimidated."

"A ball-breaker doesn't sound like our man's type."

"She's not a ball-breaker."

"Huh. By the way she was flaunting her success—"

"She wasn't *flaunting*," Drex said, making his irritation plain. "Why don't you get a clue, Mike?"

"About what?"

"Societal shifts."

"What?"

"Never mind. You're hopeless."

Gif interceded. "Drex, I think what Mike is clumsily and stupidly—"

"Hey!"

"—trying to get out of you is your sense of Jasper Ford's wife."

"I just told you," Drex said. "For a woman her age—"

"She's thirty-four."

Mike and his research. He would know her birthday, too. "Okay, then. She's accomplished a hell of a lot in her thirty-four years."

"She attractive?"

"You could say so, sure. All his victims have been. I thought you were looking for Shafer Travel ads from back before she sold it. No luck?"

"Found the ads," Mike said, "but they featured a family crest–looking logo, no photos of her. I did find some pictures of her on Google, but none that good or that recent. The business has social media accounts, but they're also under the logo. If she has personal accounts, they're private." After a portentous pause, he continued. "I did scare up a slick business journal that did a feature article on her shortly after she sold out. There was a picture. Close-up. Professional photographer. The piece was published a few years ago, but I doubt she's gone to seed since then."

Gif said, "Come on, Drex, level with us. One could say that she's several notches above 'attractive.' Or was that magazine photo air-brushed?"

"I doubt it was," Drex mumbled. A trickle of sweat slid down over his ribs. "She's a looker, okay? What of it?"

"What of it is, you like to look," Gif said.

"I confess. But this lady is married, remember?"

"Gif and I remember fine," Mike said. "Question is, do you?"

No one said anything. Drex wasn't about to defend himself when he hadn't done anything inappropriate. Unless lusting counted.

It was Gif, in his mediating role, who asked, "What are they like together, as a couple?"

"Comfortable. For all the attention he showered on Elaine, he was solicitous to Talia."

"Were they affectionate?"

"A kiss on her cheek. His hands were on her shoulders when he gave her a turn at the wheel. She kissed the back of his hand when he served her chocolate mousse. I think she must be a chocoholic. She eats Nutella straight from the jar."

"So do I," Mike said.

"Yeah, but I doubt she finishes the jar in one sitting," Drex said. He knew sure as hell that Mike wouldn't look like Talia licking the spoon clean. Which Drex had fantasized. In detail. In slow motion. With sound effects.

Gif asked, "You didn't get a sense that she was afraid of him?"

"Not in the slightest."

There had been that moment when she'd looked down at her wedding band and turned it around her finger. *And here I am.* She'd spoken so softly, the words were almost inaudible above the wind. Her expression had been, what? Not fearful. Not wary. Wistful?

Maybe. Or maybe that was the emotion Drex had wanted to see. His pals would probably conclude that, so he didn't mention it. Instead, he pitched his idea. "I don't know if or when I'll be with them again to observe. Elaine mentioned another get-together soon, but that could mean tomorrow or a month from now. The only way I'll learn what they're like alone together is if I plant a bug."

"I'm a freaking genius," Mike said around a groan. "I knew you were going to say that."

"Drex, you can't," Gif said. "Rudkowski would shit."

"It'll be good for him. I'll bet he's been backed up for years."

"This is nothing to joke about."

"You're telling me. Rudkowski has known about the discovery of Marian Harris's remains for three months. Did he inform me? No."

"For your own good."

"I'll decide what's for my own good. And what would be for my own good right now would be to eavesdrop on the couple next door."

Mike harrumphed, his way of saying that it was a foregone conclusion that Drex would break the rules and do it, and that trying to dissuade him was pointless.

Gif wasn't ready to give in. "If you're caught—"

"I'll take my chances. It's worth the risk. It was before. But now, knowing what he did to Marian Harris? Yeah. It's worth the risk."

"Are you sure, Drex?"

He said, "If it's him—"

"Big if."

"—and if we nail him—"

"An even bigger if," Mike said.

"—then it'll be *more* than worth it."

"No matter the personal cost to you?" Gif said.

"No matter the personal cost to me." In the ensuing silence, he felt the weight of their disapproval. "Guys, he has victimized eight women. Eight that we know of. My mother may not have been his first. Don't think about the consequences to me. Think about those women. Think about Marian Harris trying to claw her way out of that crate."

"We get it, Drex," Gif said. "But you'll be breaking the law."

"I'm aware. But you won't be. If I'm caught, I'll take full responsibility. You have my word on it."

"That's not what concerns me," Gif said.

"Well, it concerns me big time," Drex said. "I won't let you two be blamed. Not by Rudkowski or anyone."

After a lengthy silence, Mike heaved a heavy sigh and asked Drex if he needed any equipment shipped to him.

"No. I brought it with me."

"So this idea didn't just pop into your head."

Drex didn't respond.

"How do you plan to plant it?" Gif asked. "Where inside the house? When?"

"All TBD. I'll keep you posted."

He hung up before they could try further to talk him out of it.

The eyeglasses Drex wore were a prop. So was the ream of typing paper on the kitchen table next to his computer. Alongside the stack of blank sheets were the couple hundred pages of rubber-banded manuscript that had been typed by a woman in his office. Her name was Pam something. The text had been taken directly from a historical paperback novel set during the Civil War.

When he approached Pam with the request, she'd regarded him dubiously. "What do you want it for?"

"Something I'm working on."

She quirked an eyebrow. "You can't share?"

"Not yet."

She'd thumbed through the yellowed pages of the paperback. "What about typos? Does it have to be perfect?"

"No. In fact, a mistake here or there would be good. I'll be marking it up."

The single mother of two had a deadbeat ex. She'd agreed to do the transcription for three dollars a page. When she delivered it, Drex had given her a hug and a fifty-dollar bonus.

He marked up the pages with red pencil, dog-eared some of the sheets, dripped coffee over several, left puckered water rings on others.

Now, his setup looked very "writerly," should anyone be surreptitiously observing, which he sensed someone was.

While seated at his computer as though working on his book, he was actually reading additional material excavated by Mike. Marian Harris's parish church had held a memorial mass. After the forensic pathologist had completed his examination and turned his findings over to the authorities, her remains were cremated and placed in a vault in the church cemetery.

Although her will had specified allocations for various charities, there was nothing in the coffers to bequeath. The only asset not liquidated prior to her disappearance had been her yacht. As stipulated in her will, it was sold at auction, the proceeds gifted to the parish.

Drex hadn't asked Mike to research all that, but he was grateful to him for doing so. Marian Harris hadn't been confined forever in that shipping crate. Drex took some comfort in that.

But not much.

He wanted the son of a bitch who'd done that to her. With an instinct that was almost feral, he felt he had found him.

Throughout the evening, lights in the house across the lawn came on and went off. Shadows moved across window shades. Drex watched Jasper make himself a sandwich. He ate it at the kitchen table while perusing the Sunday newspaper. He saw Talia switch on a light as she entered a room upstairs.

He got only a glance before she shut the door behind her, but he saw that her hair was messily piled on top of her head, and that she had changed out of the oversize white linen shirt and wide-legged pants she'd worn on the cruise.

When they were on deck, and the wind had struck her just right, it had blown aside the fabric of her shirt, affording Drex a glimpse of a white tank top with skinny straps, a fragile-looking collarbone, an oh-so-slight suggestion of cleavage above the snug tank.

Nothing had actually been revealed. Which had been as frustrating as hell. Also as erotic. He'd wanted to unwrap her and explore the tantalizing terrain his imagination had mapped out.

Evening descended into night. Shortly after ten o'clock, he set aside his eyeglasses, folded up his computer, and turned out the lights inside the apartment. But he stayed at the window. He watched and waited until the house across the way remained dark for half an hour.

As he slipped out of the apartment and down the exterior staircase, his pistol was a reassuring pressure against the small of his back.

———

Jasper, sitting in the deep shadows of his screened porch, watched Drex ease through the door of the apartment, close it silently behind himself, and quickly descend the stairs. In total darkness. Even though there was a light fixture mounted on the exterior wall at both the top and bottom of the steep stairs, which Drex had referred to as killers.

He reached the ground without mishap. He didn't go to his car. Instead, he made a hard right turn and moved along the far side of the garage and eventually out of Jasper's view. Moments later, he reappeared from behind the garage at the opposite corner.

Jasper didn't move or do anything else that would give away his presence, watching as Drex continued along the back boundary of his lawn, moving parallel to the house, staying in sight except for those seconds when he was swallowed by a deep shadow or blocked from view by a tree trunk.

And, one of those times, he didn't reappear. He remained behind the trunk of the largest tree on the property.

Jasper lunged from his chair and barreled through the screen door. With long, rapid strides, he covered the distance between him and the tree. He almost collided with Drex has he stepped out from behind it. Jasper clicked on the flashlight he'd brought with him and aimed it directly into Drex's face. "What are you doing?"

Drex rocked back on his heels. "Jesus, Jasper. You scared the shit out of me."

He smiled his boyish smile. It had made Elaine's heart go pitter-pat. It made Jasper suspect that it was artificial and aptly employed whenever it suited him.

Currently it was meant to distract him when Drex reached behind his back with his right hand. He raised his left to shield his eyes from the flashlight's beam. "I thought you were probably in bed by now."

"I ask again, what are you doing out here?"

"Look, man, I'm sorry. I—"

"What have you got?" Jasper directed the light down, and leaned around to try to see what Drex was concealing behind his back.

Drex took a hasty step backward.

"What's in your hand? Let me see." Jasper thrust out his left hand, palm up.

Drex hesitated, then brought his hand from around his back and dropped a dead mouse into Jasper's palm. Jasper yanked his hand back. The mouse fell to the ground.

"I would have waited till morning to throw him out, but he was stinking up the apartment."

Jasper reigned in his temper as well as his rapid breathing. "Where were you taking it?"

"That community dumpster in the next block? I thought I'd throw him in that. Save him rotting in our trash cans at the curb. I guess I should have gone the long way, used the street. I opted for the shortcut across your yard. I'm sorry as hell I bothered you."

"I didn't know it was you," he lied. "All I saw was a tall, dark figure," Jasper said, forcing a smile. "If you take a shortcut again, you should identify yourself."

"I didn't think I'd be seen."

"Oh, I'm always watching."

They held each other's gaze for several beats, then Drex bent down and picked up the lifeless mouse by the tail. Holding it between them, he gave a jocular shrug. "Guess I won't need a cat, after all."

Jasper chuckled.

"Well, good night." Drex started off.

Jasper let him get only a few yards away before calling out, "Hold it."

He turned.

"Take this." Jasper walked forward and passed him the flashlight.

"Thanks. There wasn't one in the apartment."

Jasper smiled. "What are neighbors for?"

When Drex returned from depositing the mouse in the dumpster, he took his third shower of the day and went to bed, pulling the sheet only to his waist. The fan, aimed directly at him, hummed from the side of the bed.

His mission that night had been to get a different perspective of the layout of the Fords' house, in an attempt to figure out a way to get inside. From behind the tree, he'd been using the zoom on his phone's camera to try to spot security devices on windows and doors. When Jasper had burst from the house like a man possessed, he'd had no choice but to brazen it out.

Fortunately, he'd thought to take along the dead mouse as his excuse for being in Jasper's backyard, should he be caught. He didn't believe Jasper had bought the excuse entirely. But they'd played out the scene as though he had. It hadn't been easy for Drex, make-believing with a man whose heart and mind were darker than he'd initially thought.

He still didn't know how he would breach the castle, but he had come away knowing that Jasper was vigilant to an extraordinary degree. Meaning that Drex would be damned lucky to succeed in planting just one bug. He wished he could plant one in every room.

But even if he could manage that, there were some areas he'd rather not infiltrate. Mainly the bedroom shared by Jasper and Talia. He didn't think he could stomach listening in on an intimate conversation or, God forbid, lovemaking.

He believed that Jasper was the man he sought. Which meant that Jasper's rich, successful wife was in jeopardy. But until every element of doubt had been erased, until Drex had irrefutable proof that Talia was living with a man who had buried another woman alive, he couldn't risk warning her.

He wouldn't call in the cavalry with Rudkowski leading the charge. That would spell certain disaster. Rudkowski, who didn't know the definition of finesse, would bungle it, give them away, and then God knew what Jasper would do. It chilled Drex to think of it. He was dealing with a personality that had a very sharp tipping point, one who was in control...until he wasn't.

His short-term goal was clear: maintain his cover while keeping Talia safe from the man she lived with. He would do whatever he could to prevent her from becoming victim number nine and meeting a fate like Marian Harris's. He was committed to protecting her life, regardless of how she looked.

But she looked like Talia Shafer, and he would be lying not only to his friends but also to himself if he didn't admit that her appeal upped his level of commitment to spare her life. If Jasper Ford was who he suspected, seeing him brought to justice would no longer be sufficient or satisfying. Drex wanted to engage in mortal hand-to-hand combat. He wanted to eviscerate him.

Of course he acknowledged that such macho thinking was juvenile, stupid, and dangerous. If he went at Jasper Ford for any reason other than getting justice for eight women, he would be in hock with Rudkowski for the rest of his life.

Beyond that, allowing emotions to call the shots was a recipe for disaster. Emotions messed with a man's mind. They either weakened his resolve or made him so determined, he grew reckless. One misstep, one reflexive reaction or unplanned remark could expose his playacting. Because Jasper would be watching. A single mistake, no matter how slight, could lead to failure. Worse, it could lead to Talia's death.

Sure as hell, Weston Graham, aka Daniel Knolls, aka Jasper Ford would be at the top of his game, staying cool, playing it smart.

So must Drex be.

But, God, that was going to be difficult when he couldn't rid his mind of Talia's brandy-colored hair, the skin that tended to freckle, the gray eyes that bespoke intelligence and goodwill, but also hinted at an irresistible elusiveness.

The loose-fitting clothes she had worn on the yacht hadn't been provocative or revealing, but Drex had imagined the shape inside them to be compact and sweet. When she'd talked about desiring chairs that conformed to the human body, he'd desired to have her human body conforming to his, her bottom nestling against his middle, seeking the perfect fit, finding—

Christ!

He slid his hand beneath the sheet. He was hot. He was hard. He was going to hell for coveting his neighbor's wife. He would burn for committing whatever the biblical term was for the sin of sexual self-gratification.

He wasn't deterred.

Chapter 6

Bill Rudkowski entered his office carrying a sixteen-ounce thermal container of coffee in one hand, his briefcase in the other, and the imperishable chip on his shoulder.

He wasn't overly fond of mornings in general, but he downright despised Mondays. He greeted his assistant with a brusque nod. "Anything?"

"Everything needing your attention is on your desk."

"I can hardly wait."

"Guessing by your glower, I'm thinking your team lost yesterday."

"They suck." He entered his private office and kicked the door shut with his heel.

On his desk was more paperwork than he wanted to tackle before he'd finished his coffee. Once fortified with caffeine, and resigned to it being the beginning of another week, he started working his way through the pile.

He sorted the callback messages according to levels of urgency, scrawled his illegible signature on documents requiring it, and scanned updates on several active cases. When done, he spun his chair around to his computer and booted up.

The third email in his in box drew his attention immediately because of the name in the subject line. Marian Harris.

A case number followed her name. There was an attachment. The brief message in the body of the email read: *I thought you might want to see this again, too.* It was signed by an individual he had never heard of, a Deputy Randall Gray. His official contact info was that of the sheriff's department, Monroe County, Florida, but he had included his cell phone number.

Rudkowski opened the attachment. He recognized the photograph as the one taken aboard Marian Harris's yacht during a cocktail party at sunset. Following her disappearance several months later, everyone in the snapshot had been identified, tracked down, and interviewed by Key West PD, the sheriff's office, and/or FBI agents.

Rudkowski, who had closely monitored the case, had requested colleagues in south Florida to keep him in the loop of their investigation, since the Harris woman's mysterious disappearance bore similarities to other unsolved missing person cases with which he was familiar.

The case cooled and then went cold. Two years, give or take, had passed.

He had heard nothing further until her body was discovered, roughly three months ago. It had been a grisly find. Because of the swampy environment in which she'd been buried, her body was badly decomposed. It had yielded no clues as to who had nailed her inside the crate. The bloody claw marks on the inside of the lid indicated the unsub was a sicko of the lowest order.

While authorities in Florida were investigating there, Rudkowski rounded up a team of agents and used every criminal database, domestic and abroad, to search for a connection between Marian Harris and perps known to have buried their victims alive.

A distressing number of known suspects were still at large. Some remained unidentified. Of those who had been captured and convicted, a number of them were deceased. Several had been executed for their crimes, one had been killed by another inmate during a prison riot, others had died of natural causes while incarcerated. Which left those living out their remaining days behind bars. Rudkowski saw to it that all among that number were questioned.

One had actually confessed to Marian Harris's abduction and murder, but he was a schizophrenic and habitual confessor, who liked to brag about gory atrocities he hadn't committed. He had, in fact, been incarcerated in San Quentin when the Florida woman disappeared.

Of those questioned who denied ever having heard of Marian Harris, there wasn't any incriminating evidence to indicate otherwise. None could be linked to her.

The investigation again had stalled.

Rudkowski wondered why he'd been sent the familiar photograph now without a note of explanation. If newfound evidence had regenerated the investigation, why wasn't there an accompanying brief bringing him up to speed?

He closed the attachment and went back to the email. His gaze snagged on the last word of the brief message. *Too.* I.e., in addition to. Also.

His Monday morning tanked.

Muttering foul epithets, he snatched up the receiver of his desk phone and told his assistant to get Deputy Gray on the line. Then he waited, drumming his fingers on his desktop until the call was put through.

"Gray?"

"Yes, sir, Agent Rudkowski. Good morning."

Like hell it was. "I'm calling about the photograph you emailed me last night."

"Yes, sir?"

"Has there been a development in the Marian Harris case that I'm unaware of?"

"No, sir. Well, I don't believe so."

"You just emailed me this on a whim? Out of the blue? Why?"

"Well, because your name came up during a conversation I had with Special Agent Easton. I assured him that you had been notified when Marian Harris's remains were discovered. Your contact info was on the last communiqué between the FBI and our department, so I had your email address."

Rudkowski was seeing red, but it wasn't the deputy's fault, so he kept his voice as level as possible. "When did this conversation take place?"

"With Agent Easton? Yesterday."

"Did he say what had prompted him to call your department?"

"He said that, like you, he specializes in missing persons cases."

"Um-huh."

"He was calling specifically about the missing person case in Lexington. I'm sure you've heard about it."

"Over the weekend, I unplugged from the office and just now came in. I haven't seen anything about it."

"Well, Easton said there are similarities to Marian Harris. He wanted to compare the cases."

"Of course."

"He asked me to access the case file on Harris and give him an update. I asked for a few hours, because I had other stuff to do, but I had it all in front of me when he called back."

"I'm sure he appreciated that."

"I guess, but...I don't think he knew her remains had been found. He seemed upset when I told him about her being buried alive and all. Y'all must not work that closely together, or else he would have known."

"No, we don't work closely together at all," Rudkowski said, straining the words through his clenched teeth.

"He asked me to email him the picture. Later, I got to thinking that if he was investigating this new case, you might be in on it, too, being in the same state and all. That's why I sent the picture to you."

"Good thinking, deputy. Thank you. I'll give Easton a call. Do you have his cell number in front of you?"

"It's a private number, sir. Blocked. You know, because of all the classified and undercover work he does."

Rudkowski closed his eyes and rubbed the sockets, which had begun to throb. "Of course. I forgot. Never mind. I've got his private number here in my data bank. I can look it up. Thanks again."

"Sure."

Rudkowski dropped the telephone receiver back into the cradle, picked up his cell phone, and pulled up the last cell number he had for Easton. He called it. Got his voice mail. No surprise there. The jackass wasn't about to answer if he saw the name Rudkowski in the LED, especially if he was up to something.

Rudkowski pushed back his desk chair and marched to the door of his office, yanked it open, and barked to his assistant, "Call the SAC in Lexington."

She raised her eyebrows and, under her breath, said, "Must be Easton."

"Verify that they have a local missing person. Woman, probably middle-aged and well heeled. Then call Easton's office. He's not answering his cell, and I want to talk to him. Now. No excuses. If someone else there answers, have them drag him to the phone."

He went back into his office and slammed the door.

He could hear his assistant's muffled voice as she placed the ordered calls. He fumed. Maybe he should have told Easton about the gruesome discovery in Florida, but, dammit, this is precisely why he hadn't. He'd known Easton wouldn't leave it alone.

He'd been a thorn in Rudkowski's side for years, ever since he'd shown up in Santa Barbara, uninvited and without sanction, and had poked his nose into Rudkowski's investigation into a disappearance and probable kidnap case.

Easton had been young, idealistic, determined, clever, and passionate, as though designed to make Rudkowski appear old, jaded, lackadaisical, dumb, and indifferent.

To Rudkowski, Drex Easton didn't represent a righteous crusader, but rather an accusatory finger pointing out his inadequacies. He was a recurring rash. A major pain in the ass.

Only once had Rudkowski gotten the best of him, but it had been an empty victory, which ultimately had made him look petty and Easton self-sacrificial.

His assistant opened the door, but only by a crack in which her face appeared, as though she feared he might throw something at her.

"No missing person case this week in or around Lexington, except for a man in his eighties. They put out a silver alert. He had sneaked out of his retirement home and was found a few hours later doing tequila shots and ogling the waitresses at a Hooters."

Rudkowski had figured the missing person case was a hoax used by Easton to light a fire under the deputy in Florida. "You reach Easton?"

"He's on vacation."

"Excuse me?"

"He's on—?"

"I heard you," he barked. "Since when?"

"He cleared out midday last Friday."

"For how long?"

"Two weeks."

"Where did he go?"

"He didn't say. Nobody knows."

Chapter 7

———◆———

"Knock-knock?"

Talia came from the kitchen onto the enclosed porch, a dish-towel slung over one shoulder. She smiled at Drex, who stood on the step on the other side of the screen door. "Hi. You're early."

He looked at his watch. "I thought I was ten minutes late. Wasn't the invitation for six?"

"Six-thirty."

"Oh. Sorry. I'll come back."

"Don't be silly. Come on in." She went over and pushed the door open for him. "Jasper had to make a quick run to the store. I forgot to get buns."

Drex knew Jasper wasn't in the house, which is why he had arrived early. He'd already been showered and dressed when he saw Jasper backing his car out of their driveway. He'd pushed his bare feet into his docksiders, forewent grooming his hair, picked up the box of cupcakes he'd bought earlier at the bakery, dashed down the perilous stairs, and crossed the lawn in a gait that wasn't quite a jog, but close.

As he stepped inside, he handed Talia the bakery box.

"What's this?"

"I told Jasper I'd bring dessert."

Jasper had come over in the early afternoon to extend the invitation. Drex had seen him coming, and, by the time Jasper had climbed the stairs, Drex appeared to be an absentminded writer, unaware of everything except his manuscript. He pretended to emerge from a creative fog and had accepted the invitation, but only on the condition that he provide the sweets.

Talia raised the box's lid. "Cupcakes! Great! Dibs on one of the chocolate ones."

"I'll flip you for the second one."

She smiled at him, her eyes shifting up to his hair. He scrubbed his knuckles across the crown of his head and gave an abashed grin. "Is it a mess? Sorry. Hazards of my trade."

"Mussed hair and what else?"

"Forgetting my hair is mussed."

She scrutinized him for a moment as though unsure what to make of him, then nodded toward the bar. "Help yourself. I'll take these into the kitchen."

"What can I mix for you?"

"I already have a glass of wine."

She went into the kitchen, leaving him alone, and presenting him with an ideal opportunity to plant the listening device. The room transmitter weighed practically nothing, but he was as aware of it in his pants pocket as he would have been of a boulder.

Talia and Jasper spent a lot of time on their porch, sitting side by side in twin rocking chairs. He would like to be privy to those conversations, but the environment wasn't an ideal place to hide the electronic transmitter. It would be susceptible to humidity and dust. Inside the house would be less corrosive and better for clearer reception.

He poured himself a bourbon on the rocks and took it with him as he wandered over to the open door of the kitchen and looked in. "Ah. You *can* cook."

Talia shot him a glance over her shoulder from where she stood at the range. "I can boil water. Which is what I'm doing for corn on the cob."

He went inside and walked over to her. Three ears of corn, still in their husks, lay on the counter. "They're better cooked in the microwave."

She turned toward him and slid the towel off her shoulder. "Jasper wouldn't hear of it."

"Jasper isn't here." He set his drink on the counter. "Where's your microwave?"

She pointed to where it fit inside the cabinetry. "Are you sure about this? These are all we have, so if you ruin them—"

"I won't. Observe and learn. Step one. Pick ripe ears of corn off stalks in field. Oh, done that already."

She laughed.

"Step two, place ears of corn into microwave."

"Shucks and all? Without washing them or anything?"

"As demonstrated." He used flourishing motions like a magician to place the ears of corn in the oven. "Close door."

"That's step three?"

"No. That's the second part of step two."

"I see," she said with a seriousness belied by the smile she couldn't contain.

"Step three is to set the timer to cook on high for four minutes for each ear of corn."

She counted on her fingers. "Twelve minutes."

"Very good, sous chef. Maybe you should be writing this down."

She tapped her temple. "Taking notes."

"Good. Because you'll want to remember."

"Says you."

"Trust me."

"Not as far as I can throw you."

This time her serious tone wasn't phony, and it took Drex aback. His teasing smile collapsed. "Why not?"

She ducked her head and gave it a small shake. "Never mind."

"No. I'd like to know why you said that."

Raising her chin, she looked him straight in the eye. "You're way too cool."

"Way too cool for what?"

"Way too cool to be real."

"Oh, I'm real, Talia." He spoke in a low and vibrating tone that coincided with him dropping his gaze to her mouth. She didn't step back, but her breath caught and held.

The moment lasted for only a heartbeat, then he looked back into her eyes and resumed the ribbing manner. "I'm real *hungry*. Let's get cooking." He set the timer on the microwave and dusted his hands.

"Now what?" she asked.

She tried to sound as jocular as he but didn't quite manage it. He hadn't touched her, but his closeness had shaken her, and the male animal in him wanted to purr with satisfaction.

But he wasn't there to seduce her. He didn't want her to become even more mistrustful of him than she'd already admitted to being. He needed her to be relaxed around him. Comfortable and chummy and chatty. He needed her to talk about her husband, so he could determine if Jasper Ford, seeming law-abiding suburbanite who had run a husbandly errand, was in actuality the twisted fuck who had buried Marian Harris alive.

So he tamped down the surge of testosterone and reclaimed his drink. Raising it in a toast, he said, "Now, I drink my bourbon, and you drink your wine while you anticipate the best corn on the cob you've ever eaten."

She peered dubiously through the microwave window at the ears of corn rotating inside, then shrugged. "Okay. How about out on the porch?"

Following her from the kitchen, he tried not to fixate on how nicely her light denim skirt molded to her bottom. From those enticing curves it flared out and stopped short of her knees by several inches.

Her top was a black, body-hugging, stretchy thing with arm-holes cut high enough to reveal a lot of shoulder. He spied a few freckles beneath the strands of hair that had escaped her topknot and curled against her neck.

He wanted to give all of it a thorough, hands-on inspection.

She sat down in the rocker that he knew to be hers from having spied on her and Jasper. He was about to take the other chair, but hesitated. "Should I save this for Jasper?"

She motioned him into the chair and took a sip of wine. As they settled into their seats, she asked, "Did you write today?"

"For several hours."

"You were at it for a long while last night." He gave her a quizzi-cal look; she looked embarrassed. "Your shades were up and the lights were on. I saw you sitting at the computer."

He groaned. "I didn't do anything uncouth or indecent, did I?"

She gave a soft laugh. "Not that I saw."

He thought about what he'd done in his bed inspired by fan-tasies of her, and it wasn't entirely faked when he swiped his brow with the back of his hand as though greatly relieved. "Whew."

"I think writing must be harder work than most people realize."

"I can't speak for other writers, but for me, it's damn hard. I did a run on the beach this afternoon just to work the kinks out."

"Muscles tend to kink after sitting at a computer for long stretches of time."

"True, but I was referring to the kinks in my plot."

"Oh," she said, laughing. "Did the run work them out?"

"After a couple of miles, some of them smoothed out a little."

"Good."

He extended his legs in front of him and crossed his ankles. "What about your work? Are you off again any time soon?"

"Next week. In the meantime, I'm pulling together an itinerary for a client who wants to take his entire family to Africa for a month-long tour. First class all the way. Several countries, game preserves, Victoria Falls, Cape Town, photo safaris in the bush."

"Sounds scary."

"I don't send my clients anyplace that I deem unsafe."

"No, the scary part would be traveling for a month with family."

"Eight adults, eleven children."

He shuddered. "Terrifying."

She laughed, then turned more serious and looked into her glass of wine as she ran her index finger around the rim. "Jasper told me that you're divorced. Any children?"

"No."

She said nothing for a time, then, in a lighter tone, "He also told me about your encounter last night."

"Next time, I'll phone ahead before I come prowling across your backyard. When Jasper came barging around that tree, I thought I was a goner."

"The poor mouse was."

"Yeah. He must've gone peacefully, though. Saved me from having to trap him. Or get a cat."

She tilted her head and took him in from his hair to the scuffed toes of his shoes. "You don't strike me as a cat person."

"I'm not. But I'm not a mouse person, either."

She smiled.

"Which are you?" he asked. "Cat person or dog person?"

"I'm fonder of dogs."

"I haven't seen one around."

"Jasper is allergic."

"Too bad." He turned more toward her, tipped his head to one side, and gave her the same assessing treatment she'd given him. Nodding toward her glass of wine, he said, "Red over white?"

"Yes."

"Tropical climes or cold?"

"I was brought up in Charleston."

"Tropical then."

"Right."

"*Star Wars* or *Star Trek?*"

"*Star Wars.*"

He stroked his chin. "Let's see, what else? I already know chocolate over vanilla. Land over sea."

"My turn. I know very little about you, not even the basics. You don't talk much about yourself."

He spread his arms wide. "My life is an open book." He glanced across the lawn toward the apartment. "So to speak."

"Will your novel reveal aspects of you?"

"Undoubtedly. It'll be subconscious, but some of me will probably sneak in there."

"Then in order for me to know you better, I'll have to read it."

He arched an eyebrow. "You want to know me better?"

Realizing she'd stepped into a trap of her own making, she repositioned herself in the rocker as though reestablishing boundaries. She took a sip of wine. "Yesterday on the boat, you were stingy with your answers to Elaine's questions."

"Hard to get a word in edgewise when talking to Elaine." He hoped that would put her onto another track. It didn't.

"See? That's a perfect example of how you deflect any discussion about yourself. Why?"

He raised his shoulders. "There's nothing interesting to tell."

"I don't believe you, Drex."

"Believe it. Even I am bored with me."

She smiled at his quip, but she wasn't dissuaded. "Let's begin with where you grew up."

"If I told you, you wouldn't believe me."

"You were raised by wolves."

He laughed. "Not quite. But actually, the guess isn't too far off."

She raised her wine stem to her mouth and took another sip, holding his gaze, letting him know with her eyes alone that she was going to persist until he told her.

He weighed the risks, thought *to hell with it.* He would go for broke. "Alaska."

She lowered her wineglass, her surprise evident. "You were born there?"

"No. We moved up there before I turned three. I stayed through high school."

"It's a long way from there to here."

He snuffled a laugh. "Longer than you can imagine."

"I wasn't talking about the geographic distance."

He met her gaze. "Neither was I." Their stare held, and he was the first to look away. He shook the remaining ice cubes, drained the bourbon, and set his glass on the table. He thought that would be the end of it, but Talia wasn't finished yet.

"Where did you live?" she asked. "The town."

"Nowhere you ever heard of, and never for very long in any one place. We were migratory."

"What did your parents do for a living?"

"My dad worked on the pipeline. That's why we moved a lot. We lived in some places so remote, I'm not sure they were on the map."

"Life couldn't have been easy."

"Wasn't. Hard work. Long hours. Isolation."

She looked at him as though expecting him to continue and expand on that. When he didn't, she said, "Was there anything to recommend that lifestyle?"

He gave her a wry grin. "For dad? Hard work. Long hours. Isolation. And the pay was good."

"He left you an inheritance. Jasper told me."

He drew his feet in and leaned toward her. Squinting one eye, he said, "It seems I've been the topic of a lot of conversations between you and Jasper. Any particular reason why?"

"No. Just curious."

"Huh. I rarely arouse that much curiosity in people."

She squirmed in her seat, raised her wineglass as though to drink from it, then changed her mind. "Based on your description of your upbringing, it sounds like a very male-dominated environment."

"It was."

"Your mother was okay with that? With the frequent moves, the isolation?"

He gave her a long look before saying quietly, "My mother never set foot in Alaska."

Her lips parted with surprise, and she seemed about to ask another question, when Jasper's voice came from behind them. "The minute my back was turned."

Chapter 8

———◦———

Jasper's voice startled Talia. What was left of the wine in her glass sloshed as she left the rocking chair to meet her husband halfway. Although Jasper's tone hadn't been one hundred percent teasing, she responded as though it had been.

"You caught us red-handed." She took the grocery sack from him and kissed his cheek. "Thank you for making the run."

"You're welcome." He returned her kiss. Then, "Drex," he said, smiling and motioning toward the empty highball glass on the table. "Looks like you need a refill."

"I wouldn't say no to one. Let me pour yours while I'm at it."

"Thank you." Just then the microwave dinged. Jasper turned toward the kitchen. "What's that?"

Talia laughed. "It's called a microwave. Great invention. Not the abomination you've called it."

"That's a matter of opinion."

"Well, you'll be able to form another opinion soon. Drex has cooked the corn."

———◦———

Drex poured Jasper and himself each a bourbon, then joined him and Talia in the kitchen, where they were making final preparations for the meal. With the same amount of fanfare as he had used to put the corn in the microwave, he pulled on a pair of oven mitts and demonstrated how to get the ears out of the husks.

"Whack off the end with the silk." He severed it from the cob with one hard chop with a butcher knife and had a bloodthirsty desire to plunge it into Jasper's heart. "Hold it upside down by the stalk. Annnnnd, out it slides, clean as a whistle."

Talia applauded. "I'll get the butter."

She set the small dining table on the porch and placed lit citronella candles around. Jasper grilled the burger patties on a smoker that probably cost more than Drex's car.

Jasper kept one eye on the burger patties, the other on Drex, following his every move, which made Drex wonder if he'd given away his increased antagonism. He decided to test the waters. Drink in one hand, the other in his front pants pocket, he strolled over and joined his host at the grill.

Wielding his spatula, Jasper flipped the patties. "That was quite a trick with the corn. Where'd you learn it?"

"A friend showed me. He's a—"

"Foodie?"

Thinking of Mike's bulk, Drex laughed. "No. That suggests a refined pallet. This guy will eat anything."

"Has he taught you any other tricks?"

"Nope. My culinary skills end there. That smells great, by the way," he said of the sizzling meat. "You obviously have the knack."

"Was the UPS delivery for you or Arnott?"

Drex gave him a sharp look.

"I saw the truck as it pulled into the drive."

"Huh." Drex swirled the ice cubes in his glass. "I ordered a box fan. I would have returned yours tonight when I came over, but I had a handful of cupcakes."

"You didn't need to buy a fan. Ours was yours to use for as long as you needed it."

"Thanks for that, but I'm beginning to feel like a mooch. In fact, I'd like to treat you and Talia to dinner. Don't panic. We'll go out. I don't think you'd enjoy a dining experience at my kitchen table."

Jasper smiled. "Don't feel like you must pay us back."

"I want to do it. But I'll need you to suggest some good local restaurants. I haven't tested any yet, and I don't trust online ratings."

"I'll jot down some of our favorites."

"I'd like to include Elaine." Drex paused before adding, "If that's all right with you."

Jasper turned his head and gave him a bland look. "Why wouldn't it be all right with me?"

Again, Drex's pause was calculated. He glanced over at Talia, who was fiddling with a vase of flowers she'd set in the center of the table. When he came back to Jasper, he said, "Just wanting to make sure I wasn't setting up an awkward situation."

"For whom? I'm not following."

Like hell you aren't. "I thought maybe you and Elaine…?" Drex raised his eyebrows.

"Are just friends."

Ignoring Jasper's icy tone, Drex broke a wide grin. "Great. I thought so, but, you know." He gave Jasper a light sock on the shoulder. A man-to-man, "we understand each other" tap. "Provide me that list of favorite restaurants and we'll double date."

Talia approached with a platter for the burger patties. Without taking his eyes off Drex, Jasper said, "Perfect timing, darling." Then he leaned over and kissed her solidly on the mouth, a stamp of ownership.

When he ended the kiss, Talia turned away, appearing flustered and surprised by the sudden amorous display. Drex gathered it wasn't something Jasper often did, and that he'd done it now for his benefit, not Talia's.

I get the point, you son of a bitch.

Recovering quickly, and showing admirable poise, Talia graciously invited them to take their seats at the table. They assembled their burgers according to personal preferences. When they were ready to eat, Talia noticed that she'd forgotten the skewers for the corn.

"I'll get them." Drex shot from his chair. "I spotted them on the counter."

Before either she or Jasper could stop him, he was already through the kitchen door. He swept the skewers off the counter into his palm, then glanced through the open door onto the porch. Jasper and Talia were debating the merits of ketchup over mustard. She laughed at something he said. They clinked wineglasses above one of the flickering candles.

Drex dropped to one knee, bent down toward the baseboard beneath the cabinetry, and felt along the seam connecting them.

"Looking for something?"

Drex tensed, then swiveled around and smiled as he came to his feet. "Found it." He held up a skewer. "One had rolled off the counter and under the cabinet." He took the skewer to the sink and rinsed it off.

Staring hard at Drex, Jasper stood blocking the doorway for what seemed to be an eternity, then his smile returned. He stood aside and motioned for Drex to go ahead of him. "I hope the corn hasn't gotten cold. I'm eager to sink my teeth in."

"I think he was talking about my neck, not the corn."

After returning from dinner, Drex had lowered all the window shades in the apartment. Half an hour later, he'd turned off the lights as though he'd gone to bed. He put in the call to Mike and Gif and immediately told them what they'd been standing by to hear: He had succeeded in planting the bug, and it was working. "I listened in as they cleaned up the kitchen."

Dual sighs had expressed their relief.

"How was it?" Mike asked now. "The corn on the cob."

"So scrumptious it pissed him off."

"He said that?" Gif asked.

"No, but I could tell."

Jasper had become even more piqued when Talia all but swooned as she licked melted butter from her fingertips and declared that Drex had delivered as promised. Her husband's genial expression never changed, but as the evening progressed, his dialogue became more terse, and his smiles began to look forced.

"Even if he's not Weston Graham, I don't like him," Drex said. "He has this air of superiority. All-knowing. I admit that it amuses me to prick with him."

"You're amused. He's controlled and all-knowing, which, by the way, you've told us are characteristics of serial killers. This quasi-friendship is making me nervous," Gif said.

"I've got to play it as I see it, guys. If I went in and tried to match him in a chest-thumping contest, he would have nothing to do with me. Instead, he's intrigued. Talia told me as much. He keeps having me back because he hasn't figured me out yet."

"God forbid he does."

"Cheer up, Mike. If I go missing, you'll know where to start looking."

"That's not funny," Gif said. "Do you go armed on these dinner dates?"

"He's not going to engage in a shootout. That's not his style."

"Nevertheless," said Gif, the guru of practicality.

"Tonight was the first time my weapon and badge stayed home. All I had with me was the transmitter. Keeping it concealed was worry enough."

He'd told them that he'd taken advantage of Jasper's absence by arriving early, but he hadn't said much about the private conversation that he and Talia had shared. He had revealed more to her than he should have, perhaps. But talking about himself might have earned him her trust, which was necessary if he was ever going to get her to open up about Jasper.

It had been risky to tell her the truth about his upbringing, rather than inventing one. But what he'd described might have sounded to her more fiction than fact. If she relayed it to Jasper, he might dismiss it as pure fabrication.

Even if Jasper accepted it as truth, it was unlikely he would ever draw a parallel between Drex Easton, would-be author next door, and the toddler who'd been whisked off to Alaska by his father after his mother's abandonment. Drex wasn't even certain she had ever told Weston Graham about her previous marriage. He might never have known of Drex's existence. His mother's perfidy then might well be protecting Drex from exposure now.

"So," Gif said, "what's your second impression of them?"

"Nothing they said or did triggered an alarm. They acted like a married couple."

Mike said, "Since neither of us has experience with matrimony, could you be a little more descriptive?"

"They're familiar. She brushed a crumb of hamburger bun off his beard. He flicked away a mosquito that landed on her arm. Like that."

"Were they affectionate?"

"To an extent."

"To what extent?"

"Look, Gif, if you want me to talk dirty to you, you'll have to pay me sixty bucks a minute."

"You don't have to bite my head off. Just give me a for-instance."

Drex swore under his breath. "Okay. For instance, when Jasper returned from his errand, she thanked him with a wifely kiss on the cheek, and he repaid it." *Then he kissed her on the mouth. Hard. And, swear to God, I believe he did it to see how I would react.* But he didn't tell Gif and Mike that because they would want to know how he had reacted.

"Did you get the night vision binoculars?"

"They were delivered today. Along with a new box fan. Good thing I added the fan to the order. Jasper mentioned seeing the UPS truck."

"Like he wanted to know what you'd had delivered?"

"That was my take. I explained it away by telling him about the fan. Returning his gives me a reason to go back to their house at least once again. And I invited them out to dinner, along with Elaine."

"When?"

"Soon as I can swing it. I tried not to sound too eager. Mike, what have you learned about Elaine?"

"Mr. Conner of Delaware was husband number two."

"What happened to number one?"

"Marriage fizzled early on. No substantial funds to divide. He remarried before she did. Mr. Conner was an older widower, pillar-of-the-community type, died of cancer. They were married for thirteen years."

"Kids?"

"Not together. He had one son, who was killed in a car wreck on his twenty-first birthday. Lost his son before his wife died."

"So Elaine inherited everything?"

"Right," Mike said. "But the net worth isn't as staggering as we estimated. She's rich. She'll never have to clip coupons. But she's not über-wealthy. Nowhere close to Marian Harris or Pixie, or to most of the others, now I think about it."

"How do her assets compare to Talia Shafer's?"

"Exactly which assets are you referring to?"

"Back off, Gif," Drex snapped. "I'm working here, not pining over a married woman. Don't start with that crap again."

"Is it crap?" Mike said. "Her name comes up, you act like you've been goosed with a cattle prod."

"No, I don't."

"Make that two cattle prods," he continued. "Why is that? Why so touchy?"

"I'm not touchy."

"I stand corrected. More like hot under the collar."

"I am not."

"You are."

"If I'm hot," Drex said, "it's because there's no AC in this fucking apartment. And every once in a while, I catch a lingering whiff of dead rodent. All I do all day is pretend to be writing a book, which entails sitting in a kitchen chair till my ass goes numb."

"I suppose that could explain your bad mood." That from Gif.

"I'm not in a bad mood."

"Well, whatever," Mike said. "What I'm about to tell you isn't going to improve it."

Drex pinched the bridge of his nose, only now realizing how exhausted he was. The unrelenting tension—guarding against making a mistake that would give him away, the constant observing and being under observation, not to mention lying by omission to his friends—was taking a toll on him physically.

Fatigue had no place is this undertaking. Shaking it off, he took a deep breath. "What now?"

Mike said, "That woman you got to type your faux manuscript?"

Drex had been prepared to hear much worse. "Pam? What about her?"

"She called me today. Said you'd given her my number."

"I did."

"Why?"

"Because for obvious reasons I didn't want to give her mine. I told her that if something urgent came up in the office and she needed to reach me, you were my go-to person."

"Well, something came up in your office."

Drex's heart bumped, but he didn't ask. He waited Mike out.

"Rudkowski called there, looking for you."

"*What?*"

"Three times, after his assistant put in the initial call. He worked his way up the chain of command, demanding to know where you were and how he could reach you."

"Shit!"

"This Pam thought I should know so I could inform you. She offered to help in any way she could if you were in a jam and needed her to cover for you. She asked me to tell you that. Made me promise I would. She seemed earnest."

"She's earnestly man-hungry," Drex said absently as he tried to process this news about Rudkowski. "She wants a stepdaddy for her two kids. Maybe she thought the project I gave her was an inroad to...something."

"Is it?"

"Hell no," he replied with impatience. Then, "Did Rudkowski try to reach either of you?"

"Not yet," Gif said. "But Mike gave me a heads-up, and I dodged calls for the rest of the day."

"That'll work for only so long," Drex said. "If he doesn't show up at your desk himself, he'll dispatch someone. If you're asked— when you're asked—you haven't seen me, didn't know my vacation plans."

"The regular drill," Gif said. "Play dumb."

"Which he won't believe," Mike remarked.

"Play it for as long as you can get away with it," Drex said. "Stick to your day duties, but it's red-alert time, boys."

"What's worrisome—" Gif began.

"Is the timing of the asshole wanting to talk to me today."

"That's what rattled Mike and me," Gif said. "How long has it been since you two had any contact?"

"Not long enough."

Drex came out of his chair and went over to the window. He pulled the edge of the shade away from the framework, creating a crack just wide enough to focus the new binoculars on the house across the way.

Gif said, "I don't think Rudkowski's call is a bizarre coincidence."

"But what roused him?" Mike asked.

"Must've been that deputy in Florida," Drex said. "Rudkowski's
name was in the case file. Gray sounded green, eager to help. If he
was doing some kind of follow-up and couldn't reach me, he'd likely
contact Rudkowski."

Mike sighed. "If you're right, you need to destroy the phone you
used when you called him."

"Already have. It's on the bottom of the Atlantic. After talking to
him, I threw it out the porthole in the head." Thinking of the yacht
reminded him. "Any progress on that picture, Mike?"

"A team of photo experts in Bombay are working on it for me.
I've got TV dinners in my freezer that are older than them, and I
don't understand a damn thing they do, but they're good. I passed
along what you said about wanting to see the pores on his face."

They fell into a thoughtful silence, then Gif said, "We know your
impressions of the couple next door. What do you think their impressions are of you?"

"While they were cleaning up the kitchen, he commented on my
attire."

"Your attire?"

"That's the word he used. He said I dressed like a frat boy on
his way to a keg bust."

They chuckled. Gif asked, "What did she say?"

"That they were almost out of dishwashing soap."

"Nothing more about you?"

"That was it. They finished up, turned out the downstairs lights.
I think they've called it a night." He didn't want to think about
them in bed together doing anything except sleeping. Or even that.

The optimistic Gif said, "Well, you've made some progress."

Mike, ever Eeyore, said, "You've only got ten more days to determine whether or not it's him."

"It's him."

"You want—"

"It's him, Gif. He smiles, he's pleasant, but open a vein and ice water would pour out of it. He's abnormally vigilant. Like last night. It was like he was waiting and watching to see if I would venture onto his property. Who notices when a UPS truck is on the block and where it stops?"

"I do," said Gif.

Mike snorted with disdain.

Drex continued. "He doesn't give me access to anything he's touched."

"Like what?"

Only now did he share with them the business about the beer bottle. "It was a neighborly gesture, but why would he take back the beer when I hadn't drunk but half of it? He didn't want me to have that bottle with his prints on it."

"But our unsub is a ghost. Nobody has his prints. Nobody even knows who he is. These women up and disappeared, but there's never been a crime scene."

"Until Marian Harris's body was found," Drex said. "Less than one hundred days ago. That's bound to have fueled his innate paranoia and put him on edge."

"But forensics didn't yield anything."

"We know that, Gif, but he doesn't."

Mike made a grunting sound acknowledging Drex's point. "That niggling doubt would make him wary of anyone moving in next door."

"Exactly."

Gif wasn't convinced. "I don't know. That's all conjecture. We've gotta get something solid."

"I'm aware of that," Drex said. "Mike, in any of the disappearance cases, was there any evidence with handwriting on it? Not the victim's. Not a named someone's. Handwriting that investigators never attached to a specific person. Could be anything. A note, shopping list, receipt. Anything."

"I'll have to check it out."

"Do. I asked Jasper for a list of recommended restaurants. He told me he'd jot some down. He—Hold on. What the hell's this?"

"What?" Gif had needlessly lowered his voice to a whisper.

"While we've been talking, I've been trying out my new binoculars. Jasper just walked into their kitchen."

"A midnight snack," Mike said.

"In the dark?" Drex said. "He hasn't turned on any lights. He's using his phone's flashlight."

"That's weird."

"Maybe not," Drex said.

"Why? What's he doing?"

Drex blew out his breath. "He went straight to the spot where he caught me crouching down."

"Oh, shit," Gif groaned.

Mike muttered something more profane.

Drex watched Jasper go down on one knee and bend toward the floor until his head almost touched it. He shone the light along the baseboard and underneath the cabinet. "He's looking for it. Feeling around."

"He didn't buy your lost skewer excuse."

"We are royally screwed," Mike said.

Drex lowered the binoculars and grinned into the darkness. "We would be if that's where I had planted the bug."

Chapter 9

"Talia?"

She raised her head from reading off her tablet and looked across the breakfast table at Jasper. "Sorry. I was catching up on the news."

He was staring thoughtfully into his coffee cup. "When I got back from the store last night, you and Drex were so engrossed in your conversation, neither of you realized I was there until I spoke. What were you talking about?"

"His boyhood in Alaska."

Jasper looked at her and sputtered a laugh. "Alaska?"

"Of all places."

"Anchorage?"

She shook her head. "Remote, off-the-map spots. Another cup of coffee?"

"No thank you."

She left the table to make herself a refill using the fancy machine she'd given Jasper for Christmas. It had taken her weeks to learn how to operate it, and she was still intimidated by the technology. While she waited for it to go through the brewing process, she filled Jasper in on what Drex had told her about his upbringing.

He said, "Sounds very rugged and romantic."

"Or bleak."

"It strikes me as a woeful tale spun by an aspiring novelist who's creating a rakish persona for himself, fashioning himself after Jack London or Ernest Hemingway."

She returned to the table and curled a leg beneath her as she sat down. "You think he made it up?"

"Talia, it reeks of hogwash."

She laughed, sipped her coffee, picked up the one remaining bite of cupcake on her plate, and held it out for Jasper. "Last chance, or it's all mine."

"I wouldn't dream of depriving you."

She popped the bite into her mouth. "Ummm. Chocolate cupcake. The breakfast of champions." She washed down the cake with another sip of coffee. As she returned her cup to the saucer, she said, "If Drex is lying to impress, why hasn't he regaled us with stories of derring-do in the wilds of Alaska? He does the opposite. When it comes to talking about himself, he artfully changes topics."

Jasper said, "One wonders why."

"Apparently *you* wonder why."

"You don't? You've been taken in by the dimple?"

She frowned with exasperation. "Please. Give me some credit. I see through his practiced charm, and I've told him so." She moistened the tip of her finger and used it to collect the remaining crumbs on her plate, then licked them off, the action giving her time to formulate an opinion.

As she moved aside the empty plate, she said, "I think the basics of the childhood he described are probably true, but he might have embellished them for dramatic effect."

"That's what bothers me. Why would he want to create an effect?"

"For his own amusement?" she said, raising a shoulder. "Or, as you said, to make his biography more colorful and adventuresome, a marketable background a publisher would jump at."

"I hope that's all his evasiveness amounts to."

She crossed her arms on the edge of the table and leaned forward. "So what if he stretches the truth a bit? Why does that concern you so much?"

"I'm amazed that it doesn't concern you." He gestured toward the garage apartment. "Without notice, a stranger moves in next door. He's unknown even to the Arnotts, yet he's living practically in the shadow of our home. The day we met, he told me he'd come to the area to soak up color and soul for his novel. Doesn't that imply that he would be out and about, observing and experiencing the culture? Instead, he rarely leaves the apartment."

"He's absorbed in the writing."

"Is he? Perhaps. But I get the feeling that he's not as devil-may-care as he wants us to believe."

She looked down and studied the wood grain in the tabletop. "In all honesty, I get that impression, too."

"Then we'd be wise not to believe everything he tells us and to be guarded about what we tell him. Don't you agree?"

"Yes." Then, lifting her gaze back to his, she said, "On the other hand, we could be overanalyzing and becoming paranoid when there's no cause to be. Maybe Drex was merely testing his story-telling ability last night. He wanted to see if he could weave an engaging history for himself and make me believe it."

"Possibly. After all, when you boil it down, fiction writers are glorified liars, aren't they?"

"I wouldn't put it quite like that."

He didn't ask how she would put it. Seeming to have closed the discussion to his satisfaction, he got up and carried his dirty dishes to the sink. It rather irked her to be dismissed, but she let the subject drop. She didn't want to engage in an argument where she would be placed in the position of defending Drex, whom she didn't know and who was possibly the blatant liar Jasper suspected him of being.

However, as Drex had described to her that period of his life, he had appeared to be telling the truth. There had been no teasing glint in his eyes or devilish smile to suggest either a white lie or a whopper.

My mother never set foot in Alaska. When he'd said that, his eyes, his whole demeanor, had conveyed stark, heartbreaking reality. "He grew up without his mother."

"Pardon?"

Caught musing out loud, she repeated, "He grew up without his mother."

"She died?"

"I don't know. That's when you barged in. I'm left with a cliffhanger."

"Regrettable. The unknown facets of Drex Easton are the ones I wish I knew."

He folded the dishtowel he'd used and draped it over the edge of the sink, then lifted his gym bag off the floor and slid the strap onto his shoulder. "All right with you if I hang around the club after my workout? I may stay and have lunch there."

"I could meet you."

"I thought you planned to work on the African trip for your client."

"Those plans are flexible."

"Better to leave them in place. I'm not sure when I'll want to eat." Her expression must have revealed her letdown. In a crisp voice, he asked, "Is that a problem, Talia?"

It was a problem that she must be made to print out an itinerary to leave with him whenever she went out of town, but that he got piqued if she asked about his plans for an afternoon.

She replied with comparable curtness. "No problem."

He moved to stand behind her chair, placed his hands on her shoulders, leaned down, and whispered in her ear. "Instead of lunch, how about I take my favorite girl out for dinner tonight?"

She was being placated, and it angered her. She was inclined to shrug his massaging hands off her shoulders. But, for the sake of marital harmony, she smiled back at him. "Your favorite girl would enjoy that."

He kissed her behind the ear. "I had better stay on my toes. Because I think our new neighbor spun that sad tale about his boyhood in order to woo you."

"Don't be ridiculous."

"It's not at all ridiculous. I believe you're too smart to fall for his adolescent seduction, but I also believe he's ballsy enough to try."

As he was about to pull away, she reached up and placed her hand on his arm. "If you're seriously worried about Drex's integrity and intentions, we don't have to continue being sociable."

"I've already obligated us to at least one more dinner. A double date with him and Elaine."

"Elaine?" she exclaimed. She came around in her chair and faced him. "This is the first I've heard of it."

"He extended the invitation last night."

"And you accepted? Jasper, Elaine—"

"It's okay. He more or less asked my permission to make a move on her. He thought she and I might be carrying on illicitly." Jasper winked at her. "Funny, isn't it?"

———

Drex thought, *Not that fuckin' funny*.

He pushed back his chair and went over to the window in time to see Jasper's car backing out of their drive. Through the surveillance receiver, he could hear Talia moving around the kitchen. Cabinet doors being shut. Water running. The sun's glare on the windowpanes prevented him from seeing her. He wondered what she'd worn down to breakfast.

"Jesus." He was becoming a peeping Tom. He pushed the heels of his hands into his eye sockets in an attempt to blind himself against envisioning her in some kind of soft sleepwear, disheveled and barefoot, hair in tangles, eyes drowsy.

Before dawn, he'd been awakened by an erotic dream featuring her. Images of her were unformed and ephemeral. He could feel more than he could see, but the sensations were intense. He woke up painfully aroused, the sheets saturated with sweat despite the gale powered by the new fan blowing across him.

He was out of sorts and troubled despite last night's success.

When he'd told Mike and Gif that Jasper's search for the transmitter was futile, that he was looking in the wrong place, they'd congratulated him on his ingeniousness.

"He thought he had me," he'd said, "but he's the one who got hoodwinked." When Jasper had come up empty-handed, Drex had felt like shouting at him across the lawn, *Gotcha, sucker!*

"He gave himself away," Drex told them. "Who goes looking for hidden surveillance after having a neighbor over for burgers? Nobody, that's who. I'm telling you, he's our man."

Mike and Gif had pressed him to tell them how he'd achieved hiding the bug, and where. He'd refused. "For me alone to know. It's my crime. If caught, only I will take the fall."

At that point, Gif, in his reasonable way, had resumed his argument that Drex should notify Rudkowski. "What you're doing is high-risk, Drex. You might give yourself away and not even be aware of it until it's too late. If not Rudkowski, alert somebody to what you're doing. Think of the additional resources that—"

"No, Gif. I tried that once, and it backfired. Big time. Remember?"

"Vividly," Mike grumbled.

"Okay, then. Before I involve Rudkowski this time, I'm gonna have the suspect hogtied and squealing confessions."

Gif sighed in defeat. "In the meantime—"

"I'll watch my back."

"Better yet, don't turn it to him."

After ending the call, Drex had gone to bed, but hadn't slept that long or well before the dream woke him. Giving up on going back to sleep, he'd gotten up, made coffee, and, restless and edgy, turned on the receiver and waited to hear something from the house next door.

Jasper had come downstairs first and cooked himself breakfast. Drex could hear a TV news show in the background, pans clanking, coffee beans grinding. Finally, Talia joined him. She'd told Jasper good morning in a voice slightly hoarse from sleep. Drex had imagined them exchanging a hug, a pat on the rump, a light kiss. That was as far as he'd let his imagination run.

Then for close to an hour, he'd listened to their breakfast dialogue. For the most part, it was inconsequential. She reminded Jasper that he needed to consult an arborist about one of their trees. His tailor had called; the clothes he'd had altered were ready to be picked up. He made polite inquiries about the family who were off to Africa, but he didn't sound that interested in Talia's answers.

There were also stretches of companionable silence.

Drex hadn't sat up and taken notice until Jasper had asked her, from out of nowhere, what she and he had talked about last night while alone. His heart had skipped a beat, not because the question made him anxious, but because he wanted to hear how Talia would respond.

He told himself it didn't matter. Lately, he was lying to himself a lot.

It came as no surprise that Jasper was leery of him. But Jasper hadn't emphasized to Talia just how mistrustful, had he? He hadn't told her that he had gone downstairs in the dark to search for a listening device that he suspected Drex of planting.

Had he omitted mention of that because he hadn't wanted to appear comically foolish? Or because he couldn't explain to her why such a notion would even enter his mind?

Drex was already aware of Jasper's suspicion, but it was helpful to learn the extent of it.

Talia also harbored doubts about his honesty, but she'd given him the benefit of the doubt, seeming more inclined to think he was exaggerating rather than outright lying. She'd also sounded sympathetic when she spoke of his mother.

After that, the tone of their conversation changed, subtly but noticeably. Having it piped into his ears through the headset seemed to have amplified the silent subtext as well as their spoken words. He wished he could have watched their expressions during that exchange, to gauge whether the testiness he'd sensed between them was real or imagined.

After Jasper left the house, there was no point in eavesdropping. Drex stored away the audio surveillance gear, booted up his laptop, and began rereading the information he had collected over the years about the eight women who had disappeared. If the material were converted to hard copy, the contents would fill a moving van.

Today, he applied what he now knew or sensed about Jasper Ford, searching for a connection to his victims. Had one of the women been a gourmet cook? Had one favored the bourbon Jasper drank? Had one shared his preference for Dijon mustard over ketchup? One small thing, previously overlooked, could be the link Drex was desperate to find, especially now that he feared his culprit had an even darker side.

Was it invisible to his victims until it was too late? Had his victims sensed it but ignored it? What had made them susceptible? What had made Talia susceptible?

He was still dwelling on that question several hours later when there came a knock.

———

He sat with his hand cupped over his mouth, absorbed in whatever was on his computer screen. When she tapped on the doorjamb, he came out of his chair so abruptly, it went over backward and landed on the hardwood floor with a loud clack.

"Mercy." Talia pressed her hand against her thumping chest. It would be hard to say which had startled her most: his sudden reaction, or seeing him shirtless and barefoot, wearing only a pair of cargo shorts. Flustered, she said, "I didn't mean to scare you."

"I scare easily."

She doubted that. A man with reflexes that lightning quick would have little to fear.

He righted the chair, closed his laptop, and came over to the door. She asked, "What are you most afraid of?"

"Failure."

She'd been teasing, but he hadn't paused to think about it, and he'd answered so unequivocally, she knew he was serious. Feeling awkward and rethinking the wisdom of coming over, she said, "Should I have called ahead?"

"You don't have my number."

"Oh. Right."

He smiled. "If you've come to borrow a cup of sugar, I'm all out."

"Oh. Well then . . . " She heaved a sigh and turned as though to leave.

He chuckled. "What's up?"

She came back around and glanced beyond him at the setup on the table. "I don't want to pull you away from your work."

"Please. Rescue me."

"I'm not bothering you?"

He looked on the verge of saying something, but apparently thought better of it. To this point they'd been talking through the screen door. "Want to come in?"

"Only to be nosy."

He grinned and unlatched the lock.

"I've never been up here," she said as she stepped inside.

"I doubt you'll think the view is worth the climb up those stairs."

She stood in the center of the room and pivoted to make a complete circle. When she came back to him, he grimaced and reached up to rub the back of his neck.

"I know," he said. "It's not even—what's the term?"

"Shabby chic?"

"This is shabby shit."

She laughed. "It has potential. With a can of paint and..."

"A hundred thousand dollars."

They shared another smile. She gestured behind her toward the window. "The tree is lovely, though. The moss seems to have been draped by a decorator."

"Yeah. It gives me something to stare at while I daydream." He wasn't staring at the Spanish moss in the tree, however. He was looking into her eyes. Abruptly he said, "Excuse me a sec."

He went around her and into the bedroom, pushing the door partially closed. She walked over to the window. He didn't exactly live in the shadow of their house as Jasper had said, but through the branches of the tree, she could see the back of it almost in its entirety. Screened porch, kitchen windows, the windows of the master bedroom upstairs. Since the Arnotts' departure in June, she hadn't had to concern herself with keeping the window treatments closed at night. She realized the need to now.

Hearing him reenter the main room, she turned. He'd put on a faded t-shirt and his docksiders, but she didn't comment on the change, because it would make them each mindful that she'd caught him bare-chested and wearing a pair of shorts that hung tenuously from his sharp hipbones. It seemed best to pretend she hadn't noticed.

The t-shirt was faded. His chin was bristly. He had bed-head, the saddle brown strands even more unruly than they'd been the night before. But his eyes—agate in color and ringed in black like those of a tiger—looked anything but sleepy as they focused on her.

"I didn't know you wore glasses," she said.

He took them off and, with a puzzled expression, inspected them. "Who put those there?"

She laughed.

He set the horn-rims on the table next to his laptop. "What's Jasper up to this morning?"

"He went to our country club."

"He's a golfer?"

"No. The club has an Olympic-size pool. He swims laps. A serious number of laps."

"Every day?"

"Unless it's lightning and they close the pool."

"Huh. That explains his well-defined traps. You swim, too?"

"No."

He snapped his fingers. "Your aversion to sun exposure and water."

"Right. I can stay afloat, but I don't really get anywhere."

"So what do you do for exercise?"

"Spin class. Stationary bike."

"Ah. That explains your well-defined..." He stopped, looked away from her, tipped his head down and scratched his eyebrow with his thumb. Then said, "Would you like something to drink?"

"Sure." She said it brightly, maybe a bit too brightly, because she was wondering what of hers he found well-defined and why he'd changed his mind about telling her.

The kitchen was open to the rest of the room, demarcated only by a rectangle of vinyl flooring. The handle on the refrigerator door was loose and rattled when he pulled on it. "Water, Diet Coke, beer."

"What are you having?"

He looked at her over his shoulder. "Wanna play hooky and have a beer?"

She raised her eyebrows in a yes.

He uncapped two bottles and brought them over. They clinked bottles before drinking. The beer went down cold and bitter. "Playing hooky is fun."

He studied her for a second, then snuffled.

"What?"

"Be truthful now," he said. "You've never played hooky a day in your life."

She ducked her head. "My parents had great expectations."

"You sought their approval."

"Yes, but I was stricter on myself than they were on me."

"No naughtiness? Not ever?"

"Not *often*."

"Hmm. I see potential here. Stick around," he drawled. "I can corrupt you in no time at all."

"Jasper said you'd be ballsy enough to try."

"He said I'm ballsy?"

"He did."

"Remind me to thank him."

He saluted her with his beer bottle, and she saluted him back, then walked over to the table. She set her index finger on the blank top sheet of a stack of paper that had seen wear and tear. "Your manuscript?"

"Or a pile of manure. Hard to differentiate."

"I doubt it's that bad."

"Trust me."

"Is this your only copy?"

"Only hard copy. I back up each day's work on two thumb drives."

She ran her finger up the curled corners of the sheets. "I don't suppose you'd let me take a peek."

"Absolutely not."

"I'll give you an honest assessment."

"I already have an honest assessment. Mine. It sucks."

"Then a second opinion could be beneficial."

He shook his head. "Not yet."

Jasper was patently suspicious of Drex. Her reservations weren't that steep, but she admitted to being intrigued by his reticence. Reading his book, even though it was fiction, could provide insight into the man behind the disarming dimple. But even as she had asked to read it, she'd known with near certainty that he would refuse. She didn't try to persuade him. Rather, she said, "I Googled you this morning."

His brow arched eloquently. "I've fantasized being Googled by a beautiful woman."

Without acknowledging either the compliment or the innuendo, she set her bottle of beer on the table and crossed her arms over her middle. "Another joke, another deflection. Aren't you going to ask me why I plundered the Internet in search of information on you?"

"I'm not that vain." Then he seemed to reconsider. "Well, I guess I am. What about me sent you plundering?"

"Is Drex Easton a *nom de plume* or your real name?"

He formed a slow grin. "You didn't find anything, did you?"

She didn't admit it, but her silence confirmed his guess, and his grin widened.

"I told you last night, Talia. Even I'm bored with me."

"Is it your real name?"

"Yes. Given to me by my dad."

She hesitated, then asked softly, "What happened to your mother?"

"I haven't the faintest."

She flinched. "What do you mean?"

"Exactly what I said. It's the God's truth, and that's all I'm going to say on the subject."

"Why the secrecy?"

He set down his beer bottle hard enough to make a thump against the tabletop. "What difference does my past make to you? Or, for that matter, my present and future?"

"Because of Elaine."

Chapter 10

—◦◦◦—

Drex seemed taken aback by her answer, which wasn't the whole truth, but it had moved them off the track that she'd been following—his past. It was the one subject that made him restive and annoyed.

Now, his forehead wrinkled with perplexity. "Elaine? Am I missing something?"

"Jasper told me you planned to invite her to dinner."

He raised his shoulders in a silent *So?*

"I'm not sure... That is, I hope..." She stopped, pushed her fingers through her hair, and said, "I'm botching this."

He placed his hands on his hips and tilted his head slightly. An attitude of impatient waiting.

She took a deep breath. "In the time I've known Elaine, she's had a string of romantic disappointments. A man expresses interest, she tends to become infatuated very quickly and then falls hard, only to discover that he was less attracted to her than to her—"

He held up a hand. "I get it. You want to protect her from a man like me who has no visible means of support and is looking for a rich..." In search of an appropriate word, he twirled his hand. "Patroness?"

"I've insulted you."

"No shit."

"That wasn't my intention, Drex. It's just that Jasper and I have become very fond of Elaine. Because she's innately affectionate and generous, she sets herself up to be taken advantage of. We don't want to see her hurt."

"By a snake like me."

She blew out a breath. "Insulted *and* angered."

He didn't say anything.

"I'm sorry. I shouldn't have interfered." She turned to go, but he hooked his hand in the bend of her elbow and gently brought her back around.

"Look, taking Elaine to dinner seems like an appropriate way to thank her for her hospitality on Sunday. That's my only agenda. Okay?"

She looked up at him with chagrin. "Now I feel small."

He let several seconds lapse, then placed his hand flat on the top of her head before drawing it toward his chest to measure her height against his collarbone. "You are small."

With him looking down on her, and her looking up at him, they smiled at each other. Smiles that didn't show teeth. Small, olive branch–extending smiles that faded with continuance and, as they aged, assumed a different, uncertain, and unsettling nature, until they didn't count as smiles at all.

He was the first to speak. Huskily. "What night?"

"What?"

He cleared his throat. "What night would be best for you and Jasper? You say, then I'll check with Elaine. And, yes, she gave me her number. But, no, I didn't ask for it."

Talia figured she deserved that dig. "Thursday?"

"Perfect. What are you in the mood for?"

"Oh!" She thumped her forehead with the heel of her hand.

"That's the reason I came over. Jasper told me that you had requested a list of good restaurants. He asked me to compile one for you."

She took a sheet of notepaper from the front pocket of her jeans and passed it to him. "These are within a reasonable driving distance. They're all reliably good. I prefer the Italian."

Without even glancing at the list, he said, "Italian it is."

She began backing away from him toward the door. With a flick of her hand toward the table, she said, "Thanks for the beer. I don't remember when I last drank one."

"See? You're already halfway to being corrupted. A cupcake for breakfast. Beer for lunch."

She laughed and moved toward the door. He got there first and opened it for her. She stepped out onto the landing, where she halted and came back around, standing in the wedge between the threshold and screen door he held open. "How did you know I had a cupcake for breakfast?"

His parted his lips to speak, but nothing came out.

"Drex? How did you know that?"

Again, he hesitated before raising his free hand and whisking the pad of his thumb across her cheek near the corner of her mouth, then holding his thumb up to where she could see. "Chocolate icing."

Following Talia's visit, the afternoon dragged on torturously. Drex almost wished she hadn't come. Almost. Because now he couldn't escape seeing her in this tacky room. She'd stood there. She'd touched that. Her voice and laughter echoed off the ugly wallpaper. Her scent permeated the stuffy air.

He tried to immerse himself in the case files, but having studied them for years, he knew their contents almost by heart. By reading the first few words of a sentence, he already knew its ending. The material held his attention for only minutes at a time before his mind drifted to something Talia had said or done.

At dusk, he gave up, shut down shop at his computer, and went for a run through the neighborhood. As he was returning, the Fords were backing out of their driveway in Jasper's car. Both waved to him.

He smiled and waved back, when what he felt like doing was to drive his fist through the windshield. Despite the difference in their ages, he had to admit they made a striking pair.

Before showering, he carted Jasper's box fan down the staircase and to the door of their screened porch, where he left it outside. He used a corner of it to anchor a note of thanks he'd written on a sheet of typing paper. He added the name of the restaurant where he'd made a reservation. *Thursday night. 7:30. Party of four.*

Elaine had accepted his invitation. It would worry Talia to know how exuberant her acceptance had been.

He watched a detective show on his laptop while eating his dinner of frozen pizza. The apartment's antique oven had given it an old grease-smoke taste. He didn't finish it. He wasn't hungry anyway.

He didn't go out, fearing that Talia and Jasper would come home during his absence, and he would miss an informative conversation.

Ten o'clock came, and they still hadn't returned. Ready to climb the walls, he called Mike and Gif. "They're still out, but I thought I'd go ahead and report the day's events."

He started by relating the breakfast table conversation and concluded by saying, "Jasper's nursing suspicion of me, but hasn't come after me with a hatchet."

"Yet," Mike said.

Drex asked if there had been anything out of Rudkowski. Not a peep.

"Which is a good thing," Gif said.

"Or not," Mike intoned. "If we'd heard rumblings, at least we'd know what he was up to."

Drex agreed. "It'll be eating at him that I inquired about Marian Harris, and then left for a two-week vacation to an unknown destination. He'll be looking for me. I'm on borrowed time here."

He cited the little he had to show for the time he'd already spent in residence and, pursuant to that, finally worked his way around to telling them about Talia's visit. "She just appeared, took me completely off-guard."

He told them about scrambling to close his laptop before she could see what was on the screen, making himself decent, and ensuring that his pistol, ID, and night vision binoculars were out of sight. "Fortunately I'd already put away the surveillance equipment."

Mike gave a grunt. "She came uninvited?"

"Like I said. She was hand-delivering a list of good local restaurants. I had hoped to get a sampling of Jasper's handwriting. Instead, Talia brought over a typewritten list she had compiled. At his request."

"How long did she stay?"

"Hmm, ten, twelve minutes." At least twice that long.

"What all did you talk about?" Gif asked.

"She asked to read my manuscript. I told her no way in hell. Words to that effect. Then she started in on me, asking about my past. I turned the tables on her and asked why she should care."

"Why *should* she care?" Mike asked.

"She's afraid her friend will develop a crush on me."

"Her friend Elaine?"

"Yeah. Talia was mother-henning. I set her straight on why I asked Elaine to dinner." He gave them the basic info, skimmed over the details.

He skimmed over a lot. He didn't describe to them Talia's old, holey jeans and how perfectly they fit her well-defined buns. Did they really need to know what her high, round B-cups did for a plain white t-shirt? He didn't mention the beer. For sure as hell he didn't tell them about lifting the speck of chocolate off her face with his thumb and wishing he could have licked it off and then stayed to tease the corner of her lips until they parted for him.

Because he didn't go into any of that, he couldn't account for the solemn silence that ensued when he finished. "Guys? Have you nodded off?"

Mike asked, "You at your computer?"

"No. In the bedroom."

"I just sent you an email. Call us back after you've looked at it."

He disconnected before Drex could say anything more.

He rolled up and off the bed, went into the main room, and opened his laptop. The subject line of Mike's email was empty, nor was there any content in the body of it. It had an attachment.

Drex opened it, and his heart blipped with excitement when the photograph taken aboard Marian Harris's yacht came up full screen. The boys in Bombay were geniuses and worth every penny they charged. The picture had been clarified and enhanced, and the quality was far better than Drex could have hoped for.

He zoomed in on the figure of the man he suspected was Jasper Ford. "Damn!" He'd hoped for a *voilá!*, for an unmistakable image of the man living next door.

But the improved color density had sharpened the contrast between the brilliant sunset and the male figure silhouetted against it. His features remained dark and indiscernible. His hair wasn't a sleek ponytail, but a wreath of frizzy curls. The nose in profile? It could possibly be Jasper's, but Drex couldn't swear to it, and, besides, he could have had rhinoplasty. Even a slight alteration could make a significant difference in his appearance.

He studied the close-up for several minutes before admitting that if there was something new and revelatory to see, he was missing it.

He returned the photo to its original size, sat back in his chair, and took it in as a whole, wondering what it was in particular that Mike and Gif had wanted him to see. Little of the yacht itself was visible in the picture, and Drex didn't see anything of consequence from what was shown. The enhancement hadn't changed Marian Harris's image that dramatically. There was nothing to see in the background except for the blazing sky.

The partygoers? The doctored chromaticity had deepened some hues, lightened others, making it easier to delineate forms within the mishmash of faces and limbs. Individuals were now distinguishable. One in particular on the fringe of the crowd caught Drex's eye because of a slender shaft of light shining on her hair and—

And matching it to the golds and reds that threaded through the sunset.

He sat perfectly still for a long time because he was too sickened to move. He could only stare at the face, which was out of focus, but dreamworthy, unquestionably lovely, and indisputably identifiable.

He got his *voilá!*, after all.

Chapter 11

———◆———

Starting from the time he received that initial call from Deputy Gray in Key West, it took Rudkowski three days to find the hotel.

During that seventy-two hours, he'd pulled together every resource at his disposal in an attempt to tree Drex Easton without causing too much of a stir. He wanted to keep the higher-ups unaware that Easton was at it again.

The son of a bitch.

Rudkowski was tempted to let him move forward without intervention. Why not sit back in his La-Z-Boy, overdose on ESPN, and allow Easton to self-destruct? Rudkowski's life would be simpler once Easton was completely wiped off the landscape.

But in the process of destroying himself, Easton would create a shit storm. Some of it was bound to blow back on Rudkowski. He wasn't one of those rah-rah, diehard agents who thought the FBI was an exalted company of which he was fortunate to be a member. He wasn't a blindly loyal disciple of the bureau.

He was, however, fanatically devoted to his pension.

He didn't give Easton the satisfaction of calling Mike Mallory or Gifford Lewis, demanding to know where the hell he was and what he was up to. His cronies would report straight back to him that Rudkowski was on the warpath, and Easton would get a kick out of that. Even more, he would enjoy knowing that, so far, he was winning this current game of hide-and-seek.

But Rudkowski had agents surreptitiously keeping a close watch on Mallory and Lewis. For the past three days, they had reported for work as usual. After office hours, each had gone directly home. Neither was married, both lived alone, they seemed not to have any social life or any friends except for each other and Easton. On the surface they appeared to be the two biggest dullards on the face of the earth.

Rudkowski wasn't fooled. He sensed that behind the closed doors of their drab apartments, they toiled into the wee hours, diligently working underground for their ringleader, Easton.

Rudkowski would continue to have their activities monitored, although he knew it was futile. Neither of the men was likely to make a slip-up, and neither would betray Drex Easton, not even if his life depended on it.

Rudkowski knew that because there had been a time when their lives had depended on it, and neither had caved.

Twice over the course of the past three days, Rudkowski had called Deputy Gray in Key West to inquire if he had heard anything more from Easton. He hadn't. Rudkowski pulled rank and got a sergeant in the sheriff's department down there to see if he could retrieve the telephone number that had called there twice on Sunday, the calls several hours apart. It took a while, but the sergeant came through and passed the number along to Rudkowski.

It was a short-lived victory, because when Rudkowski called the number, he got a recording telling him that the call couldn't be completed as dialed. Unsurprising, really, considering the savvy bastard he was dealing with. Easton would have destroyed that phone within minutes of speaking with Gray.

Miracles did happen, however. Rudkowski's shrinking belief in them was fully restored just that morning soon after he had arrived at his office. Another agent who'd been helping him on his search popped in. "You still on Easton's tail?"

"What have you got?"

"That last cell number you had for him?"

"No longer good."

"Not any more, but it was nine days ago. He sent a text from it."

"To who?"

"Mike Mallory."

"Shocker. From where?"

"A chain hotel in Lexington. I got the address."

———————

Rudkowski signed out for the remainder of the day and recruited another agent to drive him the seventy-something miles from Louisville to Lexington. When they reached their destination, Rudkowski left the second agent waiting in the car, preferring to handle this interview alone.

When the double automatic doors opened, a group of uniformed men and women filed past him pulling roll-aboards toward a waiting van. Flight crew, Rudkowski figured. Their departure left the lobby empty.

The receptionist greeted him as he approached the check-in desk. "Good afternoon, sir."

"Hi." He produced his badge and gave the young woman time to read his name on his ID. "It's pronounced just like it's spelled, short u. I need to speak to the manager, please."

"She's at lunch. She left me in charge."

He leaned across the counter and read her name tag. "Ms. Li?"

"Yes, sir."

"I'm here to ask about a guest—"

"Special Agent Easton?"

Rudkowski scowled. "How'd you know?"

"Because he's the only FBI agent I've checked in." She beamed a smile. "He'd be hard to forget anyway, because he was so nice."

Rudkowski wanted to grind his teeth. "Yeah. Hell of a guy."

"Are you—"

He cut her off. "I'll ask the questions, Ms. Li. If you don't mind." Her warm smile turned cooler. She bobbed her head.

"How many nights did he stay?"

"He didn't."

"He checked in but didn't stay?"

"They were here for only a couple of hours. But Mr. Easton paid for a full day."

"'They'? Did he bring a woman?"

"Nothing like that," she said, her lips pursing primly. "He was here for a meeting with two associates."

"Mallory and Lewis?"

"I didn't get their names."

"Was one of them a fat guy, face like a bulldog?"

Seeming to be offended by the description, she said, "He was...heavyset. Not a handsome man."

"Not handsome and nice like Agent Easton."

She didn't say anything to that, only looked at him with unblinking eyes.

He asked, "What about the third man?"

"I don't remember him very well."

Gif Lewis, Rudkowski thought. That guy faded into the woodwork. Rudkowski worried his lower lip between his teeth. "Easton used a credit card?"

She answered with a curt nod. "He reviewed the bill to make certain I had added the minibar charges. Plus the cake."

"Cake?"

"He called down and asked me to have room service deliver—"

"Cake?"

"Yes."

No more "sir," he noticed. Not that he cared about her opinion of him, but he added a bit of saccharine to his next question, because it was the most important one. "Ms. Li, after settling the bill with the additional charges, did Easton happen to tell you where he was going from here? Did he make a reservation at one of your chain's other hotels?"

"No. But he left something for you."

"For me?"

"That's what I was trying to ask you at the start before you interrupted. I was about to ask if you had come to pick up the envelope. Mr. Easton said that you might be coming by for it within a few days. Honestly, I was about to give up on you. Wait just a moment, please."

She disappeared into an office and returned shortly with a letter-size envelope. "Here you are."

He plucked it from her hand. "Thanks."

"I've already been thanked. By Mr. Easton. I was happy to provide the service for him." She turned her back on him and went back into the office.

Rudkowski stalked across the lobby and through the double doors, waiting until he was outside to rip open the envelope and pull out the single sheet of hotel stationery. In the center of it was printed: *Hey there, Rudkowski. Kiss my ass.*

Chapter 12

⬦⬦⬦➤◆➤⬦⬦⬦

Stroking her cheek to remove the speck of chocolate icing had been one thing. Licking it off his thumb had been another. If Drex had stopped at the former, and hadn't done the latter, she would have forgotten the incident by now. Probably. Maybe. But because he had done it, she was still thinking about it two days later. With each replay of the scene in her mind, the scintillation was magnified. As was her unease over it.

Because it hadn't been a reflexive action that could be laughed off. He hadn't noisily smacked his lips or wisecracked about her chocolate addiction. It wasn't wittiness that had simmered in his eyes as they'd held her gaze. Nothing like that.

No, licking it off his thumb had been provocative. Which compelled her to report it to Jasper.

But she hadn't.

She hadn't told him later that afternoon when he returned from the country club, or during their dinner out that evening, or when they'd come home to find that Drex had brought back their fan, along with a note regarding tonight's reservation.

On any of those occasions she could have mentioned the incident to Jasper in an offhanded manner, made light of it, and given it no significance. But she hadn't slipped it into a conversation, and now too much time had passed, during which it had acquired significance.

Of late, there had been a mounting tension between Jasper and her, made even worse because neither of them acknowledged it. Telling him about the incident with Drex might force them to expose problems within the marriage, which, to this point, neither had been willing to do.

In any case, telling Jasper about it now would feel like a confession. He would want to know why she was just now getting around to informing him of it when they were an hour away from joining the man for a double date. She didn't want to get into anything with him just before leaving for their evening out.

As predicted, Elaine was as giddy as a coed who'd been invited to the prom by the varsity captain. She'd called Talia within minutes of Drex's inviting her and had recounted word for word all he'd said, speaking as though every sentence ended in a pair of exclamation marks. Over the course of the past two days, she had called Talia no fewer than a dozen times in a dither over what she should wear tonight.

Meanwhile, Talia hadn't seen or heard from Drex since leaving him on his doorstep. Without taking time even to say goodbye, she'd gotten the hell out of there. Several times, she had noticed that his car wasn't in the driveway, but hadn't caught sight of him leaving or returning. When she casually asked Jasper if he'd crossed paths with him, he'd said with disinterest, "No."

Now, soaking in a bubble bath, chin-deep in scented suds, Talia wondered if Drex shared her disquiet over the incident. If he had dwelled on those few moments as much as she had, he might regret what he'd done and could well be embarrassed when he saw her tonight. Would it make for an awkward situation?

No. There wouldn't be any awkwardness because she wouldn't

allow there to be. She would treat him as she had before: friendly, but with boundaries clearly drawn.

She was probably making far too much out of it anyway.

Having resolved that, she climbed out of the tub and proceeded to dress for the evening. She and Jasper had offered to pick up Elaine at seven. At fifteen minutes to, Talia checked her reflection in the mirror one last time, picked up her handbag, and, as she emerged from her dressing room, called to Jasper, "I'm ready."

Elaine lived in a classy community of townhouses, Georgian in design, which afforded owners ample and pricey square footage, but zero lot lines. Talia parked at the curb and went up the walkway connecting the sidewalk to Elaine's front door, which was made private from the street by an iron picket fence lined with shrubbery.

Within seconds of Talia's ringing the bell, Elaine opened the door and exclaimed, "Oh my God, you look stunning!"

"Thank you. So do you."

"It's new." Elaine pinched up the full skirt of her dress and curtsied.

"It's lovely."

"I can't do slinky anymore," she said wistfully, eyeing Talia up and down. "Is Jasper parking the car? Come in, come in so the mosquitoes don't eat us alive. Drex, will you please tend bar?"

Talia drew up short just as she stepped across the threshold and spotted him lounging on the sofa. A great cat, having feasted on a fresh kill and lazing in the sun, couldn't have appeared more satiated and indolent as he unfolded himself and stood up. "Hello, Talia."

He was wearing dress slacks and a necktie, but the tie had been loosened, his collar button undone. She hadn't yet braced herself to look him in the eye for the first time since last she saw him and was so taken off guard to find him here that the first words out of her mouth sounded like an accusation. "I thought you were meeting us at the restaurant."

"He called and asked if he could come by early," Elaine said. "And look what he brought me!" She pointed to the coffee table on which lay a rubber-banded manuscript.

"He had a copy made and asked me to read it and give him an honest assessment, which I swore I would do."

Talia's gaze moved from the manuscript back up to Drex. His smile was smug, his eyes glinting with insinuation, and she was certain he shifted them ever so subtly to the spot near her mouth that he'd touched with his thumb.

Before she gave in to the temptation to cross the room and slap him as hard as she could, she turned her back to him and addressed Elaine. "I'm sure he'll benefit from your opinion."

"He already has. He bounced several titles off me, and we decided on one just before you got here. Am I at liberty to tell her, Drex?"

"I'd rather keep it between us for now."

Taking in the scene, Talia noticed that Elaine's high-heeled sandals were lying on their sides in front of the sofa. Drex's suit jacket was folded over the arm of a chair. Two half-filled highball glasses were on the coffee table. A gas fire flickered in the fireplace. It lent a romantic ambiance, but wasn't radiating any heat.

Talia's cheeks, however, were. She was furious over the way he had played her. It was an insult that he had asked Elaine to read his manuscript when he had soundly rejected her offer to do so. He was also playing Elaine in the very manner that Talia had warned him against.

"What's keeping Jasper?" Elaine asked.

Talia hid her anger behind a rueful smile. "He sends his regrets."

"He's not coming? Why?"

"I would have notified you, but I didn't know myself until we were due to leave. He waited until the last minute to tell me so I wouldn't cancel on you. He insisted I come on. Besides, the plan was for us to drive you tonight. He didn't want to stand you up. As it turns out..." She let the statement go unfinished except for a one-shoulder shrug and a backward nod toward Drex.

He said, "Why isn't Jasper coming?"

She turned around to face him. "Tummy issues."

"A bug?"

"The oysters he had for lunch."

Elaine said, "I used to warn my husband against eating them raw."

Neither Drex nor Talia contributed anything to that. He was still looking at her as though they shared an inside joke. A naughty inside joke. Spending an evening in his company would be intolerable.

"I hate to bail on you, too," she said to Elaine. "But I really feel I should go home and make certain that Jasper is all right."

Elaine stepped forward and hooked arms with her. "Nonsense. You know how men are when they're sick. They're either pitiful and want their mommy or they're ornery. I believe Jasper would fall into the second category. Besides, I'm not about to let you waste that knockout dress. Drex, you don't mind escorting both of us, do you?"

The dimple appeared. "It'll be my pleasure. And I would hate to waste one of the desserts I took the liberty of pre-ordering."

"Oooh, what?" Elaine said.

"Chocolate soufflé."

The sly look he gave Talia set her teeth on edge.

He walked over to the bar, turned to her, and arched his brow. "Can I pour you a nice red wine?"

Ungently she tossed her handbag into the nearest chair. "No. Vodka martini. Dry. Straight up."

He wanted to kill her.

But first, he wanted to fuck her.

No, he wanted to fuck her, then torment her, then kill her.

Drex had been experiencing these violent urges ever since he'd seen her in that photograph taken aboard Marian Harris's yacht, separated from Jasper Ford by several yards, but *there*. The two of them.

"All that bullshit about the client complaint, the email exchange, the hand-delivered roses, was just that: bullshit," he'd told Mike and Gif when he'd recovered from the shock and was composed enough to call them.

"You're sure it's her?" Mike had asked. "I mean, Gif and me thought so, but we're going only by pictures. You've been up close and personal."

They didn't know how up close, how personal. "It's her."

"So what do you think?" Mike had asked. "Is she her husband's next victim, or his accomplice?"

"Hell I know," Drex had muttered in reply.

After seeing her and Jasper in such close proximity on the yacht's deck, when they weren't even supposed to have known each other at the time, he had methodically reviewed each of his own encounters with Talia, assessing them in a new light. Especially her unannounced visit to his grubby living quarters.

Providing him a list of restaurants had been an acceptable excuse for her coming over, but it was just as likely that Jasper had sent her on a fact-finding mission. If she had come to his door wearing a see-through negligee, it couldn't have looked any sexier than her jeans and t-shirt. But maybe that downplayed wardrobe had been calculated to make the visit seem neighborly and innocent.

Was the speck of icing an accidental and unnoticed leftover from breakfast, or had she dabbed it on deliberately, placing it in a spot that couldn't possibly escape his notice? A spot that had made his loins achy and tight.

The question about her culpability hung there unanswered until

Mike said, "Drex, let me pose a question that might simplify and clarify your thinking."

"Shoot."

"If she's in the dark about her husband and his past misdeeds, why did she lie to you about how they hooked up?"

The three of them had pondered the question in silence.

It was Drex who finally spoke, grumbling, "Here I've been losing sleep from worrying about her safety."

And here he was now, topping off Elaine's wineglass with the last of their second bottle. He'd never endured such a long dinner in his life. It was torture. From the instant Talia had come through Elaine's front door, he'd been baiting her, and it had worked. She had flung her small purse into the armchair as though throwing down a spiked gauntlet.

Inside that dress—which, by the way, *was* a slinky knockout worn with no detectable undergarments—she was steaming. Her entire body vibrated with indignation every time she looked at him, which wasn't often. In fact, for most of the dinner, she ignored him completely.

He wondered if her obvious ire had anything to do with that laden moment on his threshold, from which she had run like the apartment had burst into flames. Maybe his suggestive action had offended her.

But he figured her truculent mood tonight had more to do with Elaine, who was reacting to his courtly attention as forecast, which was exactly what Talia had wanted to guard against.

Elaine's effervescence made her impossible to dislike, but, as though sensing the strain between Talia and him, she'd appointed herself social chair of the trio and couldn't leave even the briefest silence alone. She filled any gap in the conversation with prattle. Drex responded as though delightfully entertained by every inanity, which fed Elaine's flirtatiousness, which fueled Talia's anger.

When they finished their entrées and were waiting for the soufflés to be served, Elaine excused herself to go to the ladies' room, leaving him alone with Talia for the first time that evening. She took her cell phone from her handbag and typed a text.

"To Jasper?"

She said a terse yes. While waiting for a reply, she took a slow visual survey of the drapery valance, the chandelier, the weave pattern of the tablecloth. She picked at her slender diamond bracelet as though discovering that it had been clasped around her wrist without her knowledge. She did not look at him.

"You seem out of sorts tonight."

She stopped inspecting her bracelet and looked across at him, but didn't say anything.

"Why are you in such a sulk? Missing Jasper?"

On the heels of his taunt, her phone dinged. She read the text, then clicked off.

"How's he doing?"

"Better."

"Puked it all up?"

"Drank a ginger ale." Then, with full-blown hostility, she said, "You really are a piece of work, aren't you?"

Drex didn't have time to respond because Elaine's return to the table coincided with the waiter delivering their soufflés.

They ate them, their conversation limited to comments about calories and how some foods were worth the splurge. They had coffee but didn't linger over it, and when Elaine suggested after-dinner drinks, Talia bowed out.

"I hate to cut the evening short," she lied. "Jasper says he's feeling better, but I really should get home to him."

Elaine had insisted that they all ride together to the restaurant, leaving Talia's car at the townhouse. When the restaurant valet brought around Drex's car, Elaine got in the front seat, as before. Talia sat in back.

Their positions were such that Drex could observe her in the rearview mirror. She kept her head turned toward the back seat window.

As they neared Elaine's neighborhood, she expressed regret that Jasper had missed such a luscious dinner. "If he's up to it, let's have a foursome lunch at the country club tomorrow."

Talia continued to stare out the window. "It will depend on how he feels in the morning. I'll have to let you know." She didn't sound at all enthusiastic about the prospect.

"I'll make a ressie for four in the hope that you can make it. Noonish? Or a bit later?"

Drex said, "Sorry, Elaine, but I have to decline."

"Oh, no."

"I'm stuck at a pivotal part of the novel and much in need of inspiration. I'm thinking of going in search of some."

"Where does a writer begin looking for inspiration?"

"Holy ground."

"Church?"

"Hemingway's house in Key West."

Talia's reaction was instantaneous. Her head came around. They locked eyes in the rearview mirror.

"Have you been there?" He addressed the question to her, but Elaine responded.

"My husband and I docked there. But only once. The vibe was a little too bohemian for him."

Drex acknowledged that with a nod but never took his eyes off Talia, who, after holding his stare for several seconds, had turned her head aside again. *Un-huh. No way,* he thought. He wasn't going to let the question go unanswered. "How about you, Talia?"

Without looking at him, she lowered her chin slightly. "I was there a couple of years ago."

"And?"

"And..." She raised a nearly bare shoulder. "It was all right."

"Just all right?"

"Not my worst destination, but not one of my favorites, either."

"What didn't you like? The food? The nightlife? What?"

With discernible impatience, she said, "Nothing I could put my finger on."

"Hmm. Did you tour Hemingway's house?"

"No, but I'm not surprised that you plan to."

"Why's that?"

She met his gaze in the mirror. "Jasper theorized that you want to create a professional image for yourself that's reminiscent of Jack London or Hemingway."

"Jasper devoted that much thought to me and my aspirations?"

"He made the comment after I told him about your upbringing in Alaska."

"Alaska?" Elaine chirped. "How fascinating."

"Not really," Drex said.

"I've never known anyone from there. You must tell me all about it. Come in for a nightcap?"

He pulled the car to the curb in front of her townhouse, put it in park, but left it running. "If I'm going to Florida, I'll need to get up early tomorrow and start making arrangements. Rain check?"

"Of course. Besides, you probably should follow Talia home."

He glanced back at her. "I planned to."

"I wouldn't dream of inconveniencing you. Besides, I'm a big girl." She got out of the car and shut the back door.

By the time Drex alighted and had come around to open the passenger door for Elaine, Talia was impatiently bouncing her key fob in her palm. "Thank you for dinner, Drex. It was lovely." Her drop-dead glare put her sincerity in doubt. "Good night, Elaine." She leaned in and air-kissed Elaine's cheek. "I'll be in touch."

"Give Jasper my regards. Promise to call me tomorrow and let me know how he's doing."

"Yes, I will." Without another word or glance at Drex, she turned and started walking toward her car, her high heels tapping the sidewalk with a marching cadence.

Elaine gave his shoulder a nudge. "I don't care how big a girl she is, I can tell she's upset. She hasn't been herself all evening. Make sure she gets home safely."

"After I walk you to your door."

"Nonsense. It's all of twenty steps."

"You sure?"

"Go. I think she must be more worried about Jasper than she's letting on."

He gave a grim smile at the unintended irony. "I'm sure you're right." He kissed Elaine lightly on the cheek and bid her good night, then quickly got back into his car and peeled away from the curb in pursuit of Talia's taillights.

Once he caught up with her, he stayed close and pulled into his driveway seconds after she pulled into hers. She opened the garage door remotely and lowered it as soon as her rear bumper cleared the opening.

Drex got out of his car and went around to open the trunk. He took out a duffel bag, closed the trunk, then headed up the path toward the garage apartment.

"How was the evening?"

Startled, he whipped around. Jasper was sitting in the dark on the screened porch, idly rocking in his chair. Drex gave him his good-neighbor smile. "You were missed. Feeling better?"

"Much."

"Bad oysters, Talia said."

"Must've been. Did you like the restaurant?"

"Superb. Thanks for the recommendation."

A light came on. Talia appeared as a silhouette in the open doorway between the kitchen and porch. She looked at Drex but didn't say anything. Jasper turned to her and extended his hand. She went to him and linked her fingers with his.

The gesture spoke volumes, the message was clear: We're a pair, a united front.

Drex covered a yawn with his hand and hitched his chin toward the staircase. "Well . . . I'm bushed. Good night."

Jasper responded with a good night.

Talia said nothing.

Drex climbed the staircase. The screen door was unlocked, but he used his key on the solid one. Inside, he crossed the living area in darkness, went into the bedroom, and switched on the lamp on the rickety nightstand. Then he returned to the bedroom door and shut it, preventing prying eyes from seeing him unzip the duffel he'd retrieved from his trunk. He took from it his laptop, binoculars, the audio surveillance equipment, FBI ID, and pistol.

Since connecting Talia to Jasper in Key West, he'd taken these items along whenever he went out. As a precaution. Just in case someone came searching the apartment. Someone to whom a locked door wouldn't be a deterrent.

And if someone did come snooping, he wanted to know it.

So he'd taken another precaution.

He picked up the lamp by its base and lowered it to the side of the bed where he had sprinkled talcum onto the floor, but not so much that it would be noticeable unless one was looking.

"Huh."

Between the time he'd left for his dinner and now, the powder had been smeared, as though someone had knelt at the side of the bed, perhaps to look beneath it or between the mattress and box spring.

He set the lamp back on the nightstand and switched it out, picked up the binoculars, opened the bedroom door, and went into the living room. At the window, he focused on the house next door. There were no lights on inside, but that didn't mean that he wasn't being watched.

Jasper had never intended to make that dinner date. He'd had other plans for the evening.

Drex huffed a soft laugh. "Bad oysters my ass."

Chapter 13

———◆———

Talia never touched the latte.

She had bought it only to rent a table, which were in short supply. The coffee shop was an offshoot of the ground floor lobby of the multistoried medical building. This morning the place was crowded; the baristas were bustling to fill orders.

Talia surmised that countless patients had come here following medical procedures or examinations, the outcomes of which were either cause for celebration or cause for an immediate reevaluation of one's priorities.

At a table near hers, a young couple was laughing into a cell phone, sharing obviously happy news on FaceTime. Also nearby was an older couple. The woman was crying softly into a tissue while the man sat with shoulders slumped, his features haggard, his eyes glazed with despair.

Talia's emotions fit somewhere in between. She wasn't happy, but she refused to let hopelessness set in.

"Talia?"

She raised her head. Drex Easton was standing over her.

"I thought it was you. I spotted you from..." He paused in jerking his thumb over his shoulder in the direction of the lobby and leaned down to take a closer look at her. "What's the matter?"

She bowed her head again and pressed her fingertips against her forehead. He was the last person she would wish to bump into right now. She simply wasn't up to dealing with him. Rather than engage at all, she chose to retreat. She picked up her handbag and stood. "I was just about to leave. You can have the table."

But as she moved away, he closed his hand around her biceps, stopping her. "What's wrong?"

"Nothing."

"Don't say nothing. Something. Are you sick? Did Jasper have a contagious bug after all?"

"No. I'm fine."

"You don't look fine."

"Let go of my arm."

"Talia—"

"Let go." She pulled her arm free.

He reached for her again.

"Everything okay here?"

Talia hadn't noticed the approach of the other man until he was right there with them. He divided a concerned look between her and Drex, landing on Drex, a frown of stern disapproval forming between his eyebrows. She then became aware that other customers had stopped what they were doing to observe them.

Drex said, "Yeah, pal, everything's cool."

The man didn't excuse himself or back down, but continued to glower at Drex with suspicion.

Drex glowered back. "I *said*, everything's cool."

Ignoring him, the man looked at her, asking softly, "Ma'am?"

She swallowed. "Everything's fine." Her smile was wobbly and unconvincing, so she added, "I'm was upset, am upset, about... about..."

"About her dad's diagnosis," Drex said. "They're close."

Talia marveled at the ease with which he lied. Going back to the stranger, she said, "I appreciate your concern. Truly. But I'm fine. I just needed some air."

"Sure, honey." Drex shot the man a dirty look as he brushed past him, then, cupping her elbow, maneuvered her out of the coffee shop.

He guided her across the lobby to a seating area that was sectioned off by a row of potted plants. They lent some privacy, but Talia didn't want privacy with Drex. Nothing good had come of the times when they had been alone; Jasper seemed not to like it, and, besides, Drex's smarmy behavior of the night before was still fresh in her mind.

He motioned for her to sit down on one of the padded benches. She shook her head. "I have to go."

He looked at her with consternation. "You're upset."

"I wasn't until you intruded."

He just stood there, an imposing presence she couldn't go around without creating another scene. She plopped down on the bench. He perched on the edge of another that faced hers. She moved her knees aside so they wouldn't be so close to touching his.

"What's going on?" he asked.

"Nothing. You're making way too much of—"

"Something's wrong. I can tell."

"How can you tell? You don't know me well enough to gauge my moods. You don't know me at all."

In a sudden move, he leaned forward and said with heat, "And that's eating at me. A lot."

The change in his bearing was discomfiting. She reclined back to compensate for his nearness. "Why should it? If my whole world is caving in, what business is it of yours?"

"Is your whole world caving in?"

"No!" she exclaimed.

"Then why were you sitting there, staring into your coffee so morosely?"

"Morosely?"

"Till I looked it up, I didn't know what it meant, either."

"I know what it means, and so do you."

"All right then, what made you morose?"

"Lord," she said, huffing a breath. "You're not going to let it go, are you?"

By way of an answer, he folded his arms over his chest and settled on the bench as though in it for the long haul.

She closed her eyes briefly, then, resigned, said, "I had just come from the dentist. Top floor." She raised her hand to indicate the stories above them. "I was still a bit woozy from the chill pill they gave me. I thought a latte would perk me up before I started the drive home."

Gingerly she touched the side of her face. "The numbing began to wear off. I wasn't feeling all that great. Then you show up and make a spectacle of me." She paused, took a breath, and narrowed her eyes on him. "Don't ever grab me like that again."

"I didn't grab you."

She gave him a withering look.

He raked his fingers through his hair, turned his head aside and looked at the yellowing leaves on the nearest ficus tree, then came back to her. "I didn't mean for it to be a grab. I didn't mean to make a spectacle of you. I apologize."

He appeared to mean it. "Apology accepted." After a short silence, she said, "I thought you were going to Florida."

"I thought so, too. That was until I checked the airfares this morning."

She gave him a wan smile.

"Hemingway's house is still on my bucket list," he said, "but I may not make it down there until I publish."

"I'll keep an eye out for discount fares and alert you to them."

"Definitely a benefit to having the MVP of travel agents living next door."

The grin he flashed was too attractive, too rakish, too…too everything.

She looked away from him toward the bank of elevators where a car had just opened up. A group flowed out, another filed in. The building was full of people, yet they had the seating area to themselves, making it feel as though they were alone.

It occurred to her then what an odd coincidence it was that he had turned up here.

She regarded him with misgiving. "What are you doing here, Drex?"

"Downtown, you mean?"

"I mean in this building. Why are you here?"

"I was in search of the main library. Got turned around. Saw the sign for the coffee shop, came in for a shot of espresso and to get my bearings." He dismissed all that with a shrug, then his eyes sharpened on her face. "Still feeling woozy? You gonna be okay?"

"The latte worked."

"You didn't drink it. Not one sip."

It disconcerted her that he had noticed. It made her uneasy to wonder what else he might have observed that would be much more consequential. "I should go." She slid the strap of her handbag onto her shoulder and stood.

So did he. "Did the dentist give you any pain pills?"

"A prescription. But I doubt I'll need it. It was just a filling."

"Get the pills. Take one before you need it. Head off the pain."

"I think all I really need is a nap." She moved away. "See you around, Drex."

"Where's your car?"

"Parking garage."

"This building?"

"Third level."

"I could escort—"

"No, thanks." She raised her hand in a halfhearted wave, then turned and walked quickly toward the elevators.

Drex watched her progress across the lobby.

He wasn't the only one who did.

From his vantage point on the bench facing Talia's, Drex had looked beyond her shoulder and spotted the do-gooder in the coffee shop. He had claimed a table just the other side of the glass wall, which gave him a view of the seating area. For the duration of Talia and Drex's conversation, the guy had been eyeing them as though poised to rush to her rescue if necessary. It galled Drex no end.

Now, while the good Samaritan was watching Talia board the elevator, Drex ducked into the fire exit door that opened into the seating area. Leaping over the treads two or three at a time, he took the stairs down to the third level of the parking garage.

It smelled of motor oil, gasoline, and rubber. It was ill-lighted. The ceiling was low and foreboding. It could have been a parking garage in any city, anywhere in the world. Except that in this one, Talia Shafer was leaning against the driver's door of her car, crying.

Not wanting to frighten her, Drex made sure she heard him approaching. She came around quickly, and, upon seeing him, anger shimmered in her eyes along with unshed tears. "What are you doing here?"

"I told you. I was looking for the public library, got turned around—"

"You're lying!"

"So are you," he fired back, taking a step closer to her. "There aren't any dentists on the top floor. It's devoted to gynecology and obstetrics."

Seeming to deflate, she clamped her lower lip between her teeth and turned her head away. A tear escaped and rolled down her cheek all the way to her jawline, where she wiped it off.

Drex swallowed the knot in his throat. He didn't want to know, but had to ask, "Are you pregnant?"

She shook her head, then said a husky no.

Relief made his knees go weak, although five minutes ago, he wouldn't have credited that physical phenomenon. Then, a worse thought struck him. "Is something..." Awkwardly, he motioned toward her middle. "Wrong?"

"No." When he looked at her doubtfully, she repeated *no*. "And even if there were, I certainly wouldn't discuss it with you." She rubbed her fists across her eyes, bolstered herself by standing up straighter, and looked directly into his face. "You followed me here. I know you did. Tell me why."

"I was a butthole last night."

He stopped there, and, when he didn't continue, she said, "Are you waiting for an argument from me? If so, you're waiting in vain."

He gave her a wry half smile. "I saw you leave your house. I followed you in the hope of getting an opportunity to apologize."

"For beguiling Elaine?"

"For all of it. The manuscript, the smirks, the innuendos, the setup. I staged a scene for you to walk into and draw a conclusion."

"Well, I did."

"I know."

She gazed at him with bewilderment. "But why did you do it?"

"To see if you'd be jealous."

She took swift breath, then, lowering her head, stared at the gritty, oil-stained concrete between their feet. "I can't be jealous, Drex. I'm married."

"Yeah, I know. It's all I think about. You being married. You being married to him."

She raised her head and looked into his eyes. "You don't have cause, or the right, to think about it."

"But I do." He extended his arm and braced his hand against the roof of her car. He pressed his forehead against his biceps and expelled a long breath. "I think about it all the goddamn time, and it's making me crazy."

For the longest time neither of them moved. They scarcely breathed. Did she share his fear that something as negligible as a blink could cause a cataclysm from which they could never recover or escape? He couldn't read her thoughts. All he had to go on was her stillness.

Until finally, he heard her hair brush against her shoulder as she turned her head toward him. "I'm sorry, Drex," she murmured. "I don't know what to say."

He lifted his head from his arm and turned it toward her. Their faces inches apart, he focused on her mouth as she added, "I don't know what you expect me to say."

"Don't say anything." By the time the last whispered syllable had passed his lips, they were brushing hers.

She yanked her head back. He slid his hand off the roof of the car and raised both in surrender as he stepped away and continued to back up. "Out of line. Way out of line. I'm sorry."

He turned and took several steps away before he stopped and came back around. He looked at her for a count of five. "Bloody hell," he growled. "If I'm going to be sorry, I'm damn well going to make it count."

He covered the same distance in half the number of strides. When he reached her, he took her face between his hands, tilted it, and kissed her. But good. Without sweetness or timidity. Deeply. Boldly. Sexily. Pouring into the kiss all the frustration, anger, and lust she had aroused in him.

Then he released her abruptly, turned, and walked away.

He made it into the elevator and rode it down to the next level of the garage where he'd parked. But as soon as he alighted, he placed his back to the concrete block wall and knocked his head against it hard enough to hurt.

What the hell was he doing?

When he'd seen Talia backing her car out of her driveway, he'd given no conscious thought to following her. He'd just reacted. Fortunately, he'd planned on going out later, so the items he had begun taking with him whenever he left were already zipped into the duffel bag. He'd had the presence of mind to grab it before he'd bolted from the apartment, nearly breaking his neck getting down that blasted staircase, certainly breaking speed limits to catch up to her and then to keep her car in sight.

He hadn't planned on her knowing that he was tracking her. Between her getting into the elevator to go up and when she came back down, forty-seven minutes had elapsed. Forty-seven minutes during which he'd examined his motives for acting so rashly.

After a heated debate with himself, he concluded that he wasn't simply a man obsessed with a woman but that this additional surveillance was justified. She was as much a suspect now as Jasper. He needed to know where she went, whom she saw, and why.

Right?

Right.

So he'd continued to amble back and forth across the lobby, keeping a close watch on everyone the elevators disgorged, and trying not to attract the attention of the rent-a-cops posted at all the building's entrances.

When Talia reappeared, he'd ignored the bump his heart gave. From across the lobby, he'd monitored her activity in the coffee shop. After several minutes passed, he decided that no one was joining her. She hadn't consulted her cell phone. She hadn't glanced around periodically in anticipation of someone's arrival. Rather she sat alone, looking forlorn and in need of a friend.

He was good at that, too, he'd reminded himself. Role-playing. Wasn't that one of his best honed skills?

So into the coffee shop he'd gone.

But at that point, he'd known he was kidding himself. Her apparent anguish had taken precedence over her being a suspect in at least one capital crime. The more he saw of her, the looser his grip on objectivity became, until, as of now, it was virtually nonexistent. He'd gone so far as to admit his crazed obsession to her.

Aw, well. It was too late to rethink it. Too late for a do-over. He couldn't take back any of it. He didn't want to take back the kiss.

He pushed himself away from the wall and started down the

ramp toward his parking spot. As his car came into sight, he drew up short. *"Shit!"*

Standing in the deep shadows, the do-gooder from the coffee shop was leaning against the hood of his car, obviously lying in wait.

Anger propelling him, Drex didn't break stride but walked straight up to him and demanded, "What the fuck, Gif?"

Chapter 14

———◆———

Drex sat slumped in the driver's seat of his car. For as long as he could, he withstood the weight of Gif's stare from the passenger side, then turned to him. *"What?"*

Gif the unflappable said, "You have to ask?"

"Why were you tailing me?"

"Why were you tailing her?"

"Surveillance."

"Surveillance?"

"Surely you're familiar with the word. Derived from the French—"

"Drex—"

"—verb—"

"Drex," Gif repeated, putting some oomph behind it.

He lapsed into angry silence and stewed, then snidely asked, "Did you and Mike toss a coin to see who would be the monitor, and you won? Or did you lose?"

"He and I discussed who should come and decided that—"

"You're a sneakier spy."

"Indubitably."

Drex scoffed. "Hate to break it to you, buddy, but you're slipping. The first rule of working undercover is to stay the hell undercover. Don't let the tailee know that he's being tailed. In the coffee shop, what the hell were you thinking?"

"That I should intervene."

"Why?"

"Because of the lady's apparent distress."

"I didn't cause her distress."

Gif conveyed his doubt by raising his eyebrows.

"I didn't," Drex said.

"Okay, but your manhandling wasn't helping."

"I didn't manhandle her."

Again the eyebrows went up.

Drex ignored them. "From now on, stay invisible, or you may forget how to."

Gif gave him a rare, and somewhat smug, smile. "I had the veal Milanese and a glass of Brunello."

Drex stared at him as though struck dumb, then shook his head with incredulity. "I never saw you."

"You weren't supposed to."

"How did you even know where we were having dinner?"

"I got here yesterday afternoon, parked down the block from your apartment, and waited until you came out, so spit-and-polished you could've been a groom. I followed." He shrugged as though it had been too easy. "The dinner seemed to go okay."

"If you don't count the smoke coming from Talia's ears." He explained about the manuscript. "That ticked her off. She didn't like me schmoozing Elaine, either. She sees me as an opportunist who'll prey on Elaine's affections and her bankroll."

"Now there's an irony."

"Tell me," he said. "Anyway, as I'm sure you saw, I followed Talia home, but didn't talk to her after parting company at Elaine's. Jasper was on the porch. We exchanged good nights."

"Why wasn't he at the dinner?"

Drex explained but stopped short of sharing his certainty that the untimely illness had been a fabrication devised to give Jasper an ideal opportunity to search the garage apartment. Informing his partners of that would only contribute to their distress. They were already discontented over something, or Gif wouldn't be here.

If they had issues with either him or the situation, they should have aired them, talked them over with him, rather than to go about checking up on him so underhandedly. He didn't like it. Not one bit.

"Why, Gif?"

"Why what?"

Drex gave him a droll look. "Something has your noses out of joint, or you wouldn't be here."

Gif grimaced as though troubled by intestinal gas. "That dinner date you arranged worried us."

"How come?"

"You were reluctant to talk about it."

True. He hadn't elaborated on the plans for the date because he didn't want his cohorts questioning his reasons for setting it up. Which indeed had been questionable. But Gif could sense an evasion and sniff out a lie from a mile away, so his straightforward answer came as no surprise to Drex.

He felt a mix of admiration and agitation. "It pisses me off that you two appointed yourselves my babysitters. Did you come to see if I was behaving myself? What are you going to do? Put me in timeout? Am I grounded?"

"Don't get riled."

"I'm already riled."

"Then I had just as well lay it out there."

"Do."

"Did you arrange this dinner just so you could spend more time with her?"

"Yes! So I could spend more time with her and *her husband*. Who we believe to be a serial killer. Isn't that why I'm here?"

Gif raised his hand in a peacekeeping gesture. "We just wanted to make sure that your eye was still on the target and not on... something else."

"And now you can be sure. Go home."

Gif tugged on his earlobe. "The wasn't the only reason for my coming."

"What else?"

"Not what, who."

"Rudkowski?"

"He's got a periscope up Mike's ass."

Drex cursed under his breath. "Well, that's just fabulous. How far up it?"

"He showed up at Mike's office yesterday morning all bluster and self-importance. Hauled Mike away from his desk and into a conference room. He grilled him about the meeting we had in the hotel. Remember the enchanting Ms. Li?"

Drex couldn't help but chuckle. "She delivered my note to Rudkowski?"

Gif didn't see the humor in it. "I think you're missing the point here."

Sighing, Drex pressed his thumb and middle finger into his eye sockets and rubbed them. He was suddenly very tired. "I get your point. Rudkowski isn't just following up on my mysterious vacation, he's micromanaging a pursuit."

"Precisely."

"I saw this coming and warned you of it. If he failed to find me, he'd come after you. I advised you to be on alert."

"Agents are watching us, night and day. We've pretended not to notice. But coming to Mike's workplace, putting him through the wringer? That takes Rudkowski's zeal to a new level." He studied Drex for a moment. "You left him a bread-crumb trail to follow to that hotel."

"You and Mike urged me to contact him."

"Through official channels, Drex. Making him the butt of a joke isn't what we had in mind."

Drex put up no defense. He figured he deserved this particular hand-slapping. "Rudkowski found the hotel by tracking the text sent from my old phone?"

"Isn't that how you planned it?"

He shrugged, as good as an admission.

"Rudkowski went to the hotel in person," Gif said. "Conversed with Ms. Li."

"I made certain she would remember me. The birthday cake and all."

"Likely she would have remembered you even without that."

"She's new on the job. Eager to accommodate."

"Nevertheless, I doubt she would have been quite so accommodating had you not been quite so suave." He paused. Then, "What did the note to Rudkowski say, anyway?" Drex told him, and Gif smiled in spite of himself. "I would have paid good money to see his expression when he read it. But it would have been nice for you to let Mike and me in on the joke before it was sprung."

Drex shook his head. "This way, you can truthfully claim ignorance and innocence."

"Makes no difference what we claim. We could take a blood oath, and Rudkowski still wouldn't believe us."

"Probably not. But, on the plus side, your consciences remain clear." He shot Gif a grin, but Gif wasn't in a jesting frame of mind.

"This is serious, Drex."

He dropped the grin. "Yeah, I know."

"You don't know the worst of it."

"There's more?"

"Rudkowski didn't stop with the grilling. He alleged that Mike had tampered with evidence, stolen classified documents, breached secure email accounts. He reeled off a laundry list of offenses."

"Shit."

"Right. On and on."

"How did Mike respond?"

"By bending over backward to cooperate. He surrendered his work computer for Rudkowski's flunkies to tear into."

"There's nothing on it relating to any of this."

"No, but Rudkowski threatened to get a search warrant for his apartment and to seize everything it in, from roof to basement."

Drex steepled his fingers and tapped them against his forehead. "He can't get a warrant based on a hunch. A judge would ask for cause, and Rudkowski doesn't have it."

"He would cite our history. Your obsession. Our loyalty to you. The—"

"Okay, okay. It's worrisome, but Mike will take care of it."

"He already has. When we first heard that the sleeping giant had been awakened by that deputy down in Florida, Mike took the precaution of emptying everything off his hard drives, then destroyed them."

"What about you?"

"Rudkowski considers me less of a problem than Mike. I'm not the computer genius. But immediately after Mike tipped me, I got out of Dodge before Rudkowski could ambush me, too. I took a week's worth of personal days."

"With what excuse?"

"Hemorrhoidectomy."

"You have hemorrhoids?"

"That's why I used it. My superiors may be skeptical, but who's going to ask to see proof of the necessity?"

Drex chuckled again.

"It's still no laughing matter," Gif said. "I left my workspace and apartment clean as a whistle. They can turn them inside out and won't find anything. But as long as you and I are off the grid, Rudkowski is going to plow on."

"No doubt."

Gif hesitated, then said, "You could still put in a call to him—"

"No."

"Okay then, skip Rudkowski and alert one of his higher-ups."

"Who would either throw it back to Rudkowski or send someone else down here to check it out, who would probably screw up, then we'd be blown, and Jasper would get away."

"If you explained the delicacy of the situation—"

"Not doing it, Gif. Not yet."

Gif relented. "All right. But please stop pricking with Rudkowski. Because whether we succeed or fail at getting Ford, Rudkowski isn't going to forget your making him look foolish. He doesn't think your pranks are funny." He paused for effect. "What really has Mike and me worried—"

"We're back to that?"

"We're afraid that one of these days, one of your inside jokes is going to blow up in your face."

Sobered by his friend's tone, Drex thoughtfully scraped his thumb across his stubbled chin, repeating quietly, "One of these days."

"Or has one already backfired?"

When Gif looked at someone the way he was looking at Drex now, it cut through bullshit like a cleaver. He was referring to Talia, of course. Drex answered as truthfully as he could. "I don't know."

"I think you do."

Drex faced forward and laid his head against the headrest, inwardly cursing Gif and his damn uncanny ability to read people.

A long silence ensued, then Gif said, "Why *her*? You could go back to Lexington tonight and, with a crook of your finger, have that pretty hotel receptionist at your beck and call."

Drex rolled his head to the side to look at Gif. "You think she's pretty? And enchanting? Why don't you go back to Lexington? When's the last time you got laid? Oh, no, wait. You've been too busy keeping tabs on my sex life to have one of your own."

"Don't do that. Don't try to turn the tables here. Mike and I have stuck our necks out for you—"

"You can quit at any time."

"That's it on a nail's head, Drex." The uncharacteristic volume of his voice was indication of his anger. "We don't want to quit. We're all in. We made our choices, and they've cost us huge. But now, when we're close to a payoff, it could all go to hell because of your hard-on for the suspect's wife."

"We don't know that she's complicit."

"We don't know that she isn't."

Although he knew Gif was right, it was infuriating to be scolded like a kid caught with his hand inside his pants. "You can relax. Nothing has happened." Gif didn't back down. Hell, for all Drex knew, Gif had been standing within a yard of them when he'd kissed Talia. He amended his denial, muttering, "Nothing much."

"Doesn't matter," Gif said. "If you only *want* something to happen, you're compromised."

"Hell I am. There's a gulf of difference between thinking on something and acting on it."

"Your dinner date—"

"Was an attempt to learn more about her. Is she friend or foe? Guilty as hell or pure as the driven snow? Would she be appalled to learn of her husband's crimes, or did she snicker from the sidelines while he was nailing shut that box on Marian Harris? I've asked myself those questions a thousand times."

"Mike and I get that."

"Then why'd you hustle down here to check on me?"

"To make certain that you hadn't lost perspective."

"I haven't."

"No?"

"No."

Gif looked at him and said nothing for a time, then, "What were you two talking about while hiding behind the ficus trees?"

"If you were able to see us, we weren't hiding, were we? But, as to what we were talking about, I tried to get out of her why she was upset."

"And?"

"Something female."

"Oh. That narrows it down to about a million different things. Could you be more specific?"

"I tried. She wasn't having it." Losing patience with the inquisition, he said, "Anything else? Did you save the best for last?"

"In fact I did." Gif's eyes narrowed a fraction. "I have to ask. What was predominantly on your mind when you whisked her out of the coffee shop? Were you trying to determine if she's Ford's accomplice, or were you wishing she wasn't his wife?"

Damn him. Leave it to Gif to strike straight to the heart of the matter. It was a question Drex dared not answer. He didn't know how he would answer even if he were inclined to. Gif was right: His attraction to Talia was a hazard. But knowing that didn't stop him from wanting her. His better judgment, integrity, and resolve were tested every time he got near her.

However, he wasn't going to discuss this personal conflict with Gif. It was his problem to solve, and he would work through it alone, without Mike's bullying or Gif's counsel

He said, "Earlier, you mentioned a blood oath. Have you ever taken one?"

Gif shook his head.

"Well, I have." He thrust his arm across the console and held his hand palm up where Gif could see the thin scar that spanned it.

"I swore to my dad that I would get the son of a bitch who stole my mother from him and then killed her. He never recovered. He'd been dead on the inside for decades before he took his final breath." He stabbed the console with his index finger. "I will—I *am*—going to get the fucker responsible for their mutual destruction."

"No matter if—"

Drex cut him off. "I've said it, Gif. I've sworn it. No more questions."

Chapter 15

———◆———

Elaine bobbed her head to the waiter in thanks for the cosmopolitan he set in front of her, then smiled at her companion, who was seated opposite her at the low, round cocktail table. "I'm glad you called."

Jasper said, "I felt terrible about missing last night's dinner. I know how much you had looked forward to it."

"It wasn't the same without you."

"Come now."

She giggled. "It was a lovely evening, but you were missed."

"Thank you." He raised his bourbon highball to her, then took a sip. "Since I couldn't make lunch today, either, I didn't want you to think I was avoiding you."

"It never occurred to me to think that. The important thing is that you're feeling better. Was it ghastly?"

"I'll be avoiding oysters for a while."

"Poor baby." She sipped from her martini glass. "What's Talia up to this afternoon?"

"Absolutely nothing. She had an appointment earlier today. When she got home, she excused herself and went upstairs to take a nap."

"Was she all right?"

He leaned forward and whispered, "I think she might be a bit hung over from last night."

Elaine grinned knowingly. "It wouldn't surprise me. She's not a heavy drinker, or as conditioned as I am. We killed two bottles of wine over dinner, and, before that, Drex gave her a generous pour on a vodka martini."

Jasper's teeth clenched, but he smiled. "Drex was tending bar?"

"I hosted a happy hour."

"I thought Drex was going to meet you and Talia at the restaurant."

"That was the original plan, but he called and asked if he could come a bit early and bring his manuscript."

"Whatever for?"

"He left it with me to read. Talia didn't tell you?"

"We didn't talk much after she came in. I was up, but still queasy. She shooed me back to bed and slept in the guest room in case I had a virus and not food poisoning." He took unnecessary care readjusting the coaster under his glass. "Odd that Drex asked you to read his book. He's been so protective of it."

"I was flabbergasted! Delighted, but flabbergasted. I'm hardly qualified to critique it."

"I'm sure he asked because you showed such interest in the subject matter and writing process."

"I guess. But if he asked anyone among us to take a look at it, I'd have thought it would be Talia."

He sipped his bourbon, then asked with nonchalance, "Why's that?"

"She's so much brainier. I'm not the intellectual that she is."

He *tsk*ed. "You don't give yourself enough credit. Besides, I doubt Drex's novel is that complex and literary."

"Between you and me, it isn't. I read a few chapters before going to sleep last night, and a few more over my morning coffee. I'm surprised that it isn't... hmm... what's the word? Heftier?"

"Heftier will do. But in what way isn't it hefty?"

"I don't know how to explain it. He's so…"

Jasper tilted his head. "So…?"

"Well, manly."

"The book doesn't reflect his manliness?"

"You're goading me," she said, pretending to slap his hand. "But the truth is, no, it doesn't shout masculinity. I mean, it does, but not to the extent…Oh, I don't know what I mean."

"You expected a book written by him to read differently."

"Yes. It's not as meaty as I thought it would be." She seemed embarrassed to have expressed her opinion and tried to laugh it off. "But who am I to say? It's light fare. Fast paced. Overall, it's enjoyable reading, and that's what I'll tell him when he asks for my feedback. As I said, I'm no critic. Far be it from me to dampen his ambitions, and I wouldn't hurt his feelings for the world."

"Which may be why he asked you to read the novel instead of Talia. She would have been candid in pointing out its weaknesses."

"No doubt you're right, and that would not have set well. Already they rub each other the wrong way."

As she drained her glass, she dribbled a bit on her chin and was now dabbing at it with her napkin. Otherwise she might have noticed that Jasper's right eye ticked in reaction to her last statement.

"Hold that thought," he said and signaled the waiter for another round.

Elaine demurred. "I really shouldn't have two."

"I agree." He gave her a sly wink. "Three minimum."

"You are *bad*."

"My dear," he said silkily, "you have no idea." Then he motioned for her to pick up where she had left off. "You were saying something about Talia and Drex rubbing each other the wrong way?"

"It's probably just me, but—"

"No, I've also noticed it."

She sat forward, her bosom nearly knocking over her empty

martini glass. "You have? I thought I was imagining it. The minute she arrived last night, I sensed the antagonism, and it only got thicker as the night wore on."

"He must have said or done something to offend her."

"I don't think so. He was his charming self."

The waiter arrived with fresh drinks. As soon as he walked away, Jasper asked, "How do you explain this hostility between them?"

"They weren't hostile, exactly. Just not comfortable with each other like they'd been that day on the yacht. Remember, they talked for a long time out on the deck. I thought maybe something had happened that I was unaware of. A disagreement of some kind."

"Not to my knowledge. In fact, we hadn't seen Drex for a couple of days leading up to last night."

"Hmm." She gave an elaborate shrug. "Who can explain why we like some people and detest others? Although Talia's aversion is understandable if you compare Drex to you. You're polished and sophisticated. He's—"

"Manly."

She gave a gusty laugh. "That's not at all what I meant to imply. If Talia weren't in the picture, you'd have dozens of women lined up at your back door bearing casseroles, and I would be leading the charge. You know I adore you."

He placed his hand to his chest and humbly tipped his head.

Smiling at him, she sipped her drink, but as she lowered her glass, her smile became a thoughtful frown. "It's unlike Talia to be snippy. Even with someone she doesn't particularly like."

"Talia? Snippy?"

"I know, right? But on the drive from the restaurant back to my house, she got really short with Drex."

"What provoked it?"

"I have no idea. We were talking about Key West."

With great care, Jasper set his highball glass on the table, then left his fingers cupping the rim and turned the glass idly. "How did that come up?"

"Drex wants to visit Hemingway's house. He asked if we'd been there. It was a casual conversation. And then it wasn't. I'm not sure at what point it went downhill or why it did." She sipped at the ice crystals floating on the surface of her drink. "I think his questions began to pester her."

"Questions?"

"Basic ones that a prospective tourist would ask a travel agent. He kept at it even though she made it clear she didn't want to talk business."

"She didn't want to talk about Key West."

Noticing his shift in tone, Elaine's gaze sharpened on him. "Oh? Why?"

"It's a private matter. Not something that Talia is comfortable talking about, even with me. All I'll say is that she had a client who became a close friend. But the relationship ended abruptly." He paused before adding, "And badly."

"I'm sorry."

"It was a while ago but remains a sensitive topic with her. I trust you'll never bring it up again."

"Of course, Jasper." She picked up her glass and raised it to him. "On the subject of Key West, I'll be as silent as a grave."

Jasper could barely contain an eruption of laughter.

"Jasper?"

Talia flipped on the kitchen light and was greeted by a startling sight. Dressed in pajamas, Jasper was crouched on the floor, running his hand along the baseboard beneath the cabinet. "What on earth are you doing?"

He came to his feet, dusting his hands. "I dropped an ice cube." He shaded his eyes against the overhead light. "Please switch that off. I think we're being watched."

"Watched?"

"Turn off the light, Talia."

She didn't appreciate his imperious tone but did as asked, then waited for him to explain his bizarre behavior.

He asked, "Have you been asleep all afternoon and evening?"

"No, I woke up to an empty house. I found the note you left on my dressing table. You and Elaine must have been enjoying yourselves. Your get-together for drinks extended into the dinner hour." She looked at the clock on the stove. "And beyond."

"I called to invite you to join us. Your phone went to voice mail."

"Oh. Right," she said with chagrin. "I silenced it when I lay down and forgot to turn it back on."

"Assuming you were asleep, I left you in peace rather than call on the house phone."

She nodded absently. "How was Elaine?"

"Enlightening. Did you skip dinner?"

"No. After reading your note, I ate a peanut butter sandwich and went back to bed. When did you get home?"

"An hour ago. Give or take."

"I didn't hear you."

"You were virtually unconscious."

She must've been. She felt as though she were coming out of a coma and discovering that while she'd been out, everything had gone awry. Nothing felt right or familiar, in particular this disjointed conversation with Jasper. He was prowling the room, stopping at every window to look outside.

She shook her head to try to clear the lingering cobwebs. "Are you going to tell me what's going on? What did you mean when you said we're being watched? Watched by whom?"

"By Drex."

Her heart gave a telltale bump. She'd returned home from their encounter in the parking garage shaken to her core by what he'd professed, by the kiss. She'd taken a mild sedative in the hope of sleeping off the conflicting emotions that assailed her. They'd run the gamut from fury—*how dare he?*—to shame. Even now, she felt the tingling, throbbing effects of that kiss.

She looked in the direction of the garage apartment and remembered standing at the living area window, looking through the branches of the live oak, and realizing that the rooms on the back of their house were open to his view. "Why would you think he's watching us?"

"Let's sit." There was enough ambient light for them to see their way around. They sat adjacent to each other at the dining table. "I think Drex Easton is a fraud at best. At worst…doesn't bear thinking."

"Jasper—"

"Hear me out."

Her heart was beating abnormally fast. Her hands had turned cold and clammy, made even more noticeable when Jasper reached for her right one and clasped it between his.

He said, "Elaine told me she's reading Drex's book, and that it's dreadful."

"She said that?"

"She put it a bit more kindly."

"Does she intend to tell him that?"

"Elaine wouldn't be that blunt. Even if she were, I don't think he gives a damn about her opinion or anyone else's. I don't think he's a writer at all."

"But he works at it. I've seen him. So have you."

He gave his head a hard shake. "He's pretending. He's only posing to be a writer until he finds someone, specifically a woman of Elaine's ilk, to support him."

While she didn't want to believe it, she herself had virtually accused Drex of having those intentions. "He has been tight-lipped about his work."

"About everything."

"But why a writer? If he's going for seduction, there are occupations much more fascinating and exhilarating."

"But not as easy to emulate. It's one occupation where he doesn't have to exhibit any notable skills. All he has to do is sit on his ass all day."

"I've seen him working. The day I went over to give him the list of restaurants, he was immersed in something on his computer."

"Are you sure it was his novel?"

"He said it was."

"Did you see what was on the monitor?"

"No. He closed the laptop."

"He could have been immersed in pornography. Online poker. Anything." He looked down at the hand he held in his. "Speaking of that day, Talia, did anything improper happen while you were over there?"

"No."

He lifted his gaze to hers. It was an effort for her to stare back without blinking. She could practically feel the brush of Drex's thumb against the corner of her mouth.

"The reason I ask," Jasper said, "is because Elaine also told me there was a strain between Drex and you last night, a hostility that became more palpable as the evening progressed. Was she imagining that?"

"No."

He looked at her as though expecting her to elaborate.

"I'm thirsty." Withdrawing her hand, she got up and went to the fridge. "Would you like a bottle of water?"

"No thank you."

She returned to the table with one, twisted off the cap, and took a drink.

"Talia? How do you explain this tension between you and Drex?"

"He brought up Key West. Not in a random way, either. And he wouldn't drop the subject."

"Yes, I know."

She jerked to attention.

"I heard all about it from Elaine. Nothing of it from you. Why didn't you tell me this the moment you got home last night?"

"Because whenever the subject of Marian arises, we both become upset. Drex's persistence unnerved me, but, in hindsight, I believe he only mentioned Key West in the context of wanting to visit the Hemingway house. Nothing more."

Jasper sat as still as a stone, but he wasn't as contained as he seemed. She could hear each deep inhale through his nose, each exhale. "I'm not so sure. Elaine said he pestered you with questions."

"I told him I didn't particularly like the place, he prodded me to tell him why. Rapid-fire questions. It was as though..."

"What?"

"It felt like he was trying to spark a reaction, make me blurt out something."

"Do you think he knows something about Marian?"

"No. Maybe, Jasper." She withdrew her hand from his and used it to rub her forehead. "I don't know."

"He's living next door, Talia," he hissed. "I should have known about this immediately."

"I didn't tell you because I predicted you would respond exactly as you are. You're jumping to a conclusion that has no real basis. You've mistrusted Drex from the start."

"As it turns out, with good reason."

"We don't know that!" she exclaimed in a stage whisper. "His mention of Key West triggered a response from me, and he noticed. I tried to shoot the topic down."

"But he persisted."

"Only to be obnoxious. Honestly, I think that's all there was to it."

And she did. Because this morning Drex had dismissed the idea of going there any time soon, and there hadn't seemed to be an ulterior motive to his mentioning it. In fact, she'd started the exchange by asking about his proposed trip.

But she couldn't tell Jasper about that conversation without telling him that Drex had followed her to the medical building. Knowing about that would reinforce his suspicion.

He'd been ruminating and now said, "Key West came up toward the conclusion of the evening. Elaine picked up on antagonistic vibes as soon as you arrived at her townhouse."

"I had told him about Elaine's history with men, of her falling hard and getting hurt. I warned him against romancing her. Last night, he flaunted that he was doing just that. He was positively oily."

"How did Elaine respond?"

"As expected. She was eating out of his hand."

Elaine's receptiveness to his flirtation came as no surprise. What Talia couldn't reconcile was the man she'd been with this morning and the Casanova of last night, who had irritated her no end.

Now, however, it seemed like a caricature, a part overplayed, and which had led to nothing. Because if he had so much as kissed Elaine before she'd arrived at the townhouse, Elaine would have found an opportunity by now to describe it to her with enthusiasm and in minute detail.

No, he hadn't kissed Elaine. He had wasted the romantic staging in Elaine's living room and, instead, had kissed her in a parking garage, a setting hardly conducive to romance. He might have been role-playing last night, but there hadn't been any artifice in his manner this morning. He'd been all too real. Every aspect of him. His anguish. *It's making me crazy.* Certainly his desire. *I'm damn well going to make it count.*

And he had. With fervency and finesse, he had penetrated more than her mouth. He had tapped into a deep-seated loneliness she hadn't realized was so acute until his own raw need had roused it and caused within her a strong tug of yearning. She could never be alone with him again.

"After today, I won't have anything to do with him."

"After *today?*"

She flinched at the sound of Jasper's voice and, too late, realized her slip. "Now that I've slept on it," she said. "Until Drex moves out, we'll keep our distance. Problem solved."

"Is it? I'm not as ready as you are to dismiss the Key West thing as a coincidence. The way Elaine described his interest, it seemed excessive."

"Did she pick up on your concern? Can I expect a call from her tomorrow, asking for the lowdown?"

"I told her it was a private and sensitive matter, and asked her never to mention it again. She promised not to."

Talia groaned.

"What?"

"Elaine loves intrigue. All you've done is entice her. She'll demand the lowdown."

"If she brings it up, shrug it off. Give her a drink, and tell her I made too much of it."

"Which you are."

He looked through the window. No lights were on inside the garage apartment. It was an indistinct dark form among the shadows. "We'll keep our distance from him," Jasper said. "If he's merely the man next door, he'll get the message and stop making overtures. If he's more than that, he'll make a nuisance of himself. That's when we'll know."

"We won't *know*."

"Strongly suspect, then. If he continues to come around, it will confirm my suspicion, and we'll be forced to take some drastic measures."

Alarmed, she said, "Like what?"

He patted her hand. "We'll wait and see. In the meantime, I've taken the precaution of changing the alarm code."

"That's unnecessary, Jasper. You're overreacting."

"Better safe than sorry. The new code is our anniversary date numerically, except backward. Got it?"

"Yes." She recited the sequence.

"Good. Don't forget it." He pushed back his chair and stood. "For now, let's go to bed."

"You go. I slept most of the day away. I think I'll read for a while. Maybe watch a movie."

"Then I'll say good night." He bent down and kissed her cheek, but as he moved away, she reached for his hand.

"Wait. There's something else. Something you should know." She wished he weren't standing over her. Looking up at him at an awkward angle made this all the more difficult. "I have a confession."

"Regarding Drex?"

"Yes." Her voice came out husky. She wet her lips. "He...he..."

"What?"

She lowered her head, took a deep breath, and, in a nanosecond, reversed her previous decision. "You asked if anything happened that day when I went over to his apartment."

"Anything improper."

"It wasn't improper, but something did happen. I offered to read his manuscript. He declined. No, not declined. Refused. Outright."

"Probably because he feared exposure as an imposter."

"Possibly. But the point is, when I arrived at Elaine's townhouse last night, found him there, learned that he had given her his manuscript to read, I behaved childishly. I was insulted that he had solicited her opinion over mine. That was the source of the tension."

"He rejected you, but was paying court to Elaine. You were jealous."

"Resentful, at least. I told you it was childish."

"But not a stoning offense," he said, chucking her under the chin.

Despite the playful gesture, his choice of words was troubling. In some cultures, one stoning offense was adultery.

"Remember to keep the lights off in the rooms within sight of his apartment."

He was almost through the door when she stopped him again. "I think I'll go to Atlanta for a few days."

The spur-of-the-moment decision was made almost simultaneous to her declaring it. Jasper turned. His face was in shadow, but she sensed that his expression was inquisitive, if not suspicious.

She said, "That new boutique hotel I told you about? It sounds like something my clients would flock to. I think I'll go and see if it lives up to the hype."

He said nothing for an interminable time, then, "Ordinarily you plan your business trips well in advance. The suddenness of this one is uncustomary, but it's in perfect keeping with your mood of late."

"My mood?"

"You haven't been yourself, Talia."

Tartly, she said, "Neither have you, Jasper."

"Me? In what way?"

"Not in a way I can put my finger on. But something."

He retraced his steps back to her. "Is the honeymoon over?"

"I could ask you the same."

"Why would you?"

"Because I suspect you're having an affair with Elaine." There, she'd said it.

"Don't be ridiculous."

"That's what every cheating partner says when accused."

"You're being preposterous. I am *not* sleeping with Elaine. Good God."

His denial didn't prompt her to back down or withdraw the allegation. She held his self-righteous glare.

Sounding frustrated, he said, "I'm not having an affair, but you're right. We need to get back on an even keel. A change of scenery would do us good. I'll come with you to Atlanta."

"Come with me?"

"Is that such an outrageous notion?"

"No, not at all. You're always welcome to come along, but you rarely do. I can't remember the last time you did."

"I've read about this place, and it does sound special. It poached a superstar chef away from a New York restaurant. We'll have each other to ourselves. No Elaine chattering a mile a minute. No bothersome neighbor," he said shooting a glance out the back window. "I don't see a downside to us enjoying time to ourselves."

The downside was that she would prefer to spend those several days alone. She needed time to think about the implications of her doctor's visit this morning and to reflect on the destabilizing events that had taken place since Sunday when she'd gone yachting on the *Laney Belle* and met Drex Easton.

She also needed to isolate a reason for the vague uneasiness that had plagued her for several months now. A premonition of doom was her constant companion, and that was a complete turnaround from the optimist outlook she'd always had. She'd arrived at no explanation for this gradual but inexorable reversal, but if the erosion of her marriage was the cause, that was reason enough to spend quality time with Jasper and try to get them back on track.

She smiled up at him. "That sounds lovely."

"Make the reservation."

"When do you want to go?"

He stroked her cheek, pushed back a strand of her hair, and curled his hand around her throat. "Tomorrow."

Chapter 16

———◆———

Long after Jasper's final word, "Tomorrow," Drex sat, staring through the darkness at nothing. Like a prizefighter who'd received a knockout jab and had made a hard landing, it took a while for him to come around.

But when at last he did, it was with a jolt of furious energy. He whipped off the headset, picked up his cell phone, and placed a call.

Gif answered sleepily. "I didn't think you were speaking to me."

"Where are you staying?"

Gif gave him the name of the motel.

"What room?"

"You're coming now?"

"As soon as I can get there."

"Has something happened?"

"It's them."

"It's them?" He sounded wide awake now. "How do you know?"

"The bug. I was listening. Heard a lot."

Gif processed that. "You said 'them.' Her, too?"

Drex unlocked his jaw enough to say, "Her, too."

He dressed in darkness, added the surveillance equipment to the duffel bag, and took it with him. He felt his way down the staircase, then scurried along the far side of the garage to the back. Peering around the rear corner of the building, he halfway expected to see Jasper charging across the lawn after him as before.

He watched and waited, remaining so still he could feel the blood pumping through his veins, hear his heartbeat thudding against his eardrums. Supercharged by adrenaline and anger, remaining motionless was torture. But he stayed as he was for five long minutes. The Ford house remained dark.

"Sleep tight," he whispered as he slipped into the darkness.

He picked his way through the green belt that buffered the Arnott property from the street behind it. It was a moonless night. The atmosphere was laden with humidity. A light mist felt like cobwebs against his face. When he reached the street, he struck out at a dead run and covered the mile to the nearest convenience store in under six minutes.

There, mindful of security cameras, he pulled the hood of his windbreaker over his head, shuffled up to the counter, and asked the cashier if he could use his phone to call for a taxi. "My battery's drained." Never looking up from his hot rod magazine, the guy slid his cell phone across the counter.

It took twice as long for the taxi to get to the convenience store as it did to cover the distance to the motel. Drex asked to be dropped off at an apartment complex across the freeway from it. He paid the driver in cash, waited for him to get out of sight, then crossed the road to the motel.

Gif had texted him the room number. It was on the ground floor. Drex rapped softly on the door, heard the bolt, the chain, then Gif opened the door a crack. Moving aside to let Drex in, he said, "I didn't dress up." He was in boxers, a white t-shirt, black socks. He secured the door, then went over to the dresser, pulled a can of beer from the plastic webbing, and extended it to Drex.

"I could use a belt of whiskey."

"No whiskey."

"Then never mind." Drex took off his windbreaker, pulled a chair from beneath the table for two in front of the window, and sat down. He propped his elbows on his knees and used all ten fingers to hold back his hair. The adrenaline was wearing off.

Gif sat on the edge of the unmade bed. "I didn't hear your car."

"I left it at the apartment so they wouldn't know I was gone." He explained how he'd gotten there.

Gif asked, "You sure you weren't tailed?"

"Of course I'm sure. I made sure."

Gif looked him over and noticed that his clothes were damp. "Is it raining?"

Drex raised his head. "You want a weather report?"

Gif opened his mouth as though to retort, but thought better of it and closed his mouth with an audible click of teeth.

Drex said a few choice words directed toward himself. He took a deep breath, let it out. "I'm sorry, man."

"Doesn't matter."

"Yeah, it does. I'm sorry. Thanks for being here."

Gif bobbed his head, then took a sudden interest in the loose cuticle on his thumb. "You're sure she's in on it?"

"Hear for yourself."

Drex took the receiver/recorder from the canvas duffel, connected it to the audio feed of the headset, and passed it to Gif. "I think you'll find the conversation telling."

He left Gif to listen and went into the bathroom. He used the toilet and splashed cold water on his face. He gave his image in the mirror a look of sheer disgust. "Even now, you'd fuck her if given the chance, wouldn't you? Dumb bastard." He tossed the towel onto the floor and opened the door.

Gif was still listening, but his expression didn't give away his opinion of what he was hearing. Drex returned to his chair at the table and used a new burner phone to call Mike.

He answered with a growl. "Who's this?"

"Is this phone secure?"

"It goes through about five rerouters. Should be okay."

"Were you asleep?"

"No. I'm watching the people who're watching me."

"Gif filled me in on Rudkowski. I'm sorry as hell, Mike. When we started this, you gave me fair warning that you wouldn't help me dig my own grave or climb in with me."

"That's what I said, but I didn't mean it." He snorted what passed for a laugh. "Actually, it's kinda fun. They're out there in their van, eating cold pizza and scratching their balls. I had a pork loin with all the trimmings. Bottle of wine. I've got all the comforts of home. Still have my toys, too."

"They haven't served a search warrant?"

"Rudkowski is blowing smoke. He knows the chance of finding anything on my computers is nil. If he made good on his threat to search, he'd be left with nothing to show for it. He wouldn't be stupid enough to go through with it, because he'd never live down being made such a fool of."

"But you've still got a team watching you."

"Not cowboys. Old guys they wouldn't trust with any other duty."

"Could you get away without getting caught?"

"Skip out?"

"Skip town."

"Sure. But that's all the excuse Rudkowski would need to put a noose around my neck. And if he did, I'd be no good to you. So why would I want to skip?"

"We have them."

That he announced it without inflection or fanfare gave it more impact than if he'd shouted it with glee. Continuing in that manner, he gave Mike a broad-strokes version of what had taken place.

When he finished, Mike said, "So, her, too, huh?"

"Yeah."

For once Mike showed that he had a human side after all. He didn't follow with *I told you so.* "Okay. So now what?"

"Stand by. Gif is listening to the conversation now. We'll get back to you."

Drex had a few questions for Google. By the time he'd gotten the info he needed, Gif was removing the headset. Drex looked at him expectantly.

"Not to dash cold water on this, Drex, but it's a long way from a smoking gun or signed confession. It was illegally obtained, which makes it inadmissible in—"

"I know all that."

"Rudkowski would cook us and serve us in Quantico's cafeteria."

"Mike referenced a noose."

"Neither appeals to me." Gif fiddled with the headset as he mulled over this new development. "Do you think he's doing Elaine Conner?"

"I don't know, but it wouldn't surprise me. They're chummy."

"The Ford marriage sounds wobbly, if not rocky."

"Doesn't mean they aren't partners in crime. Or at least they were when they killed Marian Harris."

"But did they?" Gif brandished the headset. "This isn't solid enough to issue them a parking ticket. Nobody, not the FBI, *nobody* would touch it. In fact, if we pass this along as evidence or even probable cause, any law officer in the land would laugh his ass off and then arrest us for violation of the privacy act."

"Which is why we must proceed as we have been. On our own. Under the radar."

Gif grimaced and tossed the headset onto the bed. "Drex—"

"Get Mike on the phone. Please."

When they were on speaker, Drex addressed Mike. "Tomorrow the lovely couple next door are going on a getaway to Atlanta. I need you to find out the name of a new boutique hotel that poached a chef from a restaurant in New York. If you can—"

"The Lotus."

"What?"

"That's the hotel. I read an online article about the chef."

Gif and Drex looked at each other and, in spite of the grim circumstances, smiled.

"Okay. Thanks," Drex said. "Can you get there by tomorrow afternoon?"

"To Atlanta?"

"Don't ask like that. Ever been there?"

"No."

"It's nice."

"It's nice where I am."

"You can't leave a trail, which means you can't fly. You'll have to drive."

"How far is it?"

"Far. Google says almost four hundred miles." Mike grumbled something unintelligible. Drex said, "I'm not in the mood to argue about it, Mike. It's six hours in the car. You can snack all the way. Will you do it or not? If not, good night."

After a brief silence, Mike said, "What do I do when I get there?"

"Check into The Lotus. Make a reservation tonight."

"It's costly."

"I'll pay."

"It's the weekend. What if it's booked up?" Gif asked.

"Child's play," Mike said. "I'll hack their system and cancel somebody's reservation." He paused. "I don't suppose you're sending me there to sample the five-star cuisine."

"I'm sending you there to keep tabs on the Fords."

"Are you nuts?" Gif exclaimed. "He couldn't fade into the woodwork if they had a sequoia growing in the hotel lobby."

"He's not your typical undercover operative, no," Drex said. "He's obese and ugly—"

"I'm still here," Mike said.

"—which is why no one would take him for a spy."

Drex wanted Mike in Atlanta, but not only for the reason stated. He also wanted him out of Lexington. If the shit went down, he didn't want Mike to be within Rudkowski's reach. Eventually he would corral them, but Drex didn't want to make it easy for him.

Gif, in his reasonable manner, suggested that he be sent to Atlanta instead. "I'm already in a neighboring state."

"Yes, but Charleston is roughly a hundred and fifty miles farther. I checked. Besides, if Talia saw you, she might remember you from the coffee shop."

"He's unmemorable," Mike said. "And what's that about the coffee shop?"

"We'll tell you later," Drex said, impatience mounting. "Mike, can Sammy get you an untraceable car by morning?"

"With one phone call."

Sammy—Drex wasn't sure which alias was his real last name—was a mechanic who could make a rattletrap run like a Porsche. Early in Mike's career with the bureau, he had been in on the sting that busted Sammy for transporting stolen merchandise across state lines.

Sammy had served time, but, by the time of his release, Mike was working with Drex and had seen the advantages of cultivating a relationship with a guy like Sammy, someone who was only a little crooked. They'd used Sammy and his larcenous automotive know-how more than a few times.

"The tricky part will be making the swap," Mike said. "But Sammy is creative."

"Leave as early as possible," Drex said. "I'd like you in place by check-in time."

"I'll be missed when I don't show up for work."

"Hold on, you two," Gif said. "Please. This plan has pitfalls I can see from here."

After a few more minutes of back-and-forthing, Drex called an end to it, saying, "Either you're in or out, guys. If you want out, no hard feelings. But tell me now or shut up."

Neither said anything.

After a moment, Drex resumed. "Mike, I don't know for sure how long they're staying. You'll have to find that out somehow. I'll need to know when they're on their way back. "

Gif looked around his motel room. "In the meantime, what's my job?"

"Hang around until, or if, I need you for backup, and then come running."

"What'll you be doing?" Gif asked.

"Tearing their fucking house apart."

Mike and Gif put up another argument that lasted for half an hour. But Drex was resolute. While the Fords were whiling away a few days in the luxury hotel, he would have access to their house, ergo to their lives.

He was going to search exhaustively until he found something that linked them to Marian Harris. The photo taken on her yacht wasn't indicting. The authorities in Florida had used it to identify Jasper, aka Daniel Knolls, when Marian first went missing. He'd been interviewed by police and subsequently released.

Drex now wondered if Talia had also been questioned. He made a mental note to follow up with Deputy Gray.

He relegated that to the back burner of his mind and concentrated on what today might hold in store. His cohorts begged him to reconsider going inside the Fords' home. They cited that it was a crime. They enumerated the obstacles he'd likely confront. Security alarm. Nanny cams.

"Hell, this freako might've booby-trapped the place," Mike said.

"I wouldn't put it past him," Drex said. "I'll be careful."

"Say you get in without any trouble, and it turns out to be a gold mine of evidence," Gif said. "What good is it going to do us? Anything you find will be inadmissible."

"Anything I find will justify my killing him."

That had shut them up.

After signing off with Mike, Gif packed his things in preparation of moving to another motel. "With a credit card no one knows I have," he assured Drex.

The two of them left together in Gif's car. Dawn was just about to break, but the difference between it and the night was negligible. The overcast was solid. Precipitation alternated between an all-out rain and a mist now heavy enough to make windshield wipers necessary.

Drex directed Gif to the convenience store. "Let me out there. I'll go the rest of the way on foot."

"You sure?"

"I don't want my nosy neighbors to see you dropping me off." Gif pulled over. Drex said, "Call me with your new location."

"As soon as I'm checked in."

Drex reached for the door handle, but Gif said suddenly, "Listen, Drex. I gave you some grief about her, but I had started hoping, for your sake, that we were wrong."

Drex didn't react except to say a brusque "I'll be in touch." He got out, shut the door, and tapped the roof of the car twice. Only as Gif was driving away did he murmur, "Thanks, buddy."

He went into the twenty-four-hour store. A different cashier was on duty. He made his purchase, then set out for the apartment. He was skirting the green belt, looking for a place to cut through that wasn't too overgrown, when he spotted a lone runner on the street, coming from the opposing direction, taking form in the mist.

She must have seen him at about the same time as he saw her because she slowed her pace to a walk. She looked toward the other side of the street, as though considering crossing it to avoid him. But then she squared her shoulders and continued toward him.

He stopped where he was, forcing her to close the distance between them. But he took small satisfaction in that, because, even
though he was cold with rage over how thoroughly he'd been
duped, the sight of her up close made him hot and hard. Her tights
and top were wet from sweat as well as from the elements. They
conformed to her like a coat of paint, revealing the shapeliness of
her legs, the perfection of her breasts, the small points of her nipples.

Her eyes were the color of the cloudy sky. Like the mist, they
held mysteries. Her ponytail hung heavy and damp against the
back of her neck. A bead of water dripped off a loose strand of
hair at the side of her face and rolled down her cheek like yesterday
morning's tear.

Which he'd fallen for. Like a lovesick kid. Like a damned idiot.

He suppressed a rush of renewed anger and said, "You're out
early. Couldn't sleep?"

"Thunder woke me up."

"It hasn't thundered."

"Then it must've been something else."

"Must've been." He looked her over, making her aware that he
was aware of every curve, dip, distension. "No spin class today?"

"They weren't open yet."

"You could've waited."

"I wanted to get an early start on the day. So did you, apparently." She indicated the grocery sack.

"I needed milk."

"Why didn't you drive?"

"I needed exercise."

"What's that?" She pointed at the duffel bag.

It hung against his side by the shoulder strap. He patted it.
"That? That's my bag of tricks."

"I can see you're going to be obtuse."

"Obtuse. Ranks right up there with morose."

She shot him a look of annoyance and gestured as though to say she needed to be on her way. "Have a nice day." She tried to go around him. He sidestepped to block her. "Please let me by."

"Did you tell him?"

"Tell who what?"

He gave her a smile that was insolent and, he hoped, infuriating. "Your husband, Talia. Did you tell Jasper about the kiss?"

Another squaring of shoulders. "Yes."

"Yeah?"

"Of course I told him."

"And what was his reaction?"

"The same as mine."

"Oh, I doubt that."

She read the innuendo in his drawling tone and the snicker that accompanied it. "Go to hell." She tried to move past him, but he blocked her again. "Cut it out, Drex!"

"Jasper was upset?"

"No, not upset. Outraged that you would dare."

"Really? Then why didn't he barge up the stairs, kick in my door, and tear me apart limb by limb?"

"Because he isn't governed by animal impulses."

"Neither am I. If I were, we would have done a hell of a lot more than kiss."

She slapped him. Hard. It smarted like hell, but he only laughed. "You didn't tell him, did you?"

"Stay away from me." She nudged him with her elbow as she went past and took off running.

He turned to watch her, saying under his breath, "Liar."

She stopped and came back around. "What did you say?"

He didn't answer.

Raising her voice she repeated the question, enunciating each word.

By contrast he leaned forward and spoke in a whisper just loud enough for her to hear. "I said 'pants on fire.'"

Chapter 17

Following his three-way call with Drex and Gif, Mike had been unable to sleep. He lay on his bed and stared at the ceiling until daylight, then got up, showered, and dressed without any readjustment of his morning routine.

However, for what he was about to do, he did not have a method for mentally preparing himself.

His breakfast consisted of two toasted bagels with cream cheese and smoked salmon, a bowl of strawberries floating in heavy cream, and three cups of coffee with three teaspoons of sugar each.

Thus stoked, he was as ready as he was ever going to be.

But as he held his cell phone in his palm, he was once again gripped by indecision. For the next few minutes, he did some tough soul searching, telling himself that he could still change his mind.

Ultimately, however, he determined that he was doing the right thing. Without further deliberation, which could produce more doubt, he placed the dreaded call.

A gravelly voice answered. "Rudkowski."

"It's Mike Mallory."

As though waiting for a taunt, Rudkowski didn't say anything.

Had he been shocked speechless? Or was he rigging up a way to record the call? Mike figured both.

Finally Rudkowski said, "And?"

"I think you're an asshole of the most rectal sort."

"You interrupted my breakfast to tell me that?"

"No, I just thought you should know up front what I think of you, in case you didn't know already."

"I had more than an inkling. Now if that's all, my oatmeal is getting cold."

"That ballyhoo you raised about a search warrant? All you achieved was to make me look like a victim of your peevishness and make you look like a douche."

"A matter of opinion."

"It's unanimous. Even the agents you have watching my house would agree. You won't risk a search because you know you won't find anything."

"Maybe I'll get a warrant and maybe I won't. But whatever I decide about that, I'm keeping you under a microscope until I know what's going on. Your crony Gif took time off to have hemorrhoids removed. Really? Hemorrhoids? Nobody in his office remembers complaints of such."

"It's hardly something he would discuss with coworkers over lunch."

"Don't even try to cover for him. His sudden need for surgery coincides with your ringleader's vacation. Vacation," he repeated with scorn. "I know Easton is up to something. You three musketeers are playing with fire, and you're all going to get burned. Again."

Rudkowski had given him an opening. He took it. "That's why I called you." He let that hover to be certain he had Rudkowski's undivided attention. "Drex *is* up to something. And this time, I think he's..." He paused, took a deep breath. "What he's about to do could have serious repercussions. For all of us, but especially for him."

"What's he about to do? Where is he?"

"Un-huh. Before I tell you anything, we've got to strike a bargain."

"No bargain."

"Then enjoy your oatmeal."

"Wait! All right. What kind of bargain?"

"Drex gets a scolding, nothing more. You've got to promise me that you won't come down hard on him. He hasn't done anything yet. He's only talked about it."

"I promise."

Mike laughed. "You agreed way too fast, Rudkowski. You think I'd trust that?"

"I give you my word."

"Like that counts for shit. I want it in writing."

Rudkowski thought it over. "I'll be as lenient as I can be. That's the best I can offer. It's not just me you've got to worry about, you know."

"But your influence—"

"Will only go so far. They don't call it a *bureau* for nothing. I've got to account to my higher-ups here in Louisville."

Mike knew that to be the truth. "I guess that'll have to be good enough."

"Do we have a deal?"

"Yes. But I want witnesses to my voluntary surrender of information. I'll turn over everything I have, but not before getting your sign-off on it, plus passes for Drex, Gif, and me."

"Easton won't thank you."

"That's what kept me awake last night. He'll be pissed. But I hope I can convince him that he still has my loyalty. We share a commitment to getting this guy and putting him away."

Rudkowski scoffed. "'This guy.' Nobody has proved there is a guy."

"There's a guy. You just don't want to think so because you haven't identified and captured him yourself. While he's out there rooking and killing women, you'll shuffle paper and look busy until the day you can retire."

"While Easton is a man of action."

He said it derisively, but Mike smiled. "You're making my argument for me, Rudkowski. You've always put your resentment of Drex ahead of getting the bad guy. This creep is real, and I hope to God Drex eventually nails him." He hesitated.

"But this time feels different, and it spooks me. I've felt it from the start, but new information has recently come to light. We're talking about one sick dude, not just a con man. Gif has had a bad feeling, too, and we told Drex we did."

"But he thinks he's smarter than everybody."

"He's definitely smarter than you," Mike said. "But he's also single-minded and hardheaded. In typical Drex mode, he's latched on to this intel and is running with it. I'm scared he's running toward a cliff at full throttle, and, if he goes over, he'll crash land. I told him that I wouldn't help him dig his own grave. Or mine, either. And I'm not getting any younger." He paused, cleared his throat. "I love him like a kid brother. But this time the stakes for stepping out of line are just too damn high."

"You're doing the right and responsible thing."

Reverting to his customary snarl, Mike rebuked him. "Don't sound so goddamn pious, Rudkowkski. You've already peed down your leg over this. Relish the moment. Have your field day. But I'm not feeling a bit good about what I'm doing. I'm betraying my best friend, even if it is for his own good."

Rudkowski had the good sense not to offer another platitude.

Mike took a deep breath and sounded like a bellows when he exhaled it. "Shit, let's get this done. We'll meet at my office. I like the idea of having witnesses who like me better than you."

"When?"

"I'll leave now. Before I change my mind." He glanced at his wall clock. "I usually don't head to work this early. Will your watchdogs let me out of my driveway?"

"I'll call them. See you soon."

They disconnected. Five minutes later, Mike placed another call. Drex answered after the first ring. "Did it work?"

"Like a charm," Mike said. "I'm on my way to Atlanta. Sammy said to tell you hi."

Drex called Gif to report their success. "Mike must have laid it on thick, because Rudkowski fell for it. Imagine when he showed up at Mike's office ready to get the goods."

He told Gif that Mike had given Rudkowski just enough time to call the men watching his house and then had raised his garage door so they could see his car and think that he was about to leave as planned.

He'd carried out an armful of files—filled with back issues of epicurean magazines—and placed them in the passenger seat. He'd then gone back into the house and carried out a box with back issues of *Wine Spectator* which he placed in the back seat.

He'd gone inside the house again... and out the back door. He'd walked through the houses behind his. Sammy had been waiting on the next street in a standard gray car that looked like every other make and model of standard gray car.

"Motor was running," Drex told Gif. "Mike got in. They were off."

"I wonder how long it took before those agents realized he'd split?"

"I don't know, but whenever Rudkowski learned about it, he would've combusted."

"I get the feeling that this escape plan wasn't hatched by Mike."

Drex snuffled. "I know you advised me to stop pricking with Rudkowski, but—"

"But you can't resist a chance to get his goat."

"The important thing is, Mike is out from under his thumb."

"What if they canvass the neighborhood? Somebody could have noticed Sammy and remember the car."

"We took that into account. Sammy drove Mike to a picnic area a few miles outside of town where he'd left another car. Mike preferred the gray sedan, but Sammy argued that it might not be as *standard* as it looked."

"Hot?"

"Mike didn't ask. Anyway, he's Atlanta bound in a midnight blue minivan."

The summary had taken longer than was necessary to relay the facts. They were dancing around the subject that overrode all others. Gif seemed as reluctant to bring it up as Drex was to address it.

Gif gave in first. "Have you seen them stirring this morning?"

"No." Since Gif had asked about "them," collectively, it wasn't exactly a lie of omission that Drex didn't tell him about his dawn encounter with Talia. "But I listened in on their breakfast. Jasper told her he was going to let his meal settle and then go to the club for a swim. She asked if he was packed. He said he would pack when he got back from the club, leading me to think they're not leaving until this afternoon."

"Could be they're going to drive."

"No, they agreed they could get by without checking luggage. Delta has direct flights at three forty-six and five-nineteen. I'm thinking they'll be on one of those, but we won't know which until they leave the house. Any time past two o'clock would put them in a tight squeeze to make the three forty-six."

"Are they driving themselves?"

"They didn't say, but I'll call you as they're leaving. Be ready to move. I want you stationed at the airport, near security to confirm that they go through."

"Without her seeing me."

"Without her seeing you."

"And you?"

"I'll follow them in my car as far as the airport to make sure that's where they're headed. If they take another direction, I'll continue following until you can catch up with me. If they do go to the airport, I'll let you know to watch for them, then I'll circle around, come back here, and—"

"Break and enter."

"With any luck I won't have to break anything." Gif didn't respond to the quip. Drex sighed. "Don't start again."

"It's risky, Drex. Why take such a chance?"

"Because we've established that legal channels are closed, and I don't know any other way."

"Okay. But you don't have to go it alone. After I see them off, why don't I join the search? Another pair of eyes and hands would halve the time it will take."

"Nope. It's my plan, so my neck is the only one on the block. Besides, if I'm caught, I'll need you to rush in waving your badge and getting me out of hock with the local cops."

"I'd rather you not get caught."

"Goes without saying."

"What are you doing now?"

He was doing what he'd been doing since his exchange with Talia at dawn: wishing that Jasper *had* rushed up the stairs and kicked in his door. He wished Jasper *had* tried tearing him limb from limb. He would have demonstrated to him and his lying wife what animal impulses unleashed looked like.

But to Gif he said, "Killing time till they leave."

———————

He paced. He sat. He eavesdropped on the Fords' intermittent conversations as they came and went from the kitchen, but nothing substantive had come from those exchanges. If Talia had told Jasper about seeing him that morning, and what had been said, she'd done so outside his hearing. The climate between the two of them seemed to have warmed from what it had been the night before.

It gave Drex no pleasure to speculate on what had brought that about.

At 10:05, Jasper left the house alone. He returned at 12:36.

Knowing that they could be leaving at any time soon after that, Drex posted himself at the window and began an uninterrupted vigil. At 2:07, his phone buzzed. He answered. Gif said, "The five nineteen flight?"

"Looks like. Stand by."

Three o'clock rolled around. Three fifteen arrived, and still there was no sign of them. By 3:22, with Drex on the verge of imploding, Jasper's car backed out of the garage.

Drex called Gif. "They're rolling."

"Car service?"

"He's driving."

"On it."

They clicked off. Drex watched to see which way the car turned out of the driveway, then waited at the door and counted slowly to fifty before bounding down the stairs.

He didn't pick up their tail until he reached a major thoroughfare and saw their car stopped at a traffic light. Several cars were between them. He slowed down to let more pass him to create a safer barrier without blocking them from sight. He followed them across the bridge into Charleston, then north on the freeway toward the airport.

Jasper stayed within the speed limit and stuck to the outside lane, making him easy to follow. When Jasper signaled to take the airport exit off the freeway, Drex called Gif. "Looks like it's a go. You in place?"

"Trying not to make myself conspicuous to ATF."

"We're here. Hang on." Staying a discreet distance behind Jasper, Drex followed him toward the parking garages and reported to Gif when Jasper entered the short-term one directly across the street from the terminal. "They should be coming your way in a matter of minutes."

"Roger that. Eyes peeled."

"I'm on my way back to the house."

He decided to go in through the screened porch, the obvious reason being that it couldn't be seen from the street. But, also, that was the area of the house with which he was most familiar.

The latch on the screen door didn't present a challenge. He pulled on a pair of latex gloves and had the flimsy lock busted within seconds. The lock on the solid back door took longer to pick, but he managed it easily enough. Then, with Mike's foreboding about booby traps in mind, he held his breath and pushed open the door. The alarm began to beep. He punched in the new code as he'd heard Talia recite it the night before.

The beeping ceased.

He closed the door. Moving from window to window in the kitchen, he scanned various sections of the property, looking for a sign that he'd been spotted. But there was no movement except for rainwater dripping from the eaves and causing ripples in the puddles beneath.

Satisfied that he'd gotten inside without detection, he let out his breath, and that exhalation was the only sound in the house. The silence was absolute. No ticking clock or hum of an electrical appliance, no gentle whirring of air passing through a vent. Nothing.

Adding to the eeriness of the silence was the gloom. Blinds and shutters had been left open, but the dreary day had created a premature dusk. The light that did leak into the house was so feeble, Drex had to give his eyes time to adjust to the dimness.

When Mike had recovered the real estate listing for the house, he'd printed out the included floor plan. Drex had familiarized himself with it so, even though he'd only been in a few of the downstair rooms, he knew the layout of the house. He made his way from the kitchen, through the formal dining room, and into the two-story foyer where the main staircase curved gracefully upward to the second floor.

He had decided to begin upstairs, do a general walk-through to see what each room consisted of and determine what it might yield, then search the spaces one by one in order of priority.

He climbed the stairs to the landing. Extending from it was a wide hallway, and midway down it, a set of double doors. He pushed them open and stepped into the master suite. Moving his gaze from left to right, he took in the entire room, mentally cataloguing the furnishings. The bed was positioned even with the double doorway and directly in front of him. He walked over and stood at the foot of it.

They'd left it made, decorative throw pillows attractively placed. Identical night tables bracketed the upholstered headboard. The items on them indicated who slept on which side of the bed. On Jasper's were a lamp and alarm clock only. On Talia's were a matching lamp and alarm clock, but also a crystal tray holding several pieces of jewelry, which she must have removed just before climbing into bed. Drex recognized the bracelet and a pair of gold hoop earrings that she'd worn to dinner on Thursday night.

A crystal pump bottle contained what appeared to be hand lotion. He told himself not to, but he rounded the end of the bed, leaned down, and sniffed. It was her fragrance, and it caused a twinge of longing. He cursed himself for being a damn fool.

Not allowing himself to dwell on the evidence of marital domesticity, he rapidly looked through the drawers of her night table. A hardcover fiction book, a paperback travel book on Norway, a box of personalized stationery in the name of Talia Shafer. Not Ford. That gave him a small sense of satisfaction.

The drawers contained nothing remarkable or intensely personal. Thank God. He couldn't have borne that. But maybe Jasper kept the sex toys in his nightstand.

Drex moved to that side of the bed and opened the drawers one by one. He didn't find items used for sexual enhancement or kinky bedroom antics. He didn't find anything. Nothing. Nada. The drawers were empty. He tapped on the back of the piece to see if it was false. It seemed solid, and the inside dimensions of the drawer matched those of the outside.

He looked under the bed. No doubt Jasper would find that highly amusing. There was nothing there.

Next he went to a chest of drawers. The first drawer he opened attested that it was Jasper's. Undershorts—an expensive name brand—were folded and lined up in rows that a seasoned valet would have been challenged to match in terms of straightness. The sock drawer was the same. In one drawer, the arrangement of silk pocket handkerchiefs looked like a canvas of modern art.

Drex was tempted to upend each drawer on the floor, if for no other reason than to make a mess in Jasper's pristine environment. He decided to wait until he had finished his overview, but damned if he wasn't going to start with this drawer of fancy hankies.

Jasper's closet looked like a men's store on Rodeo Drive. Impeccable. Every garment was perfectly hung with an inch of space in between. Shirts, pants, jackets were grouped by color. His shoes were aligned as though he'd used a ruler to make sure the toes didn't extend beyond the edge of the shelf.

Had Jasper arranged everything with such precision so he would know if somebody had touched his things?

Drex was pondering that when his cell phone vibrated, startling him and causing him to jump. He pulled the phone from his jeans pocket and answered in an unnecessary whisper. It was Gif.

"They didn't show."

"What?"

"They didn't show."

"What's that mean?"

Gif made a sound of impatience. "They didn't check in or go through security."

"You must have missed them."

"No, I didn't. Security is in plain sight."

"But I saw him drive into the garage."

"That may be, but they're not on that flight. I pretended to be running late and asked a ticket agent if I had time to make it. She told me the door of the plane had already been closed. It's probably taxiing as we speak."

Drex checked his watch and figured that Gif was right. His mind was careening, trying to process this. "Talia's in the travel industry. She must have some kind of escort service that bypasses regular security."

"I guess that's possible."

"What else could it be?"

"Private plane?" Gif ventured.

"They wouldn't have used public parking."

"Right."

"Can you get to the garage, check to see if their car is still there?"

"Sure, but it'll take me a minute."

"Stay on the line."

"Okay. But, Drex, if they changed their minds and are on their way home, you've got to get out of there."

"Way ahead of you." He pulled the double doors closed as he left the bedroom and hit the staircase at a run. The gloaming had turned darker but he was disinclined to turn on his flashlight. The flashlight on loan from Jasper.

Gif asked, "Have you disturbed anything?"

"No, I was saving that. Are you at the garage yet?"

Gif was puffing. "Almost. What's he drive?"

"Black Mercedes SUV. Shit!"

"What was that?"

"I bumped into a corner of the dining table. Why would they have changed their minds? Goddammit! I thought I'd have days of free access to this house."

Gif was growing shorter of breath. "Plans made on short notice get changed, canceled."

"But they were talking about it this morning. The weather forecast for Atlanta. What they should pack. How casual or dressy did they want to be. They went on for a full five minutes about—"

"Okay, I'm in the garage. Which way?"

Drex had come to a dead standstill in the center of the kitchen and repeated in his head what he'd heard himself say.

"Drex? When he turned in, did he go left or right?"

"They talked about the trip. At length. Both last night and this morning."

He pivoted toward the stove. After a second's hesitation, he went over to it and stuck his fingers in the narrow crack between it and the cabinetry where he'd placed the tiny transmitter while waxing poetic about the best way to cook corn on the cob.

It wasn't there.

He fell back a step, took several breaths, tried again, wedging his fingers in as far as they would go, but he knew where he had attached the bug, and it wasn't there.

"Drex!" Gif shouted in his hear. "Left or right?"

"Doesn't matter. You're not going to find their car."

"What? Why?"

"Hold on." He walked over to the spot where he had let Jasper catch him crouched in front of the cabinetry. He knelt down now and ran his hand along the baseboard.

And came up with the transmitter.

"Drex? Are you out of there yet? What is going on?"

"Jasper moved the transmitter."

"What? He couldn't have. He didn't know where it was."

"He found it. And, as an inside joke, he put it right where I had pretended to hide it that night." He gave a mirthless laugh. "We overheard exactly what they wanted us to hear."

"Son of a bitch."

"In spades," Drex said. "We've been played."

Chapter 18

———◈———

Gif was yelling in his ear, being a hard-ass coach, drilling him. "Get out of that house. Vacate the apartment, too. *Hurry.*"

He'd needed the drilling to knock him out of the momentary stupor he'd lapsed into upon realizing that he'd been duped.

"I'll be in touch."

He disconnected. With Gif's urgent instructions ringing in his ear, he launched himself off the floor. On his way out, he reset the alarm and locked the back door, leaving both as they'd been. He straightened the lock on the screen door so one couldn't tell simply by looking that it was damaged.

Then he ran like hell to the garage apartment. Precipitation had made the stairs treacherous, but he charged up them and into the apartment. No sooner had he closed the door behind himself than he heard the siren.

"You have got to be fucking kidding!"

He stood in the center of the room, heart booming, lungs laboring, mentally shuffling through options and discarding them until he was down to only one.

In a flurry of motion, he felt for the wall switch behind him and flipped on the overhead light. Blinking against the sudden brightness, he peeled off the latex gloves and stuffed them into the pocket of his windbreaker, exchanging them for his pistol. He shucked the windbreaker and threw it aside where it landed carelessly in the ratty easy chair.

With pistol in one hand, he unbuttoned his jeans with the other, then pogoed on alternate legs toward the bedroom, pulling off his jeans as he went. He left them on the floor and switched on the lamp. His duffel bag was on the bed. He returned his pistol to it and took out his computer and the stained original manuscript— bless Pam's heart. He carried them into the living area and hurriedly staged his workspace.

Out on the street, flashing lights created fuzzy streaks of color in the mist. The siren wailed down as the police car wheeled into the Fords' driveway and came to a jerky stop. Both doors opened.

Drex rushed back into the bedroom, stripped off his shirt, put on the fake eyeglasses, toed off his shoes, and grabbed the duffel by the strap. As he did, he spotted his FBI ID wallet lying at the bottom of the canvas bag.

He stopped to consider. He could use it now and, damn, it was tempting. But if he did, he would be blown. He couldn't revert to being the hapless writer *cum* gigolo. It was a dilly of an ace, but if he played it too early, he stood to lose the big pot: Jasper Ford.

He zipped up the duffel bag and shoved it into the closet. He then dashed into the living area and took a beer from the fridge. He twisted off the cap and poured half down the sink, then took the bottle with him to the table where he set it beside his laptop. He dropped into the chair, dry scrubbed the sweat off his face, and tried to appear tormented by writer's block.

As it turned out, he had plenty of time to catch his breath. It was five minutes before he heard them clumping up the stairs. He let them get halfway up, then scraped back his chair and ambled over to the door, arriving at the screen door the same time they did.

Looking back at him was a pair of patrol officers, the patches on their uniform sleeves designating the Mount Pleasant police department. Young. Crisp. And looking surprised to be greeted by a man in just his underwear.

Drex pretended to realize only then his state of undress and looked abashed. "Sorry, guys. What's going on?"

"What's your name?" officer number one asked.

"Drex Easton."

"You live here?"

Drex shot the room behind him a deprecating glance. "It's a roof. I've rented it for three months." He explained about the Arnotts. "Do you want to come in or . . ." He let the invitation trail to nothing.

But they took him up on it, came inside, and looked around.

"You live here alone?" number two asked.

"Yes."

"What's that?" Number one pointed to the manuscript.

"First novel."

"You're a writer?"

Grimacing, Drex said, "Not according to the heap of rejection letters."

Number one chuckled. Number two asked, "Do you know the people in the house across the way?"

"The Fords? Sure. We've hung out."

"Their security alarm went off."

Feigning puzzlement, Drex looked toward the house. "I didn't hear it. When was this?"

"Twenty minutes ago, give or take," officer number one told him. "Siren didn't sound. It cut off with the warning beeps. But Mr. Ford has an app on his phone that signals him when the alarm is activated. Since nobody was authorized to go in, like a cleaning lady or something, he called us."

Drex nodded understanding but held his tongue.

Number two asked, "Have you seen anybody around the neighborhood who looks like they don't belong?"

"Besides me?" Number one thought that was funny, too. Number two, not so much. Good cop/bad cop. Drex turned serious. "I haven't seen hide nor hair of anybody, and I've been here all day. Well, except for a few minutes early this morning. I went out for milk. What did he take?"

"Who?"

"The burglar."

"Nothing, looks like. No sign of a break-in."

"Huh. Wonder what set off the alarm. Or maybe that app on Jasper's phone is faulty."

"Could be. Because the alarm reset itself."

Drex rolled his eyes. "Technology, right?"

The two young officers looked at each other and seemed to come to the tacit conclusion that he was harmless. Number two said, "If you see or hear anything peculiar, please notify the department."

"Sure thing."

Number one wished him good luck with his novel.

"Thanks. I need it."

They thanked him for his time, said their good nights, and trooped down the stairs. A minute later, they backed out of the Fords' driveway and were on their way.

Drex drained the bottle of beer, then picked up his windbreaker from off the chair and fished his cell phone from the pocket.

Gif was beside himself. "I've called you a dozen times."

"I had company." He told him about his visitors. "If they'd arrived sixty seconds sooner, they would have caught me beating my way back up here. If I'd made a run for it when I first heard their siren, they could have seen me fleeing. False alarm."

"Close call. You need to get out of there. And I mean the apartment."

"Have you heard from Mike?"

"He got to the fancy hotel. I told him not to expect the Fords and brought him into the loop. He's standing by, waiting to see what you want him to do."

"I don't have a fucking clue."

"You need to clear out. This room has two beds. You can bunk here tonight. We'll discuss options."

"See you in a few."

When he showed up at the motel without his belongings, Gif greeted him with exasperation. "Where's your stuff?"

"I didn't clear out."

"We agreed—"

"I didn't agree."

"You didn't disagree, either."

"I'm hungry. A mile back I passed a place." Drex turned around and headed for his car. He'd left the engine running. Gif pulled the motel room door shut and followed.

On the way to the restaurant, Gif said, "While I was waiting on you, I took the liberty of calling Mike."

"Did you interrupt his five-course, prix fixe dinner?"

"He canceled his reservation."

"Excuse me?"

"I know. Shocked me too. He was in his room, working."

"Doing what?"

"If the Fords left the airport in the vehicle they arrived in, it would show up on surveillance camera video."

"That would only prove they left. Wouldn't tell us where they were going."

"Mike's going to look into it anyway."

The seafood shack was outlined in turquoise and pink neon, and had a sign with a fish jumping out of a skillet. The shrimp was hot out of the deep fryer, and the beer was icy cold. They ate in silence for several minutes before Gif again raised the subject of Drex leaving the apartment.

Drex hadn't had a change of heart. "If they return to their

house, it'll look better if I'm still there, carrying on as though nothing happened. I replaced the transmitter where Jasper had left it.
That'll be the first thing he checks. He will suspect that it was me
who triggered the alarm, but he can't prove it."

"Unless he has nanny cams."

"Even if he had me on video stealing Talia's jewelry, would he
drag the police in?" He shook his head. "No. He doesn't want involvement with the police."

"He got them involved tonight."

"Only to let me know that he's on to me. I'm sure he got a good
chuckle out of that. But it was a tactical error."

"How so?"

"Why would he play hide-and-seek if he didn't have something
to hide?"

Gif thought on that and conceded with a nod. "But what if
they've vamoosed, and we never lay eyes on them again?"

Drex tried not to give in to the dejection that thought induced.
To come away from this exercise with nothing to show for it would
be a disappointing defeat. Even more crushing would be to think of
Talia on an escapade with Jasper, the two of them laughing at him,
crowing over how effortless it had been to gull him.

"If they've flown the coop," he said to Gif, "it won't matter if
I've moved out or not, will it? He'll have vanished. We'll be back
where we started, except that I'll be out three months rent on that
rat hole."

Sensitive to his mood, Gif let the subject drop. They finished
their meal, split the tab with a twenty each, and were sipping
second beers when Drex's phone vibrated. "Must be Mike." He answered.

Straightaway Mike asked, "Where are you?"

"A restaurant. Just finished dinner."

"Gif there?"

"I'm looking at him."

"Have you seen any news?"

"No."

"Start moving."

Responding to Mike's no-nonsense timbre, Drex scooted out of the booth and motioned for Gif to follow. As they wended their way through tables of diners, he asked Mike, "What's up?"

"The yacht that belongs to the Conner woman, the *Laney Belle*, right?"

"Right. What about it?"

"Well, around nightfall a Coast Guard cruiser came upon a capsized dingy belonging to it."

"What?"

"The *Laney Belle* was located adrift about a half mile away. Nobody was on board."

"*What?*"

"And that ain't the worst of it."

Drex stopped so suddenly, Gif bumped into him from behind.

"A body has washed up on shore," Mike said.

Drex's shrimp and beer threatened to come up. "Whose body?"

"Name hasn't been released. All they're saying is…Drex, it's a woman."

Chapter 19

Tossing his cell phone to Gif, who fumbled it before securing it, Drex said, "Talk to Mike. Ask him where we need to go."

He shouldered past the cluster of people waiting for tables, made it to the exit, and, once outside, broke into a run. Gif jogged along behind, Drex's phone to his ear. By the time they were fastening their seat belts, Mike had explained to Gif the nature of the emergency and given him the name of the marina near where the woman's body had been discovered.

"Mike said the fastest route to take—"

"I know how to get there." Drex sped from the restaurant's parking lot, tires squealing as he executed a shallow U-turn onto the thoroughfare. "Put the phone on speaker."

Gif did. Mike asked Drex what he wanted him to do.

"Be honest with me." Drex's fingers flexed and contracted on the steering wheel. "If the dead woman has been identified, and you're withholding that, I'll cut your heart out."

"I swear, Drex. They haven't released her name."

Drex forced himself to calm down, push personal considerations aside, and think pragmatically. "Pack up. Leave your car—"

"Sammy's car."

"Sammy's car. We'll square up with him later." He checked the clock on the dashboard. It was going on nine o'clock. "I think the last flight from Atlanta to Charleston is at—"

"Ten twenty-nine. I already booked a seat."

"Good man."

"Figured you'd want me there. Where should I go when I arrive?"

"Hell if I know. I haven't thought that far ahead."

"I'll text when I'm on the ground."

"Any sign that Rudkowski is on your tail?"

"None."

"Do you have another phone?"

"Charged and ready."

"I'm gonna switch, too. You and Gif trade numbers."

Gif clicked off the speaker while he and Mike sorted out the new phone numbers.

Drex concentrated on driving. He wove in and out of traffic, cursing motorists who went too slow. Gif held onto the strap above the passenger window but had the discretion not to comment on Drex's speed and chancy maneuvering.

As they neared the general vicinity of the marina, it became apparent that access to it had already been restricted. Some streets had been cordoned off. On those remaining open, traffic was being redirected by officers with flashlights and reflective vests. Seeing that one was about to signal him to make an unwanted turn, Drex whipped into the parking lot of a strip center where the shops were closed for the night and announced they would go the rest of the way on foot.

"There may be barricades," Gif said.

"Keep your badge handy."

"Do you intend to muscle your way in?"

"Only if I have to."

"If you do, Rudkowski will—"

"Keep your badge handy." Drex put a lid on Gif's arguments. They would be reasonable. He would encourage prudence. He would advise that they tread carefully.

Drex didn't want to hear it.

They made it to the base of the pier without being challenged. Drex indicated a roped-off area where the media had been shepherded. "Go mingle with the news crews. See if you can learn anything beyond what Mike has told us."

"Where will you be?"

"Up there." He motioned toward the elevated pier. "Look for me at the railing."

He climbed the steps. The pier was crowded with spectators, but they were unexpectedly subdued. Drex made his way through them until he reached the wood railing and saw what they were looking at on the beach below.

EMTs were lifting a body bag from the packed sand onto a gurney. Once transferred, it was strapped down. The gurney was carried to an ambulance and placed inside. The doors were shut with a sound that had a finality to it. The ambulance drove away down the beach.

As though watching the last scene of a sad movie, the crowd remained still and hushed before gradually beginning to disperse, talking quietly among themselves, posing questions of each other, speculating, philosophizing about the fragility of life.

"Drex."

The soft-spoken voice brought him around to Gif. "It's not official yet," he said, "but they're all but certain it's Elaine Conner."

Drex felt as though his breastbone would crack and his chest cave in. From anguish over Elaine. And guilt-ridden relief that it wasn't Talia. He turned back to the railing, braced his hands on the weathered wood, and bent double, taking deep breaths through his mouth.

Gif let him have a full minute before continuing. "People in the marina saw the yacht leaving the harbor, wondered why anybody

would be going out in weather like this. According to several witnesses, there, uh, there was a man at the wheel."

"Jasper."

"Unidentified."

"It was Jasper." Drex took one last deep breath and stood up
straight. "While he had us looking the other way, he must have
come straight here from the airport and boarded the yacht." Turning only his head, he looked sternly at Gif. His friend knew the
question he wanted to ask, but he couldn't work up enough
courage.

Gif raised his shoulders, looking apologetic. "It's unknown if
anyone else besides the man and Elaine were onboard."

What went unspoken was that the last time Talia was seen, she
had been in the company of her husband, but whether as a victim
or an accomplice remained unknown. As though following Drex's
thoughts, Gif said, "The authorities have had no indication of another casualty, so the search is being referred to as a rescue, not a
recovery."

Drex stared out across the water. "They may find Talia, or her
body," he said in a voice scratchy with emotion. "But if they search
till Doomsday, they won't find a trace of him." He pushed off the
railing, turned, and started walking with determination toward the
steps leading down. "The fucker can swim."

He was pleased with his new appearance.

True, Howard Clement wasn't as dashing as Jasper Ford, husband to Talia Shafer, friend to Elaine Conner, member in good
standing of an exclusive country club, snappy dresser, and connois-
seur of fine wine and cuisine.

But his new look and persona would do. He would never be recognized among the crowd of gawkers on the pier who watched as
Elaine became a headline, her life reduced to a sound bite.

However, that was more notoriety than most people got. When looked at that way, Jasper had done her a favor. He had attained for her in death the attention she craved in life.

Her exuberance had been annoying at times, especially when his investment advice paid off in large dividends. On those occasions the two of them celebrated privately. Often Elaine had urged him to let Talia join in. He had refused.

"She's a conservative investor and would never dare to take the gambles you do, Elaine." Elaine had preened over that.

He didn't have a one hundred percent accuracy rate, of course. Whenever his advice resulted in a loss, Elaine had accepted it philosophically, patted his cheek, told him she loved him anyway, then had asked where she should next put her money.

He would trot out inch-thick analyses of various investment opportunities in the US as well as in foreign markets. He would excite her with projections, then dampen that excitement by enumerating the risks. He'd enticed her with estimated yields, but cautioned her to give serious consideration to the volatility of international trade in an unstable diplomatic climate.

Her attention span had been that of a gnat. She'd been easily confused by the vernacular and eventually overwhelmed by the volume of information. "Oh, just pick one and handle it for me."

Actually, it had been almost too easy. He'd grown a bit bored with her. Ever cheerful and optimistic, she'd rarely challenged anything he proposed.

That was up until tonight. He had called and told her about a squabble between Talia and him that had culminated in the cancellation of a getaway. He'd asked if Elaine would meet him on the *Laney Belle*. "I need a stiff drink and a good friend."

He'd been assured that she would gladly provide both.

She'd welcomed him aboard with a sympathetic hug and an open bottle of bourbon. But when he suggested that they take a short cruise, she had balked. The weather wasn't ideal, she'd said. They couldn't sightsee with the mist so heavy, and the forecast was for conditions to worsen, not improve. She would rather err on the side of safety and keep the *Laney Belle* snug in the marina.

On and on, she'd whined, whined, whined until he'd wanted to strangle her. She hadn't given in until he announced—irritably—that his coming to her for consolation after his quarrel with Talia had been a bad idea, that he was leaving.

"Oh, all right. But only for a little while."

He'd promised to make it quick. That was a promise she had forced him to break.

He'd persuaded her to let him pilot the boat out of the marina because she'd had several drinks. He'd seen to it that she had two more before suggesting that they give the dinghy a test run.

"Tonight? Talia would scalp me if I let you do that."

"That's the point," he'd said, giving her a conspiratorial wink. "She would never allow it. She's afraid of the water, you know. Let's misbehave and do it while she's not looking."

Elaine had been unable to resist the thought of misbehavior.

She'd giggled through the process of getting the dinghy into the water and climbing in. There had been a litany of "ooopsy-daisies" and hilarity over her tipsiness. She'd squealed like a little girl whenever the dinghy was rocked by a swell, and she'd been laughing when a wave sloshed into the boat and knocked her off balance.

She'd stopped laughing when he shoved her overboard. Ocean water had filled her mouth, silencing her scream as she went under. He'd gone in seconds after her and had hooked his elbow around her neck from behind as she'd struggled to the surface.

It was a lifesaver's maneuver, which she'd relaxed against, until realizing that he wasn't keeping her afloat, but holding her under. Then she'd begun to fight. He'd promised to make it quick, but she hadn't allowed it. It had seemed to take for bloody ever for her to die.

He'd let go and pushed away from her, swum back to the dinghy, and hung onto the side of it until he'd regained his breath. Once recovered, he'd peeled off his clothes. He'd practiced doing this in shallower swells. It was harder to accomplish than he had counted on, and took more time, but eventually he was down to his Speedo.

He'd sent his shoes adrift and made a tear in his shirt before letting it go. Then he'd tied his remaining garments together and attached them to a fire extinguisher he'd taken from a cabinet on the yacht. He'd placed it in the dinghy while Elaine was pouring another round. The heavy canister sent his bundle of clothing to the depths.

The hardest part of the whole ordeal had been to overturn the dinghy, which, clearly, had been designed *not* to capsize.

Then he'd swum. He'd estimated that it would take him at least an hour to reach the shoreline, although he couldn't be precise about how far the dinghy had drifted from the yacht. He'd rested periodically but pushed himself.

He was twelve minutes off on his timing, but had missed his destination by only thirty yards. As he'd walked to where he'd left the car, he'd watched the tide erase his footprints almost as soon as they were formed.

The car was a heap that he'd bought months ago off a we-tote-the-note lot. He'd paid in cash and had the title made out to Howard Clement. He hadn't bothered to register it. He'd scraped off the VIN number. He was confident it could never be traced to him.

He had parked it in a clump of scrubby palmetto with a lacy overlay of kelp that had washed onto the beach. In the unlikely event that his tire tracks were ever detected, they would be difficult to imprint. He'd pulled on the pair of latex gloves, which he'd carried folded inside his swimsuit, then reached for the magnetic box he'd secreted beneath the car and used the fob inside to open the trunk. He'd lifted out the roll-aboard he had ostensibly packed for a getaway, but which actually contained everything he needed to undergo a metamorphosis.

The backseat of the car served as his chrysalis.

When he'd emerged an hour later, gone were the ponytail and

door knocker. He'd shaved his head, leaving only a ring of hair on the lower third. He covered the tan line on his scalp with a khaki Gilligan hat.

He'd dressed in a pair of unshapely cargo shorts and a loud Hawaiian print shirt he'd bought in Key West two and a half years ago, when he'd determined that his next target would be the lovely Talia Shafer who lived in Charleston, a city that attracted thousands of tourists wearing ungodly attire. He'd padded the front of the shirt to simulate middle-age spread. He slid his feet into a pair of rubber flip-flops. He'd chosen eyeglasses that were nondescript and could be purchased for a few dollars in just about any retail outlet.

When he'd looked at himself in the rearview mirror, he'd laughed out loud. Not even his wife, not even the woman he'd just drowned, would recognize him.

He replaced everything he'd used in the roll-aboard for disposal later. Before closing it, he took out a wallet, an old and well-used one that he'd bought at a flea market, and checked to make sure the necessities were there. The driver's license had been issued in Georgia, the photo taken after disposing of the fuzzy wig he'd worn as Marian Harris's shy money manager, Daniel Knolls, and before he grew out his hair and beard to become Jasper Ford.

He had a credit card in the name of Howard R. Clement. The card was over a year old and had just enough charges on it to remain active. The wallet also contained the modest amount of currency that Jasper Ford had withdrawn from an ATM three days ago. He'd put the wallet in the back pocket of his shorts.

Last, from a zippered pocket in the lining of the suitcase, he'd taken a small velvet drawstring bag and transferred it to the front pocket of his cargo shorts, sealing it inside with the Velcro strips attached to the fabric. He'd patted the pocket with affection and smiled.

As of tonight, his collection had a new addition.

After locking the roll-aboard into the trunk, he'd driven off the beach. His initial plan had been to head straight up the coast, perhaps traveling as far as Myrtle Beach tonight, where he would get a room and lay low for several days, at least until the hubbub had died down and the search for him and Elaine was discontinued.

Then he would return and choreograph Talia's suicide. Acquaintances would conclude that she'd been led to it by grief over the deaths of her good friend and husband, whose body, regrettably, had never been recovered.

It had been a very workable plan. But as Howard Clement had been chugging along a major thoroughfare in his clunker, a convoy of emergency vehicles had forced him and other motorists to pull onto the shoulder so they could pass. They had been headed in the direction of the shore and the marina.

Could it possibly be? he'd asked himself.

Over the course of his illustrious career, he had never made a spontaneous decision. Never. But this one time, he had yielded to temptation. Acting on impulse, he had changed his route.

Now, as he gazed down at the body on the beach, he supposed it had been Elaine's fake tits, acting as flotation devices, that had caused her body to wash ashore so soon. He had reckoned on it taking a day or so, if indeed it ever did.

But there she lay, faceup, covered with a yellow plastic sheet. A police helicopter flew over. Its downwash flipped back a corner of the sheet to reveal her hand. No one except Jasper seemed to notice.

"Jesus, you just never know, do you?"

Jasper turned. Standing close behind him was a gum-smacking redneck wearing jean cut-offs, combat boots, and a tank top featuring a coiled cobra with dripping fangs. Revolting. "Sorry?"

"When you get up in the morning, you don't figure on it being your last."

"You're right there, buddy," said Howard, in the nasally twang of his newly assumed persona.

He turned away from the redneck and watched with mounting pleasure as the activity on the beach increased. The audience of onlookers on the pier expanded. Jasper delighted in the comments he overheard.

If they only knew who they were rubbing shoulders with, he thought.

He had been on the pier for over an hour when he was jostled along with others near him who were being elbowed out of the way by a man plowing his way to the railing.

Drex.

Jasper experienced a jolt of alarm.

But he soon realized that Drex wasn't looking for him. He was fixated on what was taking place on the beach. He'd made it just in time to catch the final act: that of the body being carted away.

Once the ambulance was gone, Jasper allowed himself to be shuffled along with the crowd as it vacated the pier. A bottleneck formed at the steps. Jasper waited his turn, then flip-flopped down. But he didn't go far, because Drex had stayed behind, gazing out across the water, hands gripping the railing, his body as taut as a bowstring.

Which confirmed what Jasper had suspected all along. He wasn't who he claimed to be, and he wasn't writing a novel. One didn't bug one's neighbor's house unless one had a reason for doing so. And now this drowning death had left him obviously upset, which was disproportionate to how long he'd known Elaine.

From the start, the timing of his arrival to the neighborhood had made Jasper uneasy because it had coincided so closely—mere months—with the discovery of Marian Harris's remains.

That had come as a shock. One evening he had returned home from an errand to find Talia in her study, crying her heart out.

"Remember I told you about my friend Marian who lived in Key West?"

"Of course. The one who went missing a couple of years ago."

"I just heard from a mutual friend," Talia had said as she blotted up tears. "They found her remains buried in a shipping crate. It was horrible."

It certainly had been horrible news to him. None of the others had ever been found. This was an unwelcome first, and it had rattled him. He was brilliant. He didn't make mistakes. But he would be a fool to ignore the possibility that he *might*.

He wouldn't commit a major gaffe. No, the oversight would be something minor, inane, ridiculous, something that, because of its sheer triviality, a genius like him would never think to avoid.

That evening, while Talia was mourning the grisly death of her friend, he had resolved that the time had come for Jasper Ford to evaporate.

His marriage to Lyndsay had been brief, but rife with drama. After her, he'd sworn to remain a bachelor and, for thirty years, he had. Then, ill-advisedly as it turned out, he'd experimented with matrimony again. The intimacy of the union, inside the bedroom and out, spawned risks he hadn't foreseen when he'd asked for Talia's hand. Choosing her in particular had been a miscalculation. He would have been better off selecting a bubblehead like Elaine.

Talia was far too perceptive. He had sensed her gradually increasing mistrust, which had resulted in last night's accusation of an affair. He had never slept with Elaine, but that Talia sensed *something* amiss was his cue that it was time to bid farewell to Jasper Ford.

But how to go about it had presented him with a unique problem: He had two women to dispose of this time. He couldn't leave either Talia or Elaine alive to search for him. He was confident that he was up to the challenge of their termination, but the solution had to be well thought out, methodically planned, and precisely executed.

But then Drex's unexpected appearance had thrust Jasper's strategy into overdrive. He'd sowed seeds of doubt about their neighbor in Talia's mind, hoping to thwart any interaction between them until he could formulate another plan.

Then—bless her!—Talia's mention of a getaway had opened up an opportunity.

Even better, he could broadcast it using the transmitter that Drex had planted. Talk about a backfire. It had been too delicious.

He'd acted quickly, but efficiently, and so far everything had gone splendidly.

But now here Drex was, playing fly in the ointment again.

Jasper risked making himself conspicuous by loitering near the pier, but within minutes another man joined Drex. They talked briefly, then, in a decisive manner, Drex turned away from the railing. The two of them strode along the pier and descended the steps in a hurry. They walked past him without giving him a second glance.

Jasper dismissed the other man as a sidekick.

But he was struck by Drex's unfamiliar demeanor. No jaunty gait, no dimpled smile. This Drex was no aw-shucks wannabe. There was an intensity about him, an angry determination in his bearing. It couldn't be mistaken. It definitely couldn't be dismissed.

And with that thought, the freshly cut hair on the back of Jasper's neck stood on end.

Drex Easton was him.

Jasper had been feeling him for years, an unknown entity who was invisible, but whose presence he felt. A shadow. Untouchable, but *there.* More often than he wanted to admit, he would sense him like a ghostly waft of cool air. He would awaken and imagine a menacing presence hovering over him while he slept. Sometimes, in a crowd, he would whip around suddenly in the hope—and fear— that he would spot him, that he would be able to pick him out in a sea of unknowns.

He never did, but he knew he existed. He knew he was corporeal and not just an inhabitant of nightmares and premonitions. He was real and on Jasper's trail with the unflagging purpose of a bloodhound and the fervor of a pilgrim, undeterred by time or distance or failure.

But how did one combat someone unseen? It would be like fencing in absolute blackout. He couldn't strike out without giving away his position. He couldn't beat him at his own game because he didn't know who he was, what he looked like, or his name.

Until now.

Chapter 20

Talia had been home for no longer than fifteen minutes before she was curled up in an oversize upholstered chair and sipping a glass of wine. The compact, first-floor room tucked under the staircase had a desk where she conducted her business, but she'd also furnished it with comfortable pieces, making it as much her retreat as her workplace.

She was enjoying the peacefulness it afforded when the doorbell rang.

Disgruntled by the interruption and mystified as to who would be on her doorstep this late on a Saturday night, she set aside her glass of wine, made her way to the front door, and looked through the peephole.

The two men looking back at her were strangers. With misgiving, she called through the door, "Can I help you?"

"Mrs. Ford?"

"Yes."

"I'm Dave Locke, this is Ed Menundez. We're detectives with the Charleston Police Department." Each held up a badge where she could see it. "Can we please speak with you?"

"The police department?"

"We'd like to speak with you, please."

She hesitated for a moment then disengaged the alarm, flipped the deadbolt, and opened the door. Dividing a look of perplexity between the two, she asked, "Speak with me about what?"

"May we come in?"

"What's happened?"

"May we?"

She gave Locke a vague nod of assent and stepped aside. She realized then that she'd left her shoes in front of her easy chair. The marble floor of the entry was cold against her bare feet. She shut the door and turned to the men, repeating, "What's happened?"

"Are you here alone?" Locke, evidently the spokesman of the duo, was tall and thin, with a pleasant bearing and eyes that drooped at the outer corners.

"Yes."

"Mr. Ford?"

"He's in Atlanta." The first panicked thought that entered her mind was that there had been a plane crash. "His flight...?"

"No, this isn't about a flight."

"Then please tell me why you're here."

"Are you acquainted with Elaine Conner?"

She swallowed, nodded, and replied, "Very well. She's a good friend of mine."

"We gathered that, because your name showed up numerous times in her recent calls log."

"You have Elaine's phone?"

"We discovered it on her yacht."

"I'm sorry, I don't understand. What were you doing on Elaine's yacht? Is she all right?" But even as she asked, she knew. Her eyes widened with alarm. "Has there been an accident?"

Locke extended his hand, but came short of actually touching her. "Mrs. Ford, the body of a woman was discovered on the beach tonight, washed ashore. We believe it's Elaine Conner."

Talia gaped at them with disbelief, then covered her mouth and backed into one of the straight chairs flanking the console table. She bumped against the leg of it, rocking a crystal vase so hard it would have fallen off if Menundez hadn't reacted quickly enough to stabilize it.

Locke was still talking. Talia had to focus on each word in order to comprehend what he was saying. "...ask if you knew how to contact Mrs. Conner's next of kin."

Talia wanted to wake up from this awful dream before it became any worse, but try as she might to force herself awake, the scene remained real, palpable, harsh. Her feet were freezing. Her ears were buzzing. Two heralds of dreadful news were looking down on her, awaiting a response.

"She..." She stopped, drew in two quick breaths, and tried again. "Elaine doesn't have any living relatives. No next of kin."

"Then we may need to impose on you."

"Impose on me?"

"To take a look at a sketch and verify that it's her."

Talia stared up at them, but was too benumbed to speak. This could not be happening.

Locke said, "The coroner will make a positive ID, but it would be helpful if you could identify her from a sketch. We should be receiving it shortly." He motioned to the iPad his partner held at his side.

Shakily, Talia stood up. "I'm going to get my shoes."

"I'll get them for you," Locke said. She got the impression it wasn't an offer out of kindness.

"I left them in my study. The room behind the stairs. My phone is on the end table. Please bring that, too."

He left her with Menundez, who was younger, stockier, and more all-business. He wasn't merely looking at her. He was scrutinizing her. To break the strained silence she asked him if it was still raining.

"Off and on," he said.

Locke returned with her requested phone. Awkwardly he passed her one shoe at a time. She put them on, then, feeling only slightly steadier, stood.

"Better?" Locke asked.

"I'm fine."

She knew she should probably ask if they would like to move into the living room and sit while they waited for the expected email, but inviting them to do so would make this visit seem even more official, and she was resistant to doing that.

Speaking in a low voice one would use to calm an anxious animal, Locke told her the time the 911 call had come in and the approximate location of where the body had washed ashore.

"Where the pier is?" she said. "That's near the marina where Elaine's yacht is moored."

"It left the marina a little after seven this evening."

"She took it out alone?"

"Would that be unusual?"

"Yes. She was adept at piloting it, but conscientious and careful. It wouldn't be like her to take it out on a night like tonight, especially by herself. Maybe she loaned it to someone. Or it could have been stolen."

"Mrs. Conner was onboard. Investigators have talked to several people who corroborate having seen her on deck."

"Investigators?" She looked at Menundez, whose expression remained disturbingly impassive, then came back to Locke. "Do you think the woman found on the beach was the victim of a crime?"

"We don't know yet. Several agencies are looking into it. Isle of Palms PD called us in to assist. A Coast Guard patrol discovered the dinghy."

"Dinghy?"

He told her that it had been found capsized.

"That makes no sense. Why in the world would Elaine get into the dinghy, after dark, in this weather?"

"Questions we'd like answered," he said.

They seemed to expect her to provide the answers. "There must have been an emergency onboard. Did Elaine call in an SOS or send some kind of distress signal?"

"No, ma'am."

"That yacht is equipped with state-of-the-art technology. She's bragged to me about it. At the first sign of trouble, she would have sent out an alert." Locke just looked back at her, saying nothing. With emphasis, she said, "There must be a mistake. It can't be her. Who discovered the body?" Locke told her. "Oh. How awful for the little boy."

"When his dad realized what it was, he made sure the kid didn't see it."

She tried to connect Elaine and her effervescent personality to a lifeless body washed ashore. It was impossible. "I don't believe it's Elaine."

Locke gave her a nod that could have been interpreted any number of ways, but she interpreted it to mean that he disagreed.

They all heard the beep signaling that the email had come in. Menundez opened the cover on his iPad, accessed his email, then gave Locke a nod.

Locke turned to her. "Can you give it a look?"

Talia tried to distance herself from the surreal situation, to withdraw emotionally, to become an observer rather than a participant, believing that watching from outside herself was the only way she would get through this.

"Do I need to prepare myself for what I'm about to see?"

"Are you asking if the face is disfigured?"

"Yes, that's what I'm asking."

"No. No blood, nothing like that."

She took a deep breath, then nodded, and Menundez held the tablet out to where she could see the screen.

The face as captured by the sketch artist showed no signs of trauma. But it was definitely a rendition of Elaine's face without her vitality and animation.

The detectives must have known from her reaction what the answer was, but Locke asked quietly, "Is that Elaine Conner?"

Talia nodded, spoke a raspy yes, then said, "Excuse me, please." She didn't wait for permission.

She went into the powder room, the nearest bathroom, and bent over the toilet. She retched. Hard. Repeatedly. But she hadn't eaten since breakfast, so nothing came up. The bout left her feeling wrung out and trembly.

She cupped water from the faucet with her hand and rinsed her mouth out, then used a guest towel to bathe her face with cold water. She raked back her hair with her fingers, then rejoined the detectives.

Locke said, "Can we get you something, Mrs. Ford? A drink of water?"

She understood then that their business with her wasn't finished. They weren't offering condolences and bowing out with an apology for having ruined her night. They had come to her with questions that needed answers.

She wanted to cover her head and weep over the loss of her friend with the infectious laugh and *joie de vivre*. Instead, she wearily offered the detectives coffee.

"Coffee would be good," Locke said.

"Coffee, thanks," Menundez said.

She led them into the kitchen, then stood before the elaborate coffeemaker and stared at it, dazed, as though it were the control panel on a NASA spaceship. She couldn't remember which buttons to push or in what sequence.

Noticing, Menundez stepped in. "I have one like it. Allow me?"

"Thank you." He took over for her. Maybe he wasn't an automaton after all.

She put a kettle on the stove to boil water for tea for herself, then sent Jasper a text asking him to call her as soon as possible. When she saw Locke looking at her quizzically, she said, "I texted Jasper."

"Have you heard from him?"

"No, but I didn't expect to. We had a late dinner reservation."

Simultaneously she and the detective looked at the clock on the microwave. It was almost eleven-thirty. "If he doesn't call soon, I'll try to reach him through the hotel switchboard. He'll be very upset. Elaine was his friend, too."

"Yes, mutual friends told us that they had drinks together yesterday at the country club."

"And stayed for dinner." Although she had voiced her suspicion of an affair to Jasper, she felt a need now to set the record straight: Their date yesterday hadn't been behind her back. "I didn't feel well last evening. Rather than join them, I stayed in and slept through dinner."

Locke nodded thanks to his partner, who had passed him a cup of coffee. He blew across the top of it. "Why didn't you go to Atlanta? Was it a business trip for Mr. Ford?"

"No. He's retired." Becoming increasingly uncomfortable with the tenor of his questions, she turned her back to him, opened a cabinet, and took down a box of chamomile tea. "The trip was to have been a getaway. I made it as far as the airport, then began feeling queasy. I begged off but insisted that Jasper go ahead without me. It's a new hotel. Jasper is a gourmet. He looked forward to trying out the chef."

"What new hotel?"

"The Lotus."

Menundez left his freshly brewed cup of coffee on the counter, stepped out of the kitchen into the dining room, and got on his cell phone.

"Did you get over it?"

Talia had watched the other detective leave and could now hear him speaking quietly into his phone. She turned back to Locke. "Pardon?"

"The queasiness."

"It comes and goes."

"Nothing serious, I hope."

She shook her head. "I had some dental work done yesterday morning. The prescribed pain pills must not have agreed with me."

"You were sleeping them off last night while your husband and Mrs. Conner were at the country club."

"I thought I had slept them off. I guess I didn't. The upset recurred today."

Locke set his unfinished coffee on the table. "Do you have an explanation for the house alarm going off this afternoon?"

She followed the direction of his gaze to the control box on the wall next to the back door. "The alarm went off?"

"Not the siren. It was shut off during the warning beeps with time to spare. Strange, because no one was at home."

She shook her head in confusion. "When was this?"

Menundez returned in time to hear her question. "Five oh-seven," he said. "Patrolmen were dispatched. Saw no sign of a break-in."

"A glitch in the system, you think?" Locke asked.

Menundez said, "Or else someone who knew the code was here."

If they'd been speaking in a foreign language, Talia couldn't be more confounded. "Like who?"

"We hoped you could tell us," Menundez said.

"I'm sorry. I know nothing about the alarm going off, so I can't explain why it did."

"Quite a coincidence that cops have come to your house twice in one day," Locke remarked.

Disquieted by the way the two were regarding her, she folded her arms over her middle, even knowing how defensive it looked. "Why are you asking me all these questions?"

"We have to eliminate every possibility."

"Possibility of what?"

She had addressed the question to Locke, but Menundez answered. "The possibility that Mrs. Conner's death wasn't an accident caused by misjudgment on her part. The possibility that foul play was involved."

Before Talia could process that, Locke asked, "Did you walk your husband into the airport, see him off?"

It took several seconds for his seemingly unrelated inquiry to sink in. "No. No, we said our goodbyes in the parking garage. Why?"

"Because some of the people we've talked to who saw the *Laney Belle* leave the marina said that a man was steering her, not Mrs. Conner."

Talia hugged her middle a little tighter.

Locke continued. "We were also told that Mrs. Conner often allowed your husband to pilot the boat."

"That's true," Talia said, "but it couldn't have been Jasper this evening."

"Had Mrs. Conner ever invited anyone else to take the wheel?"

"Not to my knowledge, but that doesn't mean that she didn't."

"You two were close friends."

"Yes."

"Were you acquainted with all her other friends?"

"Many of them."

"Male friends?"

"Some."

"If she had a new man in her life, would she have told you?"

"More than likely," she said huskily.

"Has she taken a romantic interest in someone recently?"

Willing herself not to glance toward the apartment across the way, she gave her head a brisk shake.

"She wasn't seeing anyone?"

"In the way you're implying, I don't believe so."

The two detectives looked at each other, then back at her. Menundez said, "Mrs. Ford, is it possible that your husband changed his mind about going to Atlanta at the last minute?"

"He would have notified me. He would have been home hours ago."

"Unless he was onboard the *Laney Belle* with Elaine Conner," Locke said.

"That's an offensive implication, Detective Locke."

"The implications to you are more dire than marital unfaithfulness. If your husband was on the yacht, and there was an emergency, an accident, he could have suffered an injury. As we speak, search-and-rescue teams are out looking for him, or his—"

The kettle screeched. Talia nearly jumped out of her skin. She turned quickly and lifted it off the burner. In the process she sloshed some of the boiling water onto her hand. She cried out. The detectives lurched forward, ready to lend assistance, but she warded them off.

"I'm fine. It's fine." She tucked her scalded hand into her opposite armpit. "You believe that Jasper is either in need of rescue or already dead? Is that what you're saying?"

Their grim expressions confirmed it.

"You're wrong. If he were going out on the water with Elaine tonight, he would have told me."

"Did they take the yacht out together often?"

"Not often. But there have been occasions." She wet her lips. "Were you given a description of the man who was with her?"

"Not a very good one. No one actually saw him board the yacht. It was a gloomy dusk. The mist limited visibility. One witness said the man he saw in the wheelhouse was wearing a baseball cap. Other than that—"

"Baseball cap?"

At her startled reaction, Locke and his partner came to attention. Locke said, "That's been confirmed. A baseball cap was found on the yacht."

Talia wilted against the edge of the countertop. "Orange, with a white capital letter T?"

"University of Tennessee," Locke said.

She covered her face with her hands.

"Does your husband own a cap like that?"

She shook her head, said *no* into her moist palms, then lowered her hands. Her throat seized. She had to swallow several times. "No. But our neighbor does."

"Next door?"

"He rents the garage apartment behind the house next door."

Menundez said to Locke, "The patrolmen who responded to the call about the alarm talked to that guy."

Locke asked Talia, "Was he acquainted with Mrs. Conner?"

"Jasper and I introduced them."

"What's his name?"

Menundez was hurriedly swiping the screen of his phone. "I've got it here."

"My name is Drex Easton."

Startled, the three of them turned as one. He was standing in the open doorway between the screened porch and kitchen. How had he opened it without their hearing him? He was wearing the same dark suit he'd worn the night he escorted Elaine and her to dinner. The same shirt and tie.

But an altogether different countenance.

His right hand was raised and open to show a small leather wallet with a clear plastic window and a gold badge. His eyes zeroed in on Talia's. "FBI Special Agent Drex Easton."

Chapter 21

———◦◦◦———

Rudkowski was sprawled on his hotel room bed, watching without much interest the dirty movie on the room's flat screen, nursing his third scotch, and wondering how a man who weighed almost three fifty could vanish into thin air. It had been some trick, but Mike Mallory had managed it, and Rudkowski was made to look like a fool. Again.

His cell phone rang. He spilled half his whiskey in his haste to mute the bump-and-grind sound track and answer his phone. "Rudkowski."

"It's Deputy Gray."

"Who?"

"In Key West. We talked a few days ago."

"Oh, yeah, yeah." Rudkowski sank back onto his pillow. "Make this quick, please. I've got a situation here."

"I'm sorry to bother you, but I'm trying to reach Agent Easton, and, like the time before, he didn't leave me his number this morning. It was my oversight. I should have made sure—"

"Hold it. This morning? You talked to Easton this morning?"

"Well, yesterday morning, officially."

While Rudkowski had been licking his wounds and swilling cheap scotch, midnight had slipped past him. "Okay. Yesterday morning. Did he say where he was calling from?"

"Well, no, sir, but he can't on account of him being—"

"Undercover."

"Yes, sir."

"Why was he calling you?"

"Same as before. The Marian Harris case."

"Specifically?"

"He asked if a Talia Shafer had been questioned during the investigation into Harris's disappearance."

Rudkowski rolled over and picked up the notepad and pen on the nightstand. "Spell the names, please. And who is she?"

The deputy gave him the spellings. "She was in the photograph of the party scene on the boat."

"So were dozens of other people. What was Easton's particular interest in her?"

"He couldn't disclose that, because it's—"

"Classified."

"Yes, sir. I thought you would know what his interest was."

What he didn't know about Easton's recent activities would fill the fucking Superdome. "Was this Talia Shafer considered a person of interest in the Harris case?"

"No, sir. Agent Easton asked if there were any notes taken during her interview, but it was just basic stuff. Date and time. Names of the officers who talked to her. Nothing came of it, nothing to follow up on. Agent Easton thanked me for checking, and that was it."

Rudkowski figured that he'd had too much to drink. He was having trouble connecting the dots. "So, if that was it, why are you trying to reach Easton now?"

"Because about an hour ago, our department got a call from Charleston PD."

"South Carolina?"

"Right."

Rudkowski listened with shrinking patience as the deputy re-lated what he knew about the death of an Elaine Conner.

"They haven't ruled out that it was an accident, but they're leaning toward foul play. A man was with her on the yacht. He's unaccounted for. Anyhow, one of the investigators up there remem-bered reading about our case down here and was struck by the similarities."

"Rich lady. Snazzy boat."

"Yes, sir. So they called our department to compare notes. I thought Agent Easton would want to look into this Charleston case, too."

"I'm sure he will. I'll tell him—"

"Especially since Talia Shafer is from there."

Rudkowski froze in the process of raising his glass to his mouth. "Say again, deputy."

"Talia Shafer lives in Charleston. At least she did. I'm not sure Agent Easton knows that. This incident in Charleston occurred only a few hours after he called me, asking about her. It's a crazy coincidence."

"Not so crazy," Rudkowski said, speaking too softly for Gray to hear.

"I figured he would want to know about this new case, if he doesn't already. Since I can't reach him, will you see to it that he gets the message?"

Rudkowski clicked off the TV and swung his legs over the side of the bed. "You can count on it, Deputy Gray. In fact, I'm going to deliver it personally."

Chapter 22

———◦◦◦———

Talia was immobilized by Drex's stare as two men eddied around him into the kitchen and introduced themselves to the detectives. Drex walked toward her, crowding into her personal space before he stopped. "Surprise."

"You're *FBI*?"

"The writing thing wasn't working out."

A cavalcade of recollections flashed through her mind. Her involuntary reactions to his deceptive charm, her nervous retreat from his apartment, her anguish over what had taken place in the garage of the medical building, the ambiguities she'd wrestled with, the times she had defended him against Jasper's reservations. All that crystalized into hatred.

Softly but emphatically, she said, "Go straight to hell."

"You tried that already." He spread his arms. "I'm still here, and you're up shit creek."

He held for a beat, then turned away from her and shook hands with Locke and Menundez. "I apologize for crashing your party, but I believe you'll welcome our intrusion. We can shed a lot of light on your investigation. Excuse me, Mike."

He nudged the enormous man aside and knelt down to reach beneath the cabinet. When he straightened up, he held out his hand to show the detectives the object in his palm.

"What is that?" Talia asked.

Drex turned to her. "Commonly called a bug. I've been using it to eavesdrop on you and Jasper."

"You bugged our home?"

"You say that like you didn't know it was there."

"I didn't! Isn't that illegal?"

She asked the group at large, but it was Drex who said, "It's not as illegal as kidnaping, conspiracy to commit murder, and murder, which is what you and Jasper stand to be indicted for, so if I were you, I wouldn't split hairs on legalities."

He wasn't teasing. He wasn't baiting her as he'd done in Elaine's living room. This wasn't playacting. He was serious, and the import of what he had alleged stole her breath. "What are you talking about?"

"We'll get to it. First, meet Agent Mike Mallory, who put me on to you and Jasper."

"A pleasure."

His response was so droll, Talia couldn't tell if it applied to the introduction or to the service he'd performed for Drex.

Drex pointed to the other man. "Agent Gif Lewis. He—"

"You're the man from the coffee shop," she said. "I remember you."

"That's a first," the heavy man said under his breath.

Gif Lewis acknowledged her with a polite nod. "Mrs. Ford."

Feeling stung and betrayed, she said, "But you seemed so nice. I truly believed you were trying to help."

"I was. Drex was coming on a little strong."

"He does that." She shifted her gaze to Drex, wondering if his fellow agents knew how strongly he had come on to her in the parking garage. He was still watching her with cool contempt, as though she were responsible for his actions, for the kiss. He didn't look away from her until Locke addressed him.

"You said you could shed light?"

Drex seemed to shake off whatever else he was thinking and got down to the matter at hand. "Has anybody checked Elaine Conner's financial portfolio, her bank accounts?"

"It was on another team's to-do list," Menundez said.

"Let me tell you what they'll find." Drex formed an O with his fingers and thumb. "Zero. Zilch. He cleans them out. He kills them. He vanishes."

"You can't mean Jasper."

Drex ignored Talia's outcry and said to his cohorts, "Take these gentlemen into the living area and start briefing them. We'll be there in a minute."

Locke looked uncertain about leaving her alone with Drex, but Menundez fell into step behind Drex's men. Locke followed. She waited until they were out of earshot before she launched into Drex. "You've been spying on us?"

"Most of it was boring. I didn't bug your bedroom."

"You bastard."

"But I make damn good corn on the cob."

Incensed, she spun away from him. "I want to hear what they're saying."

"Wait. Did you burn your hand?"

She looked back at him, wondering how he knew.

"The kettle whistled. You cried out."

"Never mind my hand." She placed it behind her back. "I want to know what's going on. First Elaine . . . " Grief, exhaustion, dismay, fear, and another dozen emotions avalanched and overwhelmed her. Hot tears filled her eyes. Her voice cracked. "I *hate* you."

"Let me see your hand."

She didn't move, so he went to her and reached behind her back. His touch wasn't rough, but still she flinched as he took hold of her hand. He examined the red splotch on the back of it, then pulled her over to the sink, turned on the cold water tap, and guided her hand beneath the stream. "Don't move."

She wanted to tell him to fuck off, but the cold water brought instant relief, so she stayed. He got ice cubes from the dispenser in the door of the refrigerator and returned with them. Placing his hand beneath hers, palm to palm, he supported it while gently rubbing the ice cubes across the burn.

She stared at their joined hands as the water spilled over them, became hypnotized by the slow circles he drew on the back of her hand with the ice cubes. "Don't be nice to me," she said, her voice hoarse. "You're ruining my life."

"You ruined your life the day you went in cahoots with Jasper, whom I first came to know as Weston Graham."

"I don't know what you're talking about. None of it."

His eyes bored into hers. "Where is he, Talia?"

"Atlanta. If you were listening in, you no doubt heard us laying plans last night. He and I—"

"He's not in Atlanta. He never went. He never intended to."

"You're trying to trick me like you've been doing since I met you." She tried to pull her hand away, but he curled his fingers up, linking them with hers and keeping her in place.

"Listen to me." His voice was low and emphatic. "All those questions the detectives put to you about Jasper, where he was tonight, and so forth? They already knew the answers. And your answers didn't mesh with what they know for fact.

"Local police, the sheriff's office, state police. They've got resources. Mike has even better resources. We've all been busy trying to determine Jasper's whereabouts ever since Elaine's body washed ashore and witnesses claimed that a man was at the helm of her yacht."

"Wearing a baseball cap that belongs to *you*."

"I didn't realize it was missing until Locke mentioned it. I'm certain that Jasper took it from the apartment the night we went out to dinner."

She opened her mouth to protest, but he cut her off with a hard shake of his head. "We'll argue the finer points later. What's im-

portant to your future, short-term and long-range, is to stop lying.
Now."

"I'm not lying."

His jaw tensed angrily. "You lied to those detectives about a
damn dental appointment and disagreeable pain pills. If you'll lie
about something that trivial, you'll lie about something large."

She lowered her head. "That was a fib, not a significant lie."

She could feel his angry breathing against the crown of her
head. "You've lied about plenty that *is* significant, Talia. Confirmed
by the airlines: Jasper wasn't on that flight, nor any other Delta
flight, private plane, or another carrier. Confirmed by TSA: His
boarding pass was never scanned. He wasn't on their security cameras. Confirmed by the Lotus Hotel: He didn't check in or show up
for your dinner reservation. All of which you told those detectives
that he did." He put his finger beneath her chin and tipped her
head up, forcing her to look directly into his incisive eyes. "Where.
Is. He?"

"If he's not at The Lotus Hotel in Atlanta, then I. Don't. Know."

He held her stare for several seconds, then dropped the remnants of the ice cubes into the sink and turned off the faucet. They
shared a dishtowel to dry their hands. "Do you want to put some
salve on that burn?"

"I think it's okay."

He motioned her toward the living area. "Remember, I gave
you a chance."

Mike, Gif, and the two detectives had drawn chairs up to the
coffee table and were huddled around it, intent. As Drex and Talia
entered the room, Locke was saying, "But no bodies were ever discovered?"

Drex said, "Not until Marian Harris."

Talia stopped in her tracks. "Marian?"

"Your friend Marian Harris." Drex pointed at the sofa. "Have a seat."

"I'll stand."

"Suit yourself, but this is going to take a while." In order to join the group, he pulled a chair over to the table, took off his jacket, and hung it on the back before sitting down. As he loosened his necktie, he asked Mike, "Have you worked forward or backward?"

"Forward. Starting with—"

"Lyndsay Cummings," Drex said. "The first we know of."

"Right." Mike shifted in his chair. "We'd just got to the Harris woman."

"Please don't refer to her like that," Talia said. "She was my friend."

Drex crossed his arms over his chest and leaned back in his chair. "You and Jasper talked at length about Marian last night. My 'excessive' interest in Key West had you both skittish."

"Did you bring up Key West only to bait me?"

"Yes. And guess what? You bit."

He turned to the detectives. "During her conversation with her husband about it, Talia admitted to getting upset over any mention of Key West and/or Marian Harris." He recapped what he'd overheard.

"This is a direct quote that refers to me. Jasper asks, 'Do you think he knows something about Marian?' Talia replies, 'No. Maybe, Jasper. I don't know.' Jasper, anxious and insistent. 'He's living next door, Talia. I should have known about this immediately.'

"They go on like that for about ten minutes. Neither confessed to nailing her inside a shipping crate, but it was a telling discussion. On the heels of it, they made plans to leave town. It's recorded. You can listen if you want."

Talia was looking at him with horror. "Jasper thought you were on a fishing expedition, that *you* might have nailed Marian inside that shipping crate." She turned to the other men. "Jasper didn't completely trust him from the start. He thought he was a phony.

"He became even more suspicious when Drex expressed his interest—which *was* excessive—in Key West. Out of the bug's range, Jasper theorized that the discovery of Marian's body might have made the culprit nervous, that he was going around to former acquaintances of hers and testing their reactions to any mention of her or Key West." Looking back at Drex, she said, "If he sounded skittish, it was because he didn't want happening to me what had happened to Marian."

She had grown heated. Drex remained cool. "The culprit did get nervous, all right. Because he feared I knew that he had bilked Marian, then killed her."

"Jasper didn't even know her!"

Drex lunged forward, almost coming out of his chair. "You two met through her."

"No, we didn't. I told you how we met."

He sat back. "Share with the detectives. Mike and Gif already know the story."

Talking rapidly, in stops and starts, she told Locke and Menundez a condensed version.

When she finished, Drex said, "It's awfully sweet, but it's a lie."

Mike addressed the two detectives. "Our guy had hooked his other ladies using online match-up services."

"That's not how he and I met," Talia said.

"Right enough," Drex said. "You were introduced by Marian Harris."

"Jasper and I didn't meet until months after Marian's disappearance."

Drex motioned to Mike, who withdrew the party photo from a file he'd brought in with him. Drex got up and walked over to the sofa, where Talia had changed her mind about sitting down. He held the picture out to her. "Ever seen this?"

"Yes. It was the last known picture taken of Marian. After her disappearance, the police interviewed everyone who was at that party, me included."

He looked at the photograph as though giving it a fresh assessment. "You're not exactly in on the merriment. How come you're out there on the fringes all by yourself?"

"I didn't know any of the other guests."

He cocked his head to one side, indicating doubt.

She said, "I went to Key West to check out a hotel. Marian was a good client. I called her to see if she and I could have lunch. She said what good fortune it was that I was in town. She was hosting a party that night and insisted that I attend."

"You didn't know anyone else there?"

"I just said that."

"You didn't mix and mingle?"

"Since I was the outsider, Marian introduced me to several people."

"What about him?" He pointed out the blurred figure silhouetted against the sunset. "Did she introduce you to him?"

She squinted. "Possibly."

"What's his name?"

"I don't know."

"Daniel Knolls."

"If we were introduced, I don't remember him."

He leaned down to her and whispered, "You're sleeping with him."

She recoiled. "That's not Jasper!"

He passed the picture to Locke, who looked at it and passed it to his partner. It made its way back to Mike, who replaced it in the file. Drex returned to his chair and gave Talia a long look. She stared back with defiance and hostility. "Say you're as honest as Abe, telling the truth—"

"I am."

"Haven't you been struck by the similarities between Elaine Conner and Marian Harris?"

He could tell by the wariness in her eyes that she had. He let that question simmer, then said, "You told the detectives that you and Jasper parted company in the airport parking garage."

"We did."

"You told Jasper that you didn't feel up to going, but urged him to go without you. You kissed goodbye and waved each other off."

She nodded, but only after a nanosecond of hesitation, which Drex made mental note to pursue later.

He said, "You drove Jasper's car out of the airport."

"Yes."

"She did," Menundez said. "I got texted a security cam freeze frame."

Mike had that, too, but Drex didn't reveal that. The local cops didn't need to be apprised of Mike's hacking talents, lest some rule-bending was soon called for. To Talia, he said, "The camera got you, but if someone was inside the trunk of your car, Jasper for instance, he would have gotten away unseen."

"Uh, Easton. He took a taxi." Menundez held up his cell phone. "They texted me the video. Shows clear that he never went inside the airport. They're checking with the taxi company to see where it dropped him."

Mike had obtained that information more than an hour ago. Drex had only used the ploy about escaping in the car trunk to see how Talia would react when she learned that Jasper truly had run out on her.

Looking stunned, she asked quietly, "May I see that video, please?" Menundez handed her his phone. Stoically she watched the brief segment of video, then passed the phone back. "Thank you."

Drex got up again, walked over to the sofa, and, this time, sat down beside her. Close beside her. Close enough to feel her trembling. "Talia, it's not too late for you to talk to us. I don't know what Jasper told you, or promised you, but it appears that he's abandoned you to take the fall."

"For what?"

"Elaine's murder."

"It hasn't been established that she was murdered. There could

have been an accident. He could be out there in the water, waiting
to be rescued."

"The man who swims miles every day?"

"He could be hurt."

"He could also be safely on shore and changing his appearance
as we speak. The next time you see him, you won't recognize him as
the man you share a bed with. You didn't recognize him as the man
at Marian's party, but that was him, going by the name of Daniel
Knolls. Marian was his most recent victim before Elaine, but there
were a lot of others before he met you. He doesn't deserve your loyalty. One last time, where is he?"

"I don't know." Her voice was so husky, it was barely audible.

He stayed as he was, peering deeply into her eyes. They were
watery, but she never looked away.

Sighing regret, Drex stood up and motioned for the other men
to follow him. They withdrew as far as the entryway. They were still
within Talia's sight, but Drex spoke so that she couldn't overhear.

He posed a question to the group at large. "What do you think?"

Locke said, "Since we first broke the news to her about the body
on the beach, she's seemed distraught and unaware of her husband's activities." He looked over at his partner.

Menundez shrugged. "I don't know. I flip-flop."

Drex looked at Gif. "What's your verdict?"

"We've laid a lot on her. I abstain."

Drex gave him a sour look. "Mike? Your take?"

Mike addressed the detectives. "How much do you know about
her? You know she's not hurting financially?"

"We haven't been given figures," Locke said, "but word is that
she's worth a bundle."

"Well, up to this point, me, Gif, and Drex have been agonizing.
Was she going to be this asshole's next victim? Or was she in on his
fleecing scheme?" He raised one beefy shoulder. "She's still breathing. Elaine Conner is in the morgue. Which is answer enough
for me."

"Victim or accomplice," Drex said, "we've reached a stalemate with her."

He looked into the living room, where Talia sat, hands clasped in her lap, rocking back and forth, staring vacantly into space. She looked frail and afraid. But he thought of how hot and cute she had looked when she'd paid him the surprise visit to the apartment. That could have been calculated. It had worked. He'd wanted what was inside those ragged jeans.

This sad victim could also be a pose that appealed to another instinct. He wanted to be her protector, to hold her, reassure her, comfort her over the tragic loss of her friend. His susceptibility made him mad at her, but absolutely furious with himself.

He turned back to the other men. "I'm thinking a night spent in the detention center might make her more forthcoming."

Chapter 23

———— ◆ ————

Drex's suggestion caused Locke to wince. "We don't have anything to hold her on."

"Seriously, Drex?" Gif said in a stage whisper. "Jail?"

"It would be a short night," he argued. "Only a few hours. Just long enough to convince her that we're not messing around."

"One major discrepancy is gnawing at me," Gif said. "The audio surveillance." He told the detectives about Jasper's finding the transmitter and moving it. Looking back to Drex, he said, "If he knew you were eavesdropping, why did he talk about Marian Harris at all?"

"Because he can't help himself from bragging about killing her and getting away with it." He turned to the two detectives. "I've been after him for a long time, but having spent time with him and learning the unspeakable circumstances of Marian Harris's murder, it's evident to me that he has the characteristic ego of a serial killer. He doesn't want to be caught, but his ego compels him to flaunt how smart he is."

With chagrin, he added, "Much as I hate to admit it, he outsmarted me this time. He said just enough. Stopped just shy of a

confession. He knew that a defense lawyer would shred the recording in court, even if it were admissible, which it isn't. Jasper used it
to get me running in the wrong direction, and now he's laughing
up his sleeve."

"I guess you're right," Gif said, and the rest nodded in grudging
agreement.

Drex asked the group, "So what's it to be?"

"If we mention jail, she'll lawyer up," Menundez said.

"Shit." Drex dragged his hand down his face. "You're right. In
which case, our involvement would become known. Sooner or later,
if not already, the FBI will get in on this investigation. There's a resident office here, right?"

Locke nodded.

"Good men and women, I'm sure, but I would rather continue
operating independently if at all possible."

"We could use their help, Drex," Gif said.

"True, but here's my thought. Jasper knows that I'm screwing
with him, but he doesn't know why. I could be a crook trying to
poach his territory. I could be a gigolo after his hot wife. I could be
a cop trying to nail his murderous ass. As long as he's unsure, we
have an edge."

"How's that?" Locke asked.

"Because I don't think he'll be able to stand not knowing. I don't
think he'll go too far afield without either dismissing me because
I'm no real threat, or dispatching me because I am. But if I'm at the
epicenter of a bureau investigation, he won't risk sticking around.
He'll leave me to the devil and vanish."

Mike said, "I predict he'll vanish if you put his wife in lockup.
As you told her, he'll turn his back and let her take the fall."

Drex scowled. "Thanks for those words of wisdom, Mike."

"I'm just saying—"

"And you're right," he snapped. "I just don't trust her not to take
off, and we can't strap on an ankle bracelet."

"Good God, no," Gif said.

Looking troubled, Locke said, "How about this? No lockup, but make it clear to her that she's not to go anywhere. Get Mount Pleasant PD to send over a policewoman to stay inside the house with her."

"With us right next door, that would be overkill," Drex said. "Besides, someone shows up in a uniform, she'll clam up even tighter until she can summon a lawyer. Gif, Mike, and I'll take turns standing watch till morning."

"She won't like it," Locke said.

"I don't give a fuck what she likes." Drex thought on it, then added, "But having a couple of patrolmen outside wouldn't be a bad idea. They'd be two extra sets of eyes for us and give her peace of mind."

"How will I explain the three of you to them?" Locke asked.

Drex shrugged. "Tell them the truth, but emphasize that we're undercover and that if they tell anybody we're here, even within their own department, we'll cut out their tongues."

"In other words, use subtlety and tact," Gif said.

"I'll get on it." Menundez took out his phone, but before placing the call, he read another text. "You were right, Easton. Local FBI is now assisting," he told the group, then continued reading. "Word got out how similar our case is to Marian Harris's. Tomorrow, an agent familiar with that investigation is flying in to talk to Mrs. Ford."

Mike groaned.

"Rudkowski?" Drex asked Menundez.

"How'd you know?"

Gif, Mike, and Drex exchanged looks of disgust. Drex said, "He's a blowhard. All mouth. No brains. The three of us took personal days, using phony excuses, just to follow this lead on Jasper Ford before Rudkowski could barge in and muck it up. Mike eluded him yesterday, made him look like an ass, which isn't difficult to do. He won't be happy to see us."

"Who has seniority?" Locke asked.

"He does. In years, not know-how. What time is he due?"

"Around ten. Wants to interview Mrs. Ford right away."

"They say where?" Mike asked.

Menundez shook his head.

"Find out and let us know the location," Drex said. "We'll have her there." Seeing the consternation registered by Mike and Gif, he said, "It was only a matter of time, guys. We're lucky he didn't run us to ground before now."

Talia had remained seated on the sofa. When the group of men broke up, the two detectives came over to her and expressed their condolences regarding Elaine. "I'm sorry we had to put you through that identification procedure," Locke said.

"You were only doing your job."

He thanked her for her cooperation then said, "We're still relying on your cooperation, Mrs. Ford. Please don't leave town."

"I have no intention of going anywhere until my husband is accounted for."

He nodded and gave her his business card. Menundez also passed her his.

Locke said, "Call either of us if you think of anything that could be useful to the investigation."

Although Drex's arguments were damning, she wasn't ready to concede that it had been Jasper onboard the yacht with Elaine. "Are they still searching for the man?"

"Yes, ma'am. We'll notify you if there's something to report."

"Please. No matter how bad the news may be."

He gave her a bland smile. "Try to get some rest. We'll see you tomorrow."

Menundez nodded a quasi goodbye, then followed Locke out, leaving her alone with Drex and his partners.

Gif said, "I'll take first shift."

Talia shot to her feet. "What do you mean first *shift*?" She walked over to Drex. "You're my jailers now?"

"Protectors."

She scoffed at that. "I feel less safe with you than with anybody."

"Then you'll be relieved to know that two police officers will be parked on the street. If you feel unsafe, you can signal them for help, and they'll come running."

"Am I allowed to go upstairs to my room? Alone."

Ignoring her snideness, he said, "Of course. In fact I recommend it. Tomorrow doesn't promise to be your best day. Get some sleep if you can. See you in the morning."

He turned away and walked from the room, the large man lumbering behind him. Gif passed her his business card. "That's my cell number. Text me if you need anything during the night."

She took the card but was still looking at the arched opening through which Drex had left. "Does he always wear that gun?" She'd seen the holster clipped to his belt at the small of his back.

"While on duty."

"Is he a good guy or bad guy?"

"Depends on who's asking."

She looked at Gif. "*I'm* asking. Can I trust him?"

"You can trust his commitment to catching Weston Graham."

"You mean Jasper?"

"To Drex he'll always be Weston Graham."

"Why?"

"You'll have to ask Drex." He backed away. "I'll be in the kitchen."

He left her. She turned toward the staircase, which, in her exhausted state, looked as daunting as Everest. Using the bannister for support, she climbed it slowly.

She got into the bath but sat beneath the shower and rested her head on her raised knees. From the detectives' arrival until now, she'd been required to function with some level of composure and reasonableness.

Now that she was alone, the reality of her circumstances crashed down on her. Elaine was dead. Jasper was a multifaceted mystery. And she? She was trapped in a mercurial situation that defied her attempts to grasp it.

As the water pounded over her, she wept. Hard. Copiously. In wracking sobs. When the water ran cool, she got out and pulled on an old pair of cotton pajamas that she hadn't worn since her marriage. The printed fabric, baggy bottoms, and loose-fitting top had been designed for comfort, not seduction.

She left the master bedroom in favor of the guest room across the hall. She got into bed and lay motionless in the darkness, staring at the ceiling.

Where was Jasper? If it was true that he hadn't gone to Atlanta, why hadn't she heard from him? If he had survived the accident that killed Elaine, was he struggling to hold on until he was rescued? Or was he dead? Why had he gone to Elaine tonight? Which of them had suggested that they take the yacht out? Why were they in the dinghy? What had he done*?*

She had cried her eyes dry over Elaine, but, as she was assailed by unthinkable possibilities about her husband, they stung with the need to cry more. Questions swirled through her mind like a swarm of fireflies, blinking on, blinking off before she could arrive at an answer.

When the door opened, she knew who it was before he spoke. "You didn't get your tea."

She pushed herself up onto her elbows. "What?"

"I noticed the tea bag in an otherwise empty mug on the counter. You burned your hand when you lifted the kettle off the stove and never got your chamomile."

She switched on the bedside lamp. He held the steaming mug in one hand. A fat accordion file was secured in the crook of his other arm. He came into the room without invitation, but she was too depleted to put up an argument. He set the mug on the nightstand and laid the file on the foot of the bed.

"What's that?"

"Some light reading in case you can't sleep. But beware. If you start on it, I doubt you'll sleep at all."

"Thanks for the tea."

To her annoyance, he drew an armchair over to the side of the bed and sat down.

"Don't feel like you have to stay."

He didn't bother to acknowledge the hint that he leave. He asked how her hand was.

"Hardly stings anymore."

"Good."

Still, he didn't go. He spread his knees and clasped his hands between them. Head down, addressing the floor, he said, "I'm sick about Elaine. You have every reason to doubt my sincerity, but I mean it, Talia. I had my eyes on Jasper. On you. But I should have seen this coming. Warned her. Something."

"She wouldn't have believed you, especially if you had warned her off Jasper."

"Probably not. But I should have made an attempt. A word of caution might not have saved her, but I wouldn't feel so rotten about failing her." He sat up straight and looked at her directly. "Were they having an affair?"

"You were listening. You heard me ask, you heard Jasper deny it."

"I heard you ask and heard him deny it. But were you asking for my benefit, or yours? Were you playing to the bug, or did you really nurse suspicions about the nature of their relationship?"

"It didn't know anything about that damn bug! And I don't know whether or not to believe Jasper's denial. What I *do* know is that I would rather have Elaine alive and cheating with my husband than lying dead in the morgue." Her voice cracked. "Can we postpone talking about this please? At least until morning?"

"All right," he said with surprising empathy. "For whatever it's worth, I liked her. A lot, in fact."

"She was impossible not to like. I'll miss her...her..."

"Verve and vivacity."

She gave him a weak smile. "Good words. Maybe you should have become a writer."

"In my next life."

After a long stretch of silence that grew awkward for her, he looked around with curiosity, taking in the bedroom, which she had left intentionally uncluttered for the convenience of overnight guests.

But no guests had ever used the room. Jasper wasn't keen on inviting friends to stay over for a weekend or holiday. He'd never given her a satisfactory reason why, always brushing off her protest with something like, "I prefer having you all to myself." She'd never pressed the issue, and instead had visited out-of-town friends when she went on business trips.

As she had visited Marian when she made the trip to Key West. On the heels of that thought, she said, "I don't remember meeting that man in the party picture. If it was Jasper, I didn't know it."

He hiked an eyebrow.

"I'm telling you the truth. I didn't pick him out that night as someone I'd like to get to know."

"Maybe. But I'm certain he picked you out that night."

"What do you mean?"

"We'll circle back to that. Tomorrow. There's a lot of ground to cover tomorrow."

Miffed by his reticence, she said, "All the more reason for us to say our good nights now."

"Why are you sleeping in here? Why not in the master?"

"I didn't want you spying on me. You can't see into this room from your living room window."

"Fair comeback."

His wry smile gave her a hint of the dimple, and that irritated her. "You don't know fair from foul, Drex. You accuse me of lying, when that's all you've been doing."

"And now you know why."

"In the line of duty, I suppose."

"Yes. What's your excuse?"

She let it drop, too tired to fight back.

He motioned down to the mug. "Drink your tea while it's hot."

"It hasn't steeped long enough."

"What was the doctor's appointment about?"

The swift change in topic was tactical, intended to take her off-guard, and it did. "That's personal."

"So's murder."

"Don't bully me. Haven't I had enough to deal with tonight?" She reached for the mug of tea, but her hand was unsteady.

He took the mug from her. "You're going to scald yourself again."

"As if you care."

"I do care, goddammit!"

"That's not what you told your buddies!" Perhaps she had a reserve of fight left in her, after all. "I have excellent hearing and, clear as a bell, I heard exactly the regard you give my feelings, my likes and dislikes."

He looked about to defend himself, but she raised her hand to stop him. "Never mind." With a weary sigh, she pressed her head deeper into the pillow and looked at the ceiling. "Leave me alone, Drex. If you want to know about my appointment with the gynecologist, I'm sure one of your friends will unearth the information for you, even if it breaches ethics."

"Mike's already offered. I told him no."

She shifted her gaze back to him.

"I would rather you volunteer it," he said.

She didn't see what harm could come from him knowing. If she confided this, maybe she would win a measure of trust, which she feared she might need in the days to come.

"I would like to have a child. Jasper asked for time to adjust to the idea of parenthood at his age. But I'm not getting any younger, either. Biological clock. All that. So I had eggs harvested to be frozen until he...until the time was right to have IVF."

Drex didn't move, speak, blink.

"When you approached me in the coffee shop, I had just received the disappointing news that some of the eggs—and the number wasn't abundant to begin with—weren't robust. Which means much lower odds for success, should we decide even to try fertilization."

She was looking down at her fingers as they pleated the edge of the counterpane. His hand came into her range of vision. He was holding out the cup of tea with the handle toward her. She took it from him, sipped. The tea had grown tepid, but she continued to take small drinks of it. It gave her something to do besides look at him.

Since becoming involved with Jasper, she hadn't been alone with many men, but certainly with no one who unsettled her as Drex did. He posed an indefinable, but very real, threat. She'd felt it from the moment she met him. Instinct had cautioned her to Keep Away, not out of fear that he would endanger her intentionally, but as though she were getting too close to open flame. The light source that attracts the moth isn't responsible for its innate heat, nor can it be blamed for the moth's compulsion to fly into it.

While confident in every other circumstance of her life, when near Drex, she felt unsure and self-conscious. He made her aware of everything about herself. As now. She could feel every inch of her skin inside the soft pajamas, everywhere the cotton conformed to her shape, every place it abraded her with no more friction than a warm breath.

She was even more keenly aware of him. He had taken off his necktie. His collar button was undone, his shirt cuffs rolled back, his shirttail pulled out. At best, his hair had been finger combed. The dishevelment only made him more attractive. She flashed back to the sight of his bare chest and abdomen and the dusting of hair that tapered to a strip that disappeared into his low-slung waistband.

This awareness of him created a pressure against her chest, which she wanted to shove away...but also to hug tightly.

"One more question and I'll let you go to sleep," he said. "Why didn't you kiss goodbye?"

Her head came up. She met his gaze. She exhaled through her mouth. "What?"

"You and Jasper didn't kiss goodbye at the airport, did you? And the reason you didn't go on that trip had nothing to do with an attack of queasiness. Jasper picked a fight on the way to the airport, didn't he?"

"No."

"Talia."

She returned the mug the nightstand, threw off the covers, and tried to get up. He placed his hands on her shoulders. She resisted, but his eyes held her more imperatively than his hands.

"Jasper picked a fight," he said quietly but with intensity. "You quarreled. You didn't kiss goodbye and wave him off, did you? That was a lie."

She glared at him, breathing hard, but she would die before admitting that he was right.

"What was the fight about? You wanted IVF, he didn't?"

She shook her head. "I hadn't even told him I was having the harvesting procedure. I still haven't."

"Why not?"

"An opportunity hasn't presented itself."

"Bullshit. You've had plenty of opportunities to tell him. You haven't because you're afraid he'll be relieved, and his relief will break your heart."

"I'm not talking about this with you. It's personal. Furthermore, it's irrelevant."

"Is it?"

"Yes."

"Okay, so what did you quarrel about on the way to the airport?"

"It was a spat, over *nothing*. Nothing important."

"It was important enough for you to nix a romantic getaway."

"I wish I had it to do over again."

"Well, you don't!"

The incisiveness of his tone shut her down. She turned her head aside. He took hold of her chin and brought it back around. "Who started the quarrel?"

She pushed his hand away from her face. "I don't remember."

"Yes you do."

"What difference does it make?"

"A monumental difference. It was Jasper, right?"

She remained stubbornly silent.

He was just as stubbornly persistent. "Right?"

"All right, yes! He got angry."

"At what?"

"At me."

"Over what?"

"Over you!"

He recoiled and dropped his hands from her shoulders, then sat very still. "What about me?"

She reached for the mug of tea, changed her mind, and let her hand fall back onto the bed. She wet her lips. "While we were driving to the airport, Jasper picked up where he had left off the night before. He went on and on about how you couldn't be trusted. I came to your defense. Erroneously, as it turns out." She paused and took a swift breath to stave off a sob. "I should have listened when Jasper said you weren't who you claimed to be. You've been lying all along. Everything has been a lie. You played us. Jasper. Elaine. Me."

She jerked the covers back up and patted them into place, getting them just the way she wanted before looking at him. "Either arrest me and haul me to jail, or get out of here and leave me alone."

She rolled onto her side and faced away from him.

She kept her eyes squeezed shut. For the longest time he didn't move, but eventually she felt the shift of air when he stood. He switched out the lamp. In the darkness, she sensed him bending over her.

He whispered, "The kiss wasn't a lie." His fingers threaded through her hair and rearranged it on the pillow.

Then he left the room, closing the door softly behind him.

Chapter 24

—◦—

In the kitchen, Gif was sitting at the table eating a bowl of cereal. "I helped myself," he said to Drex, crunching.

"I'm sure she won't mind."

"What did you help yourself to?"

Drex, who was on his way to the back door, stopped, turned, and gave his associate a berating look.

Unfazed, Gif spooned another bite into his mouth. "I go to the bathroom, come back. You're nowhere to be seen. I texted you. No reply. Texted Mike. He said you hadn't shown over there. You weren't in any of the rooms downstairs, so—"

"You've made your point."

Gif polished off the cereal in two slurping spoonfuls, then pushed the bowl aside. "Is that why you maneuvered this situation? You got the detectives out of here so you could tuck her in?"

"That's not why."

"'I'm thinking a night spent in the detention center,'" Gif quoted and gave an eye roll. "As if."

"Thanks for putting up the arguments against it. They made my suggestion more credible."

243

"I've worked with you long enough to know when you're manipulating someone."

"This way they went away thinking it had been their idea to leave her in our charge."

"Oh, I get why you did it. Just don't try to manipulate Mike and me."

"You're too smart for me."

"Question is," Gif said, and shot a glance toward the ceiling, "is she too smart for you?"

Drex backed up against the counter and crossed his arms. Staring at the toes of his shoes, he replied, "I don't know, Gif."

"Mike thinks she is."

"He's made that abundantly clear, but he mistrusts all women."

"And all men."

"And all men," Drex said around a chuckle. Then, back to serious, he said, "I took her a cup of tea, that's all. She looked weepy and vulnerable. I took advantage and tried to worm something out of her."

"To what avail?"

"Zip. She's either genuinely shaken by Elaine's death and mystified by Jasper's vanishing act—"

"Or?"

"Or she's a damn good con."

"She would have learned from the master."

"That's what I can't discount," he said, no joy in his tone. "So, tomorrow morning, you and Mike will deliver her to Rudkowski."

"Where will you be?"

"Making myself scarce."

Gif shook his head. "Drex—"

"Don't start, Gif. If I get anywhere near him, I had just as well cut off my dick now and deny him the pleasure."

Gif's silence indicated that he concurred. "What about Mike and me? What do you want us to do after dropping her off?"

"Has to be your decision, and each of you has to make up

his own mind, independent of the other and me. I can't ask you, nor do I expect you, to stick with me on this. You know the shit storm this is going to raise. Don't underestimate Rudkowski. We did before."

"This isn't like that."

"No, it's worse. Sleep on it. Sleep on it good." He pushed away from the counter and moved toward the door.

"Drex?"

He came back around.

"While Mike and I contemplate whether or not to stick with you or throw ourselves on Rudkowski's mercy, it would help if we knew how you were going to deal with her if it turns out that she's her husband's partner in crime."

The question was an insult. Damned if he was going to answer. "Mike will relieve you in a couple of hours."

The following morning when Talia entered the kitchen, the three men were gathered around the dining table, so deep into their discussion that she'd been there for a while before they noticed her.

When they did, they fell silent and stared, no doubt taken aback by her appearance. She'd pulled a robe on over her pajamas, but hadn't taken the time to groom herself before coming down.

Gif pushed back his chair and stood. "Good morning. Can I get you some coffee?"

The aroma of freshly ground beans was thick in the room, as was the yeasty scent of doughnuts. A box of them was in the center of the table. Gif nudged it in her general direction.

"Mike went out for them," he said. "Help yourself."

Disregarding Gif's offers, she walked straight to the table and thumped the thick file in front of Drex, nearly upsetting the cup of coffee in front of him. "I couldn't sleep, so I followed your suggestion to do some light reading."

He reached for the back of the chair that Gif had vacated and motioned her into it. "Get her some coffee, please, Gif."

She sat down in the proffered chair, not having taken her eyes off Drex since she'd come into the room. There were dark crescents under his eyes. He hadn't slept, either.

Gif set a cup of coffee within her reach, asked if she needed anything to go in it, and she shook her head. Drex took a chocolate-covered doughnut from the box, placed it on a paper napkin, and slid it over to her.

Ignoring the coffee and doughnut, she gestured at the bulging file. "You believe that Jasper had something to do with these women who went missing?"

He folded his forearms on the table, leaned upon them, and talked for half an hour virtually uninterrupted. Occasionally he asked Mike to verify a date or place. Gif elaborated when invited to. Otherwise, her attention stayed riveted on Drex, and his on her.

"He made himself fit into the lifestyle of an oil heiress in Tulsa. By those who knew Pixie, Herb Watkins was described as having short black hair, a goatee, and liked Native American art, for which Pixie had a passion.

"For Marian, he adopted frizzy hair, probably permed, because he knew it would be reminiscent of her hippie stage and that she would find that appealing.

"Then he spotted you at her party. Learned you were very well off. Saw you as a prospect. Through Marian and his own research, he learned everything he could about you. He probably followed you, Talia. Logged where you went, where you ate, what you drank, where you shopped.

"He deduced that, as a world traveler, you would be attracted to a sophisticated gentleman who would hand-deliver flowers even if it meant driving one hundred and fifty miles. Classy dresser. Gourmet cook. A man who appreciated expensive bourbon, all the finer things in life. Goodbye Daniel Knolls and his frizz, hello Jasper Ford with the cosmopolitan ponytail."

When he finished, she looked at each of the men in turn. Their expressions were grave. All too apparent was the depth of their conviction that Jasper was the man they sought. She didn't deny the allegations, didn't defend her husband, because to do so would be tantamount to accepting the horrific implication that he was indeed their culprit.

Drex asked if Marian had ever confided to her anything about her friend Daniel Knolls.

"No."

"Nothing?"

"She was a proud and private woman. If in fact the two of them had met online, she might not have wanted it known."

"That fits," Drex said. "He doesn't want a woman who would be open about it and, by talking about it, put someone on to him. If not for Mike's memory, he wouldn't have found the thread."

"Must have been a boon when you introduced him to Elaine Conner," Mike said. "He didn't have to work quite so hard."

She bowed her head and massaged her brow. "Before coming downstairs I called Detective Locke. They're certain that Elaine and the man onboard the yacht got into the dinghy together. His identity and fate are still unknown."

"I know his identity," Drex said. "It was Jasper, and he swam ashore. I'd bet my life on it."

She wanted not to believe it. She wanted to hear from Jasper that he had changed his travel plans, had gone somewhere else, and, after spending a remorseful and restless night, was on his way home for a reconciliation.

She wanted to rewind the clock to when they were newlyweds and she didn't harbor a single doubt as to his character. Or, if what these federal agents believed to be true, she would wish to revert to the life she'd had before meeting him.

But time couldn't be reversed. This was her here-and-now, and she must face this calamity head-on.

She looked at Drex. "Say that's true, that it was Jasper on the yacht with Elaine. How did he get to the marina? Locke told me that the taxi he took from the airport dropped him at a hotel out near there."

"He didn't check in," Mike said.

Locke had also told her that. "According to Locke, Jasper instructed the taxi driver to let him out a distance from the entry. I can't fathom why."

"To avoid security cameras," Drex said. "He had left a car either on the hotel property or somewhere in the vicinity. He drove it back to Isle of Palms, to a predetermined spot on one of the beaches. Remote. A place that would be dark as soon as the sun went down, but within reasonable walking distance of the marina.

"He went there on foot, chose his time, and managed to board the *Laney Belle* without being seen. If anyone had happened to see him, they would describe a man wearing an orange baseball cap, not a man with a gray ponytail."

"Locke said that Elaine's neighbors at the townhouse had seen her leaving it, alone, at around five-thirty. I suppose she and Jasper had a date to meet on the yacht."

"Not necessarily," Drex said. "He may have called her, told her that the two of you had squabbled, and asked if he could nurse his misery, or anger, on the yacht. Something like that."

"She would have dropped what she was doing to lend him a shoulder."

"He would have counted on that."

"But Elaine would have been disinclined to take the boat out in bad weather."

"Jasper appealed to her spirit of adventure. Or sweet-talked her. 'Please, Elaine. The ocean air will clear my head.' Once in open water, he convinced her that there was a malfunction of equipment, or an emergency onboard that spelled peril for them if they didn't abandon ship. Somehow he persuaded her to get into the dinghy."

"Without her cell phone? Or his?"

"Negligible," he said without forethought. "He would have

come up with something. The weather was interfering with cell service. They were out of service range. If she questioned him about the phones, providing a logical answer would have been easy. After he killed her—we won't know until after the autopsy by what method—he swam to shore."

"Clothed?"

"Possibly. But maybe after dispatching Elaine, he stripped down and used something to sink his clothes. He had a change waiting for him in the car on shore. I'd wager that those articles of clothing would be nothing like what the Jasper you know would wear."

Gif said, "He was probably long gone by the time Elaine Conner's body was discovered."

Talia wanted to clamp her hands over her ears and hear no more. But she had to hear it, had to deal with it, had to prepare herself for accepting the unimaginable. "Everything you've said is plausible. But every bit of it is assumption."

Drex conceded that with a nod.

"You could be completely wrong."

"Yes."

"Then how can you theorize with such certainty that it happened that way?"

"Because that's how I would have done it."

The statement caused her breath to catch. All along she had intuited that there was more to Drex Easton than he let on, that he was shrewder than he pretended to be, not nearly as laid-back, that there was a dark side camouflaged by the dimple.

But she had miscalculated just how much intensity he concealed with his superficial posturing. He was a man on a mission. One had to respect his commitment. But it also filled her with foreboding.

"How long have you been after him?"

"Long time."

"Since—?"

"Seems forever."

"And you won't stop until you catch him, will you?"

"Never doubt it."

She gestured at the file lying on the tabletop between them. "And if Jasper proves not to be him?"

"He is, Talia. He is."

His tone left no doubt of that, either.

Chapter 25

———❦———

"Talia, when you left the airport where did you go?" Drex asked.

"I came home."

"At ten o'clock."

"Was it?"

Mike said, "Ten oh-three to be exact."

"How can you be exact?" she asked.

"I was about to board a flight."

Drex took up the explanation. "Mike was in Atlanta, waiting on you and Jasper to show up at The Lotus."

"So he could spy on us?"

"Yes," he replied without apology. "But when we learned that you and Jasper never got on the flight, and that a body had washed ashore, plans changed quickly. Gif and I went straight to the marina. We got there in time to see Elaine's body taken away. From the marina, we came to the apartment and were on the phone with Mike giving him an update when you drove into your driveway."

"At ten oh-three," the large man repeated.

She ignored him. "When I got home, there weren't any lights on

251

inside the garage apartment. But then, if you were spying on me, there wouldn't have been, would there?"

"No. Spying is easier with the lights off."

"Don't make fun of me."

"I'm not. None of this is fun or funny, Talia. Do you want to hear the rest?"

Tamping down her humiliation and anger, she bobbed her head.

"Gif and I were debating what to do about you when Locke and Menundez showed up. The transmitter was too far away to pick up what they were saying until you moved into the kitchen. For all we knew, they'd come to arrest you. We know now they asked you to make an ID."

"If you already know all that, why are you bringing it up?"

"The time gap. Surveillance cameras show you leaving the airport at four forty-seven."

"Eight," Mike said.

Drex gave him a frown but corrected himself. "Four forty-eight. Talia, where were you between then and ten o'clock?"

"Does it matter?"

"It'll matter to Locke, Menundez, and every other investigator on this case, county, state, and federal, including our own Bill Rudkowski."

Mike said, "It'll matter a lot if, during that five hours, you hooked back up with your husband, say on the beach, where you were flashing a light so he would know where to make landfall after ensuring that Elaine Conner was no longer breathing."

Talia was developing a tremendous dislike for this man, and hoped that the drop-dead look she gave him conveyed as much. She went back Drex. "From the airport I drove downtown."

"And did what?"

"Walked around."

"Such a nice night for a stroll," Mike said. "In the drizzle and rain and all."

"I was unmindful of the weather."

None of the men took issue, but they were regarding her with patent doubt.

"Where did you walk?" Drex asked.

"Along Bay Street. I went into a restaurant and lingered."

"Lingered, why?"

"There was no rush to get home. I believed Jasper had gone to Atlanta."

The men looked at one another and seemed to conclude that her answer was at least credible, if not truthful.

"Where did you park downtown?" Gif asked.

"I got lucky and found an empty parallel spot on one of the side streets."

"Fucking lucky, I'd say," Mike muttered.

Her temper snapped. "I've had it with you and your snide editorials. If you want to accuse me of lying, do it. If not, stop with the mumbling, all right?"

Drex patted the air in a *calm down* gesture and suggested that Mike dispense with his remarks unless they were pertinent. He asked Talia for the name of the restaurant. She told him.

"The waiter will remember me. I had two glasses of wine and ordered dinner. But I didn't have an appetite and never touched the plate. The waiter noticed and asked if the food wasn't to my liking. He offered to bring me something else. I declined, tipped him well, and left."

"Did you pay with a credit card?"

"Yes."

Drex turned to Gif. "Relay all that to Locke. Their guys can do the fact-checking."

Gif left the room to make the call. Drex glanced at the clock. "Menundez texted that Rudkowski is going to interview you downtown at police headquarters." He looked her over, taking in her dishabille. "You'll need to be ready in twenty minutes or so in order for Mike and Gif to get you there by ten o'clock." He pushed back his chair and stood.

"Aren't you coming with us?"

"No."

"Why?"

"I've got other things to do."

She stood up. "Such as?"

"Such as going after your husband without being hamstrung by red tape. Good luck."

"Wait. What's going to happen with this Rudkowski?"

He shrugged. "I don't know."

"Guess," she said tartly.

"Well, if I were to guess, he'll spend most of today taking turns grilling you hard, then leaving you alone for long stretches of time to search your conscience, to ruminate on and perhaps reassess your position. Don't say a word unless a lawyer is with you."

"You're worried about my welfare?"

"No, I'm worried about testimony being tossed out because it was obtained without counsel present. Rudkowski may claim you as the feds' own, but if Locke is also allowed to interrogate you, he'll be the good cop. Menundez is young and yet to prove himself, so you can probably count on him to be tougher. But you probably won't see anyone familiar. Except your lawyer. I hope you have a good one."

"What about them?" She indicated Mike, who was inspecting what was left of the doughnut selection, and Gif, who'd just returned and announced that Rudkowski's plane had landed.

In answer to her question, Drex said, "The three of us are out of Rudkowski's favor and unsure what form his payback will take. Could be a slap on the wrist, or much harsher discipline. Mike and Gif have volunteered to face his wrath and that of the bureau, giving me a head start tracking down your lawfully wedded husband."

"Who could be dead!"

"He isn't."

"You don't know that."

"Yes, I do. Furthermore, so do you, Talia."

"I know no such thing."

"Come on. You don't believe for a second that he's foundering out there in the ocean, praying for rescue. Know how we know? Tell her, Gif."

The other man said, "If you thought that your husband was in a struggle to survive a watery grave, you would be hysterical."

Drex rounded the table and bore down on her so that she had to grab hold of the back of her chair to maintain her balance. "Hysterical. As in out of your mind. Frantic. You'd be tearing at your hair and raising hell with the Coast Guard, with every damn body, to *find* him, *save* my husband." He leaned in closer, and added softly, "You haven't."

She angled away from him, but he only made a countermove to keep his face within inches of hers. "When you were told there was a man at the helm of Elaine's boat, and I was ruled out, it was no mystery to you who it was. Which leaves Mike, Gif, and me, and all the other cops working this case, with only two possible conclusions.

"One, you knew who the man was all along because you two conspired to kill Elaine. Or," he said, slapping his palm against the file lying on the table, "you believe Jasper Ford is the latest incarnation of our man. You believe he harmed these eight women. Now nine. He befriended them, robbed them, killed them, and disposed of them."

She hiccupped a sob. "I don't want to believe it."

"But you do, don't you?"

Drex was stirring her long-held, secret fear that she didn't really know her husband. Ambiguities and uncertainties, which she had staved off, rationalized, chalked up to an illicit affair, and even taken blame for, were now closing in on her. They were so cruel and frightening, she tried to keep them at bay. "What evidence do you have against him?"

"Not a frigging bit."

"Then—"

"But answer me this. Do you honestly believe they're going to find Jasper or his body? In a dire emergency, would your water-savvy husband have left a vessel as tricked out as that yacht? Even if their phones weren't working, even if all fail-safe systems *had* failed, he wouldn't have swapped that yacht for a damn dinghy.

"Do you actually expect him to come staggering through that door battered and bruised, embrace you, and give you an account of a harrowing experience? No. You don't. You strike none of us as a lady who's waiting in desperation for her missing and feared-dead husband to return."

He jabbed the space between them with his index finger. "He took Elaine on that excursion with the intention of killing her. And he did. Deny it till hell freezes, but you know it, and so do we."

Pressured by her own doubt, feeling the weight of their vile allegations, she hugged her elbows and sank into the chair.

———

Her failure to respond immediately, along with her self-protective body language, spoke volumes to Drex. Now was the time to apply the thumbscrews. He said to Gif, "Call the PD. Stall them."

"How?"

"Shit, I don't know. Try to get Locke. He's tenderhearted. Tell him she's not feeling well, that we can't get her out of the bathroom, something. Ask him to pacify Rudkowski. Say that we'll have her there soon. Ish. An hour at the outside."

"Will it be an hour at the outside?"

"Remains to be seen." Gif left the kitchen to do as instructed. Drex motioned at the box of doughnuts and said to Mike, "Take those to the officers posted outside."

"I already took them a box of their own when I brought these."

"Then ask them if they need a bathroom break. Water. Sodas. Tell them Mrs. Ford is currently indisposed, but we're working on her."

"Rudkowski won't hold out forever."

"Neither will Mrs. Ford if she knows what's good for her."

That roused her. She straightened her hunched shoulders and looked up at him. He said, "They're champing at the bit to interrogate you. And make no mistake, that's what today will be. One long, grueling interrogation. I suggest you be thinking of what you're going to say."

"I need time to—"

"You've had time, Talia. I gave you time last night. You're out of time."

"Allow me to absorb all this. Please."

Drex considered, then said to Mike, "Buy me a few minutes with those guys outside."

Mike limited his opinion to a harrumph and a scowl then left through the door connecting to the garage. They heard the automated door going up. Drex resumed his seat at the table. He stared at her until she squirmed and asked, "What?"

"You're using up your minutes."

She raised her hands in a gesture of helplessness. "It's all so much." She looked at the file. "So horrendous. I don't know where to start."

He got up from his chair and dragged it over near to hers. He straddled it backward so they were facing each other. He met her gaze directly and waited. Waited longer. Then said, "This will come as no surprise. I've wanted you since I first laid eyes on you."

Her lips separated, but she didn't say anything.

"When we were alone on the deck of Elaine's yacht, I was staring at you, all right. Engaging in polite conversation, but in my mind all your layers of white clothing were dissolving, and I was seeing you naked and on your back in an unmade bed. During your surprise visit to the garage apartment, I honestly don't know how I kept my hands off you. Touching your face was all I allowed myself, and it was torture. I still taste that kiss, your mouth. I want to taste you all over. I want to—"

He broke off, dropped his head forward, and finished in a rough voice. "I want to do it all." Then he raised his head, and, in a soft but insistent voice, said, "But if you fucking lie to me now, I'll see to it that you go to prison for a long, long time."

She swallowed. Faintly, she said, "Everything I've told you is the truth. I swear it. How Jasper—that's the only name I've known him by. How we met, all of it, true, Drex. Elaine was my friend. Marian. How you could think that I would…"

She had to swallow again, then recovered and faced him with a small measure of defiance. "I have fibbed to you about inconsequential things. But I am not a criminal. I never conspired to hurt anyone."

"Okay. Okay. That still leaves us with this. The man you're married to is a serial killer. I've been after him for years. I've crawled inside his twisted brain, put myself in his place, and it's a hellish, diabolical place to be. I loathe it. I detest it. I don't want to live the rest of my life inside his fucked-up head.

"Until I moved next door and met him face-to-face, he was a phantom. Vapor. No more tangible than fog and just as impossible to capture. I feared I never would. But now I know he's human."

He raised his hand and squeezed it into a fist. "He's flesh and blood. He eats and drinks. He puts on his pants one leg at a time. He sweats. He's real, and he lives among us. I can touch him, and I'm going to catch him." He paused and inhaled deeply. "Where could he be, Talia?"

"I don't know. I swear I don't."

"Hometown?"

"He claimed none. He told me his parents were itinerant workers."

"Where?"

"I got the impression of southern California. But I don't know if he told me that, or if that was conjecture on my part."

"His parents' names?"

"He wouldn't talk about them. He said he'd risen above his

roots, and didn't want to revisit the past. Ever. And, anyway, they were both deceased."

"No family?"

"None."

"Old friends?"

"No."

"Convenient." He had expected as much. "Did he mention past relationships, former marriages?"

"He was married once, a long time ago. She died."

"She didn't die. He killed her. Her name was Lyndsay Cummings."

Talia glanced at the file. "She was the first of the eight?"

"First that we know of." He wiped his damp upper lip with the side of his index finger. "Did he ever talk about her and their marriage?"

"He said the memories were too painful."

"No doubt."

She rested her hand on top of the file, staring at it. "No bodies were ever discovered, Drex."

"Which doesn't mean they weren't killed. What it does mean is that we haven't had forensic evidence that could connect the disappearance of one woman to another, and then to another, establishing a pattern that would ultimately point us to an individual. Not until Marian Harris, that is."

She pressed her fingertips to her lips. "He couldn't have done that."

He didn't argue with her, but she gained some breathing room when Gif returned. "A message from Rudkowski. He says we either deliver the material witness within half an hour or he's coming here after her, and woe be to us."

"Shit!"

"Locke's patting his hand, but you know Rudkowski. Where's Mike?"

"Hand-patting the patrolmen outside."

"How long are you willing to wait, Drex?"

"Five more minutes."

Gif divided a look between him and Talia, took in the seating arrangement, and must have concluded that Drex was putting on the full court press. He said, "I'll check to see if there's anything I can do to further Mike's cause." He left by way of the garage door.

"You heard," Drex said. "You've got five. So think and talk fast. What did Jasper bring into the marriage?"

"Sorry?"

"Possessions, Talia."

"I don't understand what you're asking."

"The guys I profile are sociopaths, and they share characteristics. No conscience. Above the rules. They're smug and have overblown egos."

"I overheard you describing that to the detectives last night."

He nodded. "They're also compulsive collectors."

"Collectors?"

"They take souvenirs."

He watched her face as she reasoned out what he was saying. Her gaze dropped to the file. "What were they missing?"

"We don't know, and that's been damn frustrating. None of the women had the same body type, no common feature like blue eyes, crooked teeth, long hair, short hair, a beauty mark. They were physically different, and lived different lifestyles. No common hobby.

"Nothing alike except healthy bank accounts that were emptied within days of their disappearances. He could collect safe deposit box keys, ballpoint pens, locks of hair, fingernails. We don't know. But I would bet my career that there's something he takes from them. And saves. And takes out on occasion and fondles. Possibly masturbates."

She looked nauseated at the thought.

"Does he have a safe, sealed packing box, tool box, tackle box, anything that he asked you not to open?"

She was shaking her head before he finished. "He told me he had sold everything when he moved to Savannah."

"From Florida."

"He said Minnesota. He told me he no longer needed heavy clothing and cold weather gear, so he had disposed of everything."

"A logical lie. But didn't he have any personal items? Photographs? Memorabilia? Stamp collection? Coins? A cigar box of postcards?"

"Nothing, Drex."

He looked at his wristwatch. "*Think*, Talia."

"He had his car, his clothes, some cookbooks."

He shot to his feet. "Where are they?"

"They're *cookbooks*."

"Where are they?"

But by the time he had repeated the question, he had remembered the shelf above the stove. He went over to it and picked one of the books at random. It was a two-year-old edition with a glossy cover. The spine was unbent. The pages were so new and unused, some stuck together. He remarked on its newness.

"When we met, he hadn't been a foodie for long," she said. "It was a hobby he began after his retirement."

"Books are good hiding places. I'll have Gif tear into them." She seemed on the verge of protesting, and he pounced on that.

"Do you *want* him caught, Talia?"

The file held her interest for a ponderous moment, then she looked up at him. "If he did what you allege, then, yes, of course. Those women deserve justice."

He said nothing, just looked at her.

"You don't believe I'm sincere?"

"You married him, Talia, and shared all that the state of matrimony implies. I think you'll have a difficult time convincing Rudkowski, et al., that you never felt something was off about your husband."

"I felt he kept secrets," she said softly and with reluctance. "More lately than at first. I attributed it to an affair."

"Had you ever accused him prior to night before last?"

"No."

"You showed your hand with that accusation. You're lucky he went after Elaine first. When I came tearing down here to South Carolina, I thought I was rushing in to save *you*. You're loaded. All of us figured you were next. But you weren't."

"You sound disappointed."

"No, I just want you to understand what that means to you. If the authorities don't find his body, and they won't, they'll keep their eye on you. They may not call you a suspect, but there'll always be that shadow of doubt as to what you knew or didn't know, what your level of participation was, if you had any compliance whatsoever."

"I didn't!"

"Okay."

"You don't believe me," she exclaimed. "What do I have to do to prove I'm innocent?"

"Die."

She slumped against the back of her chair and looked at him with incredulity over his bluntness.

He said, "If you turn up dead, the authorities will reason that he killed you to shut you up, whether or not you were culpable. If you go on living, untouched, there'll forever be that question mark beside your name."

She looked around her, taking in various perspectives of the room as though it had become alien territory. When she came back to him, she said, "I realized this last night, although I didn't want to acknowledge it."

"Realized what?"

"That no matter how this ends, I'll never regain the life I lived before. Will I?" He didn't say anything, but she got the message. She nodded, then straightened her spine and asked, "Will they hold me in jail?"

"I don't know."

"If it were up to you?"

"It won't be. Not entirely."

"If it were. Entirely."

"I would rather have your full cooperation with the investigation. I'd want your input, your gut instinct, your recollections, your unconditional help in catching him."

"What if I offered my unconditional help?"

"That would go a long way with them."

She looked down at her lap in which her hands rested. "You're good at this, aren't you?"

"At what?"

"Manipulation. Bending people to your will."

"Yes. I'm very good at it. But I'm not trying to manipulate you. I'm telling you like it is."

"Why should I trust that that's true?"

He couldn't come up with an answer. "The clock is ticking, Talia."

She looked at him with appeal. "Are you a good guy?"

"I could tell you I am. I could cross my heart and hope to die. Swear to my goodness on a stack of Bibles. But you'd be crazy to take my word for it."

"Who was Weston Graham to you?"

The question took him aback, but he answered without pause. "Not was, *is*."

"Who is he to you?"

"The man who killed my mother. Lyndsay Cummings." She registered wordless shock. He let it sink in before adding, "That's why I want him, Talia. I want to see him burn. And whether that makes me a good guy or a bad one, I really don't give a shit."

He was aware of the seconds passing as she stared into his eyes. Finally she said, "I offer my unconditional help."

He pushed out of the chair. "I'm sure they'll be glad to have it."

"I don't offer it to them. I offer it to you."

Mike, Gif, and the two young cops trooped single file up the exterior stairs to the apartment. The patrolmen took turns using the bathroom, then Mike and Gif doled out bottles of water from the refrigerator. They raided the cabinet and found an unopened box of Nutter Butters, which the cops took with thanks. The four trooped single file down the staircase. Mike and Gif waved the officers back to their squad car and started toward the house.

As they crossed the lawn, Gif admired the rear perspective of the Ford's house. "Pretty place, isn't it? Makes me question my life choices."

"Not me. All this grass to mow? No thanks."

"Do you have one aesthetic inclination, Mike?"

He thought on it. "I like my steak tartare garnished with fresh parsley."

Gif laughed, but as they got closer to the screened porch, he lowered his voice and asked, "What do you think they're talking about?"

"He's trying to squeeze as much information out of her as he can before she lawyers up."

"You think she's dirty, don't you?"

"Dirty or not, she's dangerous."

"Dangerous how?"

"To Drex," Mike grumbled. "His head is under her skirt. That makes a man stupid."

"About that, I think we should back off."

Mike stopped and turned to him. "Back off?"

"Stop nagging him about it."

"Let him screw her and pretend not to notice?"

"That's right, Mike. It's not our business."

"Since when?"

"Since he hasn't screwed her already. When have you known him not to when he wanted to?"

Reading between the lines of what Gif had said, Mike grunted a sound to express his contempt for the frailties of human beings since the fall of Adam, then continued on without further comment.

They went in through the back porch. The kitchen was empty. The two looked at each other. Gif called, "Drex?"

The name echoed throughout the house. Mike elbowed past Gif and went as fast as his waddle allowed into the dining room and then beyond into the living area. "Check upstairs."

Gif mounted the staircase in a run. He checked all the rooms—empty rooms—before coming back down and shaking his head at Mike, who was returning from an inspection of all the first floor rooms. "Damn!" he said, wheezing. "It's a friggin' curse, being right all the time."

Gif stepped past him. "What's this?"

On the dining table was a cookbook with a note in Drex's handwriting lying on top of it. Gif read it aloud. "Tear apart all the cookbooks. Hiding place for souvenirs?"

In addition to the cookbook was a manila envelope with a brass clasp. Drex had written on the envelope: *Special Agent Rudkowski, congratulations. You're getting your heart's desire.*

Mike and Gif looked at each other with dread. Gif unfastened the clasp and shook out the contents of the envelope.

It was the wallet containing Drex's badge and ID.

A sheet of notepaper drifted out along with it. On it was written: *P.S. I'm keeping my gun and the girl.*

Chapter 26

———— ⊰◦⊱ ————

"His *resignation*?" Locke exclaimed.

Gif and Mike regretted having to lay this on the detective, who seemed like a conscientious cop and overall nice guy. They had anticipated the disbelief he expressed. It matched their own.

Gif said, "There's more." He then read aloud the last line of Drex's note.

"You're telling me he left and took Mrs. Ford with him?"

"Looks like."

"The two of them just up and left?"

"Looks like."

"Where would they have gone?"

"Your guess is as good as ours," Gif said. "Last we saw of them, he was trying to wear her down, and I think making progress. Maybe he thought if he got her alone——"

"He gave up his authority to do that when he surrendered his badge. Which car did they take?"

"They didn't. All four are still here. Hers, her husband's, Drex's, and mine."

"They left on foot?"

"Unless they sprouted wings."

"How in hell did they manage it? *Why?*"

"I'm sure there's a logical explanation."

"There is," Locke said, speaking with more vexation than they'd heard from him before. "Easton is either harboring a material witness who requested him to do so or he's kidnaped her, and I lean toward the latter."

"Drex wouldn't force or coerce her to go with him. I'm certain of that." Gif looked over at Mike, who gave him a telling look back, and Gif amended his statement. "Fairly certain."

Locke said, "Last night that woman was afraid of him."

"She was apprehensive of all of us, not just Drex." Gif didn't share that Drex had spent a good half hour in a bedroom alone with her. "But he has impressed upon her that it's her missing husband she should be scared of."

Locke heaved a sigh. "On that, I'm afraid Easton is right. Following the autopsy, the coroner ruled Elaine Conner's death a homicide. She didn't drown; she was choked to death."

Gif received the news without comment. Mike muttered a string of obscenities. Neither took pleasure in having foretold her fate.

Locke was saying, "When your call came in, I had my phone in my hand about to call Easton with this update. We don't know that the perp was Jasper Ford—"

"We do."

"The search-and-rescue for him is still on."

"You won't find him."

"Well, right now I need to locate his wife," Locke said with asperity. "She is key to this investigation. Pass this latest info along to Easton. He's bound to come to his senses and bring her back before anyone else notices that they're gone."

"We've called his phone a dozen times," Gif said. "He isn't answering."

"Do you have Mrs. Ford's number? If not, I do. I'll call her."

"Won't do you any good. We've tried it. Out of service."

Locke said, "He would've removed the battery so it can't be used to lead us to her."

"In all probability."

"That's not something an innocent person does, Agent Lewis."

"An innocent person would if they were frightened enough of a guilty person. If we can't track her phone, neither can Ford. To us, to Drex, he isn't *missing*. He's *at large*. The difference in terminology is significant."

"It hasn't been established that he was the man on the yacht. "

"Who else could it have been?"

"Anybody."

"You don't believe that. Fingerprints?"

"We lifted them from the wheel. But even if we match them to Ford's, he had steered the boat many times. The circuit solicitor would tell us to try again."

"Who?" Gif asked.

"DA. That's what they call them in South Carolina," Mike explained. He'd been listening on speaker, but until now hadn't spoken. "Locke, if you need something on Ford to take to the prosecutor, get a warrant to search this house, inside out."

"We tried," Locke said. "Judge declined to issue one. Ford hasn't been positively identified as the man on the yacht. Mrs. Ford's alibi checks out. The waiter remembers her just like she said. There's no probable cause. But maybe, now that she's made herself scarce, I'll go back to him. Press it."

Gif could tell that Locke was beginning to feel the pressure of what this turnabout with Talia meant to him. He would get a lot of departmental backlash for losing a material witness and possible suspect.

In addition to that, Rudkowski was going to blow a gasket. He would require appeasement, and the only appeasement that would satisfy him would be to have Drex's head served on a platter.

Above all, Locke was confounded by what Drex had done, which to the detective would seem outlandish. It didn't fit his code of professional conduct or conform to the rules of law enforcement.

Gif took pity. "Detective, listen. Drex isn't playing a dirty trick on you, although it may feel like that. I guarantee that somehow he'll make it up to you. Menundez, too. Believe me, he wouldn't have surrendered his badge unless he was convinced that it was the best, maybe only, course of action left to him. Something compelled him to whisk Talia out of here, or he wouldn't have done it.

"Don't make the mistake of discrediting him, or questioning his commitment to capturing the serial criminal we acquainted you with last night. Drex has never been this close to getting him, and he won't squander the chance. He'll go for broke. He'll go to any lengths, even if it means his own downfall."

With reluctance, and what sounded like grudging respect, the detective said, "I sensed all that. The guy's passionate. But you've worked with him for a long time. I just met him. Has he ever done anything this out of line before?"

Gif looked over at Mike, who gave a shrug that said Locke would hear of Drex's shenanigans sooner or later. Gif said, "I'm sure Agent Rudkowski will be all too glad to fill you in."

"I'll relay this latest news to him on our way there."

Gif started. "You're coming here?"

"Rudkowski had already made up his mind not to wait on Easton to deliver Mrs. Ford. He was coming to the house to question her. After I break this news to him—"

"Duck when you tell him," Mike said.

"—he'll want to begin the search for her where she was last seen. How will he react to Easton's resignation?"

"With glee. And he'll want to kill him for pulling this stunt. I'm glad it's you, not me, who has to tell him. Good luck. We'll see you when you get here." Gif clicked off.

"Poor guy."

Mike had his back to the room, looking out the front window.

In a low rumble, and a rare show of empathy, he said, "Chalk up another victim to this son of a bitch."

"Number nine."

"Shit, Gif."

He sighed. "Yeah. And we have no way of knowing how many we've missed."

"I don't want to think about it."

Gif said, "I'll text Drex about the coroner's ruling. It won't come as a shock. He already knew." He sent the text to the last cell number he had for Drex, not knowing if that phone was still in existence.

The news about Elaine Conner had cast a pall over him and Mike. They maintained a lengthy silence, then Mike snorted with his customary disdain. "Those two uniforms are searching the bushes across the street." They had asked the two young officers who'd been guarding the house to take a look around the immediate neighborhood for a sign of Drex and Talia. "Do they really think they're going to find them in the thicket?"

It was a rhetorical question, which Gif didn't bother answering. Mike turned away from the window and posed another. "How the hell did they disappear in such a short amount of time on foot? Even for Drex, it was slick as owl shit."

"She knows the neighborhood, and you can bet he has committed it to memory in the time he's been here. He got to my motel the other night by jogging to a local mini-mart and calling Uber. I dropped him back there the next morning."

"Should we drive over, check it out?"

"He wouldn't use the same location, and I doubt he'd use the same method."

"I don't think so, either," Mike said. "I only suggested it because I've got nothing else."

Gif did some rough calculation in his head. "When I came through the kitchen, they were nose-to-nose in conversation."

"Was she still in her pajamas?"

"Yes, but they had a good ten, twelve minutes after I joined you," Gif said.

"Enough time for them to make their getaway while we were waiting for peeing cops and fetching Nutter Butters. Jesus," Mike said, ridiculing his own gullibility. "How did he talk you into leaving him alone with her?"

"He didn't. I volunteered to check on you."

"You only thought you volunteered," Mike said. "You were manipulated."

Gif shot him a grim smile. "And here just last night, he told me that we were too smart for him."

"Not this morning, we weren't."

"What worries me?" Gif said, idly scratching his frowning forehead. "This time he might have been too smart for his own good."

"Worries me, too," Mike said. "I told you the woman was a hazard to Drex's thinking. He's off to God knows where with her, which, mark my words, will lead to nothing good. Not only that, he's left us to Rudkowski."

Gif's gaze shifted to the cookbook still on the dining table. "He also left us with an assignment."

———————

The envelope addressed to Rudkowski was waiting for him on the dining table. He fingered the mocking note from Drex as he glared at the two young police officers who'd served as guards the night before.

"Where are they?"

His bellow made one of the officers jump. "We don't know, sir. We've been combing the neighborhood. A lady down the street knows Mrs. Ford, but she—"

"Not them," Rudkowski barked. "Mallory and Lewis."

"Oh. They left. About—" The officer consulted his partner, who said, "Twenty minutes ago. About."

Rudkowski looked over at Locke. "You told them we were on our way?"

"Lewis said they would see us when we got here."

Rudkowski walked a tight circle, holding onto his temper by a thread. When he came back around to the young policemen, he asked, "Did they happen to say where they were going?"

"To meet you."

"What car did they leave in?"

"Must've been Lewis's. He was driving."

"Did you happen to get a license plate number?"

"No, sir, b-but why would we?"

Menundez stepped forward. "Signals got mixed is all."

Rudkowski's blood pressure spiked. "After everything I told you on the drive here about this trio, you think mixed signals is the reason Mallory and Lewis have also flown the coop?"

Locke came to his younger partner's defense. "They may have heard from Easton and had to leave in a hurry. Before we jump to conclusions, why don't you call them?"

Rudkowski snapped his fingers. "Good idea. Why don't *you*?"

Locke bobbed his head at Menundez. As the younger detective moved away to follow the directive, he shot Rudkowski a look of contempt, which Rudkowski ignored. "You two," he said to the uniformed officers, "get back to what you were doing, which was precious little."

"Do you want us to call our department or the FBI, get more officers—"

"No," Rudkowski said. "For the time being, I want to keep this under wraps."

He didn't want to appear more of a buffoon than he already did. He'd jumped the chain and placed a call to the SAC of the field office in Columbia, asking him to call him back on a matter of some urgency. He didn't know whether to look forward to speaking with him and alerting him to Easton's latest chicanery or to fear the flak he himself would catch for being outwitted again.

Left alone now with Locke, he said, "Show me around."

"We don't have a warrant yet."

"We have a material witness who has skipped out to avoid being questioned."

"That hasn't been ascertained."

"She ran off dressed in pajamas. Wouldn't you say that indicates flight?"

"Or coercion," Locke said.

"Which Easton is more than capable of, and, ethically, he's not above it. But there were four other men on this property. If he was forcing her, why didn't she scream bloody murder? There's no sign of a tussle. No, detective, she left of her own volition. Now show me around."

They went upstairs. From the master bedroom window, Locke pointed out the garage apartment. "There's a window behind that oak. Easton had a good vantage point. He could surveil them without being seen."

Rudkowski snorted. "If you call window-peeping and illegal bugging surveillance."

Locke turned tight-jawed but didn't comment.

They walked through the rooms on both floors, finding nothing of particular interest. They concluded the tour in a small room behind the main staircase. "Mrs. Ford's study," Locke explained. "When she came to the door for us last night, she left her shoes in here. I came to get them for her."

"Do you extend that kind of courtesy to every murder suspect?"

"We didn't know then that it was a murder. She wasn't a suspect."

"Well, it was, and now she is."

Menundez joined them. "I called the numbers I have for Mallory and Lewis. They go to voice mail."

"Um-huh. You still think signals got mixed?" Rudkowski huffed a sardonic laugh. "Apparently you haven't absorbed what I've told you. Easton is Peter Pan. Lewis and Mallory are the lost boys. They weren't always. They were good agents. Lewis has always been a nerd, but Mallory actually did field work before he turned to blubber.

"Then the two started working with Easton. He recruited them with flattery, told them he needed men with their individual and unique skills. He's corrupted them. They have no families, no social life, no nothing. Their world revolves around him. They would walk through fire for him. They *have*."

"Because they believe in what he's doing," Menundez said. "It seemed to me that they're every bit as committed as Easton."

The young detective's admiration of the three inflamed Rudkowski. "Committed to breaking rules, yes."

"Sir, regardless of their methods, the perp is real. They've gleaned a lot of—"

"Save it, Menundez," Rudkowski snapped. "For years Easton's been piecing together a scenario and molding it to fit an imaginary bogeyman." He spread his arms at his sides. "He doesn't even have the bodies to prove the women are dead."

In contrast to his shout, Locke's voice was low "The Harris woman in Key West is dead. You can't deny the parallels between her case and Elaine Conner."

"That photo, right? With the fuzzy-haired guy in the background? And in the foreground—as has recently been brought to my attention—Talia Shafer Ford. We can't confirm that the man in the picture is Jasper, but we can sure as hell tell it's her. Two friends of hers, both rich, both dead.

"I'm not saying that the Marian Harris case and this one aren't connected. I'm saying these two aren't connected to any of Easton's others. What's the common denominator here, fellas?" He snapped his fingers several times as though to hurry them to provide an answer.

"Talia Shafer. Maybe her old man drowned after killing the Conner woman. Maybe a shark got him. Or maybe he escaped and left her holding the bag. However it happened, she was in on it."

"I'm not convinced of that, Agent Rudkowski," Locke said.

"Well, if we get a search warrant for this house, maybe we'll dig up something that will convince you. Twist that judge's arm. Send those rookies outside home. They're useless. Easton is long gone."

"His car is still here."

"He's long gone," he repeated. "Even after everything I've told you, it still hasn't sunk in, has it? You've never come up against somebody like him, and, in your career, you probably never will again."

He divided a look between them, but ended on Menundez. "Keep in mind that his preoccupation is psychopaths." He stabbed his temple with the tip of his index finger. "He thinks like they do. He's cunning, unprincipled, egotistical, and relentless."

He let that hover, then said, "Find him, you'll find your suspect. You'll have all the help you need from the bureau. I look forward to reading Easton's eloquent resignation letter to the SAC in Columbia. He'll be pleased. Easton has built a reputation for himself through the rank and file. He's been a blight on the FBI for more than a decade."

He moved to the doorway. "Call the judge back and tell him we need that warrant. While we're waiting on it, we can grab some lunch." He turned to go, then stopped and came back around. "Does Mrs. Ford look like her picture? Young? Fair of face and form?"

The two detectives consulted each other with an exchanged look, then Locke spoke for both of them. "You could say."

Rudkowski snuffled. "Easton's got the devil's own luck with pussy."

Drex sensed that Talia was about to utter a sound of protest over Rudkowski's vulgarity. He stopped it by placing his finger lengthwise over her lips. Even the slightest sound, an intake of breath, could have given away their hiding place.

Chapter 27

────◆────

It had been agony to remain perfectly still and silent for the duration of Rudkowski's conversation with the pair of detectives, especially when listening to the harsh things he'd said about Gif and Mike.

Drex was glad to hear his stamping footsteps moving out of the study and down the hall. As soon as he was out of earshot, Menundez said something under his breath in Spanish. Locke asked him for a translation. What he'd said was unflattering to Rudkowski and his ancestry, but less of an insult than the jerk deserved.

The two detectives remained in the study while Locke called the judge, who must have been unavailable. The detective said, "Tell him there's been a development. Ask him to call me back. Thank you."

After a pause, Menundez asked, "Where do you think they went?"

"You'll have to be more specific."

"Mallory and Lewis."

"On a mission for Easton."

"That's what I think, too. What about him and her?"

Locke said, "Maybe she tried to escape, and he had to chase after her."

"Is that what you really think?"

"Hell, no."

"Easton's got balls. Gotta give him that. Would you have the nerve to pull something like he's doing?"

"No."

"I admire the guy."

"Don't let Rudkowski overhear that."

"What an asshole. Even after what we now know about Easton and his team, I would choose them over that guy to lead the charge or cover my back."

"Easton called him a blowhard. That description doesn't come close."

"How'd he make it into the FBI and manage to stay on?"

"Must've been a nephew," Locke said. "I'll get the search warrant for him, but, between you and me, I think it's a waste of time."

"How's that?"

"If Jasper Ford *is* Easton's guy, and he's as canny as Easton says, he wouldn't have left anything incriminating behind. He never has before."

"Maybe he did, and the investigators missed it."

"But Easton wouldn't have." Following Menundez's unintelligible agreement, Locke said, "We'd better rejoin Rudkowski."

"Do we really have to eat with the guy?"

"We're his ride."

Menundez continued to mouth about it. Their voices faded as they left the room.

Tension ebbed out of Talia. "Close one," Drex whispered.

"I'm not cut out for adventures like this."

"Me neither. I'm too tall. I'm getting a crick in my neck." He'd had to keep his head lowered in order to fit beneath the ceiling.

"How's the bump?"

"I'll live." He'd banged his head as they'd squeezed into the small space. "You could have warned me about the low ceiling."

"There wasn't time."

"Sure there was. We had maybe a second and a half to spare."

Inside the enclosure, it was pitch black dark. He couldn't see her, but he felt the silent laugh that caused her breasts to shift against his chest, then resettle in the hollow between his ribs. They were soft, unbound, and enduring this forced alignment with them had been both agony and bliss.

Except for pressing his finger against Talia's lips, he hadn't dared to move. He estimated that two hours had elapsed since her offer of unconditional help had launched him into action. Through the back porch screen he'd seen his partners marching up the stairs to the apartment, the two young patrolmen trailing them.

"I've got to get you out of here," he'd told her. "Now. Before they come back. They'll try to stop me, and they would be right to."

He'd gnawed on the problem as he watched the quartet disappear into the apartment. How could he and Talia leave, either from the back or front of the house, without being seen? Taking any of the cars would result in a chase.

Then he'd remembered something from the floor plan he'd studied before breaking in the first time. "There's a sizeable unlabeled space beneath the stairs," he said to Talia. "Storage closet?"

"Safe room."

"Where's it accessed?"

"My study."

"Who knows about it?"

"Jasper and me."

"Well, unless he's in it, that's where we're going, and we've gotta be quick."

They had rifled a kitchen utility drawer to find a pen, some notepaper, and an envelope. After seeing why he'd requested them, Talia had exclaimed, "You can't resign!"

"We'll discuss it later." He'd hastily assembled the items on the dining table, then hustled her down the hallway and into her study, where he'd drawn up short. "Where is it?"

She stood her ground. "Drex, you can't throw away your career."

"I'm not. I'm fulfilling it. How do we get into the safe room?"

Through the window, he'd seen that Mike and Gif had parted company with the officers and were making their way across the expansive lawn toward the house. "Talia? It's gotta be now."

She'd hesitated, searching his eyes, then went over to a built-in bookcase and reached between two books. With a metallic click, a section of shelving had popped out a few inches. Drex had propelled her toward it. "Is it ventilated?"

"Yes."

"Get in." He'd taken one last glance out the window. His partners were approaching the porch.

Talia had slipped into the space. He crowded in behind her. "How do I shut us in?"

She'd turned to face him, reached around him, and pulled the door closed with a handle that had been digging into his right kidney ever since. Both being breathless by then, he'd asked in a whisper if she was all right.

"A little claustrophobic."

"Close your eyes."

"I'm thinking about Marian."

He'd put his lips to her ear. "Don't. Just close your eyes. Breathe."

They'd said no more after that because footsteps were heard thudding upstairs and others approaching the room from the hallway. Judging by the heavy tread, it had been Mike who'd come looking for them in the study. They'd held their breath until they heard him head back down the hallway toward the front of the house, where he and Gif had discovered the items left on the dining table.

Drex still felt a twinge of conscience for hoodwinking them, but

they could never be held accountable for something they didn't
know about. He would beg their forgiveness later.

He and Talia had remained sealed in darkness. He, too, had
spent some of that time dwelling on Marian Harris's final minutes.
Hours? Who knew how long she had struggled to free herself, to
survive.

That was justification enough for what he was doing. It was
rash, unadvisable, and irreversible. No apology or rationale would
be adequate to pacify either the FBI or the local authorities. But he
was prepared to live with the consequences of his action. Whether
or not he was wrong about the others, Marian Harris was dead,
and now Elaine Conner. He would die before letting Talia be
added to their number.

To call this a safe *room* was inaccurate. It was no larger than a
telephone booth. They couldn't change positions without risking
making a sound. The slightest bump, thud, or scrape would carry
through the walls and give them away. Because they couldn't be
sure who was inside the house at any given time, they'd had to remain perfectly still.

Time crawled. Sounds reached them, but they were indistinct
and not always identifiable. Occasionally they'd caught a word or
two spoken by someone in the front rooms, but then there would
be stretches when their light breathing was the only sound.

During one of those silences, Talia had whispered, "How long
do we have to stay?"

"Longer."

She'd sighed but hadn't complained.

At that point he hadn't known whether or not his partners were
still in the house or perhaps had returned to the garage apartment.
They could have posted the two young cops to stand guard duty inside. He'd felt it prudent to stay put.

Then Rudkowski had made his grand entrance. Drex had
sensed his arrival even before he could be heard chewing out the
patrolmen for letting Mike and Gif leave. Learning that they had

gotten clear before Rudkowski descended on them had made Drex smile.

Talia and he had tensed when Rudkowski and Locke came into the study. It had put additional strain on their already strained muscles, but Drex was glad he had gotten to hear the game plan.

Of course he'd wanted to rip out Rudkowski's jugular with his teeth over the crude comment, not because it was an insult to him, but to Talia. It had made him feel better, knowing that Locke and Menundez had accurately sized him up. They hadn't even wanted to share a meal with him.

After their footsteps had faded to nothingness, Talia whispered. "Have they gone?"

"Let's give them a few more minutes before chancing it."

"Chance sneaking out?"

"Chance searching the house before they return with the warrant."

"Oh. Then what?"

"*Then* we chance sneaking out."

"Will we be able to?"

"That's the hope. We're not out of the woods yet."

When she gave a small nod, her hair brushed against his cheek. He thought strands of it got caught in his scruff.

"I was afraid my stomach was going to growl," she said.

"You should have eaten your doughnut."

"It was a matter of principle not to touch it."

"Because I'd given it to you?"

"Exactly."

"Next time, you'll know better than to let pride get in your way."

"Next time." With those words, she drooped, as though the prospect of what they still faced sapped her strength. "I'm scared, Drex."

"Fear is healthy."

"It's draining. Exhausting. I'm so tired."

"Lean against me."

She did.

God, he was going to die. "Just a few more minutes, then you can stretch."

"No, I meant I'm so tired of living the way I have been."

"How's that?"

She took time to choose her word. "Watchfully. For a while now, I've treaded very carefully around Jasper."

He thought on that. "I want to hear about it. Everything. Later. When we're out of here. All right?"

Again she nodded. Again he thought strands of her hair were caught in his whiskers, and the thought of that alone, in addition to their proximity, sent heat rushing to his center.

He tried to stay focused. "Say it out loud. 'All right.'"

"All right. I'll explain later. For now, I'll just say thank you."

"What did I do? Other than cram you into a closet."

"You forced me to acknowledge what I had intuited about Jasper but refused to accept. I feel unburdened, liberated from my own denial, by your browbeating. I realize you were only doing your job, but you have my gratitude anyway."

"Talia." He bent his head lower and nuzzled her just below her ear. "This isn't only doing my job." He caught the lobe of her ear between his teeth.

She stirred and whimpered his name. He followed the soft expulsion of breath to its source, her parted lips, and covered them with his. Her mouth was hot and wet and receptive when he pressed his tongue inside.

Unlike when he'd kissed her before, this time she didn't turn her head aside and angle away. Instead she leaned into the kiss, not just with her mouth but with her body.

They shifted instinctually, matching up parts that had been created to complement each other. Still, it was a tease to what it could be. He had believed there wasn't room enough to reposition themselves, but he discovered there was, as he curved his arm around her waist.

In doing so, his elbow knocked against the wall. The giveaway sound would have alarmed him earlier, but now he disregarded it and focused only on splaying his hand over Talia's ass and pulling her closer, up, onto him. She responded by arching up even higher until—God!—the fit stole their breath. Until then they hadn't broken the mad kiss, but they did now, gasping in unison.

A heartbeat later, their mouths fused, and, again they were governed by carnal instinct. His palm followed her shape from her waist to the top of her thigh, caressing bare skin that felt like warm silk against his hand, although he didn't even remember sliding it inside her pajama bottoms.

He couldn't say when she had raised her hand to his head, yet her fingers were imbedded in his hair, urgently tugging on it to pull him closer.

Beneath his circling thumb, her nipple was hard, but how had he found it beneath her pajama top? He didn't know, but he loved the feel of it, of her, of her excitement, and knowing he had kindled it.

He hadn't thought to thrust against the welcoming V between her thighs, but he was, and it was killing him not to be inside her.

These incredible sensations coalesced in an instant of clarity, and he realized that if he didn't stop now, there would be no stopping.

He lifted his mouth away from her hungry kiss and clasped her head between his hands. "Talia, Talia." With his forehead pressed to hers, he kept repeating her name on gusts of breath until she stilled against him. "God knows I want to," he groaned. "But I can't. Not under his roof."

He let go of her, fumbled behind his back for that son of a bitching handle, and flipped it up. The wall popped open behind him. He ducked his head and stumbled backward out of the enclosure and into the room. Reaching for her hand, he guided her out of their hiding place.

The house was silent and, he sensed, empty save for the two of them. It was another gray day. The blinds were partially shut. The room was dim. He thought it was probably best that they couldn't see each other clearly. She couldn't have missed his erection. He'd never been this hard without having a woman under him or straddling him or sucking him.

In her dishevelment, Talia had never looked so sexy. Her lips plump and damp. Hair a mess. One side of her shapeless robe was hanging off her shoulder. Her nipples were peaked beneath her pajama top. She looked ravishing. Ravish*ed*. If only. Jesus, was he *crazy*?

No. He'd been right to stop.

"I had to," he said, his voice hoarse. "I would never have gotten over being with you here. In *his* house."

She swallowed with apparent difficulty and drew her robe back into place, then crossed her arms over her front. "I understand. I do. I probably would have hated myself afterward, too. I shouldn't have let it go that far."

He scrubbed his hands over his face.

"Right. And besides all that, I've placed us in a serious situation. It's not too late for you to change your mind. You could stay here, wait for Locke and company, tell them that I had talked you into splitting but then you saw the light."

"No. I'm going with you."

"I have your trust now?"

"It was hard-earned, but yes."

He took a deep breath, dropped his head forward, and for several seconds stared at the floor. When he raised his head, he spoke with unmitigated gravity. "Also trust this, Talia. If given an opportunity to kill him, I'm going to."

"I hope so," she said gruffly. "Because if you don't, he will surely kill me."

Chapter 28

―――――•◉•―――――

As Drex had gathered, there was no one inside the house, but a police unit was parked at the curb with two officers keeping watch.

"I hope Rudkowski didn't want fast food for lunch," he whispered as he turned away from the window. "No lights, no unnecessary sound, and we've got to make these minutes count. Where should we start? I've already searched the master bedroom."

"When?"

"Yesterday after you left for the airport."

"It was you who set off the alarm."

"Thought I was so clever to know the new code. Jasper laid that trap for me. Were you aware of the app on his phone?"

"App?"

"Never mind. Doesn't matter now." He thought for a moment. "Any other spaces like that safe room?"

"No. Until today, there's never been cause to use it."

"Whatever Jasper's trophies are, they're small, easily hidden, and he would keep them close to him, not where you would have better access. Where does he spend most of his time?"

She led him upstairs to a room at the end of the hallway. It was similar in proportion to her study. It was furnished with a desk and computer, a leather recliner, and a wall-mounted flat-screen TV. Like any ol' man cave. Except that it was sterile, a stage setting lacking enough props to make it look lived in.

The hardwood floor was bare of carpet or rugs. Drex didn't have time to see if any of the planks were loose, but he didn't detect any cracks that would suggest a hidey-hole underneath. And, anyway, Jasper wouldn't be that mundane.

He pulled the chair from beneath the desk and powered up the computer. "Do you know his password?"

Talia gave it to him. He typed it in. "If he gave you his password, we won't find anything. Is this the only computer he has?"

"That I know of."

Drex accessed Jasper's email. Talia identified the names she recognized, most of whom were vendors they used for various services or acquaintances from the country club.

"Friends of Jasper's?"

"Sometimes he plays doubles tennis and will have lunch with the group afterward. That's about the extent of it. He's not a mingler."

He'd had several exchanges with Elaine, but they didn't amount to anything. The most recent email from her had come in on yesterday morning, the day of her death. She'd thanked him for drinks and dinner the night before. There was no mention of an evening excursion on her yacht.

Drex went to the history of websites Jasper had visited. Most were for foodies or wine enthusiasts. Nothing exotic or noteworthy.

He was shutting down the computer when, from behind him, Talia said, "Drex, our picture is missing." She was looking down on a round cocktail table next to the recliner. "Jasper made a ceremony of putting our wedding photo on that table the day we moved in."

"Touching."

"I thought so at the time."

"Who had the picture framed, you or him?"

"I did. Why?"

"It could be significant that he took it with him. His souvenirs would be stashed in something portable, like a picture frame. Unless he hid his collection inside the walls for retrieval later."

"If he'd torn into walls, I would have known."

"When you were having the house decorated?"

"We didn't make structural changes."

"While you were out of town? He never had any 'repair' done, anything like that?"

"Not to my knowledge."

"Any other pictures?"

"Of me. None of him."

"Figures. The only one I know of in existence was the one taken on Marian's yacht. I doubt he knew he was in the shot."

He asked Talia to check the front of the house. Keeping out of sight, she peered through the louvered blinds. "They're still there. Just sitting. No other cars on the street."

Drex, who'd been surveying the Spartan room, noted all the bare shelves. "He doesn't like clutter, does he?" he asked wryly. "DVDs? Books? Coffee mugs with funny sayings?"

"I told you, he didn't bring much with him."

"Yeah, but who doesn't have *stuff*?" Then he realized that he didn't. Mike and Gif were on him all the time about how barren his apartment was. Shaking off the thought that he had anything in common with Jasper, he asked Talia where the attic access was.

"In the garage. A ladder pulls down from the ceiling."

"No time for that."

"I need to put some clothes on," she reminded him.

He nodded. "Wear something dark. Nothing fancy. Comfy."

"Can I bring some things with me?"

"If you pack them in a bag you can carry in one hand or on your shoulder. Go. I'll finish in here."

She rushed out. Aware of the clock, Drex checked the closet but found only a couple of tennis racquets and a pair of swimming flippers, all hanging from the rod by specialized hooks. He tapped the back wall of the closet. It didn't sound particularly hollow, and even if it were, he didn't have any way to tear into it. There was nothing on the closet floor, not even a pair of sneakers past their prime.

In frustration over the shortage of time, he gave the room one last scan, then crossed the hall and entered the master suite. Since Talia hadn't slept in here last night, everything appeared to be exactly as it had been when he'd searched it yesterday. The crystal tray holding Talia's jewelry was still on her nightstand.

On the outside chance that Jasper had returned undetected, Drex checked his night table drawers again. All were still empty. Underwear, socks, the artistically folded handkerchiefs—nothing had been disturbed in the bureau. Nor had anything in the closet.

Staring into it, Drex muttered, "Fucking whack job."

"What's that?" Talia had moved up behind him.

"I was saying this looks exactly like my closet."

She laughed, but it lacked mirth. "When we first married, I teased him about being such a stickler for order." She ran her hand along the sleeves of the jackets so precisely hung. Drex figured she enjoyed disturbing the perfection. "Actually I'm surprised he was willing to leave this wardrobe behind," she said. "He's so particular about it. He changes it frequently. Almost everything is custom made. He keeps his tailor in business."

"Custom made for Jasper Ford. Another of his incarnations wore blue jeans, flannel shirts, and cowboy boots. He went horseback riding and fly fishing."

"How do you know all that?"

"I know a lot more. What I know right now is that we've got to get the hell out of here."

"How do you propose we do it?"

"I have a route out the back."

"They could see us."

"They're guarding against someone coming in, not going out." While talking, he'd been tapping in Gif's cell number.

He answered immediately. "Well, well. We'd about given up on you."

"I need you to come pick us up."

"Us? So she's still with you?"

"Yes. Remember how to get to the mini-mart?"

"Sure."

"How long will it take you to get there?"

"About forty-five seconds."

Drex thought about it, then chuckled. "Who figured it out?"

"Mike. Said you had to be inside the house because a woman couldn't possibly have dressed that fast."

Talia had changed into jeans, a black t-shirt, and a rain jacket with a hood. A small bag hung from her shoulder. "You'd be surprised," Drex said and winked at her. "We'll meet you at the mini-mart."

"You don't have to go there. We're on the next street. Where you and Talia had a four-minute chat that morning after I let you out at the mini-mart."

"You sly dog."

"Don't get caught."

They clicked off. Drex motioned to Talia's bag. "I hope you chose well. I don't know when you'll be able to come back."

She walked over to the nightstand and worked her wedding ring off her finger. With a plink, it landed on the crystal tray. "I'll never come back."

———

As they exited through the kitchen door onto the screened porch, Drex paused to set the alarm.

"Why are you doing that?"

"To piss off Rudkowski when he comes back."

"He'll know you've been in here."

"That's the beauty of it."

"What's with the two of you?"

"Long story. I'll tell you sometime."

He wasn't as confident of making an escape unseen as he'd made out to be to Talia, but it had begun to rain harder. That helped. Plus he had cut through the lawn and the green belt enough times to know what areas of the back of the property were visible from the street in front.

Gif's sedan was parked where he'd said it would be. He and Talia scrambled into the back seat, shaking off rainwater. "In the nick of time," Gif said. "A convoy of squad cars just went through that intersection behind us." He headed in the opposite direction. "Where to?"

"Just away," Drex said. "Let me think."

"We got a room at a suite hotel," Mike said. "Within minutes of checking in, I figured out you'd never left the house. Where did you hide?"

Drex told them.

Mike grumbled, "Should've remembered that space from the floor plan."

As though sparked by that comment, Talia spoke for the first time. "I've remembered something." She turned on the seat toward Drex. "Were you watching us that day before we went to the airport?"

"Like a hawk."

"Jasper went to the country club to swim that morning."

"He left at ten something."

"The time isn't so important. Did you see him return?"

"I saw him pull into the garage, around—"

"But you didn't see *him*?"

"Only the car."

"I don't think he came back with his gym bag."

"Maybe he left it in the trunk of his car."

"He didn't. I was with him when he loaded our suitcases for the airport. The bag wasn't there." She leaned forward and said to Gif, "Do you know where the country club is?"

"No, but I can take directions."

She told him the first turn to take, then said to Drex, "I have the code to his locker. He left his wristwatch in it once. I was at the club having lunch with a couple of girlfriends. He called and asked me to retrieve his watch. He didn't trust the attendant with the code to his locker, so he gave it to me, then alerted the attendant that I would need brief access when no one was in there."

"He might have changed the code since then." That from Mike.

Talia said, "It's worth a try."

"How will you get into the men's locker room?" Drex asked.

"Can't you tell that I'm on the verge of a meltdown, worried sick over what's become of my husband, frantic over the failure of the authorities to find him? Possibly there's something in his locker that would prove helpful to the search. Who's going to deny me access?"

Mike harrumphed his opinion of the plan. Gif raised his eyebrows in the mirror. Drex grinned. "I'm rubbing off on you."

"God help us," Mike grumbled.

She insisted on going in alone. "If we all go, it'll look like a parade and call attention."

"Not all of us have to go. Just me," Drex said. "If I'm with you, and someone denies you access, all I have to do is flash my—" He broke off.

Talia gave him an arch look.

Gif offered to go in with her. "If the occasion calls for it, I'll use my badge."

"Since you're not stupid enough to have surrendered it," Mike said, turning his head to glower at Drex. "Still, somebody should go with her."

She addressed the back of Mike's head. "So I won't skip out on you?"

"Just sayin'. Somebody should go."

By the time they'd reached the country club, it had been decided that Gif would accompany her into the clubhouse. As she got out at the entrance, Drex wished her good luck and squeezed her hand. He waved off the valet and took Gif's place behind the wheel. "I'll park over there." He pointed out an area of the lot.

Talia was recognized by staff, but all seemed shocked to see her looking so bedraggled. Her trek through the green belt in the rain had contributed to the overall impression of a woman in desperation.

The attendant on duty at the desk outside the men's locker room seemed downright alarmed. "Mrs. Ford?"

"Hi, Todd. It is Todd, isn't it?"

"Yes, ma'am." He was young. Gauging by his physique, he availed himself of the club's weight room often and for hours at a time. "Any word about Mr. Ford?"

"No. Which is why I'm here. Is anyone in there?"

"In the—?"

"The locker room, the locker room." With impatience she thumped the countertop in beat with her words. "I need to go in there." For good measure, she made her voice thready. "I want to check my husband's locker. Maybe something he left in it will—"

"It was empty."

"What?" Talia said with genuine dismay.

"Two detectives already came."

"When?"

Todd scrunched up is face. "About an hour ago, I guess. They had the club manager open your husband's locker. It was empty. Saw inside it myself."

She opened her mouth to speak, but Gif stepped forward and laid a cautioning hand on her shoulder. "They explained that to her, Todd. Or tried to. Sergeants Locke and Menundez?"

"I never got their—"

"Was Special Agent Rudkowski with them?"

"The third guy? I think he was their boss."

"Yes, he thinks so, too. They assured Mrs. Ford that her husband's locker was empty, but she's, uh, terribly distraught, as you can imagine. She insisted on checking it for herself. I volunteered to bring her."

"You're a detective, too?"

"Police chaplain."

"Oh."

"If it wouldn't be too much trouble..."

"Well, sure. Sure." The young attendant gave Gif a reassuring wink. "Of course you can go in, Mrs. Ford," he said, speaking to her as though she were deranged. "I don't think anyone's in there. Weather's keeping the golfers in the card room. But let me double-check. I'll be right back."

Gif commended her performance. Talia commended his. But as they left the country club, dejection settled over all four of them. Feeling dispirited down to his bones, Drex gave the responsibility of driving back to Gif, leaving him free to concentrate.

The abbreviated search of the house hadn't yielded anything. The trip to the country club had been a bust. He had nothing to work with. Nothing. As before. As always. Jasper had left nothing behind to come back for. Except Talia.

He'd taken only a wedding photo and...and what?

He stirred, stilled, stirred again. "Talia, you and Jasper took roll-aboard suitcases to the airport, correct?"

"Yes."

"One each?"

"Yes. To carry on."

"Did you pack for him, or see what he packed?"

"No. By the time he came home from the club, I'd finished packing. I left our room to him and went down to the study to catch up on emails and business-related calls. I worked right up until time to leave for the airport."

"Mike, in that security video showing Jasper getting into the taxi?"

"Yeah?"

"He had his roll-aboard with him, right?" Drex thought he remembered correctly, but he wanted to check Mike's computerized memory to be sure.

"He placed it in the back seat with him."

Drex resettled, turned his head, and stared out the rain-streaked car window. Jasper had left behind a custom-tailored wardrobe and took with him only what he could pack into a roll-aboard. He fit his whole life into a piece of carry-on luggage. With the tip of his finger, Drex followed a rivulet of rainwater as it trickled down the outside of the glass.

What had he packed into that roll-aboard? Where was it now?

Gif drove them to the suite motel where he and Mike were already checked in. Gif pulled under the porte cochere. Mike said to Gif, "I've got this, Reverend Lewis." He turned to Drex. "Every suite has two bedrooms."

Drex didn't rise to the bait. "Then it works out even."

Mike shot a look at Talia, then squeezed himself out of the passenger door and lumbered into the lobby.

"Understating the obvious," she said to Drex, "he doesn't like me."

"Don't take it personally. He doesn't like anybody."

A few minutes later Mike returned and passed a card key to Drex. "Not that you asked, but we brought all your stuff from the garage apartment."

"Thanks."

"We didn't figure you'd be returning for it," Gif said.

In a lame attempt to lighten the mood, Drex said, "I miss the place already." No one reacted.

Gif said, "What about your car?"

"Temporarily abandoned. They may impound it. I don't know. Don't care. I'll worry about that after ... After."

Gif parked. They all got out. Mike said, "Here's ours. Yours." He pointed to another of the suites, facing his and Gif's from across a gravel courtyard dotted with dwarf palmettos.

"I'll see Talia in, then come and get my things," Drex said.

Without further discussion, he walked Talia to their door, unlocked it, and told her he would be back within a few minutes. "Keep the chain on." Looking as downcast as he felt, she nodded.

He waited until he heard her secure the lock then, heedless of the rain, strode across the courtyard and rapped on the door. Gif opened it. Drex went past him and made a beeline to Mike, who was sprawled in a chair in the living room looking not dissimilar to Jabba the Hut.

"Cut it out, Mike."

"What?"

"Give me a fucking break. You know what."

"All right." Mike raised his hands as though in surrender.

"I mean it," Drex said, stressing the words.

"Be nice or take my leave?"

"I couldn't have phrased it any better. I need *you*. But I don't need your shit. The situation is bad enough without it. Be nice. Or leave."

Mike raised his hands higher. "I said, all right."

Drex backed away. Now that the air had been cleared between them, he said, "Rudkowski has probably already blacklisted you. Do you think you can hack the autopsy report on Elaine?"

"Won't have to." Mike nodded toward Gif. "He bullshitted it out of somebody in the coroner's office."

"Email it to me, please, Gif."

"Sure," Gif said.

Drex spotted a stack of cookbooks on one of the living area end tables. "I see you got my message. Start digging into them."

"They don't look used enough to hold secrets," Gif said.

"Maybe not, but check anyhow."

"In the meantime, what are you going to do?"

They both looked toward Mike as though expecting an innu-endo involving Talia. He raised both hands again. "What? This is me, being nice. Besides, that setup was so easy it was beneath me."

Drex actually gave him a grudging smile as he lifted his duffel bag off the sofa. "I'm going to my room to think."

"About what?"

"About what I would do now if I were Jasper."

Chapter 29

———◆———

Talia released the chain and opened the door. She looked so forlorn that Drex asked her what the matter was.

"I'm sorry my brainstorm didn't pay off."

"Most brainstorms don't. We celebrate the odd occasions when they do."

"Those odd occasions are what keep you going?"

"What keeps me going is that I haven't caught him yet."

"It's going to be more difficult now that you've resigned. Maybe if you appealed to Rudkowski, he would disregard what you did this morning."

"You heard him. Does he sound like a man to whom a *mea culpa* would make a dent?"

"No."

"However, I might attempt it except for the time it would cost."

"And you think time is of the essence, don't you?"

Not wanting to alarm her—yet—he hedged. "I need to shut myself off and think. Are you going to be all right for a while?"

"After the night and morning I've had? I need some downtime, too."

He gave a strand of her hair a tug then kept hold of it. "I wish I'd seen you in action in the locker room. Gif said you struck just the right note. Somewhere between a pit bull and pitiful."

"I'm out of my league."

He tucked the strand of hair behind her ear and rubbed the lobe he'd taken a bite of earlier. "I'm afraid I am, too."

"Why do you say that?"

He lowered his hand. "Jasper's been at this for three times longer than I've been chasing him. He's had more practice." He gave her a grim smile as he checked his watch. "We're regrouping at six o'clock. Gif's going to bring in dinner."

They climbed the stairs. The two bedrooms were separated by a short hallway, the shared bathroom between them. "I put my things in here." She pointed to the bedroom on the right. "I'll see you a little before six."

She turned away, but before she'd taken a single step, he reached for her and brought her around. He pulled her to him and wrapped his arms around her.

"I want to lie down with you so bad." He kissed the side of her neck. "But you wouldn't want to go where I've got to go now."

He hugged her tighter, then his arms relaxed and finally dropped to his sides. He left her, entered the darkened room, and closed the door behind him.

———

Gif had brought in Chinese. They divided the cartons and sat around the dining table to eat.

The cookbooks, Drex noted, had been ripped apart. Pages from them formed a snowbank in a corner of the room. Nodding toward it, Drex said, "Nothing?"

"Not a single notation," Gif replied. "And we went through each book page by page. Nothing glued into the backings. We turned up *nada*."

"Some of the recipes look good, though," Mike said. "I saved those."

"You can add that to the paper pile." Drex pointed his fork at the phony manuscript he'd set on the bar when he'd come in. It had been included in his belongings that Mike and Gif had brought from the garage apartment. "I won't be needing it anymore."

"Did you actually write all that?" Talia asked.

"I had it copied from a paperback book."

"Elaine told Jasper it wasn't very good."

"Pam will be crushed," Mike said as he polished off an egg roll. Talia looked at Drex. "Pam?"

Drex shot Mike a warning look. "A woman at the office typed it for me. I never even read it, only messed up the pages to make them look authentic."

"You had me fooled," Talia said. "That day I came over to the apartment and asked..."

Becoming aware that Mike and Gif were listening with rabid interest, Drex said, "That was the point. To fool you."

After that, conversation lagged, and they focused on eating. When they were finished, they made quick work of cleaning up then chose their seats in the living area. Mike claimed the largest chair, Gif straddled one of the dining chairs, Talia curled up into a corner of the sofa. Drex perched on the opposite arm of it.

He had decided how he was going to call the meeting to order, despite how tough it would be on Talia. He had to be straightforward, perhaps even harsh, because it was essential to erase any lingering doubts in his partners' minds about her culpability.

"Talia?"

She took a breath and let it out slowly. "This is the 'I want to hear it all later,' isn't it?"

"Yes. Speaking for all three of us, we need it explained how you couldn't have known that you were married to a psychopath."

It was the opening Mike had been waiting for. "When I saw you in that picture taken at Marian Harris's party, that did it for me."

"And you haven't changed your mind," she said.

"Say you didn't meet your husband that night—"

"I didn't."

"—and that everything else you've told us is true, didn't he ever strike you as not quite right in the head?"

"I'd like to hear that myself," Gif said, quieter and less judgmental than Mike.

"Yes, I sensed something wasn't quite right," she said. "But I couldn't isolate what it was. You three think in terms of criminology and psychopaths every day. That's outside my realm. So, no," she said, addressing Mike, "it didn't pop into my mind one day that my husband was a serial killer."

"Okay," Drex said. "Take a breath. This isn't an inquisition. We're trying to analyze and understand him more than we are you. What first sparked your feeling that something was off?"

"It didn't spark. It came on gradually. Initially, I talked myself into believing that it was the difference in our ages. Three decades' difference."

"But you married him anyway," Drex said.

"The strangeness didn't start until *after* we married. Soon after, though, I began to notice oddities. For instance the way he phrased things. Words and expressions seemed to have a double meaning that escaped me. I felt particularly uneasy when we were alone, but I couldn't account for it. I thought it might have been hormonal. I was going through some procedures." She glanced at Drex. "But my uneasiness persisted. Over the past few months things he said and did became even stranger."

"Did this strangeness intensify around the time Marian's remains were discovered?" Drex asked.

Her brow furrowed. "Now that you mention it, yes. About that time."

"That fits," he said, getting nods of agreement from Mike and Gif. "That would have agitated him. Made him second-guess burying her alive."

"Maybe it wasn't his intention to," Gif said. "When he nailed shut that box, he mistakenly thought she was dead."

Mike jumped on that. "'Mistakenly' is the key word. A blunder like that is anathema to him. It would have set him off."

Drex had followed their exchange with interest, but he didn't want to address the particulars of it yet. "It would have set him off in either case. The discovery of that grave spoiled his perfect record."

Back to Talia, he said, "You went out to dinner together one night this week. I waved at you as you were leaving."

"Yes."

"You two seemed simpatico. All dressed up. Hubby taking his best girl to dinner."

"So you heard that conversation?"

He nodded.

She looked embarrassed. "The invitation surprised me. That was the first date night we'd had in weeks."

"He was playing to me?"

"He must have been. But what I thought was that he was trying to cover an affair."

Drex looked at his cohorts to gauge their opinions. Gif looked interested but as yet undecided. You could have cut Mike's skepticism with a knife.

Drex turned back to Talia. "What shape did his strange behavior take? What did he do to make you think something was really out of joint?"

"Nothing threatening or overtly weird. He never mistreated me. On the contrary, he was solicitous, often to an annoying degree. But sometimes, when he looked at me in a certain way, it would cause a chill to creep over me. I began making up excuses to avoid intimacy."

"How did he react?"

"Casually."

"Not violently?"

"Not at all. Just the opposite. He was indifferent."

She pulled one of the sofa's throw pillows into her lap and hugged it against her chest. A shield, Drex thought, against what she was still reluctant to admit.

"His indifference seemed abnormal," she said.

"It's all kinds of abnormal," Drex said, "because he is. Some of these guys can't function sexually unless it is violent. But Jasper isn't about sex. It's the mind fuck he gets off on. Except for my mother, his relationships with the women have been platonic." Mike and Gif looked like they'd been goosed. "Yes, I told Talia this morning, and I trust her not to reveal it to anyone else. But back to the point I was making. None of his other relationships have been characterized as love affairs."

Mike said, "Even the solicitations he put on the match-up websites didn't reference sex or romance. Only companionship."

Looking at Talia, Drex said, "For whatever it's worth, I doubt he was romantically involved with Elaine. I don't believe she would have betrayed you. However, to you, an affair was a logical explanation for his quirky behavior."

"Why was I the exception to his platonic relationships?" Talia asked.

"We'll come back to that," Drex said. "Go on with what you were telling us earlier. How did his strangeness manifest itself?"

"Small things, any one of which could have been overlooked, but collectively they bothered me. Like his obsession with his clothes, his closet."

For the benefit of the other two, Drex described it.

"He was fanatical about the fit of every garment," Talia continued. "He fussed over sleeve length, buttons, everything. I was never allowed to fold his laundry and store it. He had a 'system,' he said. I teased him about the way he lined up utensils in the kitchen drawer."

"He didn't laugh it off," Drex said.

"No, he took umbrage. His obsessions like that began to wear on me. Walking a fine line twenty-four/seven is exhausting. I started inventing reasons to go out of town. My business trips came to feel like escapes. I could only relax when I was away from him. Which should have told me something, shouldn't it?"

She asked it of all three men, letting her gaze light briefly on one before moving to the next, until she came back around to Drex. He said nothing, wanting to hear how she answered her own question.

"We're supposed to trust our fear. That's what we're told. I didn't. I rationalized it away or denied it altogether." She waited a beat, then added, "Until you moved in next door. Then everything changed."

Mike shifted in his seat. Gif cleared his throat. Drex didn't move, just continued to look into Talia's troubled eyes.

"Jasper was mistrustful of you right from the start, although you'd given him no reason to be. You'd even returned the fan he loaned you. I couldn't understand his aversion."

"He saw Drex as competition."

She nodded at Gif. "Male assertion, protecting his territory, that would have been understandable over time, and if Drex and I had given him reason to be jealous. But Drex has been here all of a week, and Jasper turned paranoid almost from the day he moved in."

"'Suspicion always haunts the guilty mind,'" Drex quoted.

"What?"

"Shakespeare," Mike said.

"But don't be too impressed," Drex said. "I only know that line because it applies to a mind like Jasper's." He held up his index finger. "*Except* that he feels only the suspicion, not the guilt. In his mind, whatever he does is sanctioned.

"Oh, he's subtle," he went on. "He doesn't pull the wings off houseflies or eviscerate kittens. Although he may have in his youth, or in secret now. But when he's 'working,' he assumes all the trappings of normalcy.

"He expresses remorse when it's called for. 'Shame about your dog getting hit by a car.' He apologizes for minor offenses like being late for an engagement or forgetting a birthday. He takes a small gift to a hostess. He invites a new neighbor over for dinner. Because that's what civilized people do.

"But he's role-playing. He's condescending. Behind his hand, he's snickering at everyone who falls for his act. He's had nine personas that I know of, but they all originated and were governed by the same distorted psyche, in which he's far superior to everyone else, and rules do not apply to him."

"I feel so stupid, so foolish."

"Don't, Talia. He played you brilliantly. 'Not tonight, honey'? Fine. He was the perfect gentleman about it. The epitome of consideration. Never got pissed off, never complained, ultimately stopped asking. Right?"

She gave a small, self-conscious nod.

"That fell right into step with the way he wanted your relationship to be. He mastered without being masterful. What wife would complain about such an ideal husband? That closet, those pristine drawers made you want to scream, but you didn't, because most wives would regard it a miracle if, for once, their slob of a husband picked up his dirty underwear from off the bathroom floor.

"Jasper deliberately used words and phrases that were disturbing, then contrasted them with utmost thoughtfulness. That kept you off balance. Made you...What was the word you used today? *Watchful.* That was the turn-on of all turn-ons to him. He sensed your mounting wariness. Nurturing it was his foreplay."

"Leading to what?"

"Killing."

"Nucking futs," Mike mouthed.

Distressed, she hugged the pillow closer. "I'll never forgive myself for not heeding my instincts and saying something, doing something, sharing my misgivings with Elaine. If I had, she might still be alive."

"And you would be dead."

After Drex's sobering declaration, a silence ensued. Then Gif said, "No doubt he would then have turned to Elaine for condolence."

"And snuffed her, too," Mike said.

"That's one of the points I want to broach with you," Drex said. "These circumstances were different from all the previous ones. This time there were two women. One, he married. Marian Harris was also a departure from the norm."

"In what way?" Gif asked.

Drex stood up and went over to the eating bar that separated the living area from the kitchenette. He planted his hands on the surface of it and used his arms as struts.

"I don't think he buried Marian alive by mistake. I think he had become bored with his routine and wanted to try something new. He challenged himself. He wanted to see if he could do it and get away with it. And so far he has.

"Talia represented another challenge. She wasn't middle aged, wasn't meek or insecure, wasn't an heiress. Not at all like her predecessors, she was much younger, more beautiful, and her fortune was self-made. Could he lure a woman like that? Or, better yet, the biggest coup of all, get her to marry him? He succeeded.

"He was introduced to Elaine. Independently, she wouldn't have been a challenge. But going for two? Two who knew each other, were friends, who saw each other frequently and could compare notes about him?

"Ah, that was a risk to beat all risks. Even riskier than leaving Marian to die on her own before someone heard her screams. The challenge of Talia and Elaine combined was too tempting to resist. Dare he try?" Drex dropped his head between his shoulders. "He did, and has accomplished half his goal."

No one behind him moved. No one spoke. Finally, Gif said, "This is his way of escalating."

"I believe so. It's his middle-age crazy we talked about. He's taking chances he's never taken before, and it scares me shitless." He paused, then said, "See if you can get Locke on the phone."

As Drex predicted, the other three in the room reacted to the request with a start. Before anyone could ask why or object, he said, "We need somebody inside, feeding us information, and keeping us updated. Rudkowski? Forget it. Lost cause. Do either of you have a contact in any of the FBI offices in South Carolina?"

They replied with shakes of their heads.

"So you can't call in any favors. Besides, you can bet that Rudkowski has by now soured them on all of us. Same goes for Charleston PD, sheriff's office, state police, Homeland Security. Every law enforcement agency."

"Locke is a member of that fraternity," Mike said.

"As well as Menundez," Talia said.

"Yes, but you heard them talking when they were alone in your study." He briefed Mike and Gif on what he and Talia had overheard from inside the safe room. "They saw through Rudkowski's bluster and neither likes him. Us, they admire. I believe Menundez would jump at the chance to assist."

"So why not call him instead?" Mike asked.

"Because Locke is more experienced, more mature, the deeper thinker, the less impulsive, the more senior guy, and, for all those reasons, that's who we need."

Gif hesitated, but took his phone out, went to his log of recent calls, and placed one to Locke. "Put it on speaker," Drex said, then pointed to a place on the bar, and that's where Gif set the phone. He scooted his chair closer to the bar and resumed his seat.

Mike stayed where he was. Talia moved to Drex's side. He turned his head toward her and spoke softly. "Sorry I had to put you through that."

"It was healthy for me, actually. Better than keeping it bottled up. I want him expunged, Drex."

"Me too."

She searched his eyes. "You put yourself through much worse, didn't you? In that dark room for hours with the door shut?"

"That's what they pay me for."

"They *did*."

He gave her a wan smile just as Locke answered with his name, sounding world-weary.

Drex addressed the phone and identified himself. "Can you talk to me without an audience?"

"Give me five minutes and call back."

"Nope. Now or never. Yes or no? I made off with your material witness. Don't you want to know why I called?"

"To negotiate a prisoner exchange?"

"All right, be an ass. Goodbye."

"Wait!" They heard muttered cursing, followed by a lengthy pause, some muffled sounds, then, "Okay, I'm alone. Why did you call?"

"Do you think Jasper Ford killed Elaine? And please don't give me the toe-the-department-line answer. Yes or no?"

"Yes."

"That's good news. Bad news is that you're never going to catch him by looking for him."

"How's that?"

"You're going through the routine. Airlines. Rental car companies. Hotel check-ins. Tell me I'm wrong."

Silence.

"What I thought," Drex said. "Listen to me. He is no longer Jasper Ford. He's somebody else. He's undergone so complete a transformation that you wouldn't know him if he walked up to you and grabbed you by the balls." He let Locke think on that, which the detective did without comment. Drex continued. "He left the airport with his roll-aboard. Did he leave it behind in the taxi?"

"No."

"Was it found on the yacht?"

"No."

"It was in the car."

"Mrs. Ford had his car."

Drex explained to the detective his theory that Jasper had left a spare car near the hotel where the taxi had dropped him. "An innocuous vehicle that can never be traced to him. He used it to get around that night. Inside it was that suitcase. Jasper swam ashore, but it was another person who left the beach."

"You're guessing."

Drex rubbed his forehead. "I went on a trip this afternoon, into this sick shit's head. He wanted everybody to think that Jasper Ford had been lost at sea. Do you agree?"

"Okay."

"He could not risk Jasper Ford ever being seen again. Jasper Ford had to cease to exist just like his previous incarnations did. He changed his appearance and his identity somewhere out there on the beach."

"Search parties have been combing the beaches—"

"You won't find so much as a gum wrapper. He's sanitary. Meticulous. Freakin' anal. He put everything back into the suitcase. What he did with it after that, I don't know. But it contained everything he needed to transform himself into someone else."

"All right, for the sake of argument—"

"I'm not being argumentative for the sake of argument, Locke," he said with heat. "I want to catch him, but I can't fly blind. I'm trying to impress upon you that if you want him, toss the handbook on police methodology into the nearest trash can." He took a breath. "But I'm listening. What was your argument?"

"If he did change his appearance, everything you said, we've already lost him. He's gone."

Drex looked over at Gif. "Gif said that this morning. He surmised that Jasper was probably long gone even before Elaine's body washed ashore. I didn't take issue with that supposition, because, at the time, I thought it likely. I don't any longer."

"Why not?" the detective asked.

"Because I put myself in Jasper's place, and came up with three reasons why I wouldn't leave the vicinity right away. First, if I had successfully pulled off a plan that intricate, it would be irresistible to me to enjoy it. It would be like skipping the fireworks after the championship win. He wants to bask in the glow of the fallout he's created. The last local newscast I saw, he's being described as a person of interest in Elaine's death."

"It was decided to hold back on naming him a suspect. We still can't put him on the yacht or in the dinghy. It's been tossed around that an unknown third party was aboard."

"If they follow that line of thinking, he'll get away. Locke, you've got to convince somebody that this isn't a man who woke up yesterday morning and decided to knock off a lady friend. It's not a love triangle gone south. Not even common thievery. He didn't act on impulse.

"I promise you that he's been plotting this for a while. Having talked to Talia about his recent behavior, I believe the discovery of Marian Harris's grave served as his catalyst."

"Detective?" Talia said.

"Mrs. Ford?" Locke exclaimed. "I didn't realize you were listening in. Are you all right?"

"If you're asking if I came with Drex by choice, yes. There was no coercion on his part." She paused. "But I feel badly about the awkward position I've placed you and Mr. Menundez in. Last night you treated me kindly through a difficult experience. Thank you."

"You're welcome," he said stiffly. "What do you think about Easton's conjectures?"

"I don't disagree with anything. In fact, he's opened my eyes to much that I chose not to see. With no offense intended toward your department or any law enforcement agency, I believe you should listen to him and act on his advice."

The detective sighed. "Easton, you said there were three reasons why you think he'd stick around. What's the second?"

"To kill Talia."

Drex's candor took Locke aback. He cleared his throat before asking her if Jasper had ever threatened her.

"No."

"Did you ever feel threatened by implication or—"

"No," she replied, interrupting him. "That's what makes it so terrifying to me now. He had some odd habits, but I didn't perceive them as aberrant characteristics or take them as the warning signs I should have."

"We don't have time for her to rehash what she's already told me about their relationship," Drex said. "Just take my word for it. He won't leave here with her still living. It would be untidy."

"He's right, detective," she said. "I've lived with Jasper. I know his habits. He won't leave me as a loose thread."

"To say nothing of her dough," Mike said.

"Who's that?" Locke asked.

"Mallory."

"So the gang's all there?"

"Hello," Gif said.

"You know you're all screwed," the detective said. "Rudkowski has vowed to see to it. Is it true that—"

"Look," Drex interrupted. "We'll sort all that out when we have to. Right now, we've got to figure out a way to draw Jasper into the open."

Locke said, "You didn't get to the third reason why you think he's still in the neighborhood."

"Ego."

Drex pushed himself off the bar and went to stand at one of the narrow windows on either side of the front door. He twirled the wand to open the blinds. "He knows I'm on to him. Doesn't make any difference to him whether or not I carry a badge, he knows I'm after him and, because of the trouble I went to with that impersonation of a writer, he must have some inkling of my determination to nail him.

"But he pulled a fast one on me. He plotted and executed a humdinger of a murder. He duped Talia. He had me chasing my tail. He somehow swayed Elaine. None of us saw it coming. *I* didn't see it coming, and I should have. He outsmarted me, and he'll want to rub my nose in it."

"Okay, but how?" Locke asked. "By killing Talia?"

That was the question that had tormented Drex that afternoon as he lay in the dark and focused on his quarry. If he were Jasper, would he want to dispatch Talia right away and be done with it? The game would be over. Where would the fun in that be?

"What I think," he said slowly, "is that he'll want me to worry about her, to fret over when and how he'll strike. He'll want to keep her on edge and afraid, too."

"You're contradicting yourself," Mike said grouchily. "You just argued that he wouldn't leave until he'd taken care of her."

"But not yet." Drex stared out into the rain. "In order to get my attention, to let me know that he's not done with me yet, that he's still pulling the strings, he'll strike swiftly. But he'll kill somebody else."

Locke exhaled loudly. "Oh, shit."

Chapter 30

———◦◉◦———

Alerted by the detective's tone, Drex turned away from the window and looked at the phone lying on the bar. "What? Locke? What?"

Locke started backpedaling. "It's not his MO. Not at all."

Drex crossed to the bar and shouted toward the phone. "*What?*"

"A woman was found dead in Waterfront Park."

"Near the water, and you say it's not his MO? He's sending me a valentine. When did it happen?"

"First call came in less than an hour ago."

"How was she killed?"

"No visible wounds. No blood. No obvious weapon."

"Then why's she dead?"

"Her neck was broken. Looks like he killed her barehanded."

Drex plowed his fingers through his hair, then held them there, cupping the top of his head.

Locke said, "But you didn't hear any of this from me. Other detectives were assigned. It's their case—"

"Not anymore. It's mine." Drex pushed the phone toward Gif. "Get the details."

"He may not want to tell—"

"Then get them from someone else."

Gif picked up the phone and began talking to Locke.

Drex said to Mike, "Get on your laptop. It may already be on-line news. Get the buzz."

"That's what it'll be. Buzz."

"Get it anyway."

"Where are you going?"

"To bring the car around. Where's the key?"

While still talking to Locke, Gif fished the key fob from his pants pocket and tossed it toward Drex. But Talia's hand shot out and caught it in midair. "I'll drive," she said.

"You're staying here with Mike."

"Half an hour ago, you said you don't have any contacts in Charleston. You don't know your way around."

"We'll find our way."

"I'm going."

"You need to stay here."

"No, I need to do this. I *need* to do this."

He tried to stare her into compliance, but realized how unfair that would be. She had offered to help, and she needed to do something to assuage the guilt she felt over Elaine.

Mike huffed up behind them. "I got the exact location. I'm coming, too."

The four of them piled into Gif's car. Drex rode shotgun, the other two got in back. Talia was driving—speeding—toward the water-front at the confluence of the Cooper River and the Atlantic, where the so-named park, the pier, and other attractions made the area a destination landmark of Charleston.

Gif filled them in on what Locke had told him. "Locke says CID is hopping."

"CID?" Talia asked.

"Criminal Investigations Division," the three men said in unison.

Gif continued, "Two back-to-back female homicide victims within twenty-four hours sent up red flags."

"No shit," Mike said.

"Have they identified the victim?" Drex asked.

"Sara Barker. Her purse was found beneath her, strap was still on her shoulder. Driver's license, credit cards, all there. Diamond wedding ring on her finger. It's believed she was attacked from behind as she was about to get into her car."

"Age?"

"Thirty-nine. Having dinner out with three girlfriends. Her husband was at home with their two children, boy, age nine, girl, six."

Drex clenched his fist and thumped his forehead with it. "Completely random victim. Something else he hasn't tried. Or, hell, maybe he has. Maybe he's killed dozens we don't know about, and I've only spotted the ones that fit a pattern."

"Which this one doesn't," Mike said. "So you don't know this was him."

"I know," Drex said. "He's showing off. Catch me if you can, asshole. That's what he's thinking."

Talia broke in. "I see an empty space in there." She pointed out the parking lot of a busy restaurant. "This may be as close as I can get, and we'll be inconspicuous here."

Drex nodded approval. She pulled into the parking lot and claimed the space. The instant she cut the engine, Drex reached for the passenger door handle.

"Drex, you can't go," Gif said. "Neither can Talia. Last thing Locke said, he warned me that Rudkowski would bulldoze his way into this, whether CPD liked it or not. If you're seen—"

"We're had." Drex cursed Gif's rational thinking and underscored the curses with additional ones because Gif was right.

Mike said, "You stay here. Gif and me will nose around and pick up what we can."

"Thanks all the same, Mike," Gif said, "but you're too much mass to go unnoticed."

Drex said, "He's right."

"No offense taken. I'll stay here in the nice, dry car, and update you off my laptop."

Drex asked Gif for Locke's phone number, which he supplied. Before he got out, he asked Drex if there was anything specific he wanted him to look for. "Rudkowski," Drex said.

"Goes without saying."

"You see him, shrink out of sight and come right back. Also keep your eyes and ears open for a calling card from Jasper."

"What do you mean?"

"He wants me to know it's him," Drex said. "He'll have left me a sign."

"Like what?"

"I don't know. It'll be something subtle. A inside joke between him and me."

After Gif left, Drex called Locke. He could tell the detective was in a moving vehicle. "Where are you?"

"Menundez and I have been called to the scene of a homicide."

The way he said that was his way of signaling to Drex that he hadn't told Menundez about their previous conversation. "That's a boon to me," he said.

"It's not our investigation, but they wanted us to take a look, see if there may be a connection between this homicide and ours last night."

"Other than gender of the victim?"

"Yes. Something that would indicate the same perp."

"I already know it's the same perp. If you find evidence of it, call me immediately."

"I'll see how it goes."

It became plain that Locke wasn't going to talk where Menundez could overhear. Drex guessed it was as much for the younger man's protection as for Locke's own. Even though the honorable gesture was working against Drex right now, he admired the detective for not wishing to compromise a junior partner.

"All right. I'm reading you. But when you can give me more details—"

"No promises."

"Understood. But as a show of faith, I'll text you my phone number and our current location."

"How long will you be there?"

"Till we're not."

"How long will the phone number be good?"

"Till I don't answer."

"I've got to go," Locke said. "We're here."

The detective clicked off, and so did Drex. He sent the promised text immediately. Then, tapping the phone against his chin in frustration, he related to Talia and Mike what Locke had told him.

"Somebody might overlook a vital link. Dammit." He reached for the door handle and lifted it.

"Drex?" Talia exclaimed.

"I can't just sit here and do nothing," he said.

"You've got to, Drex," Mike said. "If you're caught intruding, you'll be shut down. Gif and me, too. Locke will be hung out to dry, because Rudkowski will know it was him who tipped you."

"I'm not going to let Locke catch the flak."

"That won't be your call. Do you want to cost him his job?"

Gripped by indecision, he kept the car door open but didn't get out. He looked at Talia, who said, "Mike is right." He cast a look over his shoulder at Mike, whose expression was more baleful than usual. Drex conceded the wisdom of discretion. "Okay, but I can't just sit. I'll keep to this parking lot. Stretch my legs. Clear my head."

He flipped up the hood of his rain jacket and got out.

———————

With the intention of joining him, Talia reached for the driver's door handle, but from the back seat, Mike said, "Give him a few. He'll be all right. He gets like this."

She settled back into her seat. "It pains him, doesn't it? What he does."

"It's been known to. When it does, we—Gif and I—keep our distance, let him work through it. He eventually comes out of it."

"The Drex Easton I met—good Lord. It was a week ago today," she said, amazed by how much longer it seemed that he had been in her life. "That Drex was laid back and witty."

"That's a side of him, too. He can be a real cut-up."

She watched Drex disappear into the rain. He was walking shoulders hunched, his hands crammed into the pockets of his windbreaker. "How long has he been doing this?"

"Officially? Since he got his PhD in criminal psychology."

She looked back at Mike, who took up more than half of the back seat. Seeing her surprise, he tipped his head in the general direction Drex had gone. "Dr. Easton."

"I had no idea."

"He doesn't let on."

"I take it that he and Rudkowski go way back."

"Way back."

"They had a falling out?"

"No. That implies they were once allies. They started out like oil and water."

"Over what?"

"Rudkowski's ineptitude. It became readily apparent to Drex early on, out in California. Santa Barbara woman went missing."

"Never found."

Mike nodded. "Or her money. Anyhow, after that case, Rudkowski relocated to Louisville. He hated like hell that Drex settled
in Lexington. Being that close makes it easier for Drex to keep a finger on Rudkowski's pulse, but it also makes it easier for Rudkowski
to stay on top of Drex. And he does. Like chain mail."

"Which is why Drex works around him."

"Rudkowski is a joke and knows it. He's envious of Drex. Drex
is smarter, a born leader, better looking, gets lots of girls."

He'd paused before the last phrase, and Talia understood that
he'd tacked it on only to provoke her. She opted to be provoked.
"Are you trying to put me in my place? To let me know where I
stand with Drex? With you?"

He didn't say anything.

"You know, Mr. Mallory, in the past thirty-six hours my life has
collapsed around me. It's in shambles, and I don't know if I'll ever
be able to free myself of the wreckage, or even survive. So winning
you over is not a priority. The truth is, I really don't care if I do or
not."

She didn't flinch from his sharpened scrutiny, but it surprised
her to see a twitch at the corner of his wide mouth that was as close
to a smile as she'd ever seen from him. "After that speech, you're
beginning to."

Drex chose then to return. He opened the passenger door and
slid in. "It's really starting to come down. Did I miss anything?"

Talia glanced at Mike, then shook her head no.

Mike asked Drex if Locke had called him back yet. "No, but he
probably—"

All three of them nearly jumped out of their skins when someone rushed up to the passenger side of the car and knocked hard
on the window. Menundez was looking in on them, his face a rain-
streaked grimace.

Drex opened the door. "How'd you know where we were?"

"Locke sent me to get you."

Drex already had one leg out of the car. "What did you find?"

"Lewis."

Drex froze. "What? Gif?"

Menundez shot a look toward Talia, another toward Mike, before coming back to Drex. "The ambulance just left with him."

Chapter 31

———◆———

Speaking in stops and starts, Menundez told them that Gif had been discovered lying on the pavement. "He was in excruciating pain. Couldn't talk. Barely able to breath. Somebody called 911. By the time emergency services arrived, he was unconscious."

Drex grabbed the detective by the collar and all but hauled him into the car.

"Was he still alive?"

"I don't know. I swear, I don't."

"What happened to him?"

"Nobody knows. He was in the middle of a crowd. Just dropped. People around him thought maybe a heart attack or stroke. Locke stayed to question them. Sent me to tell you."

"Thanks."

Talia already had the motor running. As soon as Drex released his hold on Menundez, she peeled out of the parking space, leaving the detective where he stood.

She navigated the streets of downtown in the direction of University Hospital ER, where Menundez had told them Gif was being taken. She made only one wrong turn, going the wrong way down a one-way street. She dodged oncoming motorists who flashed their brights and honked, but she didn't ease up on the accelerator.

In the passenger seat, Drex was beside himself, taking all the blame for letting Gif go alone. She dropped him at the entrance to the ER. He bolted from the car and ran inside while she and Mike went in search of parking.

By the time they caught up with Drex, he was threatening the personnel at the admissions desk with demolition of the hospital if they didn't inform him of his friend's condition.

"At least tell me how seriously he was injured," he shouted at the woman, who must have been the one in charge. "Was he shot? Stabbed? Bleeding? *What?*"

Unfazed, she said, "There's nothing I can tell you, sir. You're welcome to take a seat in the waiting—"

"I'm not taking a seat!"

Talia and Mike flanked him, each hooking an arm through his and pulling him away. They wrestled him toward the waiting area where Mike pushed him into a chair and told him to get a grip.

"You're not the only one upset, you know. Losing it isn't helping."

Drex told him to back the eff off, then planted his elbows on his knees and buried his face his hands.

"Keep an eye on him," Mike said to Talia. "My badge will make that harpy more accommodating."

"Hold on." She caught him by the sleeve. "Flashing your badge might draw unwelcome attention to us."

She'd become aware of other people in the waiting area, who had diverted their attention from cell phones, magazines, and pamphlets about miracle drugs, and were now observing them with avid interest, as though the personal drama that had brought them to the ER tonight paled in comparison to Drex's.

Mike's glower made most go back to what they'd been doing.

Talia crouched in front of Drex and placed her hand on his knee. "Drex, do you still have my cell phone and the battery with you?"

He raised his head and looked at her as though she were speaking in tongues. When the words registered, he nodded. "Why?"

"Put the battery in." When he started shaking his head, she pressed his knee. "One call, then you can take it out again. Trust me. I've got this."

Either he did place his trust in her or he was too worried over Gif to argue, but he began doing as she asked. She left him under Mike's watch and returned to the admissions desk.

The woman took her sweet time sorting through a stack of forms, then, without even looking up from her task, said, "Yes?"

"Is Dr. Phillips in the hospital tonight? Andrew Phillips."

She looked up then. "He's chief of surgery."

"I know. Would it be possible for you to get a message to either him or his assistant?"

She sputtered as though Talia had told a good one. "I don't think so."

"I see. Well, thank you." She gave her a pleasant smile. "I'll call Margaret."

"Who's that?"

"Mrs. Andrew Phillips." Talia held her gaze. "Or, so I don't have to disturb her, if you think it's possible to reach someone on Dr. Phillips's staff, please ask them to call me. My name is Talia Shafer."

The woman shifted her stance as though her shoes had suddenly become too tight. "Like the children's foundation?"

"Exactly like that. Margaret serves on our board."

The woman thought it over, then, "What's your phone number?"

Talia recited it; the woman wrote it down. "Please convey that I'm in the ER waiting room, and that I'm very anxious to know the condition of a patient named Gif Lewis."

The woman gave her a sulky nod.

Talia returned to Drex. She sat in the chair beside his, took her phone from his listless hand, and checked to see that he'd restored the battery and turned it on. "We should know something soon."

"Your approach must've been more diplomatic than mine."

"I didn't use diplomacy. I pulled strings."

She could tell that he wasn't really engaged in what they were saying to each other. He was staring straight ahead, his eyes bleak, haunted. She placed her hand in his, sliding her palm against his, then linking their fingers. They didn't talk.

Across from them in a facing row of chairs, Mike was overflowing the seat of his, but he looked stalwart. Talia found herself judging him less harshly. He was a disagreeable grump, but a levelheaded and reliable friend. His outward display of worry was more contained than Drex's, but she could tell that it was just as deeply felt.

At one point, Drex looked over at him and said hoarsely, "Jesus, Mike."

"I know."

"I'm wishing for a heart attack."

Mike confessed that he was, too. "They're survivable."

After that, they lapsed into a somber silence, stirring only when a stout man, dressed in scrubs and sporting a white beard, pushed through a door and strode into the waiting area with the bearing of a commanding general. Or a chief surgeon at a major teaching hospital.

He glanced around and, spotting Talia, walked straight over. She stood up, Drex and Mike doing likewise. She said, "Andy, I didn't expect you! You could have sent an underling or just called me."

"Does this have anything to do with Jasper? Margaret and I were shocked to hear about it. Has there been any word?"

"Thank you for your concern. There's nothing new to report on

Jasper's disappearance, but indirectly that's why I'm here. One of the men on the investigative team was brought here by ambulance a short while ago."

"Lewis."

"Yes. What can you tell me?"

"I can tell you that he's alive."

She, Drex, and Mike all slumped with relief. "We're all very glad to hear that," she said. "Thank you, Andy." She made hasty introductions. "Mr. Lewis is more than simply their colleague, he's their very good friend. Naturally, they've been anxious to know his condition."

"And that woman over there wouldn't even tell us what had happened to him," Drex said.

The surgeon looked him up and down. "You must be the extremely rude and vituperative individual referred to by her."

That bounced off Drex. "Is Gif going to be all right?"

Talia knew Andrew Phillips to be kind, but he was also brusque. "Come with me."

Without further ado, he turned away. They followed him through the door from which he'd entered and headed toward a bank of elevators. He jabbed the up button. "Mr. Lewis presented with a lacerated liver that required immediate surgery."

Talia covered her mouth with her hand. "Heavens."

"Knife?" Drex asked as they boarded the elevator.

"Blunt trauma."

"He took a blow to the gut?" Mike asked.

The surgeon placed his fist in the wedge where his rib cage came together. "Right here. Vulnerable spot. Ask any boxer. You catch a blow there, you'll likely go to the mat. Hurts like a mother. Excuse me, Talia. Renders you unable to move, breathe. Blood pressure tanks. Here we are."

The surgeon alighted from the elevator first and led them to a much smaller waiting room, which was unoccupied. "Whoever hit him knew what he was doing," he said. "The blow was perfectly placed and done with harmful intent. I wouldn't rule out brass knuckles or some other object. In any case, it was hard enough to cause a sizeable tear. Good news, your friend got here before catastrophic blood loss, and he had an excellent trauma team working on him. The tear has been repaired. He seems overall healthy. Barring any complications, which aren't anticipated, he'll live."

While Mike and Talia expressed their relief, Drex turned away from them and placed one hand on the back of his neck, indicating to Talia that anxiety and tension had concentrated there. Likely he also needed a moment to suppress his emotions.

"When I got your call, they were closing him up," the surgeon was saying. "So if he's not already out of surgery, it shouldn't be much longer. I'll be sure someone lets you know."

Drex came around. "Can I see him?"

"He'll be in recovery ICU for several hours."

"Can I see him?" Drex repeated.

"He'll be out of it. But if you—"

"I do."

Dr. Phillips eyed him as though he warranted his reputation for rudeness, but also with respect for a man who didn't mince words. "I'll tell the staff to grant you a minute as soon as possible."

"Thank you. For everything. I mean it."

The surgeon acknowledged Drex's appreciation with a curt nod, then reached for Talia's hand and patted it. "This business with Jasper..." He let that trail. "Margaret and I are here for you, whenever."

"You certainly have been tonight. Thank you."

He gave her hand a final pat, turned to Drex and Mike, and said, "I have utmost respect for the FBI. Good luck to your friend." Then he left them as though already late to the next emergency.

"Friends in high places," Mike wheezed as he lowered his bulk onto an upholstered love seat.

Talia said, "I'm glad I could be of some use."

"Well, thanks," Mike said.

Drex didn't thank her verbally. He simply pulled her into a tight hug.

Drex had paced miles, it seemed, before he was summoned by a nurse and told he could see Gif. He followed her to one of the ICU rooms, where she left him. Under the loose hospital gown, Gif looked fragile and pale and, if Drex didn't know better, dead. The rhythmic blinks and blips on the machines to which he was connected were reassurance that his systems were functioning.

When the nurse returned to escort him out, she emphasized that Gif was doing well, that his vitals were strong, and that she predicted a full recovery.

"Take good care of him," he said.

"I will."

"He'll complain, but don't listen. Do what's needed to get him well."

"I promise."

Drex hugged her tightly, too.

He relieved Mike and Talia of their concern immediately upon reentering the waiting room. "He looks poorly, but he's doing well. His condition has been upgraded to stable." They were on the verge of asking questions when his cell phone vibrated in his pocket. "Hold on. This may be Locke." He looked at his phone. "It is. He's sent a text."

Warning! Rudkowski here. On our way up.

Drex read it silently and then out loud. "Dammit." Gif's emergency had temporarily distracted him from the other crisis. This jerked him right back into the thick of it.

"He's still typing," he told Mike and Talia, then read the new message aloud. "'Take fire stairs. Look for M.'"

"Menundez," Mike said. "Go!" He shooed them toward the door.

Drex said, "I can't leave Gif."

"He'll never forgive you if you don't. Go!"

"What about Rudkowski?"

"I'll be the sacrificial lamb." Then, rubbing his hands over his extensive midsection, he said, "Sacrificial ox."

They hurried down the fire stairs to the ground floor. Menundez was waiting for them where the stairwell opened into a lobby. "How's Lewis?"

"Out of surgery and in ICU." Drex gave him a concise update. "I can't thank you enough for getting word to me."

"Sure, man." Menundez called their attention to the unusual amount of activity in the lobby. "As you can see, there's a large police presence."

"For us?" Drex asked.

"Busy night. Two assaults, one fatal, in the same area within hours of each other."

"Mike Mallory stayed behind to stall Rudkowski, but he'll be demanding to know where Talia and I are."

"Hear ya. Keep your heads down," the detective said, and started threading this way toward one of the entrances. Glancing around, he lowered his voice before continuing. "Rudkowski is an idiot. After this thing with Lewis, Locke brought me into the loop."

"You and he talked to witnesses who were near Gif when he went down?"

"Yeah, but didn't get much. Boatload of people had just gotten off one of the harbor tours. Word spread about the deadly assault of a woman. The crowd began migrating toward the scene of the crime. Lewis must've got caught up and swept along."

"No one saw the attack?"

He shook his head. "One guy we talked to said that at almost the same time Lewis dropped, he noticed a man making his way through the throng in a hurry. He didn't think anything about it at the time."

"Description?"

"He only saw him from the back, and all he remembers is that he had on a rain poncho. And it could have been just a man in a hurry. Security cameras may have picked him up. They're being checked."

"I'll appreciate any information you can pass along."

"You got it. Locke and me will do what we can to help."

"If you're called on it, I swear I won't let them hang you out to dry."

"Mr. Easton," he said grimly, "if it means catching Ford, I wouldn't mind if I was."

They were approaching an exit where two uniformed policemen were standing together, chewing the fat more than being vigilant. "Just keep walking," Menundez said out of the side of his mouth. "We'll be in touch."

He veered off and headed toward the officers, saying to them as he walked up, "Hey, guys. Menundez from CID. That second emergency near the wharf? It was an assault."

"Any connection to the homicide?"

"We don't know yet, but..."

That's all Drex and Talia heard before they cleared the door. At the first opportunity, Drex pulled her out from under the bright lights of the porte cochere and into the shadows of the building. There he stopped.

"I thought we were in a hurry," she said.

"Let's wait here for a minute or two, see if anybody follows us out."

"Police?"

"Jasper." Thinking out loud, he said, "He killed that woman for no other reason than to draw me out, get me to make myself visible, so he could follow me. Follow me to you. I didn't show, but he recognized Gif."

"But how? From where?"

"Hell I know. I can't figure that. Gif doesn't just fade into the woodwork. He becomes the woodwork. But Jasper picked him out of that crowd."

His eyes narrowed with wrath over what Jasper had done to Gif. "The calling card he left me was anything but subtle. If Jasper materialized in front of me right now, in any disguise, I swear to God I'd kill him."

After waiting for several minutes and seeing no one worthy of a second look, he took Talia's hand. Together they made their way to where she'd parked Gif's car. Drex asked for the key. "I'm driving."

"You may get lost."

"I hope I do. It would make a tail more noticeable."

Earlier that day, Jasper had bid Howard Clement a fond farewell. The man with a penchant for garishly printed shirts had served his purpose, but it had been time to assume another identity.

Tonight, as he'd moved among ordinary people looking very much like one of them, no one paid him any heed. Even if the woman he'd killed had seen him coming, she wouldn't have felt threatened. Had she seen him as she walked alone across the dark and deserted parking lot—such a stupid thing for her to do—she probably would have smiled and wished him a good evening before turning her back to him to unlock her car door.

But she hadn't seen him as he came out of the darkness and moved up behind her. The full nelson had taken her so unaware that she'd barely squeaked in surprise as he clamped his hands around her head like a vise, and forced it forward and down at such a steep angle that the vertebrae in her neck had snapped like twigs. Spine severed. She was dead. It had taken no time at all.

He'd left her where she fell and took a stroll out onto the wharf. It had been crawling with tourists who'd defied the inclement weather. He'd blended in. He'd walked all the way out to the end of it and stayed for several minutes to enjoy the view across the water. He had started back when he heard the first sirens' whoops and wails like trumpeters announcing his achievement. He'd wanted to stop in his tracks and take a bow.

Wanting to be near the crime scene as the curious began converging, he'd picked up his pace, but not enough to be noticed. A reasonably sized crowd had already collected and continued to grow. He'd meandered among families, teenagers groping each other, packs of rambunctious young men, all bunching together, ebbing toward the concentration of police activity.

Jasper hadn't cared to see the body. He'd seen it. He'd been on the lookout for Drex Easton.

He would come, just as he had to the beach. Of that Jasper had had no doubt. Easton would want either to confirm or rule out that this slaying was the handiwork of Jasper Ford. And Jasper had wanted him to know that it absolutely was.

Take that, Easton.

He'd wondered at what point Easton had initiated his chase? Jasper had been intuiting him for years, but he couldn't pinpoint the time he had first sensed him. The knowledge that he had a pursuer hadn't come to him in a jolt of awareness. It had been a seepage into his subconscious. When had it started? After Pixie? Before Loretta? Did Easton know of all his aliases, he wondered, going back all the way to Weston Graham?

How could he? Weston had existed thirty years ago. Easton would have been a boy.

He'd been speculating on how he had come to be the lodestar of Easton's vocation when he did a double take on a man in the crowd. He was as colorless as a person could possibly be, but Jasper had recognized him instantly as Easton's sidekick who'd been with him on the pier above the beach.

The man had been observing the scene and looking into each individual face with the same studied casualness that Jasper boasted himself capable of doing. In an instant he had realized that the man was looking for him. But for Jasper Ford, not his newly assumed identity.

Jasper had really wanted to find Easton. Find him, find Talia.

But this opportunity had been too fortuitous to pass up. The gift horse, so to speak.

Jasper had kept the man in sight and carefully stayed out of his. He'd bided his time, allowing the crowd to thicken until it had become difficult to wade through the newcomers asking what had happened and craning their necks in order to see.

Eventually he had worked his way around until he was walking directly toward the man. There was a cluster of people within touching distance of them, but no one noticed when Jasper socked the man hard.

Easton's pal went down without a sound. With all the jostling going on around them, no one noticed his collapse for a few precious moments, long enough for Jasper to put some distance between them. He kept moving, sometimes swimming upstream, sometimes being propelled by those around him.

But soon he heard the exclamations behind him, had felt the disturbance rippling outward from the spot where the man had dropped. Like everyone else, Jasper halted, turned to look back to see what this new source of commotion was.

His jab had been hard enough and so well placed that it would have incapacitated Easton's buddy. To what extent didn't matter much. Easton would get the message.

As he'd left the vicinity, he'd felt a groundswell of satisfaction inside his chest. It had been a productive night. Much more so than he'd counted on. He'd wished to mark his success, make it an occasion. But he'd foregone a celebration. He was bold, not reckless.

So he'd prudently returned to his car, added his newest trophy to the velvet bag, and zipped it back into an inside pocket of his tracksuit.

Driving away, he'd passed ambulances racing toward the scene of yet another emergency, a scene of havoc, another of his masterpieces.

He'd cruised through the city, in no particular hurry, on the hunt for new lodging.

Chapter 32

———◉———

Drex took a roundabout route from the hospital. After twenty minutes of aimless driving and doubling back several times, he was convinced that they weren't being followed.

He considered switching hotels, but that would involve a check-in process he would rather avoid. He returned them to the suite they'd occupied that afternoon and, once inside, plopped into a chair and sent Mike a text. Seconds later, his phone rang, surprising him.

"I expected something more covert than a call."

"I'm all by my lonesome."

"Rudkowski?"

"Went apeshit when he learned that you two had ducked out. He threatened to arrest me. I double dog dared him. I hadn't absconded with a material witness, had I? I was keeping vigil over my friend who *could have died tonight*.

"Locke told him that he was being unreasonable. Talia's hotshot surgeon came to see what all the yelling was about, told Rudkowski to pipe down or he'd have security throw him out. Rudkowski told me to tell you that you were ruined, that he would see to it, then he left with Locke and Menundez. I think both of them are solid."

"Me too. Have you seen Gif?"

He hadn't, but he was receiving periodic updates that Gif was holding his own.

There had been no developments in the investigation into the homicide or the assault on Gif. "They're reviewing surveillance camera videos," Mike said, "but they have a lot more of them to look at. Out of Rudkowski's hearing, the detectives promised to keep us apprised. The coroner's report on the woman killed tonight is expected in the morning. Locke said he'd shoot it to us, along with the one on Elaine Conner."

"Jasper's got people working overtime tonight."

"He must be so proud," Mike returned drolly. "Anyhow, nothing more we can do tonight except wait."

"I feel guilty for having a bed and you don't," Drex said.

"I can sleep sitting up. Do most of the time anyway."

"Let me know if there's any change in Gif's condition. I'll come immediately."

"Okay."

"I mean it, Mike. *Any* change."

"Cross my overtaxed heart." With that he clicked off.

Drex looked over at Talia. "Did you hear any of that?"

"I got the gist."

"Talia." He paused in order to give his next words heft. "Thank you." She tipped her head inquisitively. "For pulling those strings. If you hadn't, we might still be in the dark about Gif. I'd still be losing my mind."

"I believe the lady at admissions thought you already had."

"I'm surprised she didn't send for the straitjacket squad."

They smiled at each other. Then he leaned his head back and dug the heels of his hands into his eye sockets. "God, how long has this day been?"

"Long."

He lowered his hands from his eyes and slapped his knees as he rolled up out of the chair. "I'm going to shower, unless you want the bathroom first."

"Go ahead."

He trudged up the stairs, went into his bedroom, and took off his windbreaker and shoes. He unclipped his holster from his belt and considered taking the pistol into the bathroom with him so it would be within reach. But he set it on the nightstand instead. When he went into the bathroom he noticed that Talia's bedroom door was closed.

By the time he'd undressed, the water in the shower was steaming. Flattening his hands on the wall above the taps and standing directly beneath the spray, he let it pound so hard against the back of his head and neck that it stung.

Then he was shocked into awareness of a softer, gentler touch between his shoulder blades. His head snapped up.

"No, stay as you were." Talia moved up behind him and pressed her body—all of it—against his. She rubbed her center against his ass. Her breasts sandwiched his spine.

"Oh, my God. Talia—"

"Stay as you are."

"But I want to see you. And it feels so good."

"To me, too." She rested her cheek against his back. "It feels good to be needed. Allow me to do this for you. Okay?"

He answered by saying nothing and staying as he was. She backed away only far enough to reach for something. It must have been the bottle of shower gel, because her hands were soapy when she applied them to the back of his neck.

Starting at the base and working up, she kneaded out the achiness, then slid her fingers into his hair and massaged his head. On their way back down, they gently pinched the tops of his ears and earlobes, then moved across his shoulders, squeezing the tension out of them.

He sighed a long, drawn out *ah*. "That felt great. Thanks."

"You're welcome."

"Can I turn around now?"

"No."

"When?"

"When I'm done."

"When will that be?"

"When I say when."

She got a refill of gel, then pressed her hands firmly against his back on either side of his spine, rubbing circles into his lats, working her way down until her hands were on his butt, creating deep depressions in his glutes with her fingers.

"Your muscles are tight," she said. "Relax."

"Relax? Are you serious? I'm dying here."

She laughed softly. "I don't think so."

Her thumbs became twin pressure points on the small of his back. They rode the bumpy path of his vertebrae all the way down to the cleft of his ass, then teased it with feather-light brushes that caused his breath to hitch.

"Damn, Talia. Now?"

"Not yet."

Again she withdrew to get more gel. *The bottle must be near empty by now*, he thought. Then all thought ceased as her arms came around him, and she covered his pecs with her hands.

"I like the hair," she whispered, tweaking it.

"Yeah?"

"Um-huh. Just the right amount."

After her thumbs glanced his nipples, her hands took a sinuous, crisscrossing, slippery course down his torso, over ribs and abdomen, past his navel, until her fingers slid down the channels above his thighs where they met at the base of his cock.

Christ. He didn't want to beg.

He didn't have to. Her hands took turns forming silky fists around him, one massaging upward and moving off, only to be outdone by its alternate that followed just behind. When he didn't think he could withstand any more, one hand didn't slide off at the tip. It stayed. Fingers dripping lather made teasing rotations around the crest, over it, again, as though testing its tautness, and then something wicked was done to the slit.

Through clenched teeth, he strangled out, *"When."*

He turned around and hauled her against him. He tried to pause and register all the incredible sensations that holding her wet and naked against him induced, but his brain was functioning on a more primitive tier.

He gathered up a handful of her hair and pulled her head back, tilting her face up to his. He looked into her eyes, then covered her mouth with his. It was a ravenous kiss. He couldn't get enough of her, and she was as hungry.

He skimmed her breast with his palm, then claimed it, reshaping it, lifting it as he lowered his head and took her nipple into his mouth. With each tug, she whimpered in pleasure and clasped his head to hold him to her.

He skimmed her front, marveling over the feminine curves and hollows, the incredible softness of her skin. Briefly he entangled his fingers in the hair between her thighs, then parted the soft flesh beneath.

She was slick and pliant around the fingers he pressed into her. When he began stroking, her head dropped forward against his chest. He felt the scrape of her teeth against his pec. With urgency, she reached down and closed her hand around his erection.

"Talia," he gasped, pushing her hand aside and withdrawing his fingers from her. "This is going to be some fever-pitch fucking. If we attempt it in this shower, we'll be the next two patients in the emergency room. Let's get in bed."

Dazed, she nodded.

He gave himself a fifteen-second rinse, turned off the taps, and helped her out of the stall. He yanked a towel off the bar and handed it to her, then took one for himself. They haphazardly dried themselves as they stumbled into one of the bedrooms. His, he thought, although he didn't know for sure and didn't care. It had a bed.

He flung back the covers, then sat down on the edge, placed his hands on her bottom, and pulled her between his spread legs. Leaning into her, he rubbed his face against her breasts, touched his tongue to her nipples, flicked it over the occasional freckle and imagined it melting in his mouth like a speck of raw sugar. He nuzzled her middle and swirled his tongue over her navel. Moving lower, he breathed out through his lips into the damp curls.

She spoke his name in a husky whisper.

He turned her and guided her down until she was lying on her back, arms at her sides, hands at shoulder level, palms up. Taking her up on the invitation he saw in the unresisting pose, as well as the look in her smoky eyes, he knelt, opened her thighs, and kissed her with utmost intimacy, his tongue doing as his fingers had minutes earlier. He took tender love bites, applied gentle suction, tantalized her with erotic play, and only then exposed that most vulnerable spot.

Her body jerked in reaction to the first sweep of his tongue, then she began moving in response to and in anticipation of each fluid caress. They increased in frequency, the carnal friction intensifying with each one until she was arching up for more, then more, and more, until an orgasm seized her. He stayed with her, whisking his lips against her, murmuring her name, until the final aftershock shuddered through her and she lay still.

He levered himself up and above her—and was shocked to see tears sliding down her temples into her hair. She reached for him, grabbing at him until their mouths were melded and he had pushed into her.

But he went only far enough to secure himself just inside. There he waited, wanting to commit to memory this moment of feeling her around him for the first time. Then he continued pressing into her until he was solidly imbedded.

She hugged him to her tightly, and it was fantastic, but he had to move or he was going to die. He buried his face in her hair. "If I get too rough, slow me, stop me. I want...I want...Oh, God..."

The mating instinct took over. In spite of his best intentions, his strokes became faster and stronger. A slight shift in his position enabled him to reach deeper, and he did. God, did he.

"Don't hold back," Talia said on a near sob, lifting his head from the crook of her neck so she could look into his face.

He kissed her again and continued kissing her until he couldn't focus on anything except the orgasm that rocked her and caused her to bow her back and clench around him. That was his undoing. Grafted to her, he came in a burst of light.

Drowsily she said, "Moving to the bed was a good idea."

"One the best I've had lately. I might have irreparably injured us in that shower stall."

"It would have been worth it."

He hitched an eyebrow. "Yeah?"

"Hmm," she said, stretching luxuriantly.

She lay on her back but was angled slightly toward him. He was lying on his side, propped on one elbow, extremely attentive to her nakedness, but seemingly blasé toward his own.

Of course he had no call to be self-conscious. He was lean and long limbed, muscled but not bulky, clouded with lovely brown hair in all the right places.

Against her, it all felt wonderful.

"Can you get drunk on sex?" she asked.

"I could get drunk on you."

"I feel as though I'm on display."

Drex gave her a lazy smile. "I'm feasting my eyes, all right."

"Your tiger eyes."

"Tiger eyes?"

"That's what they remind me of."

He leaned down and licked the slope of her breast. "Hear me purring?"

She laughed and sank her fingers into his unruly hair. "I heard you growling. Several times." She pulled him toward her for a kiss. It was lazy, unhurried, and delicious.

When they finally broke apart, he resumed his position and continued his survey of her terrain by touching her nipple with his fingertip. "I'm going to have to coin some new adjectives to describe color...." His caress had caused her nipple to tighten. "...and texture."

His hand moved down the center of her torso, his fingers barely grazing her skin. When he reached her mound, he feathered the hair. "But some things defy description."

"You don't need descriptive words. You're not a writer."

"Hmm." Preoccupied with what his fingers were doing, he said, "I may take it up just for the research." He angled his head back and took her in, his gaze moving from her tousled hair to the tips of her toes. "You are gorgeous, Talia Shafer."

"I was going to say the same about you." She scrubbed his bristly jaw line with her knuckles, smoothed his sun-glinted eyebrows with her index finger, then trailed it down his cheek and dipped it into his dimple. He deepened it for her by smiling, and she laughed lightly.

It felt so good, so right to be with him like this, she was reluctant to bring into the open something that had been needling her. She reached for his hand and drew it up to the center of her chest, holding it between her breasts, but not provocatively. She traced the network of veins on the back of it. "Drex, what we just did was amazing."

"On a scale of one to ten?"

She smiled, but he must have sensed that she wasn't teasing, that what she had to say was serious, because he pulled the covers up over them before resettling beside her and intertwining their legs.

"I don't want to spoil this," she said. "But I must ask."

He brows drew together. "What?"

"You talked tonight about Jasper playing an inside joke on you."

"Something to let me know that he'd gotten the best of me."

She shifted her gaze back to his hand and ran her finger along the ridge of his knuckles. "Did you sleep with his wife to get the best of him?"

He became so still that she feared she had ruined something precious, and that the memory she would be left with was of him being highly offended and storming from the bed, the suite, her life.

But after a ponderous silence, he said, "Look at me." She did. He said, "No. Believe me, wanting you in my bed has been no joke, inside or otherwise. Mike, Gif, and I had words. They lectured me like maiden aunts about letting my dick do my thinking. They cited the conflict of interest this—" he said, sawing his hand between them, "—would create. You see the effect of all their wise counsel."

He turned the hand she held against her chest and linked their fingers. "If I had wanted to use you to taunt Jasper, that's what I would have done. Taunted. I would have let him *think* that we had slept together or planned to at our first opportunity."

He studied their clasped hands. "You probably won't believe me, but I swear, for all my tomcatting, I've never been with a married woman. You're my first adultery, and I wouldn't break my personal moral code just to score points against Jasper."

"But you were unfaithful to your wife."

"No, I wasn't."

"You told Jasper—"

"I've never had a wife to cheat on."

Her head went back an inch. "What?"

"I've never been married."

She was stunned by the joy that spread through her from knowing that. "No one special enough to make you stop tomcatting?"

"No time or inclination to let anything special develop. Besides, I wouldn't drag a good woman into my particular hell."

"Into that dark place you have to go?"

He nodded. "Hazard of the trade."

"You didn't drag me into it this afternoon. In fact you shut me out."

"Because it's hardly conducive to foreplay, and I was hoping to get lucky."

She smiled, but didn't let him flirt her away from the subject. "Mike and I talked."

"Oh, great. Did he go into his maiden aunt persona?"

"A little. Dr. Easton."

She recapped her conversation with Mike. When she finished, Drex said, "I started looking for Weston Graham long before I earned my doctorate."

"When you learned he had killed your mother? How did that come about?"

"Are you sure you want to hear that?"

"Yes. I'd like to know."

"You accept that Weston Graham and Jasper Ford are one and the same?"

"You've convinced me. No, actually, *he's* convinced me with his actions over the past two days."

He reflected for a moment, then said, "Although I'm not certain he launched his career with my mother, I suspect it. Maybe he hadn't consciously mapped out woman killing as a career path. But after he'd rid himself of her and walked away unscathed, he recognized his talent and saw a future in exploiting it."

She scooted closer to him and laid her hand on his chest. "I saw her picture in your files. She was lovely."

"I have no memory of her."

"How old were you when she went missing?"

"Around ten, I think. But my dad had moved the two of us to Alaska years before that."

"Tell me about it."

He took a deep breath, rubbed his legs against hers, readjusted his head on the pillow. "A lot of it I've had to piece together because Dad wouldn't talk about it. Never. But what I gather is that she abandoned us to be with Weston Graham."

"She abandoned you, too?"

"I don't know if she did so without a second thought, or if Dad was unbending on keeping me with him. He cut me off from her. Completely." He told her about the name change. "That's why I wasn't afraid to use my name with Jasper. I knew he wouldn't recognize it."

"Wasn't that a rather spiteful thing for your dad to do?"

"No doubt spite was his motivation. He made it impossible for her to find us. But it was fortuitous, because it also prevented Weston from locating us after he'd disposed of her. We might have been two of those loose threads you referred to earlier.

"I knew none of this at the time, understand," he said. "My first clear recollections are of living in Alaska, and it was always just Dad and me."

"What you described to me, all the moving around, et cetera?"

"All true."

"It must've been a lonely life for you."

He admitted as much by giving her a rueful smile. "On the other hand, I didn't know anything different. Not until I got older and saw that other dads actually talked over mealtimes. They laughed and joshed with their kids. They had male buddies they hung out with to drink beer and watch ball games. They had women they slept with. Our house was devoid of anything feminine. I began to notice the touches that my friends' houses had that ours didn't. It was the...the appealing *something* that a woman emanates."

He fell silent for a moment, then said, "My mother's desertion robbed Dad of all that enjoyment, of all joy. She stole his soul. Then Weston stole from her."

"She had money?"

"What seemed like a lot at the time. It was modest by today's standards. After her, Weston, with a new identity, set his sights much higher. But when she went missing, and investigators began digging into her life, it was discovered that all her assets, which she'd inherited from her parents, had miraculously disappeared along with her."

"How did your father learn of it?"

"It made the newspapers. I didn't know he'd saved them until later. But I remember when the change came over him. He'd never been a hard drinker, but he started drinking heavily at night, every night, long into the night. He became even more taciturn than normal. I didn't ask him what the matter was, I think out of fear of what he would tell me. But even if I had asked, he wouldn't have told me. She had been eradicated from my life."

"But your dad still loved her. He was bereaved."

"I see that now. I didn't then. Years later, when I was old enough to read up on her disappearance, I matched the timing of it to that dark period when Dad really shut down."

"And you were around ten years old? That must have been an awful time for you."

"In one respect, it was beneficial. That's when I learned to be sociable. I stayed over at friends' houses a lot. Their parents must've felt sorry for me. They took me in, saw that I was well fed. Anyway, over time, Dad stopped drinking and went back to being more himself. Which was still a level of bereavement. He grieved for my mother, for everything about her, until the day he died."

"When was that?"

"I was in my first year of college in Missoula. I was summoned home. He'd had a stroke, which didn't kill him right away."

"Did you make it home in time to be with him?"

"That's when he shared the story of my mother. He'd secretly kept all the newspaper write-ups about her disappearance. He told me about Weston Graham, who was sought as the prime suspect but never captured. Her disappearance remains a cold case of the LAPD."

He raised his right hand to within inches of her face. "See the scar?" A faint white line bisected his palm. "While my dad lay dying, I cut both our palms, pressed them together, and took a blood oath to get the bastard." Wryly, he added, "It's taken one hell of a long time. All my adult life. And I'm still working on it."

With gruffness in his voice, he continued. "I wouldn't trade for those last minutes with Dad, though. When I made that vow, he cried. It was the most naked emotion I'd ever seen from him. Ever. In my life. It was the closest he and I ever came to having a genuine father-son relationship. He died later that day."

She took his hand and kissed the palm, openmouthed. "He loved you very much."

He looked at her with doubt.

"Perhaps he took you away to spite or to wound your mother, but maybe he saw Weston for what he was and feared for you."

"Maybe," he said grudgingly. "That has occurred to me."

"Drex, if he hadn't loved you and wanted you with him, he could have dumped you anywhere along the way, and at any time. It couldn't have been easy for a single man working on the pipeline to rear a child alone."

"He felt an obligation to me, maybe. But he had lost the will to live."

"Then why didn't he kill himself and be done with it? Leave you to your own devices?" She raised her eyebrows in question.

He gave her a hard look, but he didn't say anything.

"He loved you. Believe it." She settled close to him again. "How do you feel toward your mother?"

"I vacillate between deep resentment over her letting me go and sorrow for the fate she must've suffered. Fair to say that I'm conflicted?"

"Fair to say."

They lay quietly for several minutes, then he placed his forearm across his eyes and moaned.

"What?"

"I finally got you naked in bed. I should be talking dirty to you, not blathering all this maudlin crap."

"You can still talk dirty." She slid her hand beneath the sheet. It took only one stroke to bring him erect. She laughed. "Well, that didn't take long."

"I told you a sad story. Are you doing this out of pity?"

"I don't think anyone would pity a man so well endowed."

He flashed a grin that would have done the devil proud.

"But even if it is out of pity, do you want me to stop?" she teased.

"Hell, no. Have at it."

She rolled onto him and began dropping kisses on his chest.

"Talia?"

"Don't bother me, I'm busy."

"I just want to ask—"

"Later."

She opened her thighs and guided him in. He hissed swear words as she slowly sank down onto him and began rocking. He grunted with pleasure. "And I thought the first time was good." He angled himself up in order to reach her breasts. His mouth was hot and avid, and left her nipples wet with loving.

When he lay back, he gripped her hips between his hands and coaxed her, coached her, cajoled her in the raunchiest language. Several minutes later, on short puffs of breath, he said, "Have at it. That's what I said. But, sweetheart...God a'mighty."

He slid his hand between them. His revolving thumb worked its magic, and half a minute later, she lay sated atop his heaving chest.

When she had regained her breath, she whispered, "You were saying?"

"Hmm?"

"Before I had my way with you, you were about to ask me something."

"Oh. Never mind."

"No, ask."

He combed his fingers through her hair and rearranged it on her shoulders.

"I remember you doing that last night when you came up to the guest room."

"I couldn't keep myself from touching you. I'd have rather put my hands inside those ugly pajamas, but I settled for stroking your hair."

"It was nice. The kind of touch I needed then. What were you going to ask?"

He hesitated. "When we were in the shower, you said it was nice to be needed. You practically asked permission to give me the best damn hand job ever."

"Really?"

"Don't get me off the subject. What I'm wondering is…You don't have to tell me. You owe me no explanation. I just—"

"Jasper neither invited or welcomed attention like that. He didn't…He never said, 'Have at it.'"

He didn't respond immediately, and when he did, it wasn't to pursue the topic of her relationship with Jasper. "I probably could have said something a little more romantic."

"It was romantic to me."

He tipped her head up. His eyes moved over her face, taking in every feature. He ran his thumb along her lower lip. "Sleepy?"

"I'm having trouble keeping my eyes open."

"Let's go to sleep." His reach was long enough to turn off the lamp on the night table.

Talia was about to move off him, but he wrapped his arms around her, one under her bottom, the other just below her shoulders. He raised his head and pecked a kiss, then left his lips against hers. "Stay here."

"Like this?"

"Just like this." He dabbed the corner of her mouth with the tip of his tongue. "I'm not ready to leave you yet."

"I may get heavy."

"I may snore."

She returned her cheek to his chest and closed her eyes, feeling more languid and safe than she could ever remember feeling. "You thought my pajamas were ugly?"

He answered with a soft snore.

Chapter 33

———◆———

At some point during the wee hours, Drex had disengaged from Talia, moved her off him, and turned her onto her side so they could spoon. He woke up with his arm tingling from having gone to sleep supporting her head. He checked the clock on the night table and was surprised by the time. He hadn't planned to sleep that long. It would be daylight soon.

As tempting as it was to stay snuggled with Talia, he had thinking to do.

He eased his arm from beneath her head and scooted off the bed without waking her. He took only his phone and pistol with him as he tiptoed from the bedroom and into the bathroom. Five minutes later, he emerged, showered and dressed in the clothes he'd worn the day before and which had remained on the bathroom floor all night.

Downstairs, he brewed a cup of coffee, then sent Mike a text asking for an update on Gif. Mike called him back. Keeping his voice low, Drex answered on the first ring. "How's he doing?"

"I got to see him around four-thirty. He had woken up, but was still under the influence. Wanted to know what had happened to him."

"He didn't remember?"

"Remembered a throng of people. He was making his way through as best he could toward the cordoned-off crime scene. Next thing he knew, he was on the ground, in pain like none other, paralyzed. Couldn't even breathe."

"He never saw his attacker?"

"He wasn't looking for one."

"Right," Drex said. "Did you get any sleep?"

"Couple of hours. You?"

"Some."

"Talia okay?"

"She's still asleep."

The unasked question hovered between them. Drex chose to ignore it. "Have you heard from Locke?"

"Check your email. He sent the coroner's reports about ten minutes ago."

"I haven't turned on my laptop yet. I'll get to them as soon as we hang up."

"No surprises in the one on Elaine Conner. The woman last night? He came up behind her, probably caught her in a nelson, snapped her spinal column, C-six."

"Jesus."

"Tell me."

Drex said, "What worries me most is the cheekiness of it. He killed that woman and hung around."

"In the hope that you would show."

"No doubt, but staying in the vicinity is out of his norm. He's done it twice now within twenty-four hours. Takes balls."

"No, it doesn't," Mike said. "It takes a psychopath. He's accelerating."

"Spiraling at the speed of a tornado."

"Because you've come too close."

"He's taunting me. These two dead women are his red cape."

"We've got to put this cocksucker out of commission, Drex."

"I know. But listen, Mike, you can't come back here."

"I already figured that."

"Beyond the chance of leading Rudkowski to Talia and me, I need you to stay with Gif."

"Figured that, too. At least through today to make sure he's on the mend."

"Are you okay with hanging out there?"

"I'm better off than Gif."

"I know, but—"

"Did you hug a nurse?"

"What?"

"A nurse. Gray hair, smiling eyes?"

Drex remembered her now. "She promised to take good care of Gif."

"Well, she must've enjoyed that hug. Since you aren't here, she's taken me under her wing. Fetched me a pillow and blanket last night. This morning, she brought me a washcloth and towel. I took a sponge bath in the men's room. There's a large cafeteria. I've got my laptop and charger. I'll be doing for you here what I'd be doing for you there. I'm fine. So long as Rudkowski leaves me alone, but I doubt he'll make another scene like he did last night."

"Thanks, Mike. I'll stay in touch. Let me know if you see an opportunity for me to talk to Gif."

"Will do."

They disconnected. Drex made himself another cup of coffee and set up his laptop on the eating bar. He opened the email from Locke, whose message was: *No connection between the two homicides except gender and birthdays in April. You still think it's him?*

"You bet your ass I do." But Drex knew he would need more than, "*I* feel *him*," to convince the law enforcement community that the man who was missing and feared lost at sea was on dry land, alive and well and lethal.

He opened the first attachment in the email, which was the coroner's report on Elaine Conner. He read it word for word. As

Mike had said, it didn't contain much that Locke hadn't already shared with them.

The report on Sara Barker, the woman murdered last night, was difficult for Drex to read. It was a heinously wasteful act. Jasper being his most self-indulgent.

After going through the report once, Drex left the bar and wandered into the living area, where he turned on the television. Network morning shows were in full swing. During the brief break-in for the local station, a story was aired about Sara Barker's murder. A spokeswoman for the family described her friend as a giving, loving person. "Who would do such an unspeakable thing?"

"Who indeed?" asked the young female reporter, looking straight into the camera, affecting a tragic tone and expression.

"The same man who buried a woman alive," Drex replied.

When the reporter began chatting energetically with the weatherman, Drex muted the TV and returned to the bar. He pulled up the report on Elaine Conner again. "Come on, Elaine. You loved to talk. Talk to me. Tell me what I'm missing."

It had to be here: Weston/Jasper's trademark, initial, stamp, signature. *Something.* What the hell was it?

He read the report again out loud, as though speaking the words would sharpen their definitions and make them revelatory.

And then he read a word, and, as soon as his mouth formed it, his mind slammed on the brakes. Returning to the beginning of the sentence, he read up to that word, and stopped on it again.

His hands got clammy. His heartbeat sped up. But before he let himself become too excited, he went back to the report on Sara Barker. He scrolled through the various forms until he found the one he sought. He magnified it to make the print larger on his monitor. And there it was. The same word. In a seemingly innocuous notation in the autopsy report.

He broke out in goose bumps.

In his haste to get up, he knocked the barstool over backward. He mounted the stairs two at a time and painfully banged his shoulder against the doorframe as he barged through it and into the bedroom.

"Talia!" He rounded the bed and sat down on the side she was facing as she slept. "Talia." He shook her shoulder.

She roused and blinked up at him, then smiled sleepily. "Good morning."

He placed his hands on her shoulders, as much to stabilize himself as to focus her. "Tell me again about Jasper's wardrobe being custom-made, keeping his tailor busy."

She struggled to sit up, dragging the sheet up over her breasts and pushing her hair off her face. "What? Has something happened?"

"You said he fussed over things, like buttons."

"Yes. He recently had his tailor replace buttons that he called 'outmoded.'"

Drex's gut clenched. "He did?"

"No more than a week ago. He had old buttons swapped out for new ones on several pieces."

Drex held still and let it sink in, then released her and sat back on his bent knee. Staring into near space, he said quietly, "He takes a button." Coming back to Talia, he looked into her gaze, from which all sleepiness had disappeared. "He takes a button."

Getting off the bed, he paced the length of it. "He's collected them. He puts them on garments he has custom made and wears them in plain sight of everybody. His trophies are on display, no one suspecting they came off the bodies of women he killed. That's his joke on us dumb slobs."

He ran his hand over the top of his head, then down the back of his neck. It was still difficult for him to breathe evenly. His heart was racing, and not from climbing the stairs at the pace he had.

"How did you come to this conclusion?" Talia spoke softly as though not to derail his train of thought or interrupt the flow of deductive reasoning.

"In the coroner's report on Elaine, he described her body as it was on the beach. The position it was lying in. So forth. She was fully clothed. A black, low-heeled sandal was on her right foot. The left one was missing. She was dressed in black capri pants and a light blue shirt. The coroner noted that a button on the shirt cuff was missing.

"The woman last night was wearing a skirt with decorative buttons down the left side. Here," he said, running his hand along the side of his thigh. "According to the autopsy report, which included photographs of her clothing, the last button in the row was missing."

Talia processed all that. "How does this help you?"

"It links the two homicides, Elaine's and Sara Barker's. It's a telltale signature that I never had before, because there has never been a corpse before. Until Marian Harris." He gave Talia a sharp look, then left the bedroom and clambered down the stairs, snatched his phone up off the bar, and called Mike. When he answered, Drex said, "He takes a button."

"Come again?"

Sputtering in his haste to get it out, Drex told him of his discovery.

"Possible coincidence," Mike said.

"It's possible for me to be voted pope, but how likely is it? Did that deputy in Key West send you the coroner's report on Marian Harris?"

"We never asked for it."

"Shit! You're right. Gray—that's his name—mentioned the decomposition of the remains. I was focused on the atrocity, and then on getting that party pic enhanced. I'll call him now. If Marian was clothed when the creep buried her, forensics would have a description of the garments, even if they were partially disintegrated. The report would include the detail of a missing button."

"You hope."

"I hope. But this feels right, Mike. If we can connect Marian's murder to these most recent two, Rudkowski can't deny that we're chasing a serial killer. If he does, we'll jump the chain."

"But you've still got to prove that Jasper Ford is the creep."

"One step at a time. This is a leap. Stay handy. I'm putting in a call to that deputy now."

Talia came downstairs as he was rifling through his duffel bag looking for the cell phone that had Gray's phone number logged. Her hair was still wet from the shower. She smelled of the gel, the scent of which would forever call to mind that erotic experience.

As she walked past him on her way into the kitchen, he said, "By the way, good morning back," and leaned over for a quick kiss on the mouth, then resumed replacing a battery in the cell phone.

Talia said, "Jasper had his buttons switched out recently so he could take all of the trophy ones with him when he disappeared."

"That's my theory. They're small, portable."

"When he moves on, he'll have them sewn onto other clothes, adding the newest two."

"He would, but he's not going to move on, Talia." He clicked on the back of the phone. "He's not getting away this time."

He pulled up the number of the sheriff's office in Key West and hoped to God Gray was on duty. When the main line was answered, he asked for him and, while he waited, watched Talia make herself a cup of coffee. Her hands were shaky. When she turned to face him, he said, "You okay?"

Her smile was tentative. "Yes. It's just that this pushes it beyond speculation. It's become very real."

"I know." He went over to her and stroked her face. "I'm sorry."

She covered his hand with hers, holding it against her cheek. "Don't be sorry. Don't be sorry at all." He gave her another tender kiss, then righted the barstool and guided her onto it.

"This is Deputy Gray."

Drex jerked his attention back to the phone call. "Gray, it's Special Agent Easton."

After a brief silence that teemed with resentment, the young deputy said, "Agent Rudkowski called me about half an hour ago. He told me all about you and what you've done. I can't talk to you."

"Deputy—"

"Sorry."

"Gray! Don't hang up. Listen. I need—"

"I can't talk to you." He was emphatic, but spoke in an undertone, as though afraid of being overheard. "I've been warned by the *FBI* not to talk to you, or send anything to you. Rudkowski also reported all this to my sergeant, who is furious."

"Okay. Busted. I manipulated you, and my tactics have been questionable."

"Questionable? Did you really run off with a material witness?"

"Yes, in order to try and save her life. I don't want her to meet a fate similar to Marian Harris's. Which is why I'm calling. I think I've found a link between—"

"You're not hearing me, Easton. You have no authorization. I can't help you."

"All I'm asking is that you send me the coroner's report on Marian Harris."

"That report is exempt from public disclosure because the criminal investigation is ongoing."

"That sounds memorized."

"It was. Rudkowski suggested it, so I'd have a reply if you had the gall to contact me again."

Drex spat out an expletive, but he forced himself to remain calm. Being overbearing wasn't going to work on Gray, who had been cowed by pressure coming at him from all sides. At any other time, Drex would feel bad for having exploited the green officer's initial willingness to help.

He said, "All right. I understand your reluctance to send it to me. Instead, send it to Agent Mallory. Remember him? You sent him—"

"Rudkowski said I wasn't to feed him anything, either. Or somebody named Lewis. He said you three have formed a league of your own. That you're impeding two homicide investigations. He also told me that this isn't the first time you've pulled illegal and unethical stunts."

Drex pinched the bridge of his nose. "Will you at least read through that report, and then let me ask you some questions pertaining to it?"

"I. Can't. Talk. To. You."

"I'm not asking you to *talk*. A simple yes or no. In fact, you don't even have to speak. You could cough. Once for yes, twice for no."

"Rudkowski said you'd turn it into a game of some kind or another."

"I'll limit it to one question. *One*. That's all. Will you do that much?"

"Sorry, no."

"Lives are at risk, Deputy Gray."

"Rudkowski told me you'd say that, too. He said you're—"

"I'm...?"

"Delusional."

"Do you think so?" The deputy remained silent. Drex said, "I suppose you were also instructed to pass along this phone number if I called, so Rudkowski can use it to locate me."

Drex heard him swallow hard. "I'm sorry, Easton," he said and hung up.

"Michael Mallory?"

Mike was in the process of trying to hack the police report on last night's murder of Sara Barker. He looked up, expecting to see someone on the hospital staff. Instead, facing him were two uniformed sheriff's deputies, one of each gender.

He closed his laptop. "That's me."

"We'd like to ask you some questions."

"Check with detectives Locke and Menundez, Charleston PD. They know all about it. The man attacked last night at Waterfront is my friend. I have their permission to keep vigil."

"Maybe. But it was an FBI Agent Rudkowski who told us where to start looking for you."

Mike didn't like the sound of that. "Well, you found me."

"Do you know a Sammy Markson? Also known as—"

"I know all Sammy's aliases."

"So you do know him?"

"I helped put him away for his first stint."

"A few days ago, did you drive a vehicle provided by him from Lexington, Kentucky, to Atlanta?" The woman deputy consulted her small notepad. She read off the make, model, and license plate number of the minivan. "Blue in color."

Mike scowled. "Why're you asking?"

"Did you?"

He mulishly held his tongue.

"If you're unwilling to answer," said the male deputy, "we'll have to take you in for further questioning."

"First, you need to tell me what for, and, if you're taking me in for an interrogation, once we get there, you must provide me with legal counsel before I say a word."

"This is an informal interview," the woman said.

Mike snorted. "We all know there's no such thing. What's your probable cause for hassling me?"

The two looked at each other and seemed to come to an agreement. The woman said, "Last night, Sammy Markson was arrested and charged with several counts of grand theft auto."

That little shit. He was cutting deals with the Fayette County, Kentucky, sheriff's department.

Mike had notified Sammy that he was coming to Charleston and that he had left the minivan at the Atlanta airport for retrieval at a later date. It had seemed the decent thing to do. He could now kick himself.

The male deputy said, "Markson provided your name as someone who would vouch for him."

"Vouch that he's guilty or vouch that he's innocent?"

"He didn't specify. Which is our probable cause for hassling you."

Mike gave a grunt of contempt. "Sammy would sell out his own mother."

"He did. Late last night. Let's go, Mr. Mallory."

"Wait, my friend is—"

"Agent Rudkowski is being kept apprised of Lewis's condition. By last report, he's stable. You'll be notified if he takes a downturn."

Mike saw no point in arguing with these two, who were merely carrying out their orders. His fight was with Rudkowski. He heaved himself off the love seat and tucked his laptop under his arm. Just then, his cell phone chimed. "May I?"

Again the pair silently consulted each other. The man came back to him. "Make it quick."

He answered. Drex said, "Rudkowski got to the deputy in Key West. He's clammed up, and there was no cracking him. We've lost that resource."

Mike sighed. "That's the good news."

———

Drex pitched the phone onto the bar, where it landed with an unheeded clatter. But even before that display of temper, Talia knew that Mike had relayed something Drex hadn't wanted to hear.

With a sinking feeling, she said, "Bad news about Gif? Please say no."

"No, he's still doing okay."

"Then what?"

When Drex had awakened her and told her about his breakthrough, he'd been humming like an overloaded electrical circuit. The call to the deputy in Florida had dimmed the wattage. But this call to Mike had taken all the sizzle out of him.

"In terms of helping, Gif was lost to me as of last night. Now Mike's been hamstrung. If I didn't know better, I'd think Fate was working against us. Dammit!" He picked up his coffee cup and hefted it like a baseball pitcher on the mound. He even looked at the far wall as though gauging the distance.

Before he could pitch it, she walked over, took the cup from him, and set it back down on the bar. "What's happened with Mike?"

He gave her a run-down, after which she asked, "*Was* the car stolen?"

"Probably."

"Did Mike know?"

"He didn't ask. Sammy won't incriminate him because he'll want him as a future ally, which it appears he'll need. But the point is, Mike is mired in this now and unavailable to me."

"What can I do?"

He was about to reply when one of his cell phones rang. He looked at the readout. "Locke." He answered and put it on speaker so she could listen in. "Morning."

Locke said, "You're still answering this number."

"For the time being. Did you hear about Mike?"

"No. What about him?"

"Long story, and it will keep. What's up?"

"Remember me telling you that one of the people we talked to last night noticed a man walking away from where Lewis fell?"

"Witness said he seemed to be in a hurry."

"We've isolated him on two security cameras."

Drex glanced over at Talia. "Jasper?"

"Since we never met him, and you say he'll have altered his appearance, we don't know. We need you to take a look."

"Absolutely. I've got a breakthrough for you, too."

"What?"

"I want to confirm it first. Soon. Now."

"Is Mrs. Ford still with you?"

"Hello, detective," she said. "I'm here."

"Good morning, Mrs. Ford. Are you all right?"

Drex said, "You know, every time you talk to her when she's in my company, the first thing you ask is if she's all right. It's beginning to hurt my feelings, in addition to pissing me off."

"Well, is she?"

"I'm fine," she said. "Where should we meet you?"

"Not here at the department."

"Rudkowski is still in residence?" Drex asked.

"We suggested he relocate to the FBI office. He says his business is with us."

"I doubt the local agents would welcome him."

"Anyway, we're stuck with him. Menundez and I will come to you."

Drex laughed shortly. "I don't think so."

"You told me where I could find you last night, and good thing you did."

"Yeah, but this could be a trap baited with a bogus security camera video."

"It isn't. But I wish I had thought of doing that yesterday."

Drex looked at Talia, who gave a quasi-shrug of consent.

"Okay," he said. "But I have a favor to ask. Two favors."

Sounding put out, the detective said, "I'm already doing you a favor."

"These are small ones, and nothing compromising." He asked him to call Deputy Gray in Key West. "Request the coroner's report on Marian Harris."

"I already did. Yesterday. It was emailed."

"Good man!"

"It relates to your breakthrough?"

"If I'm guessing right."

"I'll forward it to you."

As eager as he was to see that report, Drex scotched that idea. Emails left a trail. He needed Locke working for him on the inside. If the detective was called on abetting him, he would lose that vital connection to the cases. "Print it out and bring it with you."

"Why don't you just tell me what you're looking for?"

"No need to get you excited if I'm wrong. Besides, I want to see it for myself."

The detective sighed with exasperation. "What's the second favor?"

"Food. A couple of breakfast sandwiches."

"Okay. Where are you?"

Drex told him the name of the suite hotel and the street it was on.

"We'll be there in twenty minutes."

"Oh, Locke." Drex stopped the detective before he could disconnect. Holding Talia's gaze, he said, "Talia goes by Shafer."

Chapter 34

―――•◉•―――

Drex opened the door to their knock. "That was twenty-five minutes."

"There was a long line at the drive-through." Menundez came inside and passed a carryout sack to Talia, who set it on the dining table.

"What was your breakthrough?" Locke asked.

Drex said, "Let's see that report from Florida."

The four of them gathered around the table. Menundez withdrew from his breast pocket a sheaf of documents that had been paperclipped and folded together. He passed them to Drex, who hastily thumbed through them.

Talia scooted closer to him so she, too, could read the report, which described in detail the contents of the wooden crate as the coroner had first examined it where it had been unearthed. There was no mention of a button. Fighting disappointment, Drex shuffled through the other documents until he found the autopsy report.

He scanned it so rapidly, it was Talia who saw the notation first and pointed it out to him. Under his breath, he exclaimed with a bit of anticlimactic wonder, "Damn. It's actually there."

"Documenting that you were right," she whispered.

Smiling at her, he mentally did a fist pump, but then realized what he was celebrating. "Hell of a thing to be glad about, though."

Beneath the table, she placed her hand on his thigh.

Locke made a sound of impatience. "I hate to interrupt your private moment, but can we please be filled in?"

"Have either of you read this?" Without waiting for them to answer, Drex turned the report around and stabbed the notation. "Missing button."

Locke immediately made the connection. He blinked across at Drex. "Both Conner and Barker had a button missing from their clothing."

"That's his souvenir," Drex said. "That's the connecting link I haven't had before now."

Menundez beamed.

Locke was less elated. "It supports your hypothesis of a serial killer, but it doesn't prove that he's Jasper Ford."

"I realize that, which dims my jubilation a bit," Drex admitted. "Without concrete proof, this similarity could still be dismissed as a coincidence. Maybe the security video will help."

He took a bite of the sandwich Talia had unwrapped and passed to him. Noticing the detectives' sudden and obvious dejection, he stopped chewing, swallowed, and said, "What?"

"The video doesn't help us, but I'll show it to you anyway." Locke opened the laptop and turned it around so Drex and Talia could see the freeze-framed shot. "This is the guy we were curious about."

The form Locke pointed out to them was draped in a plastic souvenir-shop rain poncho and looked like a ghostly blob. Only a portion of his face was visible. Drex said, "I don't even recognize Gif in this shot."

"Here's Gif. We had to zoom to find him."

The individual in question was walking toward Gif.

"His body type is wrong," Talia said. "He's too tall and thin. I don't believe it's Jasper."

"It isn't," Locke said glumly. "The witness we talked to last night picked him out of this freeze-frame early this morning. He recognized the poncho. Turns out that the poncho man was picked up on several cameras, not just two. One on a nearby parking lot showed him with his wife and three kids climbing into an SUV. Car tag was clear as a bell. Menundez followed up."

The younger detective picked up from there. "We got a home address from his car registration. A couple of uniforms were dispatched to screen him. He admitted to being in that mob. He'd gotten separated from his family as they disembarked the tour boat. He was anxious to catch up with them. Except for those few minutes when they were separated, he was with his family all evening on an outing planned weeks ago."

Drex pushed his half-eaten sandwich aside. "So he really was just a man in a hurry."

"Looks like," Locke said. "Which leaves us with pretty much nothing."

"The search of our house yesterday must have yielded Jasper's fingerprints," Talia said.

"But we don't have those of Daniel Knolls or any of his previous personas," Drex said. "There's nothing to match." After a short silence, he asked if Rudkowski had been told about their went-nowhere lead on the poncho man.

Locke nodded with unconcealed distaste.

"His reaction?" Drex asked.

Menundez was at the ready to tell him. "He called you delusional and paranoid, and said that you'd made Jasper Ford a suspect only so you could get a shot at his wife." The young detective glanced in Talia's general direction. "Sorry."

"No apology necessary," she said. "I couldn't care less about that horrid man's opinion."

Drex didn't comment except to murmur an epithet directed at Rudkowski.

"There's something else," Locke said.

Drex sighed and leaned back in his chair. "Let's have it."

"This morning some guys fishing just off shore hauled in a man's shoe." Locke looked at Talia. "It matches the description you gave us of what your husband was wearing when you last saw him. Size ten, brown loafer with tassel." Going back to Drex, he added, "Rescue teams, including the Coast Guard, are inclined to think that's all they'll find of him."

"Sort of shoots down my theory that he's still alive, doesn't it?"

"If nothing else turns up by dark tonight, they're calling off the search."

"Shouldn't his wife have been notified of that?" Talia said.

"Attempts have been made. No one has been able to reach you," Locke reminded her, sliding a look toward Drex. He let that settle, then said, "There's more."

"Jesus," Drex said. "I don't know how much more good news I can stand."

Locke gave him a grim smile. "Both Elaine Conner's and Ms. Shafer's financial portfolios are—"

"Let me guess," Drex interrupted. "Intact. No recent activity. No sizeable withdrawals. Every cent accounted for."

Locke shrugged. "I guess if he's playing dead, he can't be cleaning out bank accounts. Either he's prepared to wait for things to blow over before he cashes in, or he's sacrificing the money altogether in order to avoid capture."

"Priceless." Drex laughed, but without humor. "You're right, of course, but he also knew that I would look to see if money was missing. That's why he left it alone."

Leaning forward again, he addressed the other three earnestly. "Don't you see? Jasper knew what I would allege, because that's been his MO. He made certain that I would be proved wrong. More than anything he wants me discredited and humiliated."

He caught the two detectives exchanging a telling look and groaned, "What else?"

"We saved the best for last." Locke withdrew a sheet of folded paper from the breast pocket of his sport jacket and laid it, still folded, on the table. "It's a warrant for your arrest."

"*What?*" Talia exclaimed.

"The deputy in Key West ratted you out for calling him this morning. Rudkowski wasted no time. He insisted. Our hands were tied."

Drex flipped back the folds and scanned the warrant. "CID detectives were sent to handle this piddling misdemeanor shit?"

"Rudkowski figured that we would see you before anyone else could find you."

"I can't believe it," Talia said.

"I can," Drex said. "The man's pettiness knows no bounds. He'll put his one-sided rivalry above catching a man who would walk up behind a defenseless woman and break her neck."

"Can he put you in jail?" Talia said.

Locke answered for Drex. "We don't have to be in any rush to get him there."

"Thanks for that." Drex stood up and began to roam restlessly. "The thing is, the resentful jerk has effectively hobbled me. *Now*, when a single hour could make all the difference. Jasper may decide that Talia's fortune and/or her life aren't worth the risk of being captured. He'll choose to disappear as he has before.

"Or, he could decide that he's enjoying this killing spree and continue it in a frenzy until he's finally treed. He would actually get off on that kind of notoriety. I guarantee you that wherever he is, he's watching all the TV stories about the woman he killed last night. He's feeling very proud of himself. The celebrity status fuels his ego, and when he's good and stoked, he'll act again."

"Let's hope not."

"You're not listening, Locke." Drex returned to the table and, bracing on his hands, leaned in. "He's beyond *hope*. Remember the Chi Omega sorority house? Bundy killed those girls, and minutes later attacked another only a few blocks away. Jasper is thumbing his nose at us in that same fashion. He proved it last night. He committed a random murder for no other reason except that he felt like it and wanted to yank my chain. The attack on Gif had to be spontaneous, because there's no way he could have planned it.

"That kind of footloose violence may not make you nervous, but it scares the crap out of me. If he kills somebody else, you, Menundez, Rudkowski may be able to sleep nights, but I won't.

"And if he says to hell with it, leaves the area, gets away, I'll never get another crack at him, because now he knows me. From now on, he'll be looking for me over his shoulder and will see me coming."

He gave a hard shake of his head. "This is the time. We've got to stop him now. We've got to catch him plying his trade. We've got to catch him with those goddamn souvenir buttons in his possession."

"Okay. I get it," Locke said, returning some of Drex's ire. "But you've been trying for years. We've been at it for two days. Any ideas?"

Drex yielded to the detective's frustration. It matched his own. "No."

Pushing away from the table, he walked through the living area to the far side of it and shoved open the panels of drapery. Outside, it continued to drizzle. For days now the skies had refused to clear. However, if it were sunny, Drex would resent it. The dreariness befitted the circumstances.

Behind him, Talia explained to the detectives the situation Mike was in. In cop-speak they answered her questions about the investigation into Sara Barker's murder.

Drex listened to the conversation with one ear, latching onto key words, but tuning out the minutiae. Most of it was irrelevant, anyway. They weren't going to apprehend Jasper using textbook police procedure.

In order to catch him, one couldn't think like a cop. One had to think like *him*.

He asked himself if he were Jasper, if he were in Jasper's situation, what would he do? What ploy would he use? A switchback? A prank? An irony? What would be the ultimate joke?

In a blinding instant, he had an inspiration.

He returned to the table, got on Locke's laptop, pulled up the freeze-frame, and was immediately annoyed by its limitations. "Is the rest of the video on here?"

The question caught Locke in mid-sentence. He fell silent and looked at Drex, who continued with impatience, "The minutes leading up to and right after Gif was attacked. Are they on this laptop?"

"No. The video was jerky. Hard to tell up from down, so I just downloaded that freeze-frame. The whole of it is back at the department."

"I need to see it. Right now. Have someone email it."

Neither detective moved, their reluctance evident.

"What?" Drex said. "Earlier you offered to email it to me yourself."

"That was before this." Locke flicked his hand at the arrest warrant. "We could get into real Dutch by sending you evidence now."

"Okay, then sneak me into the department. Let me watch it there."

"Sneak you in? We're supposed to be delivering you to Rudkowski. If we don't, we're sunk."

"I get it, guys. But, God, this timing sucks." He socked his palm with the other fist. "Jasper is escalating. Rudkowski is wound up like a top. Incredible. I have two enemies, and they want the same thing, which is to shut me down."

"Discredited and humiliated," Talia said, repeating the words he'd spoken minutes ago.

But hearing them now stopped him in his tracks. Slowly, softly, he said, "They want the same thing. They want me bested."

A plan began to take shape. He grabbed hold of it before it could evaporate. Even as it formed and became clearer, he began appealing to the detectives. "Sneak me into the police department. Let me watch the video *before* my showdown with Rudkowski."

"What do you expect to see on it?" Menundez asked.

"You were looking for somebody who was moving through the crowd in a hurry. Maybe we should watch for someone who wasn't in such a hurry." That didn't seem consequential enough to convince them, but that was all Drex was willing to tell them at this point.

"Let me watch the video, then no more favors, I swear. Please." He looked at his watch. "But decide. I need the face-off with Rudkowski to happen soon. Before he does something stupid."

"Like put you in jail," Locke said. "As soon as he sees you, that's what he'll do."

"Then it's up to me to convince him otherwise." He split a look between the two. "Cuff me if you want, just let me see the video. Do we have a deal?"

"Yes," Menundez said.

And simultaneously Locke said, "No."

"Fifteen minutes," Drex pleaded.

Locke wavered. "We've got to deliver Rudkowski something." He looked at Talia. "He's still hot to question you. That may pacify him for fifteen minutes."

Drex turned to her. She asked, "Will it help you?"

"Honestly, I can't guarantee that it will."

She smiled and raised her shoulders. "He'll track me down sooner or later. I had just as well get it over with."

When Drex moved, it was as though he'd been spurred. He reached for Talia's hand and pulled her up and out of her chair. "We'll get our stuff and be right back."

Responding to his haste, Talia shot up the stairs, Drex right behind her.

When they reached the landing, she pulled him into the bedroom and slammed the door shut. "What's your plan?"

"Time's short. I can't lay it all out for you now."

"You mean you won't."

"That's right, I won't. Listen," he said before she could argue. "Did that recovered shoe or the untouched bank accounts convince you that Jasper is dead?"

"No."

"No. If he wants to continue his illustrious career, he can't afford to leave us alive. I don't want him sneaking up on either of us like he did on Gif and Sara Barker. I've got to draw him out."

"I understand that, but how—"

"The less you know—"

"Stop that! Tell me."

He shook his head. "This has to be my thing."

"Well, in case it's slipped your mind, it's also *my* thing."

Immediately repentant, he said, "Of course. I'm sorry. That was a dumb thing to say. I made it your thing, didn't I?"

She gripped his upper arms and shook him slightly. "No, *Jasper* did. I'll never get back the year I spent with him, but I'll be damned before I'll let him control one more day of my life. Not if I can help it."

"Help by trusting me."

"I have to trust *myself*, Drex." She flattened her hand against her chest. "I didn't trust my instincts before. For all the reasons I've tried to explain, I suppressed my misgiving and lived with a man who is innately evil. Now, every instinct I have is screaming for me to trust you. But am I in denial again because of my sexual attraction to you? You say you're a good guy, but you operate outside the law. So do I doubt my instincts, or trust them?"

"Trust them." He cupped her face. "My methods are dodgy. I bend rules. I break them. But I'm a good guy."

"Those dodgy methods scare me."

"I understand. But remember what scares me most? I told you that day you came up to the apartment."

"Failure."

"Failure. Failure to catch him."

There was a hard rap on the door, and Locke shouted through it, "Easton!"

"Be right there," he shouted back. Then in a whisper, "My worst fear is that Jasper will slip through my fingers, that it will be generally accepted that he drowned, that I'm a crackpot, that the missing button connection is bunk. Then, when nobody's looking for him any longer, he'll come back to finish you. I've got to end this, Talia, and I've got to end it now. You can doubt my methods, but don't doubt my purpose."

She looked deeply into his eyes, then nodded, and said huskily, "I do trust in that."

He aligned his forehead with hers and whispered a heartfelt thank you, then said, "Sexual attraction, huh?" He pulled her to him and kissed her deeply, his hand on her bottom, pulling her close. She dug her fingers into his hair. The brevity of the kiss only heightened the passion behind it.

"Easton!"

Drex ignored the banging on the door but broke the kiss. "One last thing. Rudkowski will try to browbeat you."

"I can handle him."

"I have no doubt." Her gave her a parting kiss, then turned her about and pushed her toward the door. "Show yourself before Locke has a coronary."

Chapter 35

Locke walked Talia downstairs. Drex asked for a minute in the bathroom. He shut the door and called Mike.

"Who's this?"

"Me. Forgive my whisper. I've locked myself in the bathroom. Any news of Gif?"

"Your swooner at the hospital called me about half an hour ago. They're moving him into a private room."

"That's great news."

"I thought so." He passed along Gif's hospital room number. "I haven't been able to go see him, though."

"They're still holding you at the sheriff's office?"

"They're fiddle-farting around. I'm going to kill Sammy."

"Can't you talk your way out of there?"

"Working on it. I was trying to give an ex-con a break by renting a car from him. How was I to know that it was stolen? Live and learn. That's my story, and I'm sticking to it."

"Doesn't look good that you skipped town and left Rudkowski dangling."

"Our signals got crossed. His word against mine. And the agents who were guarding my house hate him and love the homemade lasagna I took them, so I'm betting they'll back me. In any case, these guys here have got nothing to hold me on, because Sammy, who fears my murderous wrath, swears that I was oblivious. They'll have to release me, in time."

"Any estimate on when that might be?"

"Why?"

"Well, speaking of Rudkowski..." In a rapid clip, overriding Mike's numerous attempts to interrupt, Drex updated him on the recent setbacks, ending with his arrest. "They don't have a choice but to take me in."

"That ass-wipe Rudkowski."

"True. But I need you to do something for me besides name-calling."

"Like what?"

Drex made his request. Mike's response was, "Have you lost your fucking mind?"

"I don't have time to explain why, or to argue with you about it. I've already overextended Locke's patience. I need a yes or no."

"You realize that if I do this, it can't be undone."

"Nine murders can't be undone."

There was a knock at the door. "Now, Easton."

"You gotta tell me, Mike," Drex whispered. "Will you do it?"

"It's your funeral."

When Mike said that, in that particular grumble, Drex knew he had him. "Thanks. Later."

He clicked off, snapped up the lock, and opened the door.

Locke was on the threshold. "Who were you talking to?"

He replied with a wide grin. "The hospital. Gif's being moved out of ICU into a private room."

Locke took the phone from him. He went to recent calls and pulled up the last number. "That's Mallory's number."

"Okay, so I skipped a step. I called Mike, who told me the news that he got from the hospital."

"You're giving me the runaround."

Drex sighed, looked away, came back to him. "I called Mike to ask if he would bail me out."

"What did he say?"

"You want it straight and unfiltered?"

"That would be a welcome change."

"He asked if I'd lost my fucking mind."

Drex asked if they could take Gif's car so Talia wouldn't be stranded. Locke agreed on the condition that Drex would go with him. Talia would ride with Menundez.

When they arrived at the police department, Locke parked in a designated slot. They reunited with Talia and Menundez at an entrance for personnel. Before they went in, Locke turned to Drex. "You carrying?"

"Yes."

"You're not planning to shoot him, are you?"

"Rudkowski? Hadn't planned to."

"That's too bad. But I can't let you go inside with a weapon. Give it to Menundez."

Knowing it would be pointless to argue, Drex passed the detective his pistol, saying, "Escort Talia to Rudkowski. Keep him occupied long enough for me to view that video."

Locke intervened. "You know, typically, the apprehended don't give the orders."

"You agreed to give me fifteen minutes," Drex said.

"I didn't agree to anything."

"I need to see that video before I see Rudkowski."

"You're not going to talk him out of the arrest."

"Don't underestimate my powers of persuasion."

Locke remained dubious, but he said to Menundez, "Text me which room you're in. Fifteen minutes or less, we'll be up."

Before they separated, Drex reached for Talia's hand and squeezed it. "Give him hell." She smiled and squeezed back.

Locke led Drex into a room that had a modicum of privacy. He accessed an available computer and downloaded the security camera video. Drex had noted earlier the time burn-in on the freeze-frame. He fast-forwarded to it, then backed up three minutes from there and started playing. To Drex's disappointment, the images were no more distinct on this larger monitor than they had been on Locke's laptop.

"Warned you it was lousy," Locke remarked as he watched over Drex's shoulder.

It was. Drex paused and restarted it frequently, zoomed in on still frames, zoomed out, fast-forwarded and rewound so often that Locke said, "I'm getting motion sick."

"Me too. I could do with a Coke. Got one around here?"

"Forget it. I'm not leaving you alone."

"I wouldn't cut out on you. Scout's honor."

"You've got ten more minutes. I've got calls to return."

Locke walked a short distance away, but still in sight, and got on his phone. Drex paused the video at a certain point and leaned in closer to the monitor to study one of the frozen images. He backed it up, saw the same individual. He fast-forwarded, but slowly, watching even more closely.

Locke returned. "Time," he said.

Drex pushed back his chair and stood up. "Thanks."

"Hold it. Did you catch something I should see?"

"Rudkowski's waiting."

"Look," Locke said with irritation, "you can continue bullshitting, or you can clue me to your plan."

"Plan?"

Locke gave a sigh of exasperation. "Easton, I admire you more than I like you. I think you're smart, and I think you're earnest. Menundez has a man crush on you. You appeal to his cowboy-cop ideal. When Rudkowski told us about you, the things you've done in the name of 'duty,' I thought at first that he had to be lying."

"All this to say...?"

"I would rather have you at my back, even without a badge, than that guy with one. But I've got to know the plan you're hatching."

Drex thought too much of Locke's integrity to continue pretending. "In your situation I would feel the same frustration. But I'm reluctant to discuss a plan that isn't even close to hatching. It's still embryonic."

"I could help, field ideas."

"When the time is right."

Still looking vexed, Locke said, "Have you ever met the SAC in Columbia? The one Rudkowski is reporting to?"

"No."

"Doesn't matter. Jump the chain. Call him directly. Explain this grudge match between you and Rudkowski."

"Who has painted me to be a nut case. Even if I could get through to the SAC, by the time I convinced him that I wasn't delusional and paranoid it could be too late."

"All right, how about this? I'll take you in to see our chief. He's a reasonable man, and he's had two women murdered in the past two nights. He wants the culprit. Bounce your idea...Why not?" he asked when Drex began shaking is head.

"Because, as reasonable as he may be, he'll toe the line. While he's trying to figure out what to do with me, time is running out."

"Maybe it already has. By now, Jasper Ford may be long gone."

"Do you honestly think that? If you do, say so."

"No. I think he's alive and unraveling just like you say."

"Okay then. This is the game-winning three-point shot at the buzzer, and I don't need my own damn team trying to block it."

"That's my point, we're not a team."

"We are," Drex said. "I swear."

Uncertainty in his eyes, the detective asked quietly, "Can you make the shot?"

"I don't know. I hope so, but I'm nursing no illusions. If I fail, it'll be spectacular. But it will be my own throat I've cut. *Only* mine."

"That's just it," Locke said. "If you're put out of commission for good, it'll be a hell of a waste of talent and guts. I want you to win. I just wish you would play by the rule book."

"I can't."

"Why not?"

"Because *he* doesn't."

———————

"Don't play dumb, Mrs. Ford. Don't act like you didn't know that I wanted to talk to you. You are a material witness in a felony case involving the kidnap and murder of Elaine Conner, as well as the unexplained disappearance of your husband."

Talia's only previous exposure to Special Agent Rudkowksi had been the dialogue she'd overheard while hiding in the safe room with Drex. Her opinion hadn't improved upon meeting him. Since he'd entered the interrogation room where Menundez had en-sconced her, Rudkowski had been railing at her, virtually without taking a breath.

As he continued to rant, she kept her expression as aloof as possible, her gaze steady on him. She wasn't accustomed to the cops-and-robbers environment, much less to being shouted at. Her failure to react with fear and trembling had roused him to become increasingly loud.

Menundez said now, "Ease up, Rudkowski. She's not a suspect."

"I'll determine that."

Talia seized her first opportunity to get a word in edgewise. "Agent Rudkowski, I'm well aware of the seriousness of the crimes."

"Are you? Then why have you hampered the investigation by avoiding this interview? You also tampered with evidence."

"I did no such thing. When I left my house before you served the search warrant, I took nothing from it except a couple of changes of clothing and some toiletries."

"Your husband's cookbooks. Menundez here says they filled that shelf above the stove. That shelf was conspicuously empty."

"I didn't take the cookbooks."

"Then it was Easton."

"He had nothing with him when we left the house. Not even his personal belongings."

"Then his cronies made off with them. How come? What did they do with them?"

Since Jasper's cookbooks had turned out to be a disappointing false lead, and therefore irrelevant, she saw no point in either denying the action or defending it. But Rudkowski's yammering about them was keeping him preoccupied, which was what Drex needed her to do.

The agent propped his hip on the corner of the table, crowding her in an obvious attempt to be intimidating. "What tactic did Easton use to get you to pull a vanishing act with him?"

"No tactic."

"Come on. He's a con man. Did he schmooze you with his boyish charm? Hate to be the one to break it to you, but you wouldn't be the first to fall for it, you know."

"He convinced me that my husband is a career criminal and, given the opportunity, would very likely try to kill me."

He scoffed. "You believed that?"

"If I had a grain of doubt, it was dispelled last night when Jasper killed that woman and critically injured Mr. Lewis."

"Those crimes have not been attributed to Jasper Ford. They're relative to nothing. Alleging that your husband was involved is just another of Easton's wild hares. Had your husband ever met Gif Lewis?"

"Not to my knowledge."

"Then how did he recognize him to attack?"

Drex had been unable to explain that. She refrained from answering.

Rudkowski cupped his ear. "Come again? I didn't catch that," he mocked.

"See what I'm getting at, Mrs. Ford? Easton makes up stuff to support his crazy notions. His claims of a serial killer have no basis, and never have." He poked his index finger against his temple. "He's nuts. He's obsessed with a bogeyman of his own invention."

She leaned away from him and gave him an unhurried once-over. "Then why are you so unstrung?"

He blinked. "Pardon?"

"I don't understand your agitation. If you believe that Drex is a mental case, why haven't you dismissed his wild hares as such, and gone on about your business?"

"Because he's impeding my investigation."

"Excuse me," she said coolly, "but from my perspective, it seems you've contributed very little to the investigation of Elaine Conner's murder and the search for my husband, whether he's dead or alive, innocent or guilty. By contrast, you've spent a great deal of time pursuing Drex and deriding him at every opportunity. If anyone has an obsession, Special Agent Rudkowski, it appears to be *you*."

Menundez snickered.

Rudkowski's whole body inflated with indignation. His forehead broke a greasy sweat. He pushed off the table and, placing his hands on his knees, bent down until his face was level with hers. "You had better watch it, Mrs. Ford, or Shafer, or whatever you choose to be called. I'll put you in lockup until you decide to cooperate."

"How could I possibly be more cooperative? I came here of my own volition."

"But you haven't answered my question."

"Which one?"

Rudkowski returned to his full height. "Where is Easton?"

With a pleasant smile, she said, "Right behind you."

Chapter 36

⎯⎯⎯◈⎯⎯⎯

Drex had arrived in time to overhear Talia's putdown of Rudkowski. Based on his apparent choler, she had effectively fired him up to his pressure-cooker state. From the threshold, he said, "You sound out of sorts, Bill. We could hear you from the end of the hall."

Locke nudged Drex into the room and closed the door behind them. He asked Menundez if he'd shared with Rudkowski the autopsy report on Marian Harris.

"Not yet. I saved Easton the honor." The younger detective produced the report and passed it to Drex. "I circled the notation in red."

"Thanks."

Rudkowski shouldered between them and snatched the printout from Drex. "You're under arrest. I'm considering booking her, too."

Talia uttered a sound of dismay. "What for?"

"Leaving official custody without permission. Obstruction of justice."

Locke and Menundez began protesting, but Drex talked over

381

them. "You're not going to arrest Talia," he said. "Stop being a jackass and read that."

With impatience, Rudkowski slid on a pair of reading glasses and homed in on the marked spot. "A button was missing off her blouse. So what?"

"So..." Locke proficiently explained its relevance. "This links that Florida cold case to our two here." Menundez also had print-outs of the other two reports and showed Rudkowski the notations about the missing buttons.

Rudkowski removed his glasses and said, "Well, it's a common-ality that warrants further investigation. But it could also be a coincidence."

"Our chief of police doesn't think it is," Locke said. "Neither does the sheriff's office, the state police, or the local FBI agents working the Elaine Conner case, or the SAC in Columbia."

Rudkowski said, "You went over my head and talked to him be-fore bringing this to me?"

"We couldn't find you," Menundez said, deadpan. "You must've been in the john."

Before Rudkowski could form a comeback, Drex again held up a hand that signaled for quiet. "Locke, with your permission, I'd like to speak to Rudkowski alone, please."

Rudkowski huffed. "So you can crow, I suppose."

"I don't consider the murders of three women something to crow about," Drex said evenly.

"Oh, you've gone sentimental? Must be the influence of your new girlfriend here."

Talia stepped forward as though to whale into him. Drex put out an arm to hold her back. "You're a small-minded weasel, Bill. Ask anybody. And there's a lot of bad blood between you and me. For once, put it aside. While you're standing here tossing out insults to a woman who outclasses you by about a thousand times, and try-ing to get the best of me, a serial killer remains at large."

"Even if that were so," Rudkowski said, "it's none of your concern, is it? You're over, remember?" He held the printouts directly in front of Drex's face and shook them. "By the way, this constitutes theft of a document pursuant to an active federal investigation. I can add that to your other offenses."

Drex pushed the papers away from his face. "I didn't steal that report, Locke obtained it. As per usual, you're missing the big picture. Let's talk about it, man to man."

"Sure, we can talk, but I'm immune to you. Nothing you say will change my mind."

Drex turned to the other three and motioned toward the door. "Maybe I can make him see sense, and he'll tear up that arrest warrant."

"Not going to happen," Rudkowski said.

Drex ignored him and appealed to Locke. "Give me a few minutes with him."

Locke said, "God knows you're good at talking people into doing what they don't want to do." He motioned Menundez and Talia out.

She looked at Drex with concern. He bobbed his chin in reassurance. Still looking uncertain and worried, she left with Menundez. Locke hung back. "You'll have won some favor and faith by coming here of your own volition. Don't screw it up."

"Duly noted."

Locke left them. Drex closed the door and turned to Rudkowski, who confronted him, one eye squinted, his head tilted. "You want to parley?"

"Only because all other options have been exhausted. Much as it pains me to ask anything of you, can we declare a truce?"

"What are you trying to pull? One of your pranks?"

"No."

"One of your switcheroos that you find so funny and cute?"

"Not this time. I swear."

Rudkowski snorted.

"Hear me out, Bill." Drex pulled a chair from beneath the table.

"Seat?" Rudkowski looked at the chair as though it might be a clown's collapsible prop, but he sat down in it. Drex took the chair across from him.

Rudkowski said, "Let's hear it."

"Give me back my badge."

Rudkowski's expression went blank. "Where's the punch line?

"No punch line."

"That's got to be a joke."

"No joke."

"It's the funniest thing I've heard in a decade." Then he did guffaw. "Even if I gave it back, it's worthless now."

"I need it for a day, one day, twenty-four hours. Then..." Drex raised his hands in surrender. "You can have me."

"I already have you."

Drex took a breath. "You saw those autopsy reports. Do you understand what they signify?"

"You think I'm too dense to grasp their significance?"

"I wasn't implying that. I only meant—"

"You implied that you, Dr. Easton, are smarter than me."

"Than I," Drex said under his breath.

Rudkowski glared at him with malice. "You're over and out. For good. When is that going to sink in? Maybe while you're in jail. You'll have plenty of time to reflect."

"I'll sign a confession, Bill. In blood."

"I like that idea."

"Tomorrow."

Rudkowski scraped back his chair. "Stay here till someone comes to book you."

"Wait. Please. Please," Drex repeated and held out his hand as though to keep him in his seat.

Rudkowski hesitated, then resettled.

Drex tried another tactic. "I'm this close to him." He made an inch with his thumb and index finger. "He's close."

"You know that?"

"I feel it."

"Do you think that what you *feel* is going to fly with a prosecutor? You have no *proof* that such a person even exists. That business with the buttons? Circumstantial."

"I realize that. But it's more than I've had on prior cases. He thinks he's outsmarted us. He hasn't. We're smarter. He's tripped up and doesn't even know it. This is our one chance to get him."

"By him you mean Ford? His bloated body will drift ashore one of these days."

"Could, but I don't think so. Give me twenty-four hours, with a badge. If I don't produce him, I've failed. You can lock me up and laugh your ass off. You can publicly ridicule me."

He paused to let Rudkowski savor the appetizing thought of that. "But, if I succeed, and we nail the son of a bitch, it's even better for you."

"How do you figure?"

"You get all the credit."

"What about you?"

"I take none."

"You take none?"

"I'll stipulate it in writing."

"Nothing you write down will be worth the paper it's written on."

"I'll email it. Emails are forever."

"Not yours. You've got Mallory to rig them for you." He shot Drex a smug smile. "Your friend Gif is temporarily safe from arrest, but the fat man is already being held at the sheriff's office."

"Thanks to you. But they're not going to book him for a crime committed by a repeat offender out of state."

"With a phone call from me, they'll book him for obstruction in this state."

Drex said, "Fine. Play hardball. Call now. Have Mike booked. You know what he'll do? He'll use his one phone call to speak to the SAC in Columbia. He'll reiterate everything Locke has already told him. He'll emphasize how crucial that coroner's report in Florida is to these homicide cases here, and how you, for no other reason than to spite me, delayed our access to it. He'll soon see that you've been more of an impediment to this investigation than Mike or I have been.

"At the very least, he'll have the agents in the resident office here check you out, and you'd fare even worse. They would want to know why you're not over there, lending assistance, instead of over here in the PD, distracting hardworking detectives from their two murder investigations."

He paused. "Bill. Think. Wouldn't you rather give me one more day of freedom than wind up looking bad? Stupid, spiteful, and bad?"

"You're bluffing."

"You think so?" Drex shrugged. "Then call my bluff." He let the dare stand, then added, "The only reason I haven't called that SAC myself is because I wanted to stay under the radar."

"So you wouldn't be jailed."

"Well, that. I grudgingly admit it. But I wanted to keep a low profile because you know what these departments are like. When it comes to leaks, they're sieves. I've been holding my breath, afraid word would leak to the media that we've tied these local cases to the one in Florida. If that got out, and Ford heard it, his ego would mushroom. He would—"

Drex stopped talking and looked hard at Rudkowski, whose complexion had taken on a rosier hue. "What?"

Rudkowski stayed stubbornly silent.

"What?" Drex stared him down, then lunged from his chair and leaned over the table. "Tell me you haven't talked to the media."

Rudkowski puffed up defensively. "I've agreed to grant an interview."

"Oh, God no! When?"

"At noon."

Drex swung around to look at the wall clock. "That's only ten minutes from now."

"Which is why we need to wrap this up. Anything else?"

"Bill, you can't give that interview."

"Why shouldn't I?"

"Who did you talk to?"

"A reporter named Kelly Conroe. She contacted me," Rudkowski said, boasting.

Drex recalled the reporter he'd seen that morning reporting on Sara Barker's murder. Pretty, perky, articulate, earnest. She'd struck him as eager. Someone who played to the camera, who would take the story and run with it.

Rudkowski was still talking. "Somebody here gave her my name as a spokesperson for the FBI. Which leaves you out, doesn't it?"

"Get back to her, Bill," Drex said. "Ask her to sit on the story until tomorrow."

"Why would I want to do that?"

"For the reasons I spelled out."

"Ford's mushrooming ego? I can't even say that with a straight face." He stood up. "I'm meeting her downstairs. Stay put until Locke comes for you."

"Christ." Drex turned his back, lowered his head, massaged his nape. "This is a nightmare." Coming back around quickly, he said, "Okay, let this Kelly Whatever record the interview, but ask her to hold it until the late news tonight."

"That's not the way a news operation operates."

As he headed toward the door, Drex caught him by the arm and whipped him around. "I beg you to reconsider."

"Let go of me." He tried to break free of Drex's grasp, but Drex held on. "Twenty-four hours."

"Let go, or I'll have you held on an assault charge."

"Charge me with whatever the fuck you want," Drex shouted. "I'll face the judge and plead guilty to anything you throw at me. Tomorrow. But I need today."

Rudkowski worked his arm free. "Your plans for today are an arraignment." He turned and opened the door.

Drex charged after him, bumping into Locke, who was on the other side of the threshold. He caught Drex in a bear hug, which Drex tried to escape with the fury of a madman. Locke ordered him to calm down. Drex only struggled harder to go after Rudkowski.

When Rudkowski reached the corner of an intersecting hallway, he glanced over his shoulder and shot Drex a triumphant grin.

"Don't do it, Bill!"

Rudkowski went out of sight around the corner.

Drex's head dropped forward. "The bastard's really going to do it."

The detective backed him against the wall and propped him there, keeping his hands on his shoulders. "If I release you, are you going to do something crazy?"

Drex shook his bowed head.

Gradually Locke eased his hold, then lowered his hands. "I take it you got nowhere."

"He wouldn't budge."

"Did you really expect him to?"

"No."

"I'm sorry it didn't go better for you."

Drex raised his head, winked, and flashed a grin. "It went perfect."

Chapter 37

———◆———

Jasper had learned on the morning news the name of Drex Easton's buddy whom he'd assaulted. Gifford Lewis was in guarded condition, but expected to survive the seemingly random and unwarranted attack.

"It was neither random nor unwarranted," Jasper argued with the motel room TV.

Lewis was a ten-second mention. Much more to-do was made of the woman who'd been fatally attacked without any apparent motive. The reporter droned on and on about what a wonderful person Sara Barker had been. There were heartrending pictures of her surrounded by her children and husband, all smiling sunnily.

Jasper noted that a victim of unprovoked violence was never remembered as being a wretched reprobate, a cheat and liar, a subhuman leech on society whom the world was well rid of. They were always eulogized as self-sacrificing saints.

"Call me cynical."

After watching the broadcasts, he spent the remainder of the morning making preparations to leave Charleston. But as noon approached, he grew eager to hear more about the havoc he'd wrought.

He tuned in just as the news was coming on the air. One of the anchors said, "Our own Kelly Conroe is coming to us live with an interview with a lead investigator. She files this exclusive report. Kelly, what's the latest?"

The blond reporter's mouth was a slash of carmine lipstick, which, in Jasper's opinion, was an unpleasing distraction.

"I'm here with FBI Special Agent William Rudkowski, who is assisting local authorities with their investigation into the murder of Elaine Conner, whose body washed ashore the night before last."

The camera shot widened to include a man who appeared to be in his late fifties, nothing remarkable about his appearance, although his stance indicated the bellicose attitude of a man who thought highly of himself, probably as overcompensation for inse-curities and shortcomings.

The reporter asked him to explain the FBI's involvement.

"The Conner case captured my attention because circum-stances surrounding it bear a striking resemblance to a two-year-old homicide case in Key West, Florida. We're examining the similari-ties. If it's determined that the two cases are related, it will represent a major breakthrough and move us closer to identifying and appre-hending a serial perpetrator, to whom the disappearances of at least nine women are attributed."

The reporter asked him to expand on what the similarities be-tween the cases were, and asked if any new evidence had been discovered. "I can't comment on an ongoing investigation," he said. "At this time, all I'll say is that this individual is under the delusion that he's outsmarted us. He hasn't. We're smarter. He has left us a distinct signature. He's tripped up, and doesn't even realize it."

The claim didn't rattle Jasper in the least. It was poppycock. If there had been any evidence connecting him to Marian Harris, Drex's wannabe-writer charade would have been unnecessary.

Agents would have stormed Jasper's house and placed him under arrest.

Having heard enough of the blather, he was about to switch off the TV when the reporter said, "You've taken a man into custody this morning. Drex Easton, who holds a doctorate in criminal psychology. What's his connection to these cases, and what charges is he facing?"

Drex had a doctorate? He was *in custody*?

One of the anchors cut to the heart of the matter. "He's said to have become recently acquainted with Elaine Conner, Jasper Ford, and Ford's wife, Talia Shafer. Is he considered a suspect in Conner's murder?"

"No," the agent replied. "But Easton has, over the course of many years, hindered other FBI investigations by interfering without authority. From the night Ford went missing and Mrs. Conner was killed, Easton has prevented Ford's wife from cooperating with the investigation. He was arrested this morning. Together they were brought in for questioning. He's being arraigned this afternoon, facing state charges of tampering with evidence and obstruction of justice. Similar federal charges are pending."

It appeared to Jasper that the agent wished to say more. Jasper wanted to hear more, but his curiosity went ungratified. The reporter thanked the FBI agent and turned to face the camera, which zoomed in on her.

"Easton's involvement with the key parties, which has led to his arrest, is a surprising twist in a case that already has authorities baffled."

"Kelly, what's the status of the search for Mr. Ford?" asked one of the anchors.

"Ongoing. However, there has been a development." She went on to relate that fishermen had reeled in one of his shoes. "It's looking more and more likely that he drowned. I haven't received confirmation, but the word is that the search for him will be suspended after today."

She wrapped up, and they returned to the studio. Jasper muted the television but stared at the miming heads for a full minute, trying to assimilate the shocking news that Drex Easton was to be arraigned later today.

What a well-deserved comedown! He wouldn't be so cocky when standing before a judge, would he? He wouldn't be glib and disarming. The court would not go all aflutter over the dimple that Elaine had found so dashing. Drex Easton, humbled to the level of a common criminal, would be a sight to behold.

Not that Jasper would go anywhere near that courthouse.

In his current incarnation, the chances of being recognized were slim to none. But it would be foolish to risk exposure when he was so close to being free and clear of this venture and ready to move on to his next.

He turned off the TV and wiped down the remote. Everything else in the room he had already thoroughly sterilized. His suitcase was packed except for the last two items to go into it. It lay open on the end of the bed. He'd hung the Do Not Disturb card on the outside doorknob to ward off the housekeeper, both while he remained and after he was gone.

Watching the noon news had been the last item on his agenda before taking his departure. He confessed that the half-hour delay had been a trifle self-indulgent, but he couldn't resist watching all the reports about himself, and he had enjoyed them immensely. He could leave Charleston feeling very proud.

Although it did stick in his craw that he was leaving with a major ambition unfulfilled: killing Talia. He had never before abandoned a project without completing it, and it galled him to do so now.

He was undeterred, of course. He would kill her. But the risk of doing so presently was too great. He would wait for several months, perhaps for as long as a year. Which, now that he thought on it, wouldn't be at all bad. The anticipation of ending her life, especially when she believed him dead, would ferment in his imagination like a fine wine. He could spend idle days fantasizing it.

He wondered if she and Drex had consummated their grubby, base lust for each other? Of course they had. No doubt that's what they'd been doing while she was supposed to have been cooperating with the police investigation. Jasper didn't care a whit if they'd screwed like rabbits. He only wished the two of them knew how utterly indifferent he was to it.

It also nagged him that he had to leave without learning what had drawn Drex's attention to him in the first place. *Over the course of many years* suggested that for most of Drex's adult life he had nursed an obsession so consuming that he had bucked the FBI in order to indulge it.

Jasper couldn't help but wonder what had instigated that fixation. Had it been a particular episode, an individual, or had Easton simply been born with a righteous zeal to seek justice for those who couldn't obtain it for themselves?

He would like to have had those questions answered. Strictly out of curiosity. He wasn't afraid that Drex and his fancy PhD would one day close in on him. Whatever authority Drex had possessed previously he'd been stripped of. He'd overstepped, flouted rules, and now was up to his neck in criminal charges. Jasper would love to be inside that courtroom when Drex had to answer for them.

But no. It would be unwise to tempt fate. He would leave as planned. Talia and Drex could play out the rest of their plebeian, romantic melodrama without him.

It wasn't as though he wished to be the star of it.

New challenges awaited him. He was off to meet them. The FBI was moving closer to identifying and apprehending a serial perpetrator? He had left a signature? He'd been outsmarted? That was a laugh. Who did they think they were dealing with?

"I'm not an amateur, you know. Just ask her."

He looked behind him at the dead woman on the bed. She lay facedown, her head at an odd angle to her shoulders. The back of her dress had ridden up, revealing thick thighs, lumpy with cellulite.

Stupid cow. He'd needed refuge and hadn't wanted to press his luck by checking into a hotel. She'd been so trusting. But then, why wouldn't she be? He had appeared harmless.

He loathed the idea of touching her again, but he tamped down his revulsion and used a tiny pair of manicure scissors to clip the threads securing a button to the neckline of her dress just above the zipper. Holding it by the eyelet, he twirled the small, fabric-covered sphere. What clever way could he sport it, he wondered.

He didn't have to decide now. He could take his time and be creative, as he'd had to be with some of the buttons already in his collection. But he never failed to come up with an ingenious way in which to hide them in plain sight.

He replaced the scissors in his leather manicure set, zipped it up, and placed it in his suitcase, then removed the velvet pouch from the inside pocket. Over the past two days, he had increased his collection from an even dozen to fifteen buttons. The FBI had underestimated his achievements by six women, proof that their agents weren't as brilliant as that moron on TV had boasted. Jasper's nimble mind could run circles around Dr. Easton's.

Indeed, it had, hadn't it?

He worked open the pursed top of the velvet bag and was about to drop the new addition into it when, yielding to an irresistible urge, he dumped the contents onto the top of the dresser. The hectic pace of the past few days had prevented him from looking at his souvenirs arrayed like this.

He wondered if the FBI's "striking similarities" and "signature" were the missing buttons. Had Easton made that connection? Jasper didn't see that it mattered, except that it caused another, sharper pang of regret that there wasn't a button from Talia. That would have been the best prize of all.

But he really must get over that disappointment. He couldn't allow himself to be detained by it. For the time being—and only for the time being—Talia was beyond his reach. Accept it.

He soothed his irritation by separating the buttons so he could admire them independently and reminisce on how he'd come by each one. There were three pearls, but each of a different size. Two were made of tortoiseshell. Four of various shapes and textures were solid black. The matte white one had adorned the skirt of the woman he'd killed last night. Naturally, all the brass ones looked somewhat military. One silver disk had a finish as smooth as satin. And, now, this cloth one.

He took a moment to appreciate its uniqueness, then it went first into the pouch. One by one he added the others, each joining the collection with a satisfying clink. He was about to pull the drawstring closed when something struck him as odd. He paused to consider, then upended the bag and spread out the buttons again. He counted them. Recounted. Meticulously, he grouped them into rows of five.

He hadn't miscounted. One of the rows was short a button.

With his heart knocking and a sweat breaking out over his shaved head, he squeezed the velvet pouch to see if one of the smaller buttons had become trapped by an inside seam. He didn't feel anything, but to be sure, he turned the bag inside out.

He searched among the magazines stacked on top of the dresser. He felt along the bottom of the television set, thinking that perhaps one had slid beneath it. He pushed aside the ice bucket and plastic wrapped glasses.

It wasn't on the dresser. He dropped to his knees, looked under the bed, the desk, the dresser. He crawled across the floor, madly skimming his hands over the carpet.

He stood up, breathing as though he'd swum miles. Starbursts of red exploded behind his eyes. Twin freight trains roared through his ears.

One of his trophies was missing.

Chapter 38

After his face-off with Rudkowski, which had produced the desired result, Drex powwowed with Locke, Menundez, and Talia in the interrogation room.

"You wanted him to blab all that on TV?" Locke asked.

"In the hope of luring Jasper to the courthouse for my arraignment. Once he learns I'm being publicly disgraced, I don't think he can stand to miss it."

"That's your plan?" The detective looked skeptical.

"Do you have an alternative?" When no one spoke, Drex said, "The first step worked, and it was crucial. While Rudkowski is busy being a TV star, let's take another look at that security video."

"I'm supposed to be booking you," Locke said.

"A minute or two isn't going to matter."

Grudgingly, the detective did as asked. Drex sat down at the small table. The other three gathered around to watch the video.

"As I play it, keep an eye on this person and watch how he navigates." Drex pointed to a blurred figure on the monitor. "See? He walks right past Gif, then turns and comes back. It's hard to tell with all the jostling and shoving, but I think that on that second pass, they bump shoulders. That could have been when he struck."

"How could he have done it that quickly, and without anyone noticing?" Talia asked.

"Someone did." Drex paused the video. "Now here, five seconds later, Gif has disappeared. We know that he was on the ground. A minute after that, here's the same individual, standing a few yards away, watching. EMTs arrive. He makes a slow circuit of the area."

He fast-forwarded, picking up the person at various spots around the perimeter of the camera's range. "Once Gif had been taken away—" He fast-forwarded before pausing the video again. "—he reappears briefly here before being swallowed up by the crowd. That's his back," he said, pointing.

"I don't know," Locke said, frowning. "Looks to me like just another curious bystander. There were dozens of them milling around."

"But only a very few came into such close contact with Gif mere seconds before he went down. Appearing to be a curious bystander would be good cover. He didn't make himself conspicuous by running, or even rushing to get away."

"The height is right," Talia said. "He's a little thicker in the middle than Jasper."

"He padded his clothing."

"Even with that," she said, "I couldn't swear that it's him."

"Sorry, Easton, but I don't think so, either." Menundez was squinting at the screen. "In fact, to me, your suspect looks like a woman."

Drex turned away from the screen to face the three of them and gave a sly smile. "The perfect disguise. No one was looking for a woman. No one would suspect an older woman of committing an unprovoked attack like Gif suffered. Sara Barker would have turned her back to her without reservation."

"Son of a gun," Locke whispered.

Menundez said something in Spanish that Drex figured was a bit more explicit.

Talia just looked at him, her lips parted in astonishment.

Drex asked Locke if he could round up some men within the department whom he trusted. "Who can keep their eyes open and mouths shut. Have them take a look at this video, then ask if they'd be willing to loiter around the courthouse this afternoon and be on the lookout? Best I can tell by this video, he was dressed in a generic, dark-colored tracksuit that would be appropriate for either sex. Short-haired wig."

"He might have changed identities again."

"He might have," Drex said. "But it's a damn good ruse, the kind of joke that Jasper would eat up, and it worked well for him last night."

Locke said, "I'll do the recruiting while Menundez is booking you."

—————

Over Rudkowski's protests, the detectives hadn't put Drex in lockup to await his arraignment, but had remanded him to the interrogation room with a stern warning not to betray their trust by trying to sneak out.

He gave them his promise, but they'd posted an officer outside the door anyway. Rudkowski was too busy fielding calls from media outlets to closely monitor Drex's preferential treatment. Had he, he would have created a ruckus.

Drex's phone had been confiscated along with his other personal belongings, but he was allowed to borrow Talia's to put in a call to Gif.

When Gif answered, Drex said, "Man, it's good to hear your voice."

"Drex, have you lost your fucking mind?"

"I see you've talked to Mike."

"We just hung up. Sheriff's office finally released him, and he's on his way to you. He called from an Uber car and filled me in. Said you played Rudkowski like a fiddle."

"With Mike's help. He tipped that reporter for me, anonymously. The stealth only made her more determined to seek out Rudkowski for comment. I knew he would jump at a chance to denounce me on TV. While appearing to try and talk him out of it, I spoon-fed him what I wanted Jasper to hear. He even quoted me directly. Let's hope it works to draw Jasper out."

"I understand your reasoning, but, Drex, you let the genie out of the bottle. You stand accused of breaking the law of the land."

"I did break the law of the land."

"But now the world knows it."

"Worth it, Gif, if we nail him."

"Are you in lockup?"

"An interrogation room. With visitation rights." Across from him Talia sat, unsmiling.

"How will you plead?"

"Not guilty. I'm not going to make it easy on Rudkowski. I've met with my court-appointed counsel. He's old and tired, but knows the ropes. He told me we lucked out on the assigned prosecutor, who's green, lazy, and none too bright. I was booked on misdemeanor state charges. Even if it goes to trial, which I doubt, I'll probably get off with a fine and probation."

"Rudkowski won't settle for that. He'll file federal charges and see to it that you do time. You know he will. Furthermore—"

"Gif, if you want to tell me how crazy I am, you'll have to get in line. But what I did, I did out of desperation, not insanity. Now, enough of that. How are you doing? Are you in pain?"

"They gave me one of those self-dispensing things."

"Good drugs?"

"Not good enough."

"Jesus, Gif. I'll never forgive myself for sending you to wander around alone last night, knowing that whack job—"

"Don't try to get off the subject."

"I'm not."

"Sure you are. I recognize the tactic. What does Talia think about what you've done?"

Drex looked over at her, where she sat, her brow knit with consternation. Her arms were folded across her middle, providing a shelf for her delectable breasts. Although, clearly, allure wasn't her intention.

"She's so mad at me, her freckles are about to combust."

"Why's she mad?"

"She says I'm setting a trap with myself as bait."

"Well, you are."

"Listen, Gif, all this talk is wearing you out. I can hear it in your voice. You need to rest. Don't worry about anything."

"That sounds like a brush-off."

"It is." Although Gif did sound out of steam, his voice having gone thin.

"I hate this, Drex. When you need me most, I'm laid up here, useless. I want to help, to be doing *something*."

"You're healing. That's a big something. Get well enough to lay into me the next time we see each other."

"When will that be?"

"Uncertain. Depends on whether or not I'm granted bail. Rudkowski will argue that I'm a flight risk."

"You are."

"Yeah, but maybe the judge will rule in favor of a flight risk over a buffoon."

"You're joking, but you could go to jail. After all these years, everything you've sacrificed to this, I can't stand to think of it ending with you behind bars."

"You're not going to cry, are you?"

"Maybe."

Drex smiled, but his voice was husky with emotion when he said, "You've been true blue, Gif. Thanks."

He disconnected, stared into the near distance for several seconds, then shook off his melancholia and passed Talia her phone. "Somebody was beeping in."

She pulled up the number. "Third time today. I don't recognize the number. Solicitation, no doubt." She set aside her phone and reached for his hands, drawing them across the table toward her. "Drex—"

"We've been over it," he said, interrupting what he knew would be another round of arguments, all reasonable, none he cared to go through again. "You're not to get anywhere near that courthouse. If you show up in the courtroom—"

"What will you do?" she challenged.

"It's what *he'll* do that should worry you."

"It does," she exclaimed softly. "I worry about you. You've made yourself a target. Even your best friends don't understand why."

"Yeah, they do. They argue, but they understand."

She turned his hand palm up. "You and your damn sense of honor." She lifted his hand to her mouth and kissed the self-inflicted scar. "But I wouldn't like you nearly as well if you didn't hold to it."

"Life's crammed with cruel ironies like that." He reached for a strand of her hair and rubbed it between his thumb and fingers. "I came down here in search of my nemesis, and discovered you. You were an unexpected lightning strike, Talia Shafer."

"So were you, Drex Easton."

"That last time…?" He arched his brow suggestively. "I liked the way you woke me up."

"I thought you would never notice."

He snuffled a laugh. "When a man is sleeping with a woman on top of him, and his cock starts being squeezed in that particular way, he tends to notice. Just so you know."

She ducked her head coyly. "I'll tuck that away for future reference."

"I didn't know how much I liked slow, sleepy sex."

"That was my first time for it."

"Mine, too. Which is why I didn't know how much I liked it." His gaze took a lazy tour down her front. "I had a particularly depraved encore planned for us."

"Oh?"

"Hmm. Hell of a one."

She reached across and poked her finger into his dimple. "Give me a hint."

He turned his cheek toward her hand and captured her finger between his teeth. "It was going to start out tame enough, but would end up with you seeing God and screaming my name."

"The imagination runs wild."

He gave a rueful grin. "Sadly, it'll have to keep. I'm off to the slammer."

"Don't make light of it."

"I don't," he said solemnly. "Come here." They leaned toward each other across the small table and brushed lips.

Mike chose that moment to barrel in. Seeing that he had interrupted a private moment, he halted, but only for a second before coming into the room and closing the door. "Met Menundez in the hall. He got this from the trunk of Gif's car." He dropped Drex's duffel bag on the floor.

"My suit is rolled up in it. I wanted to appear in court looking a bit more respectable."

"Locke's given you ten minutes to change before heading downtown."

"Did you get Gif's key back from Menundez?"

Mike held up the fob.

"You and Talia go back to the hotel. We didn't officially check out. See if you can get our rooms back."

"What do we do there?" Mike asked.

"Wait for word."

"You're to babysit me," Talia said sweetly.

Drex gave her a droll look, then went back to Mike. "Await word. With luck, you'll be able to bail me out before dinnertime."

"Okay, but fair warning. If Rudkowski gets another bee up his butt, I'm not going to talk him into throwing me in the clink, like a certain dumbass we know. I'm getting the hell gone from Dodge."

"Noted. Now beat it, you two, so I can change."

He went to the door and pulled it open. As Talia drew even with him, he said, "Don't forget to turn off your phone. Mike will take the battery out for you."

"As soon as I check my messages." She looked at him with a combination of vexation and anxiety. There were a thousand things Drex wanted to say to her, but the cop posted outside the door was within hearing distance. She went out into the hallway without a further goodbye.

As Mike approached him, Drex put out a hand and, speaking for Mike's ears alone, said, "If I'm incarcerated and Jasper remains at large, he'll come after Talia. She'll need a bodyguard, Mike."

"That speech of mine about getting gone?" He batted it down with his large paw. "I won't go anywhere without taking her with me."

"Thanks. You're a friend."

"Yeah, yeah," he grumbled, "and of all my bad habits, you're by far the worst."

Drex closed the door after him, squatted down, and unzipped his duffel. He took from it his suit and dress shirt. They were hopelessly wrinkled but would have to do. He forewent a tie. He was just about to start stripping down when the door opened and Talia burst in, Mike behind her.

She was brandishing her cell phone. "The call that was beeping in? The number I didn't recognize that had called three times? It was Mr. Singh."

"Who the hell—"

"Jasper's tailor."

Chapter 39

———◆———

Talia's words tripped over each other in her haste to get them out. "He'd called twice before. This time he left a voice mail. He was asking about a button."

"What about it?"

"His accent is thick, hard to understand, but he was calling to make certain that I had found it."

"Found it?"

She shook her head, indicating that she was in the dark, too. "I'm going to call him back. I knew you'd want to hear."

"Get him," he said to her then stuck his head out the door and told the cop in the hallway to summon Locke and Menundez.

"They'll be back for you in ten minutes."

"Tell them to come *now*."

"They'll ask why."

"Tell them I'm escaping."

He slammed the door. Talia had placed the return call. She, Mike, and he listened breathlessly at the series of rings before Singh answered with the name of his shop. "How may I help you?" As

Talia had warned, his accent was thick. Being on speaker amplified it and made it even more difficult to understand.

"Mr. Singh, it's Talia Shafer. Mrs. Ford."

"Mrs. Ford," he said in apparent relief. "You found the button?"

"I'm not...No. I'm sorry, Mr. Singh. I don't know what you're referring to."

"The button I stupidly failed to return to Mr. Ford along with the others."

The door swung open. Locke and Menundez rushed in, looking harried and put out. Mike shushed them before they could barrage them with questions. In a low voice, and with an economy of words, he informed them of what was going on.

Singh's manners were faultless, his deference admirable, but impatience was driving Drex nearly out of his skin. Eventually, with Talia's tactful prodding, the tailor related his story.

The short of it was that Jasper had asked him to save all the buttons that he'd replaced. Mr. Singh had put them in an envelope, sealed it, and had given it to Jasper when he'd picked up the clothes.

The following day, which would have been Saturday, the day the Fords were to have gone to Atlanta, Mr. Singh had been sweeping up his shop at closing time and had found one of the buttons on the floor.

"Behind the counter," he said woefully. "It was my terrible mistake. I must have dropped it when I was placing them in the envelope."

He continued lamenting and apologizing until Talia diplomatically coaxed him back on track. "Where is the button now, Mr. Singh?"

Immediately after making the "unfortunate discovery," he had called Mr. Ford, but got his voice mail. He'd left a message of profuse apology, but Mr. Ford hadn't responded. The next morning, Singh heard the news about his disappearance. He'd been anguishing ever since. Believing that Talia would want the button, especially now that it would have greater sentimental value if

Mr. Ford was never found, he'd gone to their home earlier today to return it personally.

"But no one was there, so I dropped the envelope with it inside into your mail slot."

Menundez high-fived the air in front of him. Locke blew a gust of breath up toward his forehead. Mike harrumphed in satisfaction. Drex closed his eyes and hoped to God he wasn't dreaming. The squeeze Talia gave his hand assured him that he wasn't.

"Mrs. Ford?"

"Yes, yes, Mr. Singh, I'm here and overwhelmed by your kindness. I can't thank you enough for calling me. I will be very happy to get the button back."

As he launched into another litany of apology, Drex motioned for her to get a description of the button. To do so, she took Singh off speaker.

The four men huddled. Drex said, "If Jasper asked to have those buttons back, they must've been his trophies. This is one of them." He gave the group at large a broad grin. "Let's go."

"Hold on," Locke said. "In under half an hour, you've got to appear in court."

"And you have got to be kidding!" Drex shouted. "I want my hands on that damn button!"

With reasonable calm, Mike said, "I'll go get it."

"I'll go with him." Talia had ended the call. "I recognize it immediately from Mr. Singh's description. Brass, round, with an embossed anchor. It was the single button on a navy blue blazer. One of Jasper's favorite jackets."

"An anchor. Nautical motif," Drex said. "Jesus. If it matches a button found in Marian Harris's makeshift coffin, it'll be hard evidence, not circumstantial." He turned back to Locke, but the detective was shaking his head.

"We're taking you to be arraigned."

Talia laid a hand on Drex's arm. "Mike and I will get it and bring it to you. Even if you're in jail."

He had no choice. "Okay. As evidence goes, it's compromised," he said to Mike. "But treat it like evidence. Safeguard it. No matter what happens to me at the courthouse, that button needs to be turned over to the FBI."

"You got it."

Drex gave Talia a meaningful look, but because they had an audience, neither said anything. With an uncustomary show of gallantry, Mike opened the door and stood aside for her to go ahead of him, then both walked quickly down the hallway.

Locke asked Drex if he still wanted to change clothes.

Drex nodded. "I won't take long."

"Five minutes."

It took him only two. He hoisted the duffel back to his shoulder and opened the door. "I'm ready," he informed the cop on guard.

"Locke said for you to cool your heels until he comes to get you."

Drex backed into the room and closed the door.

How long would it take for Mike and Talia to reach her house? He mentally mapped out their route and tried to establish an ETA. He had every confidence in them. He was less trustful of Fate. He wanted to be handy if it intervened, and he had to ward it off. And, damn it, selfishly, he wanted to be there to claim the treasure he'd spent years seeking.

But not for the world would he miss snaring Jasper. The hell of it was, he couldn't prepare for what would go down at the courthouse. Whatever unfolded was out of his hands and entirely up to Jasper. His capture could be uneventful or explosive. There was no way of knowing.

But a worse possibility was that nothing at all would happen. Weston Graham would have eluded him, likely forever.

Whether he succeeded or failed, he was ready to get on with it. The uncertainty, coupled with needing to be two places at once, was making him nuts. Psyched up and pumped full of restless energy, he made endless circuits of the meager square footage until finally the door opened and Locke motioned him out.

"What took so long?"

"That reporter who interviewed Rudkowski called me. She wants a sound bite from you when we get to the courthouse."

"Anything I said would have to be censored."

They made their way through the building. Menundez was waiting for them in the car, engine running. Once underway, Drex asked if their men were in place.

"Loitering around in plainclothes, as you asked," Locke told him.

"How many?"

"Six inside. One on each of the four sides of the building outside. They've all seen the video and know what to look for."

He would have to rely on their competence and Locke's discretion in choosing them. It all felt too loose, too much left up to Jasper. Damn! It was difficult to predict what he might do, and Drex really couldn't concentrate on it because his mind kept wandering back to that button.

"Do you have the autopsy report from Key West on your laptop?" he asked Locke, who nodded. "Can you pull it up?"

While the detective was doing so, Drex mused out loud. "There was always going to be something that tripped him up. Who would have thought a button?"

"Weirdo," Menundez editorialized from the driver's seat.

Locke passed his laptop back to Drex. "Here are all the photos we were sent. The clothing remnants they found in the crate look like a pile of rags. No loose or attached buttons are mentioned in the coroner's description of the crate's contents. Only that one was missing."

"Which means that when she was killed, Marian was wearing something with only one buttonhole."

"Like Jasper's blazer," Locke said.

"Like Jasper's blazer." On a sudden inspiration, Drex said, "Do you have the yacht party photo in your files?"

"Only the printouts your guys gave us, and they're back at the office."

"Damn." Then, "Let me borrow your phone, please. Gif wanted to help."

Locke passed him his phone. Drex tapped in Gif's number. He answered, groggy but conscious.

"You still want to be useful?"

"What do you need?"

"Do you have the yacht party photo on your phone?"

"Yes."

"If I'm remembering right, Marian is wearing a jacket."

"White. Summer weight, like linen."

"That's right," Drex said, remembering. "Zoom as closely as you can on the jacket's button."

"The button?"

"I'll fill you in later. Take a screen shot of the button. Good as you can get, and text it."

Gif came through in less time than it took for them to wait out a traffic light. It wasn't a clear or well-focused picture, but it was good enough.

Drex said, "Brass, round, with an embossed anchor."

Locke took his phone back so he could see for himself. "Well. I'll be damned."

Menundez grinned at Drex in the rearview mirror. "We have him."

"Not yet," Drex said. "We know it's him, but we still have to catch him."

Inexplicably, he felt that cheer was premature. Why? Him and his damned *whys*. He hated them, but he trusted them. There was always a reason for them.

He laid his head back against the seat of the car, closed his eyes, and looked for a distortion in this development. What didn't feel right? What was clouding this cause for celebration?

What did he know about Jasper? What did he surmise? How did Jasper fit the profile?

With the exactitude of a die-cast puzzle piece.

Drex's thoughts went back to the conversation he'd had with Talia when he'd described to her the common characteristics of serial killers.

No conscience. Overblown egos. They're smug. They're also collectors.
They take souvenirs.

He'd been absolutely certain that Jasper collected something from his victims, and that the collection would be his secret but most sacred possession. He'd emphasized to Talia that he would have a perverse affection for his souvenirs, that he would fondle the items, possibly derive sexual pleasure from them. He would treat those buttons like a cherished lover. He would never—

The realization slammed into Drex as though Jasper had sucker punched him as he had Gif.

Jasper would never, ever, under any circumstances, have left his collection in someone else's hands, not in the hands of a tailor.

"Oh, fuck, oh, *fuck!*" Drex sat up straight, banged the ceiling of the car with his fist, and yelled, "And I made sure he knew where I would be."

———

Talia had told Drex she would never come back to the house. At the time, she had meant it, but as Mike turned onto the street, she realized the impracticality of that statement. The house represented Jasper to her, and, therefore, she would never spend another night under this roof.

But there were things totally unrelated to him, her parents' effects, photo albums that chronicled her life with them and special friends, these things she would want to keep. Removing them was a project she didn't look forward to.

Now, however, she was eager to get inside.

Mike pulled into the driveway so sharply, one of the tires

bumped over the curb. "Where are the cops guarding the place?" he asked.

"Locke recalled them this morning when Drex and I went peaceably to the police station. And Jasper is considered either a corpse or a fugitive. No one expects him to return."

She popped the door handle, got out, and headed for the front door.

"Hold up." Mike squeezed himself out from behind the steering wheel. "If you open the door, it'll move the envelope. I need to take a picture of it as it was found."

"Without my remote, I can't open the garage. We'll have to go in through the back porch."

The latch on the screen door that Drex had broken was dangling loose, but the door leading into the kitchen was locked. Talia used her key. The alarm beeped when she pushed open the door.

Mike remarked that at least Rudkowski had had the courtesy to set the alarm when he left after searching the house.

"Locke, actually," Talia said. "He asked me for the code last night and had one of the guarding officers set it."

They quickly cut through the kitchen and dining room, into the wide foyer. A heap of mail lay on the floor just inside the door beneath the mail slot. "That has to be it on top," Talia said.

It was a standard white envelope without a letterhead, postage, or addressee. There was a noticeable lump in the center of it. Mike began taking pictures with his phone camera. "Do you have a sealable bag?"

Talia retraced her steps into the kitchen. She opened the door to the walk-in pantry and flipped on the light. She grabbed the box of ziplock bags from a shelf and returned with it to the living room.

"I have a variety of sizes. Is this one okay?"

Mike, who was in the process of texting, glanced up. "Fine. I'm sending these pictures to Locke. Drex will want to know we have it."

After sending the texts, he slid his phone into his breast pocket and took one of the bags from the box. Kneeling, without touching the envelope, he manipulated it into the bag and zipped it in. As he struggled to stand, he said, "Maybe we should take the blazer, too."

"Good idea. I'll get it. Unless it was confiscated when they searched yesterday."

"Let's check." Mike made to follow her upstairs. She said, "You stay."

Breathing hard from the exertion of coming to his feet after kneeling, he nodded. "Okay. I'm gonna get some water."

"In the fridge. I'll meet you in the kitchen."

She trotted up the stairs and walked quickly down the hallway, but when she reached the closed double doors of the master suite, she hesitated. She was averse to entering the toxic atmosphere of that room again. She didn't want to see the bed in which she had lain beside Jasper Ford, breathing the same air as he, vulnerable in her sleep.

But Drex was waiting for her.

Steeling herself, she pushed open the doors and was, for an instant, taken aback by the disarray. But then she remembered the search. The officers under Rudkowski's leadership hadn't done as much damage as they could have, she supposed, but things had been moved and slewed about.

Jasper would have been enraged over the present state of his handkerchief drawer.

His closet door stood ajar. She crossed to it and opened it wide. Garments had been pushed aside, sweater boxes opened and rifled through, shoes removed from the shelves and piled onto the floor. But it didn't appear that anything had been confiscated...except possibly the navy blazer.

Twice, she hastily sorted through the color-coordinated blue grouping of garments. The jacket wasn't there.

"Are you looking for this, Mrs. Ford?"

She spun around.

Jasper stood in the door opening. He was wearing the blazer.

Secure in its buttonhole was a single button. Brass, round, with an embossed anchor.

His smile was obscenely obsequious, his voice a perfect imitation of Mr. Singh's. "It wasn't lost at all."

Drex's outburst startled Menundez. He braked hard, forcing traffic around them to do the same. Tires screeched. Horns blared.

Above that additional clamor, Drex shouted to Locke, "Call Mike. Call Mike. Do it now. Tell him not to go to their house. Call Talia. It's a trap. Menundez, turn around. Head for Talia's house."

Locke looked at him with fury. "What the hell are you talking about? We're going to court."

"Jasper's not going there. Shit! I've got tell Mike." Drex lunged for Locke's phone, but the detective drew his hand back and kept it out of his reach. Beside himself, Drex shouted, "Menundez, turn the fucking car around!"

Realizing the more deranged he appeared, the less likely they were to listen to him, Drex forced himself to speak calmly. "Please. I know I lost it there for a sec, but you've got to listen to me."

"We *have* listened. That's why we're here. Everybody's in place. He's one of ours." Locke swept his hand toward a guy geared up in latex and a helmet holding up a tricked-out bicycle. He was looking at them with a cop's wariness.

Drex wanted to weep, wanted to tear at his hair, wanted Menundez to turn around!

"You've got to trust me one last time."

Locke's phone rang in his hand. Drex lurched forward again, trying to grab it. "Answer, answer, it might be them."

Locke clicked on. Rudkowski shouted through the speaker. "Where are you? They're about to call our case. Get that son of a bitch in here. *Now!*"

Drex didn't wait to hear any more. He reached for the back seat door handle.

"Don't do it!" Menundez shouted.

Drex turned his head and stared straight into the bore of the detective's pistol. "Shoot me then, just get to Talia's house." Rudkowski's screaming was acting like a power drill against his skull. "Hang up on that idiot and listen to me!"

Locke didn't move. Menundez didn't lower his pistol. Drex, his voice cracking, said, "I beg you. He set it up to kill her, and he will."

The two detectives looked at each other. Menundez continued to hold the pistol on him, but he tilted it down. Locke said into his phone, "We have an emergency," then clicked off, leaving Rudkowski raving. "You're sure?"

"Yes."

Locke, hearing Drex's conviction behind the single word, motioned for Menundez to get them underway. The younger man wasted no time. He popped a magnetic beacon on the roof of the car and, motioning frantically for other cars to move aside, cleaved a route through the logjam. At his first opening, he stamped on the accelerator.

"All right," Locke said, "you've got what you wanted. You had better have a damn good explanation for it."

"First, call Mike." The detective did so without argument. They all listened with mounting anxiety as Mike's phone rang several times without being answered.

Through clenched teeth, Drex said, "Please no, no."

"He's all right," Locke said. "He texted pictures. The envelope is there, right where the tailor said it would be."

"It may be there, but it wasn't a tailor who left it. Call Talia's phone."

Locke did. "Goes straight to voice mail."

"I told her to turn it off," Drex said in anguish. "Menundez, kick it up!"

Locke ordered Drex to calm down. "Why do you think Jasper is at their house?"

"He would never have left those buttons with a tailor. He wouldn't have left them with anybody. It was Jasper who called Talia and made her, all of us, believe in the fortuitous kindness of Mr. Singh."

Menundez swore.

Still skeptical, Locke said, "You thought you were right about the courthouse."

"A mistake I'll have to live with. Die with."

"We've skipped out on the court, on the prosecutor, Rudkowski. We're screwed and so are you if this turns out to be a bust. You had better pray to God you're right."

Heart in his throat, Drex said, "I pray to God I'm wrong."

Chapter 40

———◆———

The man standing in the open bedroom doorway was barely recognizable to Talia as the groom with whom she had exchanged marriage vows. He had shaved his head and beard. Unlike the natty dresser he'd been, he had put the blazer on over a pair of dark cargo pants and a golf shirt, both of which were ill-fitting and sloppy.

But of course the blazer was only for effect, she realized now.

How had he gotten in without Mike intercepting him? Likely, he had already been inside the house when they'd arrived. He had let himself in, turned off the alarm, and reset it.

It sent shivers up her spine to think of him lying in wait, in anticipation of springing this perfectly laid trap.

Her heart was pounding, but she tried to appear unafraid. With as much composure as she could muster, she said, "Hello, Jasper. Since we parted ways at the airport, you've been awfully busy."

"I could say the same for you, sweetheart."

"Stop talking like that," she snapped. "You sound ridiculous."

"I agree wholeheartedly. But it worked to fool you."

His smile was backed by a condescension that was all too familiar. She wondered that it hadn't made her skin crawl all those months that she had spent with him, as it did now.

"Maybe you would like the voice of Daniel Knolls better." He switched from the Indian accent to a throaty rumble. "You don't remember me the night of Marian's party, do you?"

She didn't answer.

"Marian introduced us. You responded politely, but with disinterest." He strolled farther into the room. She moved backward an equal distance. Her caution seemed to amuse him.

He said, "I, on the other hand, took a great deal of interest in Marian's young, attractive, and very affluent friend. Marian had grown tiresome. I had already solicited for her replacement on an online dating service, but I never had to pursue it because you were such an ideal candidate. You virtually dropped from that blazing sunset sky and into my lap. That very night, I began contemplating Marian's demise."

Talia's shudder was involuntary.

He noticed it, though, and her revulsion seemed to please him. "In effect, Talia, you're to blame for Marian's ghastly end. Come to think of it, Elaine's, too. If not for your friendship with them, they would still be alive."

When she flinched, he said, "What's the matter, Talia? Can't take the chastening for getting your friends killed?"

"My friends are dead for only one reason. Because you are criminally insane."

"Who told you that? Dr. Easton?"

Even as she squared off with him, her mind was scrambling to think of a way to get around him, to go through him, to overpower and disable him until help arrived. Surely help would arrive! "Where is Mike?"

He laughed. "The tub of lard?"

"What have you done to him?"

"I've put him out of his misery. He was huffing and puffing like a steam engine before I choked the life out of him."

She couldn't withhold a mewl of anguish, but she held herself upright by sheer force of will. If she cracked in the slightest, she would shatter completely. If she did that, she was doomed. She probably was anyway, but she wasn't going to give Jasper the satisfaction of watching her fracture.

"Drex knows that I'm here."

"Unsurprising. You two have become nauseatingly attached. But he's at the courthouse, waiting for me to show up." He tapped his cheek as though in contemplation. "I must say, there was a brief period of time today when I actually entertained the notion of going there to witness his fall from grace."

"Dressed as a woman and wearing a wig?" Talia scoffed. "Drex picked you out of a surveillance camera video, Jasper, and he wasn't even challenged by its poor quality. You gave yourself away. You're not nearly as clever as you perceive yourself to be."

"Yet he's there while you're here, eager to get your hands on this." He fingered the button on the blazer.

"What was in the envelope?"

"A pebble," he said, grinning. "Evidence of nothing. I confess to having experienced a brief panic attack earlier today when I thought I'd lost this beauty." He rubbed the button again. "But then I remembered that it was the one button I didn't switch out. I wanted to have one to wear until the others could be incorporated into my new wardrobe, whatever it might be.

"I came out of the panic when I realized that this blazer, button intact, was in my suitcase the whole time. But the episode gave me an idea about how lure you back here. I really hated to leave with unfinished business between us."

No doubt the unfinished business meant the finish of her if she couldn't think of a way to escape him. "Drex knows about your silly button collection. He knows how you think. He'll figure out that the call from Mr. Singh was a trick. He'll come after me."

His lips formed a rueful moue. "Meaning no slight to you at all, dearest, but I think it's me he's after. He's been on the chase for a long time, hasn't he?"

"Since he was nineteen. That's when he learned that you had killed his mother."

He reacted with a start. "His *mother*?"

"Lyndsay Cummings."

"Well, well, what do you know?" He laughed. "He's the child? Lyndsay thought her ex-husband and son were a well-concealed secret, but I knew about them, of course. Just like I know about your little eggs stored in an ice tray."

She couldn't hide her shock, and it made him smirk. "I wonder what they do with the ova if they aren't used before the mother dies. Hmm." He waved off the thought. "Anyway, after I disposed of Lyndsay, I spent several months trying to pick up the trail of her ex-husband and the boy. I didn't want to live looking over my shoulder for the vengeful Cummings men."

"Drex's father legally changed their names so you couldn't find them."

"Did he? Well, no wonder Drex's name didn't ring a bell. In any case, I bored of tracking them."

"You didn't get bored, Jasper. You *failed*. Drex, on the other hand, was tenacious. He kept at it until he found you."

"Which only underscores what a sad, wasted existence his has been. To fritter away one's life in pursuit of vengeance for a mother who abandoned him?" He shook his head and *tsk*ed. "And the really pathetic thing? He's only begun."

"What do you mean?"

"I mean, Talia, that he'll have a real bloodlust for me after I kill you."

With no more warning than that, he rushed her.

Acting on instinct, she turned and tried to make it into the bathroom, where she could put a locked door between them. But she soon realized that turning her back to him was the worst thing she could have done. From behind, he enwrapped her in a hug that pinned her arms to her sides and made her neck susceptible to the arm he crooked beneath her chin.

"Let her go, or I will kill you."

Drex's voice!

Jasper swiveled around, hauling her with him.

Drex hadn't shouted. He'd made a controlled and imperative statement of fact. He certainly looked deadly enough. His tiger eyes were fixed on Jasper. In his outstretched hands, he cradled a handgun. It was aimed at a spot slightly above and behind her: Jasper's forehead.

Jasper said, "I'll snap her neck."

"The bullet will get there first."

"You're not going to kill me."

"You don't think?"

"You're restricted by code. FBI rules. Law and order."

"If you don't let her go, there's no code, no rule, no law, *nothing* that would stop me from blowing your brains out."

"You do that, you'll never know where your mother is buried."

Drex grimaced.

Jasper laughed. "Ah, I've presented you with a dilemma. You want to save Talia, which is romantic to the nth degree. But, if you kill me, you'll never know your mother's final resting place."

"You're right," Drex said, lowering the pistol. "I'll just shoot you in the leg instead."

He pulled the trigger. Jasper's body jerked. He cried out. When his leg buckled, he dragged Talia down with him. She used that nanosecond of weakness to lunge away from him.

He caught her by the hair and tried to jerk her backward.

Rapid gunfire erupted.

His grip on her hair was released so abruptly, she fell forward, landing hard on her knees, gasping for breath, deafened by the barrage.

Then Drex was there, kneeling beside her. He took her by the shoulders and gently pulled her into a sitting position. Her hearing was still muffled, but his lips were moving, asking repeatedly if she was all right.

Dumbly, she nodded.

He kissed her forehead, then eased her toward Menundez, who was at her other side, down on one knee. A number of uniformed officers had crowded into the open doorway. Locke was motioning them back, keeping them from entering the room.

She took all this in, but her gaze followed Drex as he walked over to where Jasper had collapsed. He had crumpled against his closet door, listing at a severe angle. He was bleeding from numerous wounds in his chest and abdomen.

Drex crouched in front of him.

With cold objectivity, Drex regarded the wounds he'd inflicted. The one in Jasper's thigh was the only one that had required some shooting skill. He'd had to make it count without hitting Talia.

The others, he'd gone for center of mass. They hadn't required careful aim to do fatal damage.

Had he felt any remorse for that, he only had to look into the black, fathomless eyes, from which not a single glimmer of a human soul had ever shone. He had only to think of the women who had suffered and died and been abandoned in ignominious graves.

He said, "You're already dead. You've got minutes, if that. Weston."

Jasper's lips formed a rictus of smug delight. "Your mother liked my name. Liked me. So much so that she gave you up to be with me." He gurgled a laugh. "You'll never find her, you know."

"Probably not. But that's not my heart's desire. This is."

Drex reached out and yanked hard on the button of the blazer. With a snap of threads, it came free. Drex bounced it in his palm. "So much for your collection."

Blood had filled Jasper's mouth and coated his teeth, making his grin grotesque. He was wheezing for each shallow breath, blowing bubbles of blood, but he forced himself to speak.

"I suppose that you'll open up my brain and study it, won't you, Dr. Easton? You'll want to know what made me tick. You could write a textbook about me." His laugh was a blood-sputtering travesty. "Probe my brain, slice and dice it, dig into it till the day you die. It will never tell you where to look for your mother."

Drex leaned in a little closer. "Your brain has absolutely zero value, Weston. It will cook in an incinerator and turn to ash. It will never be dissected and analyzed. You are nobody's idea of a specimen worth writing about. Know why?" He placed his lips against Jasper's ear. "You're too fucking ordinary."

Seconds later, he watched Weston Graham die an inglorious death, carrying that crushing insult into hell with him.

Talia wept with relief when she learned that Mike was alive.

Drex wanted to comfort her, but they were kept separated while being questioned by investigators from the Mount Pleasant police department. When it came his turn, Locke advised him to let him do most of the talking. Drex was happy to oblige. He was coming down off a bitch of an adrenaline surge.

Locke and Menundez explained to the investigators what had brought them rushing to the Ford residence. "We alerted your department to a possible crisis situation," Locke told them, "but we had a good head start and arrived ahead of everyone else."

Menundez explained how Jasper had come to be shot by a small-caliber pistol belonging to him. "I carry a spare in an ankle holster. I gave it to Easton before we entered the house."

Those interrogating them turned as one to regard Drex with suspicion. One asked Menundez, "He was booked today. You didn't think twice about giving him a weapon?"

"I only thought twice about taking his," Menundez replied.

Locke picked up. "We entered through the back porch and found Mallory lying prone on the kitchen floor. He was unconscious, not dead."

Indeed, Mike's eyes had fluttered open as Drex's fingers plowed the folds of fat beneath his chin in search of a pulse. Mike had pushed Drex away with one hand and pointed them upstairs with the other.

Locke said, "I stayed behind to call in medical help for Mallory and to apprise your guys of what was happening. I asked them to approach covertly. Easton and Menundez proceeded upstairs."

"What happened when you got up there?" The question was addressed to Drex.

"We heard their voices. Approached with caution. No sooner had I motioned to Menundez that I was going in than we heard him say that he was going to kill her. When I cleared the door, he had her in a headlock. I tried to talk him into letting her go. He didn't heed. I shot him in the leg."

"Tricky shot," a policeman remarked. "You must have had excellent marksmanship training somewhere."

"Alaska. A school buddy of mine."

"A hunter?"

"A hoodlum."

Just then, Locke was pulled away from the group by a uniformed officer. Drex and Menundez continued to answer questions. When Locke returned, he reported grimly that a woman's body had been discovered in a local motel. "It's estimated she's been dead for at least twelve hours. Cause of death, forcibly broken neck. A button is missing from her dress."

The news cast a greater pall over the already somber scene. The coroner came and went. Jasper's body was taken away, but not before a velvet pouch with a drawstring was found in one of the pockets of his cargo pants. It was placed in an evidence bag. To it, Drex added the brass button he'd ripped off.

The house was cleared of excess personnel, although there were still officers and investigators milling from room to room, carrying out various responsibilities. Drex found Talia in the living room, talking with Locke.

"We both need some air." Without waiting for permission, he motioned Talia off the sofa and took her by the arm.

Locke didn't protest, but he said to their retreating backs, "Don't go far."

They made their way through the kitchen, where Menundez was availing himself of the coffee machine. They crossed the lawn to the garage apartment and sat side by side on a lower step of the exterior staircase. The wood was damp from the recent weather, but the rain had stopped. For the first time in days, the sky was clear. Moonlight shone through the branches of the live oak tree, casting shadows.

They didn't talk for several minutes, only held each other. When she did angle away from him, she said, "Mike's going to be all right?"

"I talked to him by phone about half an hour ago. The nurses are drill sergeants, the doctors prepubescent idiots, they're giving him Jell-O and calling it food. He said that he's too fat to choke with bare hands, that anybody with half a brain should know that. He was at his grumpiest. In other words, doing well."

"Does Gif know?"

"I talked to him, too. Told him everything."

"What did he have to say about it?"

Drex knew what she was referring to, but he answered by saying, "That he's wanted to choke Mike himself many times."

She smiled, and he smiled back, but the aftermath of the crisis caught up with them simultaneously, and they kissed ravenously, clutching at each other, assuring themselves that the other was there, whole, alive.

Drex felt her tears on his cheeks, or was he the one crying? Taking her face between his hands, he said, "On the way here, I died a thousand deaths. When I heard your voice—"

"I know, I know," she said, laughing and crying at once. "I felt the same when I heard yours. Thank you for saving my life."

"I gunned him down in front of you, Talia. Are you…I wasn't sure how you would feel about that."

"Oh, God, Drex." She nestled closer to him. "Profound gratitude and relief that it's over. He's done. That's how I feel about it."

He bent his head over hers and kissed her crown.

"There they are."

Instantly, they separated and looked toward the house. Rudkowski was strutting toward them, Locke, Menundez, and another man, a stranger, trailing him.

"Jesus." Drex stood up and said to Rudkowski, "We don't have to do this now."

"Not up to you, is it?" Rudkowski marched to within a few feet of them, then stepped aside and motioned to the man Drex didn't know. "Read him his rights."

The man came forward, turned Drex around, and placed a pair of flex cuffs on his wrists as he Mirandized him.

"What are you doing?" Talia pushed past the stranger and confronted Rudkowski. "What is wrong with you?" She shoved him in the chest with both hands. "Jasper gave him no choice. He was about to kill me and would have if Drex hadn't acted. Menundez, tell him. If you and Drex hadn't—"

"I know all of that," Rudkowski said snidely. "I'm arresting him for obstruction of justice, tampering with—"

"Oh, for godsake!"

"—evidence, and impersonation of a federal agent."

"That's ridiculous. He only resigned in order to—"

"He didn't *resign* from anything," Rudkowski said. "That badge he so theatrically surrendered, no doubt to impress you with his self-sacrifice, is counterfeit. It will be submitted as evidence at his trial."

"Counterfeit?"

"Oh. Like you didn't know," he said with scorn.

She turned to Drex. "What is he talking about?"

Before Drex could speak, Rudkowski practically squealed, "He's a phony. He and his merry band are imposters. They only profess to be FBI agents, flashing around fake badges and IDs whenever the mood strikes."

She rounded on Rudkowski, then looked at Locke and Menundez.

Locke cleared his throat. "He, uh, had us convinced, too. Until Rudkowski told us different."

Rudkowski said, "I assumed you knew, Mrs. Ford. Which is why I came down so hard on you. I thought you'd gone along with him, never mind that he's a criminal. Most women do."

"'Criminal' is a pretty harsh word," Locke said.

"How about lawbreaker?" Rudkowski said. "Use whatever word you like. They all mean the same thing. He commits crimes. And since he's a repeat offender, and has already served time for the *same offense*, he won't get off so lightly this time. I'm going for the maximum sentence."

To Drex, it seemed an eternity that Talia stared at Rudkowski, unmoving, before she came slowly around to him. The instant she looked into his face, she saw the truth engraved there. Her disillusionment caused his heart to contract.

Speaking low, he said, "Five years ago, I served eight months of a two-year sentence in federal prison for impersonating an FBI agent. Mike and Gif got off on probation."

She placed her hand at the base of her throat, which already showed a bruise Jasper had inflicted. Drex knew he was bruising her almost as deeply now.

"He's run a great con," Rudkowski said.

Giving no regard to him, Drex said, "I used the badge, played the part, but never for self gain. Only as a means to capture Weston Graham."

In a faint voice, she said, "You never were with the FBI?"

"Mike and Gif were until..." He hitched his chin toward Rudkowski. "They were with the bureau when I went to them and sought their help."

"Because they were corruptible," Rudkowski said.

"Because of their particular skills," Drex said. "They assisted me—"

"Covertly and illegally."

"—because they believed in what I was doing. After my release from prison, they left the bureau and started working with me."

"As accomplices," Rudkowski said. "And by the way, the FBI was happy to be rid of them."

"Why don't you shut the fuck up?" Menundez muttered.

Talia seemed unaware of them. Her wounded gaze remained on Drex. "Is the doctorate another fake?"

"No."

"Then why didn't you just use it and join the FBI?"

"Because I didn't want to be fettered by procedure and bureaucracy."

"It was easier just to act the part?" she said.

"Not easier. More efficacious."

"Efficacious." She gave a bitter laugh. "Good word. A writer's word. You certainly had gullible me fooled. Drex the writer. Drex the federal agent. Drex the good guy," she finished huskily.

"I'm the same man, Talia."

"The same *con* man," Rudkowski said. "Let's go."

The stoic stranger, whom Drex took to be another agent, nudged him forward. He went without protest, but as he came even with Talia, he stopped. "Talia—"

"Anything you have to say, I don't want to hear. I'm not listening to any more of your lies," she said and turned her back to him.

Epilogue

<hr style="width:15%" />

Drex read the discreet sign on the office door, summoned his courage, and pushed it open. Talia was seated at a desk, looking into a computer monitor. She turned her head with a smile of greeting in place. Upon seeing him, it dissolved.

He stepped into the office and closed the door.

The space was smart yet inviting. Vintage, arte-deco travel posters in matte black frames gave the light gray walls modish splashes of color. A Palladian window, virtually a wall in itself, overlooked a landscaped courtyard enclosed by ivy-covered brick walls, a burbling fountain in the center. The mix of chic and nostalgic created an environment that he would expect of her.

Her plain white shirt looked anything but plain on her. Sunlight coming through the window backlit her hair, creating a halo of red and gold.

She hadn't stood up to welcome him, but, since she hadn't yet picked up the crystal objet d'art on her desk and hurled it at him, he said, "I need help planning a trip."

"I only work with established clients."

"You came highly recommended."

"By whom?"

"Elaine Conner."

Looking pained, her gaze dropped a fraction.

He put his hands in his pants pockets and strolled over to one of the posters, studying the sleek lines of the artwork as he said, "I heard you escorted her body to Delaware."

"She stipulated in her will that she wanted to be buried there beside her husband."

"You saw to the dispersal of her estate to various charities."

"A while back, she had asked if I would be the executor. I agreed, of course, never guessing…"

When she trailed off, Drex said, "May she rest in peace."

After a respectful silence, Talia curtly changed the subject. "I heard you pled guilty."

He turned away from the poster and looked at her. "Who'd you hear that from?"

"Gif."

"He's recovered. Almost like new."

"Yes, I know," she said. "He stopped by to see me before going home to Lexington."

"Yeah? You two have a nice visit?"

"Very nice. He apologized."

"For what?"

She gave him a baleful look, which would have caused a less determined man to duck and run. He stayed.

Her desk was a sheet of gray-tinted glass supported by an iron base. Black. The same color as the high heel that was angrily tapping up and down against the floor beneath her chair, where she sat with legs crossed, providing him a six-inch view of thigh above the hemline of her narrow, black skirt.

"Where are you traveling to?"

Her question drew his gaze up from the scenery underneath the desk to her stormy eyes. "Pardon?"

"Where are you going on the trip that you came here to waste my time about?"

"Waste your time?" He thumbed toward the door. "You're open for business."

"To established clients."

"So you said."

She looked down at her wristwatch. Such a dainty wrist, with a sprinkling of golden freckles. "One of which is due here soon with his wife to discuss their African adventure."

"They haven't gone yet?"

"They had to postpone."

"Huh."

"So state your business, please."

"I told you. I'm planning—"

"You can't go on a trip!" she exclaimed, slapping her hand onto the glass desktop. "I know you were being sentenced today. Gif said—"

"You talked to Gif more than once?"

"He said you agreed to plead guilty if Rudkowski would lay off him and Mike."

He shrugged. "I was the corrupting influence. If not for me, they wouldn't have run afoul of the law."

"Rudkowski reluctantly agreed not to touch them, but tacked on several more charges against you. Horse poop, Mike called them."

"You've talked to Mike, too?"

"He said that with those additional indictments, you could face up to five years."

"I got two."

"Oh," she said on a catch of breath. The starch went out of her posture. She looked down.

"Suspended."

Her head snapped up. "What?"

"Surprised me, too. Sent Rudkowski into orbit. The judge read the sentence, then suspended it because of extenuating circumstances."

"Which were?"

"Rudkowski being an incompetent asshole. I'm putting words in the judge's mouth, but that was the essence of it. Additionally, I had a lot of people who defended my questionable actions."

"Locke and Menundez, I'm sure."

"Them. Their chief. Plus the SAC in Columbia. People at my workplace in Lexington put in a good word for me." He walked over to the desk and picked up the crystal formation, studying it from various angles, watching the rainbows it created as he turned it one way, then another. "What is this supposed to be?"

"Nothing. Put it down. So the judge just let you off?"

"Uh-hum. What really worked in my favor, what his honor found most compelling, was the affidavit you videotaped and sent to him."

Standing suddenly, she grabbed the objet from him and returned it to the desktop with a decisive *thunk*. "You were never supposed to know about that! Mike swore to me that—"

"Mike swore. Gif said. Just how often do you and those two busybodies put your heads together? What all have you talked about?"

"For one thing, your *work*."

"Work?"

"Foolish me. Because of the indictments against you, I was worried that you might be fired from your job. I wondered if you were financially able to pay your legal fees. As it turns out, my concern was misplaced."

"Which one of the blabbermouths told you?"

"You sold a patent when you were twenty years old? *Twenty*? For millions?"

"I didn't do anything for it. It fell into my lap. Literally. When I was sorting through Dad's stuff after he died, I upended a drawer, and all these engineering drawings fell out. Scores of them. I didn't even know what they were, had to ask someone. He had designed a thingamajig that went on a doodad that would improve the performance of a piece of machinery."

"A piece of machinery essential to the construction and maintenance of the Alaskan pipeline. And about a hundred other industries. Shipping. Forestry. Earth moving."

"I didn't know that when I filed the patent. I didn't have a clue what Dad had been doing all those long, dark nights when he shut himself off in his bedroom. He was the engineer, not me. I never even made a prototype of the thing."

"You didn't have to."

"No. While I was still at Missoula, manufacturing companies started calling me, wanting to buy the patent. I negotiated for months and sold to the highest bidder. To this day, I'm unclear as to what the gizmo does." He raised his hands. "Wasn't my field of interest. I carried on with what I wanted to do, got my doctorate, and went to work at the security company where I'm still employed."

"Coaching mega-conglomerates on how to screen potential employees so they don't hire embezzlers, pirates, spies, and such."

"Every day a criminal thinks up a new way to be one. It's a constant learning curve. I get paid for trying to outwit the outlaws. It's a great gig. I love the work."

"A gig." She placed her hands on her hips. "You're a major shareholder in a company that has eight branches nationwide."

He was going to kill Mike and Gif. "I go to the office every day, eat lunch in the campus cafeteria, and, just like everybody else, take my two weeks' vacation."

"Two weeks at a time. About six times a year."

"Every employee gets—"

"Stop it, Drex." She blew out a gust of breath in exasperation. "'How much more inept and underachieving am I going to feel?'" she said, quoting him from the day they had met. "And to think I felt sorry for you, a struggling writer living in that ratty apartment."

"Well, if it makes you feel any better, the one in Lexington is about that ratty. I've been preoccupied for the past fifteen, twenty years."

Her annoyance plain, she gnawed her inner cheek. "Why couldn't I find anything about you, the whiz kid, on the Internet?"

"I filed the patent under an LLC. Once it sold, the LLC was dissolved. I've conducted my other business behind blinds like that. I didn't want my name floating around out there in case Weston Graham ever got wind of it."

She assimilated all that and seemed to find it a satisfactory answer. "Is impersonating a federal agent still your hobby?"

"I was sternly admonished by the judge to give that up for good. But I was done with it anyway. Because *he's* done. It's over. Your words, Talia."

"What else don't I know about you? Are there other surprises in store?"

She was entitled to be angry. He wasn't. But a man could only take so much before becoming riled. "No," he said. "And I must say that you're very well informed for someone who, the last time I saw you, told me that you didn't want to hear anything I had to say, and, since then, hasn't answered or responded to a single call. Or email. Or text. Nothing!" He ended on a shout.

She matched it. "What would you have said?"

"I would have asked you to forgive me."

"Never!"

"Fine! Don't forgive me. Will you fuck me?"

Her lips parted. A soft breath puffed out.

He backed down and lowered his volume. "Sorry. I'd be more romantic, but that takes more patience than I've got right now." He moved aside the crystal thing so he could lean toward her.

"I have no right to ask. I never did. You were married, and I was deceiving you with every word and deed. But any time I've been near you since I first saw you coming up the hatchway of that boat,

I've wanted to claim you in a way that's...hell, almost primitive. And I honestly don't know how much longer I can stand here looking at you without acting on that impulse."

Later they would argue over who had moved first in order to get around the desk. After a brief but mad round of kissing and a wrestling match to pull out shirttails, unbutton plackets, get his knotted necktie over his head, and unhook her bra, they were against the wall, hands competing to cover the most bare skin in the least amount of time.

"Is that courtyard public?" he asked.

Reaching far to her right, Talia groped the surface of a small table and came up with a remote. She pressed a button, then dropped the device to the floor.

Drex turned his head, saw the shade silently lowering over the window, and said, "I need to get one of those."

She grabbed his hair with both hands and brought him back around to her. He began rubbing openmouthed kisses down her throat, across her chest, over her breasts. Pecking at her nipple, he asked, "What time are your clients due?"

"You're not the only liar. No one's due. But we should probably lock the door. You never know who will just wander in uninvited."

"Don't go anywhere."

On the short trip to the door and back, he worked open the button on his waistband and unzipped. Talia was bent over squirming out of her skirt. When she straightened up, he was stunned by the sight. Between her thighs was a V of material the same color as her skin, too sheer and pale to hide what was underneath.

"Damn."

He'd said he wanted to claim her. Physically, without question. But as much as that, he wanted an understanding reached, a pact made, a possession consecrated, and he wanted it *now*.

He went to her and lifted her onto him. The coupling was swift and absolute, the stroking urgent and unrestrained. They pushed and pulled against each other, with each other. When they came, it was together, with groans of gratification and sighs that spoke volumes without words.

They sealed it with a deep, ardent, soul-melding kiss.

He sat on the floor with his back to the wall, Talia lying across his lap. She lightly scratched her nails over his scruffy chin and cheeks. "I'm reading *The Count of Monte Cristo* again."

He traced the waistband of her panties from hipbone to hipbone, a tantalizing caress for both of them. "Have I told you how much I like these?"

"About a dozen times. And stop trying to distract me from the subject."

"I'm absorbed in this subject." His fingers drew lazy designs on the sheer fabric.

To get his attention, she rose up and bit his lower lip. "I wanted to kill you, you know."

"That came across."

"But I've ached to see you. I want to tell you all about me. I want to know all about you."

"There'll be time for that. We have a lot to talk out, and we will. That is, if you want you and I to be a 'we.'"

"I thought I'd spent the last few minutes proving that I do. Either that, or I'm just really slutty."

"I adore you really slutty. Take this sorry excuse for panties, for instance."

"You're incorrigible." Her scold was meaningless; her smile packed a thousand watts.

A sassy side of her was emerging now that she was no longer living under Jasper's influence, and Drex loved it. She probably didn't even realize until after he was gone how subtly he had suppressed aspects of her personality.

Drex had learned from Mike and Gif that she was completely

out of the house and that it was up for sale. They'd told him that she had withstood with remarkable aplomb the tsunami of media coverage generated by the exposure of Jasper's history. Loyal clients and friends had rallied around her, protecting her, lending unflagging support until the hubbub eventually ebbed. He saw no reason to bring all that up now. He would wait for her to introduce the subject.

However, he did ask where she was living.

"I'm leasing a townhouse while deciding on something more permanent. I needed a place to work, though, so I rented this office."

"Do you have an extra key for that townhouse?"

"I'll see if I can scare one up." She snuggled against him, burrowing her nose in his chest hair. "Where are you going on your trip?"

"Alaska."

She tipped her head back and looked up at him.

He fiddled with a strand of her hair. "Because of the buttons, all those cold cases are being revisited. Eventually one of the buttons could be connected to my mother. If it is, and I get it back, I'll put it in a hermetically sealed box, take it up to Alaska, and bury it there next to Dad."

"I think he would like that," she said, her voice rough with emotion.

"In the meantime, I thought I'd go up, plant a tree, add a headstone, something that would represent closure to me."

"The fulfillment of your oath."

"That sounds so lofty, but I guess, yeah. I would like for you to go with me."

She kissed her fingertip and pressed it to his lips. "If you would like me to, I will."

He sank his fingers into her hair and massaged her scalp, while his other hand drifted back and forth across her breasts. "I want to volunteer."

"For what?"

"To be the sperm donor when you thaw those eggs out."

She rubbed her cheek against his pec. "You already have been."

Both of his hands fell still. "What?"

"One of my eggs that wasn't harvested proved to be more robust than those that were."

His gaze moved down to the feminine landscape that had entranced him minutes earlier, then came back up to meet her eyes.

Shyly she said, "We were both a bit primitive that night." Drex just looked at her. After a time, she asked, "Are you ever going to blink?"

He did.

Then he pulled her into a hug, and they did something they had never done together: They laughed, out loud, and long.